CW01390837

AGENT REDRUTH

Michael Evans

"I found Agent Redruth hugely enjoyable – fast-paced, intricately plotted and shot through with all the authentic detail you'd expect from a journalist of Michael Evans's experience and calibre. In short, a blast! It'll fly off the shelves."

Giles Whittell, author of *Bridge of Spies*.

"Terrific story telling enriched by startling inside intel on the world of spooks."

Patrick Bishop, author of *The Man Who Was Saturday*.

"A whipcrack thriller from the treacherous world of espionage."

James MacManus, author of *Midnight in Berlin*.

"Michael Evans, a brilliant defence journalist, uses his unique knowledge to write a magnificent thriller."

William Shawcross, author of *Justice and the Enemy*, and official biographer of *Queen Elizabeth, The Queen Mother*.

"Agent Redruth is a gripping and racy thriller set in the world of high-stakes espionage, full of jaw -dropping insights into the workings of Putin's Russia, and as bang up-to-date as today's headlines, as you would expect from one of the most respected defence correspondents in the country."

Roger Alton, former editor of the *Observer* and *Independent*

"Moving at a thrilling pace, Agent Redruth is a cracking account of spying today in the midst of war in Ukraine, crackdowns in Moscow and attempts by British security services to outwit the Russians. The feel is absolutely right – the guarded dialogue of Whitehall's spymasters, the arrogance of their US counterparts, the paranoid plotting and suspicions in Putin's Kremlin and the chaos and confusion of a brutal war. Michael Evans has all the details right: the geography of Moscow streets and metro stations, the battered landmarks in Kyiv, the politics of Whitehall and the thrusting initiatives of a young British television reporter eager to make his mark. Into all this a young and pretty painter, Rebecca, is drawn into an ever more bizarre and dangerous role. The plots, cock-ups and coincidences pull us along relentlessly to a graphic conclusion. But oh the twist of those final three devastating words!"

Michael Binyon, author of *Life in Russia*.

Text copyright © Michael Evans 2025
Design copyright © Iain Hill 2025
All rights reserved.

Michael Evans has asserted his right under the Copyright, Designs and Patents Act 1988 to be identified as the author of this work.

This is a work of fiction. Names, characters, businesses, places, events and incidents are either the products of the author's imagination or used in a fictitious manner. Any resemblance to actual persons, living or dead, or actual events is purely coincidental.

No part of this book may be reprinted or reproduced or utilised in any form or by electronic, mechanical or any other means, now known or hereafter invented, including photocopying or recording, or in any information storage or retrieval system, without the permission in writing from the Publisher and Author.

First published 2025
by Rowanvale Books Ltd
The Gate
Keppoch Street
Roath
Cardiff
CF24 3JW
www.rowanvalebooks.com

A CIP catalogue record for this book is available from the British Library.
ISBN: 978-1-83584-046-7
eBook ISBN: 978-1-83584-047-4

Printed and bound in Great Britain by Bell and Bain Ltd, Glasgow

CHAPTER ONE

AN MI5 MOLE ON TRIAL

"All rise."

Rebecca Strong, sitting in the public gallery of Courtroom 1 of the Old Bailey, stood up, stretched her back and shook her shoulders. She looked around, and across the court to the press box where her boyfriend, Sandy Hall, crime correspondent of Sky News, was now standing alongside his rivals from every national newspaper and TV station.

Mr Justice John Cunningham-Brown entered. He walked steadily to his chair, bowed briefly to the clerk and barristers, and sat down. He then nodded to the clerk, Jennifer Braithwaite.

She faced the court.

"Case number 23, Government v. Amelia Prendergast. You are charged with six offences under the Official Secrets Act 1989, Section 1, that without lawful authority you disclosed information relating to security or intelligence which is or has been in your possession by virtue of your position as a member of an intelligence service. The disclosure of such information was prejudicial to the security interests of the United Kingdom and included information which would be useful to an enemy. The charges relate to alleged offences committed between August 5 2019 and December 18 2022. How do you plead: guilty or not guilty?"

As the clerk read out the charges against the defendant, Sandy and the rest of the reporters began tapping away furiously on their laptops. Rebecca smiled. Seeing Sandy working at his trade always made her smile.

Jennifer Braithwaite, a woman in her fifties with straight, grey-flecked brown hair, raised her eyebrows in the direction of the defendant, who was standing.

Amelia Prendergast, thirty-five years old, short-cropped dark hair, smartly dressed in a dark-blue skirt suit, replied in a quiet voice: "Not guilty."

At that moment, everyone in the public gallery, with the exception of Rebecca, leaned forward and started whispering and shaking their heads. Rebecca noticed that Sandy turned to a reporter next to him and grinned. This was a big story for him, especially because he had an inside track on the background to the case, thanks to his girlfriend.

Rebecca was not just an interested member of the public. She had played a unique and bizarre role in a spy drama a year earlier, which had led to the deportation from Britain of two senior members of the Russian GRU military intelligence service and the eventual discovery of a mole inside MI5. The mole was Amelia Prendergast, former personal assistant to Geraldine Hammer, director of counter-espionage at MI5.

Rebecca, of similar age to Prendergast, but taller, blonde and vivacious, with green, inquisitive eyes, knew more about the case than the majority of people in Courtroom 1. She was a commercial artist by profession but unwittingly came to know and share the bed of one of the two GRU spies who had been sent to London to assassinate Geraldine Hammer.

Following the failed assassination attempt, an internal MI5 investigation discovered that Prendergast had been acting as a secret mole for Moscow for more than three years. They found she had a Russian controller, a GRU-supplied codename, Svekla (or Beetroot), and a Cayman Islands bank account containing £750,000.

Mr Justice Cunningham-Brown sat forward, lifting his glasses from the end of his nose to the bridge. "Sir Jeremy," he said in a slow, forceful voice.

Sir Jeremy Blackburn KC, immaculate in a black suit, black silk gown and neat horsehair wig, raised himself from the polished bench and turned to the jury.

"I am lead counsel for the prosecution in this case which involves a serious breach of the 1989 Official Secrets Act. You will hear evidence against the defendant which is indisputable. She is charged with giving secret, highly classified information to a third party, namely an agent of a foreign power. As a trusted member of staff for the Security Service, otherwise known as MI5, she had access to confidential intelligence, including details relating to her immediate line manager, the director of counter-espionage, who for the purposes of this trial will be identified only as Witness A."

Sir Jeremy stopped briefly to let this sink in. The jury appeared suitably impressed. Amelia Prendergast looked straight ahead, not daring to glance at the jury of seven men and five women.

"The defendant abused her trusted position in the Security Service by acting as a mole for the benefit of the Russian intelligence services. I shall lay before you evidence, indisputable evidence, that in return for providing vital information about Witness A, including her confidential personal details and working practices, the defendant received large and regular sums of money paid into an offshore bank account held under a false name. The information she provided helped agents of the Russian intelligence services, notably the military branch known as GRU, to prepare a plot to target and assassinate Witness A."

Again, Sir Jeremy paused and raised his eyebrows at the jury. At least four members of the jury raised their eyebrows in return. The lead prosecutor allowed himself the tiniest of smiles.

Sandy noted down all these details on his laptop. Sometimes a court case, even a high-profile espionage trial, could become dry and lacking in sparkle once the prosecution got underway. The nods and winks between Sir Jeremy and the jury added a touch of courtroom atmosphere.

Sir Jeremy cleared his throat and continued: "The involvement of the defendant in this dastardly crime came to light subsequent to a series of dramatic events that took place in London throughout the month of July 2022, in which one, and later two GRU agents threatened the security and stability and safety of the capital, and in particular the life of Witness A. The perpetrators were caught and arrested as a result of intensive investigative work by the Metropolitan Police and security services. Why the two suspects were deported and not charged with criminal offences is not a matter for this trial, nor for you, members of the jury."

Rebecca pursed her lips. "Witness A" was Geraldine Hammer, although she would never be seen in the courtroom by members of the public. Rebecca remembered how embarrassed the Metropolitan Police were when vital evidence, including the gun intended to shoot Geraldine Hammer, essential prima facie evidence for a future trial, had only been found *after* the GRU would-be assassins had been flown back to Moscow.

Rebecca thought it ironic that the only prosecution the authorities had managed to put together was the case against Amelia Prendergast, a relatively low-level spy who knew everything about her boss's work diary and personal home background but was not security-cleared for operational matters. Rebecca knew instinctively that the prosecution of Amelia Prendergast was being hyped up as a brilliant counter-espionage operation because of the total failure to build a case against the two Russian spies. In her view, Sir Jeremy was playing his part in over-dramatising her role, presumably under instructions from on high.

Sir Jeremy pointed briefly at the defendant.

"It became clear to the security authorities that the information in the hands of said Russian agents must have come from some person or persons working inside MI5. There was a mole at the heart of the Security Service. I shall provide evidence that will point the finger, without any question or doubt, at the defendant.

She had the relevant access, she speaks fluent Russian, and she had the money, a large amount of money, in a bank account that could be linked directly to her betrayal."

Sir Jeremy hadn't mentioned the word "betrayal" until this moment because he wanted it to have maximum impact on the jury.

"Yes," he went on, "this is about betrayal. Betrayal of her country, betrayal of her immediate boss, who held a uniquely sensitive job vital to the national interests of this country. Instead of protecting this great nation, Amelia Prendergast was working for and being paid by enemy agents."

A veteran of high-profile Old Bailey trials, Sir Jeremy knew that those last few words would appear as the headline in every newspaper the following day. He threw a glance at the press box and saw all the reporters with their heads down, tapping furiously on their laptops.

The lead prosecution counsel was coming to the end of his opening address to the jury.

"The defence counsel will try to mitigate her betrayal by claiming she was caught in some sort of trap, pressured by Russia's intelligence services against her will," he said. "But the evidence points in the opposite direction. The defendant was a willing partner in this crime and she was rewarded handsomely. Why she chose to betray her country is unclear. But one motivation is undeniable: cash, pure and simple. She enjoyed accumulating money in her secret bank account. The evidence, members of the jury, is indisputable, and for that reason I believe you will find it relatively easy to come to the conclusion that the defendant is guilty on all charges."

Sir Jeremy nodded to the judge and sat down.

Rebecca was enthralled. Because of her unwitting association with one of the GRU spies, she had met and become close to Geraldine Hammer. She had also briefly met Amelia Prendergast in Geraldine's office. But Rebecca was not going to be a witness at the trial. Her unofficial role in the dramatic events that led to the arrest of Amelia Prendergast was buried in the files at MI5. The prosecution team, headed by Sir Jeremy, was unaware of Rebecca Strong.

As the defence counsel, Rosemary Blandish KC, rose to give her opening address to the jury, Rebecca's phone pinged. The sound broke her absorbed concentration on the trial. She checked quickly, whispering apologetically to those sitting next to her. One woman looked at her in disgust and muttered under her breath that phones were supposed to be banned.

It was a brief text:

"Need to see you. RR."

She stared at it, uncomprehending. The initials "RR" meant nothing to her. "Need" to see you? She wasn't impressed by that. Thought it pathetic, in fact. Wrong choice of word as far as she was concerned. After a few seconds, she shrugged her shoulders and turned her phone off. She wanted to focus on the trial.

Rosemary Blandish had started her opening remarks to the jury and was painting a very different picture of the defendant.

"She is a woman," she said, "with a troubled family background who found herself caught up in a personal crisis not of her making. She is not a traitor, as the prosecution claims, but the victim of a Russian intelligence blackmail plot.

"I will lay evidence before you, members of the jury, which will demonstrate how the defendant became the target of Russian intelligence agents when she was studying the Russian language at an academy in Siberia.

"She was a young, impressionable student who had no idea she was being groomed by a member of the Russian intelligence service. The prosecution claims that she was a dedicated spy intent on betraying her country, but this is a travesty of the truth. Amelia Prendergast is not a traitor. Yes, there is a lot of money in an offshore account in her name. But this was all part of the blackmail operation orchestrated by Russian intelligence. The money was Russian money but it wasn't there for my client's use and enjoyment. It was there to put added pressure on her. To force her to help with snippets of information that never for one moment put this country's national security at risk."

Rebecca studied the faces of the jury as the defendant's barrister laid out her case. It was the first day of the trial, so the jury was alert and interested. But as Rosemary Blandish attempted to portray Amelia Prendergast as a victim to be pitied, not punished, Rebecca noticed several members of the jury appeared unconvinced. Rebecca knew the barrister was weaving a story that had more to do with fantasy than reality.

As she listened to Prendergast's barrister, Rebecca suddenly sat back. She frowned. An idea had come into her head. The text she had received had been a complete mystery, but perhaps the initials "RR" made sense after all. It was just a thought, but the more she pondered on the two initials, the more convinced she became that she had cracked it. If she was right, the text had been sent from someone she had hoped never to see or hear from again.

CHAPTER TWO
A RUSSIAN AGENT MAKES A LIFE-CHANGING DECISION

Lieutenant-Colonel Mikhail Nikolayev Gerasimov, long-time GRU agent and former member of an assassination squad, was rethinking his life.

He had been selected by his superiors to join an elite team of special forces and military intelligence advisers to the president. He was to be promoted to full colonel and given an office in one of the most secure and protected parts of the Kremlin. His immediate boss would be the Secretary of the Security Council of the Russian Federation, one of the most powerful and influential figures in the country, trusted and relied upon by Vladimir Putin. For Gerasimov, aged forty-eight and with prospects of even higher promotion in the future, it was a great honour. It was also a job he could not turn down.

But after twenty-four years of serving his country as an undercover spy licensed to kill anyone on the president's list of perceived enemies, at home and overseas, Gerasimov had had enough. He knew he had reached a key point in his life, and there were two things that motivated him to consider a dangerous move.

The first was the war in Ukraine, which he considered the gravest strategic mistake of Putin's regime; and the second was a woman he had met while participating in an ultimately farcical mission in London which should have ended his career but bizarrely had the opposite effect. The woman was Rebecca Strong.

He would never forget the day he first spotted her, sitting at a table on the pavement outside a French brasserie in Kensington. She was on her own and didn't appear to be waiting for anyone to join her.

He was looking for a way of staying somewhere that would not be easily traceable by the British authorities. He had been staying at the Royal Garden Hotel in Kensington since arriving from Geneva, but now he needed a private address. The tall woman sitting casually at the table looked an independent type, someone in control of her life. He gambled that she lived alone.

"Excuse me, I wonder if you could help me?" he asked.

She looked up, and he saw curiosity in her eyes. He needed a safe refuge, but perhaps she could offer more than bed and breakfast.

He used his charm and explained that he was a visitor to London and wanted to go to the National Portrait Gallery. Rebecca showed little interest in his opening gambit but eyed him up and down, and when he suggested she might accompany him to the gallery, she put on a quizzical but amused look.

He introduced himself as Jean-Paul van Dijk, a businessman with Dutch, Swiss and Eastern European lineage, which appeared to intrigue her. When he asked, she said she was English, Scottish and Cornish.

"Cornish?"

"Redruth."

Gerasimov's disenchantment with his employers began soon after Putin ordered nearly 200,000 Russian troops engaged in a military exercise on the border with Ukraine to invade their neighbour on February 24, 2022. Like all those with privileged information about Putin's ambitions, he felt the decision to take control of Ukraine was right, both for the security and safety of Russia, and as a warning to the West to stop its empire-building expansion, threatening the very existence of his country.

Gerasimov shared the same paranoia about the West, as did most of his colleagues in the GRU. He agreed it was time to make a stand against the West, and in particular the United States. He felt they had to learn that enticing Ukraine to join the NATO alliance was a step too far. The Kyiv government had to be forcibly brought back under the wing of the Kremlin. Of that, Gerasimov had no doubts.

He also believed in the superior military power of the Russian armed forces and was convinced that the invasion would achieve its objectives in a matter of weeks, if not days. Then it all went wrong. Hopeless planning by the office of the Chief of the General Staff, poor intelligence about Ukraine's ability to fight back, and the unexpected decision by the whole of NATO and other partners to arm Kyiv to defend itself against the might of the Russian army led to disaster.

In preparation for his promotion to the staff of the Security Council, Gerasimov's security clearance was raised to the highest level, giving him access to documents branded "Of Special Importance". This classification was only used on documents which, if unlawfully released, would cause maximum damage to the whole Russian Federation. Prior to his promotion, Gerasimov had only been granted access to the lower classification categories "Completely Secret" and "Secret".

Being a former lieutenant-colonel in the KGB, Putin was obsessed with secrecy. Those with access to the highest level of classification had to go through intensive vetting, which could take up to a year and involved interrogation of every family member and anyone even remotely associated with a person's past career. In Gerasimov's case, he knew that those responsible for vetting his past would do everything they could to check out his extra-marital liaisons. Rebecca Strong would have been on their list. He had been obliged to provide her name and address.

His GRU superiors had known about Rebecca from the start. When they were informed by their own processes that he had moved into her rented top-floor flat in St Luke's Road, Notting Hill, during his London mission, they had raised no objection on the grounds that it seemed to be a practical solution. While he was engaged in his mission to assassinate MI5's director of counter-espionage, using a woman as cover was not thought either inappropriate or reckless, although Gerasimov's past lascivious attachments were noted high up on his personal file.

In a series of vetting interrogations, Gerasimov had downplayed his involvement with Rebecca, making it clear that the move to her flat was entirely justified and necessary. It was a purely working arrangement. As soon as he realised she had begun to suspect him, he had swiftly left the flat and had never seen her again. The replies to his interrogators contained one omission: he liked her. A lot.

The vetting process was an endurance test. Even though he was a long-serving and trusted member of the GRU, he was treated as if he were a potential traitor. The sense of paranoia in the top levels of the Kremlin was almost suffocating. It wasn't just a question of loyalty; anyone considered for a job in the Kremlin had to demonstrate total dedication and commitment to the Russian president and to his demands. He was asked frequently whether his covert missions abroad had given him any pro-Western ideas. The Kremlin, more than anything else, was paranoid about the West. Every diplomat sent to the United States or to European capitals was subjected to intense and prolonged scrutiny.

Gerasimov was interrogated every day for four weeks, including the weekends. One of the questions asked on three separate occasions was whether he would instantly expose any colleague he suspected of being disloyal. Gerasimov answered forcefully that he would, and pledged his loyalty to the president. But he knew his failed mission in London had awoken something in his head. He wasn't sure whether it was just frustration with the overpowering bureaucracy of the Russian system or whether it was more fundamental than that. Perhaps a deep, personal desire to experience a different way of life. His relationship with Rebecca had stirred up uncomfortable longings.

Three weeks after Gerasimov passed the vetting tests, Vladimir Putin launched his invasion of Ukraine. Two days later, Gerasimov moved into his new office in the Kremlin.

Several weeks went by before he saw the first documents marked "Of Special Importance" and headed "Special Operation Progress Report", which focused on the achievements, not the failures, of the invasion plan. The logistic nightmares that caused a traffic jam of ambushed tanks and armoured personnel carriers thirty miles from Kyiv were summed up in carefully crafted language. One document, drawn up by the senior planning officer of the personal staff of General Valery Gerasimov, Chief of the General Staff (no relation to Mikhail Gerasimov, despite sharing a surname), stated: *Following the temporary hold-up of the vanguard armoured convoy, the second phase of the operation will go ahead as planned. Four submarines positioned forty-five nautical miles north-east of Snake Island will fire a barrage of cruise missiles at five high-tech industrial targets in Kyiv.*

Another document with similar secrecy classification outlined the pros and cons of launching a nationwide cyberattack on all of Ukraine's telecommunications networks. Gerasimov read it with fascination. With such power in the hands of the Kremlin, why, he asked himself, hadn't the order been given to obliterate Ukraine's whole communications system? He raised the issue with one of his superiors, but instead of engaging in a sensible, intelligent conversation, he informed Gerasimov bluntly that it wasn't his job to question the strategy for the operation in Ukraine. The reply had sent shivers down his spine. He had to remind himself of the three key principles for working in the Kremlin: loyalty, loyalty, loyalty.

However, the cyberwarfare report stayed in his mind. Ukraine had been a satellite nation of the Soviet Union, and the country's telecommunications had been installed and updated by Russian engineers. The Kremlin knew everything about Ukraine's phone system and all aspects of the country's critical infrastructure. A mass cyberattack could have emasculated Kyiv's ability to maintain command and control of its armed forces, and would have caused widespread confusion and fear among the Ukrainian people. But Gerasimov read the full report and saw that there were misgivings at the highest level of the general staff. The quality of the army's supposedly secure military radio system was so poor that commanders on the ground as well as individual soldiers were using their personal mobile phones, and needed Ukraine's relatively modern broadband network for communications to work properly.

Although Gerasimov was not surprised by the revelation, it was another indication that planning for the so-called special military operation in Ukraine had been criminally inadequate.

As weeks went by, Gerasimov detected an increasing sense of panic and doubt in the reports from the general staff and from command HQ in Ukraine. However, the scale of the disasters, so openly detailed in Western press reports and dismissed as propaganda by Moscow, was never fully itemised. The reason was simple: Putin never bothered with the reports marked "Completely Secret" and "Secret". He only wanted to see intelligence with the "Of Special Importance" branding. The language in those reports, therefore, was always couched in as positive a light as possible. But Putin, like Gerasimov, was a trained intelligence officer and he wasn't fooled by his generals' attempts to hide the growing alarm over the way the operation was progressing.

Gerasimov had dared to question the optimistic view during a round-table conference in the Kremlin.

"I just wondered," he said, "whether we're grasping the full extent of the logistic challenges we are encountering."

His doubts were heard in silence. Not a single other individual in the room shared his opinion, or at least none had the courage to voice similar doubts. All of those present studiously looked down at the notepads in front of them. Gerasimov knew immediately he had crossed a dangerous line but he wasn't reprimanded for speaking out.

Indeed, later that day his boss thanked him for his intervention, but added: "I sincerely hope, Colonel, that your doubts are entirely wrong."

Gerasimov wasn't sure at the time whether that was a compliment or a warning, but it was at that moment he decided the leadership of his beloved country had gone crazy, and he knew his intervention at the meeting would be marked against him.

***

After a devastating anti-ship missile attack on the Russian Black Sea Fleet flagship cruiser, the *Moskva*, targeted with the help of US satellite intelligence and data from a US Navy P-8 Poseidon maritime surveillance aircraft flying over the Black Sea from Romania, a document was circulated within the top echelons of the Kremlin. It was dated April 16, 2022, three days after the *Moskva* was fatally struck by two Ukrainian Neptune missiles fired from a shore base.

Headed "The Non-Conventional Options" and written by the head of the 12 Main Directorate of the Russian Defence Ministry, the single-page document outlined the steps needed for a tactical nuclear weapons strike on eight targets in Ukraine. As a senior adviser to the Secretary of the Security Council, the newly promoted Colonel Mikhail Gerasimov was one of thirty-five people in the Kremlin, Defence Ministry, and GRU intelligence service who was cleared to see the document.

The document was drawn up for the urgent consideration of the president, who had ultimate control over the deployment and use of nuclear and other non-conventional weapons. It specified that one squadron of Sukhoi Su-30 fighter aircraft, based at

Kubinka air base near Moscow, would be moved to Millerovo, in Rostov Oblast, close to the border with Ukraine. A second squadron would be flown to Belarus.

Using long-planned subterfuge techniques developed in a programme codenamed *Taifun* – Typhoon – the required amount of air-launched tactical nuclear weapons would be transported separately from storage sites at six different bases to Millerovo and to Lida air base in Belarus, which was twenty-five miles from the Lithuanian border.

At the same time, two batteries of Iskander medium-range missile launchers based in Belarus and in Kaliningrad, the Russian enclave wedged between Poland and Lithuania along the Baltic coast, would be fitted with nuclear-tipped rockets. With a range of around 190 miles, the Iskanders could hit targets in Western Ukraine. The missile launchers in Belarus could reach Kyiv.

The chief of 12 Main Directorate had responsibility for all of Russia's tactical nuclear weapons and answered directly to the minister of defence. As part of his recommendation for resorting to the nuclear option, he emphasised the importance of putting Russia's strategic nuclear weapons delivery systems – land-based intercontinental ballistic missiles, commonly known as ICBMs, plus long-range bombers and strategic deterrent submarines – on high alert, in preparation for a worst-case scenario reaction from the US.

When Gerasimov read and reread the document, at first he was not alarmed. These were routine option suggestions. He had always known, indeed the whole world knew, that the Russian president might resort to nuclear weapons if he judged that Russia's existence was threatened. But the attack on the *Moskva*, while it certainly threatened the safety of the other Black Sea Fleet warships gathered in large numbers offshore, did not represent an existential blow to the integrity of the Russian motherland. The options document appeared to be more about revenge. Gerasimov assumed that Putin himself had demanded the nuclear options be laid before him.

It was this document more than anything else that made Gerasimov begin to doubt the whole reasoning behind the invasion. It also made him question his loyalty to the Kremlin leadership. He was in a position of absolute trust. He was one of the privileged few inside the Kremlin. He could never betray that honour. And yet the chief of the all-powerful 12 Main Directorate was coolly presenting his commander-in-chief with a nuclear plan that had clearly been worked out in detail well before the invasion of Ukraine had got underway. Gerasimov left his office that evening with the seeds of a dangerous idea going round and round in his head.

It was late. He knew his two children, son Sasha, aged twelve, and daughter Arina, ten, would be asleep in bed. As a senior officer in the Kremlin, he was allowed to take a taxi home when it was late evening. As the taxi drew near, Gerasimov suddenly felt afraid for his family. What he had in mind would put them in danger. He was proud of his family and felt responsible for them, but at the same time he loved his professional life, which was entirely separate from them and their needs. He loved his wife, Natasha, but enjoyed the excitement of associating with good-looking women who challenged him. Rebecca Strong had been such a woman.

His wife was not a beautiful woman. She was solid and dependable and loyal, like the wives of so many of his colleagues in the military and intelligence world. When he was promoted to the position in the Kremlin, they were given upgraded accommodation.

They now rented a three-bedroom apartment in a nine-storey circular building in western Moscow. The apartment block was more than fifty years old, and despite a high annual maintenance charge, Gerasimov had soon realised the managing agency for the building had little interest in maintaining anything.

Natasha had tried not to show her disappointment.

"We're lucky, Mikhail," she had said. "It's an honour to be given a bigger flat, we should be grateful, and I'm sure I can do things to improve it."

However, none of the rooms in the apartment had been redecorated since the block was opened; the carpets were frayed and several of the windows were jammed. But there was a courtyard with trees and a children's playground, which made life more bearable. It was certainly a significant improvement on the run-down Soviet-style accommodation they had lived in for five years in a southern district of Moscow with poor transport facilities.

Gerasimov trudged up the stairs to his fourth-floor apartment. It was 10 p.m. Natasha greeted him with a perfunctory kiss and asked him whether he had had a good day.

As he always did, he replied: "Fine, interesting and fine."

Natasha was so used to the response she made no comment and went to the kitchen. Gerasimov sat on the sofa in the small room overlooking the inner courtyard and went over in his mind the idea that had come to him earlier that day. He began to think he had reached a point in his life where he needed to make a decision that would place him and his family at grave risk. It was then he thought of Rebecca and suddenly realised there might be a way of changing his life forever. He had to contact her.

∗∗∗

Rebecca was lying in her bed. Alone. Sandy had been too busy to see her after the court hearing, and Rebecca wanted time on her own to think about the text she had received. It was past midnight. She had looked at the text a hundred times. Should she ignore it? *Yes, I should*, she told herself. It was from the man who had put her life in danger, the man who had caused mayhem in London for weeks. The man who had cold-bloodedly shot dead two police officers sitting in their car on protection duty outside

Geraldine Hammer's home. He had entered the house with only one mission in mind – the assassination of Geraldine Hammer – and yet had failed to carry it out. It was one of the many mysteries about Mikhail Gerasimov.

Rebecca had absolutely no wish to ever see him again. Yet those two initials ending the text were a private code, something only she would understand. It was a message reminding her of their past intimacy. *RR. Redruth.*

Why would he send her such a message? Was there something behind it or was it just a typical throwaway remark from a man who had enjoyed sharing her bed and wanted more? If it was the latter, she could dismiss it without replying. But what if there was a hidden message, what if Gerasimov had some other reason to make contact?

Rebecca knew very little about espionage but she liked intrigue. Since unwittingly becoming involved in the Russian assassination plot the previous year, she had not only sat down for a debriefing with Geraldine Hammer in her office at MI5 but she felt they were now friends. Geraldine had told her she would make a good spy. She liked that. But apart from bumping into Geraldine again by chance in a restaurant and exchanging a few friendly pleasantries, the two women had not spoken to each other since then, despite vowing to keep in touch.

The one thing Rebecca did have was Geraldine's private phone number, which meant MI5's spy supremo trusted her. Rebecca liked that, too. But should she ring Geraldine and tell her about the text she had received during the Old Bailey trial of the spy chief's former personal assistant? Rebecca had no reason to feel any sense of loyalty towards the man she had known as Jean-Paul van Dijk. But his getting in touch after all these months could be important.

She should tell Geraldine, she decided, especially since she, too, had been charmed and seduced by the same man when he had carried out a reconnaissance trip to London, posing as a European businessman under the name of Lucas Meyer.

It was too late for Rebecca to send her a message. She decided to wait until the morning. The only decision she made without hesitation was that she wouldn't tell Sandy.

CHAPTER THREE
CURIOSITY GETS THE BETTER OF REBECCA

Rebecca woke up with the decision already made: she would reply to the text but keep it simple. Nothing inviting. Just straightforward. It would probably come to nothing. Perhaps it had been a joke. Whatever it was, it wasn't important. Not to Rebecca. She didn't need or want to see the Russian ever again. A short text back showed casual interest but that was it.

She leaned across to her bedside cabinet and picked up her phone. She scrolled to the RR message and then closed her eyes. Her reply had to be pitched right.

"Why?"

She contemplated adding a few more words and ending with "RS". But the one word, she thought, was adequate.

Rebecca realised she was more than just intrigued by the unexpected text from her former Russian flatmate. In the pit of her stomach she felt the slightest of twinges. It was a sensation she had experienced the first time she met him, while sitting at the bistro in Kensington. She'd felt it again, although on a significantly larger scale, when he'd invited her up to his bedroom after lunch at his London hotel. The thought made her smile as she lay in bed.

It would be mid-morning in Moscow, assuming he had sent the text from there. Perhaps he wouldn't reply. But her last thought before she climbed out of bed to begin a busy day, completing a painting due to be hung in the foyer of a local bank, was that he definitely would reply.

Halfway through breakfast, her phone pinged.

"I have a proposal for you."

Rebecca waited ten minutes before texting back.

"I'm not in the market."

An instant response this time.

"Not that sort of proposal. Strictly business."

Rebecca was disappointed. Then she was annoyed with herself for feeling that way. She had no wish to rekindle the relationship. It would be both immoral and unpatriotic, perhaps even criminal. She could hardly contemplate revisiting a sexual relationship with a man who had not only threatened her country but also deceived her from the moment they met. So she knew she had no reason whatsoever to feel disappointed by his somewhat strait-laced reply. She should feel relieved. But if sex was not his motive for getting back in touch, what could it be about? She texted back.

"I'm not in your business."

A few minutes went by. She imagined him holding his phone and wondering how to reply.

"I'm serious."

"So?"

"Tell no one."

"Tell no one what?"

"Do you want to help or what?"

"You've lost me."

"This is serious."

"So you said."

"Would you meet me?"

"What for?"

"Not for that."

"I got that."

"You're the only one I know and can trust."

"Trust! There is no trust."

"Please, Rebecca, this is very difficult for me."

"Ha!"

Then nothing. For fifteen minutes. Rebecca thought she might have finally put him off. Whatever it was he had in mind, perhaps her unwelcoming tone had done the trick.

Her phone pinged. Gerasimov was back.

"This is risky."

"So stop texting."

"Rebecca ..."

"In fact, stop texting."

"I'd hoped you might help."

"With what?"

"Can't tell you."

"God."

"Have to go."

That was it.

Rebecca was relieved but still curious, and also slightly concerned. Gerasimov – no longer Jean-Paul van Dijk – had sounded genuinely serious. He had something on his mind which either he wasn't going to or couldn't tell her. She had the feeling that whatever it was she wouldn't want to be part of it anyway. Best to leave well alone. She wouldn't text him back.

She had plenty of work to do to take her mind off the Russian. She had been commissioned to do a painting with a London landscape, six feet wide by four feet high. It wasn't her usual style. She preferred a canvas filled with splashes of colour and geometric designs, oil, not watercolour, and nothing easily identifiable. Her commission was to be in watercolour and everything in the picture had to be recognisable. She had initially turned down the job offer. She hadn't painted a proper watercolour since leaving Goldsmiths art college in south-east London. But when she was promised £4,000 for the painting, she swiftly changed her mind. She knew she could do it. A long time ago she had painted a watercolour of a Sussex landscape which had captivated her parents. They still had it hanging in the front room of their house in Eastbourne.

Gerasimov had seen some of her work in her flat and praised her. But she knew he didn't like the paintings. He'd probably prefer the watercolour of the London landscape, which was now nearly completed. Painted from a position near the northern end of Vauxhall Bridge, it took in the river, with barges and a bright yellow ferry, and the somewhat exotic building that was the headquarters of MI6, the Secret Intelligence Service.

She spent the morning in her usual painting clothes, light-blue jeans that clung tightly to her long legs, and a white shirt, left untucked. She could have pinned her shoulder-length blonde hair into a bun or ponytail, but it hung loosely around her face. As she dabbed at the picture with a long paintbrush, she occasionally had to sweep strands of hair out of her eyes.

She had considered painting Thames House, the MI5 headquarters across the river from the MI6 HQ. But Thames House was old-style architecture and, apart from the entrance, which was quite grand, there was little to inspire her artistic talents. She also felt strangely protective towards the MI5 building. Inside, on the sixth floor, was Geraldine's office.

The chances of Geraldine spotting a painting by her, with Thames House as the centrepiece, were pretty remote. But Rebecca, for a reason she couldn't really explain, was unwilling to run the risk. In any event, the MI6 building at Vauxhall Cross was architecturally much more interesting. She liked the idea of a building that looked ostentatiously post-modern, stuffed with British spies, none of whom could be spotted from any vantage point across the river. Geraldine had always referred to MI6, which she could see from her office window, as their "sister service". Rebecca thought that was rather sweet.

Rebecca worked on the painting for three hours. It was still unfinished, but she was hungry and so she left her flat to go to a local café she frequented. Her phone pinged again as she was crossing the road. She didn't look at it until after she had reached the café and was seated at a window table with a coffee and slice of cheesecake. She was in no hurry to read the message. She knew it would be from Gerasimov.

"One last try?"

Rebecca really didn't know how to reply. She waited and ate her cheesecake.

"What do you want?" she texted after a five-minute delay.

"I have something I need to share."

"Like what?"

"Only when we meet."

"Like where?"

Rebecca knew she was probably sounding too interested. *Gerasimov*, she thought, *will be happy with my reply*. This was not what she had intended. But she couldn't help herself.

"I'll let you know."

"I can't just go off."

"Please trust me. I'll fix it all."

Rebecca felt strangely excited but also alarmed. This was going too far, too fast.

"Like a travel agency?" she replied.

"Yes."

"Sounds crazy."

"A bit."

"Not against crazy, but I have no reason to see you. Ever."

"I know, sorry for everything."

"A helluva lot to be sorry about."

"Yes. But this is different."

"You mean it will make up for all the bad stuff?"

"Potentially."

"I don't know…"

"Have to go."

Now Rebecca was in a real quandary. If she met Gerasimov, would she be committing a criminal offence? Could she be charged with consorting with a known enemy if she was found out? Crucially, why should she trust him? What could he possibly be after apart from the obvious? They had enjoyed an extremely energetic liaison during the time he lived in her Notting Hill flat. She had never specifically asked Geraldine whether she had also enjoyed her very brief fling with Gerasimov, but she suspected from the way her friend recounted her experience with him that she had been shocked and put off by his robust lovemaking. Rebecca had been taken aback by his forcefulness and lack of tenderness but she had quickly taken control and that had removed his apparent desire to dominate her.

Geraldine, by contrast, appeared to have succumbed to his domination and bitterly regretted it. She had admitted to Rebecca, in a highly personal conversation at MI5 headquarters when they compared notes about the man they had both slept with, that their encounter had been a disaster from the moment she lent him her phone to call a garage to pick up his broken-down car, parked near where she lived in South London.

For the director of counter-espionage to have fallen into such a trap didn't say much for her intuition, let alone her training. She had had to admit her transgression to the director general of MI5 and had received a potentially career-ending rebuke. Rebecca knew that if she rang Geraldine and told her about the series of texts from Gerasimov, her MI5 friend would order her to reject his advances immediately.

At that moment, Rebecca made up her mind about two things: she would meet Gerasimov and she would tell no one.

It was time to return to her flat. But before she left, she sent one more text.

"OK."

***

Gerasimov was in his office, a room with a high ceiling off a long corridor on the ground floor, which he shared with five others. His title was Principal Assistant to the Secretary of the Security

Council. The other four consisted of a secretary, Valentina Orlov, and three middle-ranking intelligence officers, none of whom had access to any documents marked "Of Special Importance", sent either electronically or by hard copy.

His computer was secured with a three-layered password system. But, oddly, it was linked to a printer that was available to everyone in the office. The general Kremlin rule was that nothing should be printed off, apart from the most mundane emails, letters or documents. All documents sent electronically marked with any of the three secrecy classifications were automatically covered by the "prohibited-printing" category, known throughout the Kremlin as the "*opasnost*", or danger, files.

Every office in the Kremlin was governed by the same security procedures. One member of the staff in each office was responsible for monitoring all exchanges of information and had the right, at any moment of the day, to check an individual's computer to ensure there were no unauthorised communications or, the worst scenario, leaks of any kind. Despite the tight secrecy regime, the staff member with the security responsibility was not allowed to check on any document on a screen that carried the "Of Special Importance" classification.

Gerasimov, being among the chosen three dozen to have access to these most sensitive of all documents, was, therefore, subject to the rigorous security checks except when the most secret documents were involved. For a loyal member of the Security Council staff, this was an accepted privilege; for anyone contemplating betraying their country, this was a loophole.

It was 8 p.m. He planned to head off home. But suddenly, he received a document electronically, which came with a red warning flash in the top right-hand corner of his screen. This meant it required urgent consideration.

He opened the document. It had been sent by his boss.

A request had come down from the office of the president to draw up a contingency plan for a special operations mission in Ukraine. The objective was to remove the leadership of the Kyiv government in order to cause maximum confusion and disruption, resulting in surrender and an end to the war.

The third paragraph of the document read:

Mikhail Nikolayev, you have been given the honour of commanding this mission, which is the most important of its kind since the special military operation was launched by the president. You are to start developing a plan immediately. You may recruit who you wish, but your team must be kept to a minimum. All support will be provided, depending on what you consider necessary to complete the mission. Be courageous for the motherland.

There was nothing in the document that defined exactly how the leadership should be removed. That appeared to be left to the designated commander of the special operations mission: Colonel Mikhail Gerasimov.

Gerasimov was astonished. He read the words on his computer screen a second time. *Any such mission would be suicidal,* he thought. Previous attempts had all failed. The president of Ukraine and his closest advisers were guarded night and day by a forty-to-fifty-strong unit of combat-veteran soldiers. Any attempt to remove the leadership would be condemned around the world, even if it ended in failure, as it was bound to do.

He was the last person in the office. He still glanced around to make sure he was alone. The document marked "Of Special Importance" stared back at him. Whatever he did next would have potentially life-ending consequences – his life, not the life of the president of Ukraine. Gerasimov needed a copy of the document. He couldn't print it. There were two possible solutions: to copy and paste it and send it to his private phone, which was easily traceable, or to photograph it with the camera on his mobile phone. But mobile phones were forbidden in the Kremlin. When he had texted Rebecca during office hours he had left the building, collecting his phone from security reception on the way.

Gerasimov decided he needed more time to think it through. He acknowledged receipt of the document, and switched off his computer.

He knew that his boss, the Secretary of the Security Council, and, indeed, the president himself, would expect a full reply detailing options for carrying out the required mission in Ukraine as quickly as possible.

Gerasimov was facing the biggest and most dangerous decision of his life.

CHAPTER FOUR
A SURPRISE PACKAGE ARRIVES

Rebecca's flat intercom rang. She had been awake for half an hour but was still in her yellow silk pyjamas. She went to the intercom and pressed the button.

"Package for you."

"Front door should be open. Just leave it on the hall table. Thank you," she replied.

She grabbed her keys and went down the stairs to the ground floor. The package was waiting on the table. She picked it up and scuttled back upstairs.

The package was heavily taped. It took her a few minutes to rip off the outer packing. Inside was a white envelope with no markings on it. She tore it open and removed the contents. Then she sat down abruptly, her mouth open. On the table were return first-class tickets to Venice from Heathrow, return tickets by water bus from Venice Marco Polo Airport to Hotel Palazzo Veneziano, a reservation for three nights' stay in a luxury double room and a booking for a gondola to travel from one end of the Grand Canal to the other. All in her name.

The dates for the trip, if she decided to go, were October 18–21, just three weeks away.

Rebecca's heart jumped. This was a big deal. It was one thing to play around with words in a text hinting at a possible meeting with a man she felt she never knew properly, let alone understood, but quite another to start packing a bag for three nights in the most romantic city in the world.

Gerasimov could have picked an ordinary modern hotel in, say, Frankfurt or Brussels or Helsinki. But he had selected Venice. Was this a move by a man who just wanted to spend three nights with her, or was there really an ulterior motive that had more to with his job as a spy? She suspected she was being conned into sleeping with him again. All the signs fitted that scenario. Otherwise, why go to Venice? Rebecca was disappointed. He was just a typical oversexed man after all. She could hardly take her eyes off the first-class tickets lying on the table, but she couldn't go. She had had her moment of excitement, but the trip was not going to happen.

Her phone pinged. It was him.

"I know what you're thinking."

"Really?"

"You're thinking 'that's all he wants'."

"Does look like it."

"I do, of course I do. How could I not? But there is much more. If Venice puts you off I'll send you different tickets. Anywhere. But we HAVE to meet."

"I don't know."

"Please, Rebecca. I chose Venice because I thought you deserved it."

"Well thanks."

"You're angry with me."

"Just disappointed."

"With Venice?"

"Well, no, not with Venice as such."

"So Venice is good?"

"Why should I trust you?"

"I've booked a separate room."

"What!"

"Separate room."

Rebecca couldn't believe it. Could this be true? And if so, what did it mean, exactly? Was she going to go all the way to Venice to sleep in a double bed on her own?

"OK."

"So you're happy with that?"

"I didn't say that."

"So ..."

"We'll see."

"So you're coming?"

Rebecca sat in her silk pyjamas feeling a mixture of apprehension, curiosity, doubt and desire. If she went to Venice, this extraordinary Russian would be sharing her bed in the Palazzo Veneziano. She knew that, and so did he.

"Yes."

She could hardly believe what she had just written.

***

In the second week of the Old Bailey trial of Amelia Prendergast, the proceedings were back in open court. Sandy Hall had been promised a ten-minute slot for the six o'clock. He had already gathered a lot of background information from his MI5 and Met Police sources to provide a pretty comprehensive report on the spy with the codename "Svekla", but because of the closed court sessions, Sandy had gaps in his prepared report. He knew that Rebecca probably had some of the answers, but she had made it clear that what she had learnt from Geraldine Hammer had to remain confidential. He understood, and in fact admired her for her loyalty, but it was frustrating.

In briefings by his MI5 sources, it had been acknowledged that the vetting procedures that allowed Amelia Prendergast access to highly sensitive and classified information had failed to uncover anything in her past life that could explain why she had decided to betray her country for money. He was told she had spent six months learning Russian at an academy in Siberia, but this had been thoroughly checked out. Nothing improper or unusual or suspicious had been uncovered, although it was freely admitted it had not been easy to gather sufficient information about her time there.

Sandy had asked during the briefing, why, in that case, they had given her a job.

"How," he had asked, "if there were any doubts or gaps in knowledge about her past life, did she pass vetting?"

The reply he got was unsatisfactory and vague. Vetting, he had been told, was comprehensive, but could never be seen as a guarantee of trustworthiness. Amelia Prendergast had seemed to be an excellent candidate for a job in MI5. She had transferred from the Foreign Office with the finest references. Sandy planned to speculate that the time spent at the academy in Siberia must have played a part in converting her into a spy for Russia. He believed there could be no other explanation.

The court case had been the biggest story for more than a week. Sandy had been so busy he hadn't seen Rebecca. He had phoned her, but she had seemed unusually distracted.

Sandy looked up at the public gallery hoping to spot her, but she wasn't there. She had watched from the gallery on the first day of the trial, and he had expected to see her for the jury's verdict and sentencing. Sandy knew how interested she had been in the trial, and her absence on the crucial day was curious. Whatever was distracting her, she had kept it to herself. When Sandy asked her if everything was all right, she had replied without much conviction that she was busy. He had left a message on her phone suggesting dinner later in the week. But so far, she had not come back to him.

Sandy adored her but he knew he couldn't have all of her to himself. There was always something held back, as if she wanted to keep her options open. She was passionate and caring and adorable, and he was in love with her. But he was never sure whether she felt the same way, even when she said she did.

"How do you feel about me?" Sandy had asked when they were eating in one of their favourite restaurants.

"Silly question," she had replied.

"So is that good or bad?"

"Another silly question."

"Rebecca, you are incorrigible."

It became his favourite word for her when they had similar conversations on other occasions. Annoyingly for him, she liked it.

He knew it was probably more to do with his own insecurity and lack of confidence in handling a relationship with someone as overwhelmingly attractive and demanding as she was. He might be one of the stars on the Sky News team but sometimes he feared she was way beyond his league.

There was also one thing about Rebecca that caused him continuing anguish and doubt. She had met the man who claimed to be Jean-Paul van Dijk, whom she had no reason to trust, and within a relatively short time had allowed him to take up residence in her flat. She never spoke about it, but he assumed they had slept together. And this man had turned out to be an imposter, a Russian intelligence agent using the refuge of her flat in Notting Hill to plot murder and mayhem in London. Sandy knew it had been traumatic for her. He would never forget the bizarre message she had left for him at Sky News: she suspected the Russian assassin the police and MI5 were hunting for was living with her. If she believed that, why had she not just gone to the police? Why had she, instead, contacted the Sky News crime correspondent? Did she feel, for some inexplicable reason, protective towards the man she feared might be a Russian assassin?

Sandy had thought about this over and over again as their relationship developed from a purely professional one to a personal and eventually romantic friendship. He admitted to himself that he was unnecessarily jealous of the Russian who had charmed his way into her life.

When he tentatively raised the issue, she was always totally dismissive, and angrily so.

"Sandy, for God's sake, that's not a part of my past I want to dwell on, and it's certainly not for you to dwell on. OK?" she told him.

She immediately wrapped her arms around him. As always, when she did that, he melted and resolved to push out of his mind any thoughts that she might have a lingering interest in the Russian.

Sandy and the other reporters in Courtroom 1 scrambled to their feet when the jury returned. The clerk of the court addressed the jury and asked if they had reached a verdict. The jury foreman stood up and said they had.

The clerk read out each charge and asked if they had found the defendant, Amelia Prendergast, guilty or not guilty. On each of the five charges, the foreman replied that they had found the defendant guilty.

Amelia Prendergast's shoulders slumped and she looked despairingly at her counsel, Rosemary Blandish, whose face expressed no flicker of emotion. Sir Jeremy Blackburn, prosecuting counsel, nodded to his team but otherwise did not register a noticeable reaction.

Mr Justice Cunningham-Brown turned to face the defendant standing bleakly in the dock.

"Amelia Prendergast," he said, "you have been found guilty on all the charges against you. It is incumbent on me to sentence you to a term of imprisonment that not just reflects the severity of your crimes but also acts as an appropriate deterrent to anyone who holds a position in an official capacity which necessitates access to and safeguarding of sensitive, confidential and secret information. A government cannot govern if those trusted with maintaining the secrets upon which the nation's security depends wilfully and deliberately pass those secrets on to unauthorised individuals or agencies or, in this case, to a representative of a foreign power, indeed a foreign power with hostile intentions towards this country. It is a betrayal of everything you should have stood for."

The judge cleared his throat.

"You have also shown no sign of remorse. Your defence that you were the unwitting victim of a devious plot has been shown to have no substance. The jury has returned unanimous verdicts in each of the five charges. Therefore, I sentence you to a term of imprisonment of fifteen years."

Several people in the public gallery gasped. Even Sandy and his fellow reporters looked surprised. In his early morning report on Sky News, Sandy had speculated she might get seven to ten years, if convicted.

"Same old Cunningham-Brown," Sandy whispered to the reporter next to him. "Always loves to make an example. Bye-bye, Amelia Prendergast."

Sandy had two pieces to broadcast for his six o'clock report. Apart from his summing up of the trial and the repercussions for MI5, he also had to provide a full background reassessment of the extraordinary series of incidents that took place in the summer of the previous year. The backgrounder was already written. With some deft rearranging of his main news piece and the sentencing moved straight to the top as his intro, Sandy was ready.

Two people had now been convicted of crimes related to the assassination attempts against Geraldine Hammer. Sandy was banned under government/media regulations from naming MI5's director of counter-espionage. Under the guidelines set out in the so-called D-Notice system, no member of the security and intelligence services could be identified, with the exception of the heads of the relevant agencies whose names had been officially announced by the government.

However, Sandy was allowed to say that the director of counter-espionage was a woman and that there had been at least two attempts on her life. The first was when a former soldier from the Royal Logistic Corps had been contracted by a Russian intelligence agency to target her as she was being driven in her official car to Thames House, MI5's HQ. Ex-Corporal Joseph

Paine had failed in his mission, had been caught and charged with attempted murder. He had received a life sentence at his Old Bailey trial.

In the second attempt, the Russian spy and trained assassin Mikhail Gerasimov had barged into Geraldine Hammer's house in Kennington and pointed a gun at her as she sat up in bed in her underwear. He, too, failed, but not because he missed. He failed because he didn't fire when he had the chance. He hesitated and was grabbed by Geraldine's bodyguard, who burst into the room.

Gerasimov had escaped only to be captured a few days later and deported when crucial evidence that could have been used to convict him at a trial proved frustratingly elusive.

Sandy had never understood, and hadn't been told by his Met Police contacts, how the necessary evidence had not been found and processed for a conviction. He didn't know that shortly after Gerasimov and the other Russian, Maxim Popov, had been escorted onto a plane for Moscow, all the evidence that the police needed was discovered packed into a heavy holdall at a Left Luggage office in Waterloo station. By then it was too late; the two men were safely out of reach on a plane that had already flown beyond the twelve-mile limit.

The Times, in an editorial, had denounced the incompetence of the police in failing to gather prima facie evidence to put Gerasimov and his fellow spy in a British jail for a long time. Sandy, in his report on camera, said a trial would have served as a stark warning for Moscow that if they sent assassins to the United Kingdom, the British authorities would not hesitate to track them down and put them on trial for all the world to witness.

Sandy broadcast live the news of Amelia Prendergast's tough sentence and his long explanatory piece for the six o'clock. His news editor was happy with both the presentation and the content. Even without help from Rebecca, he had gleaned enough from his contacts to produce a dramatic account. He hoped his main rivals, the crime correspondent of the BBC and the reporter on the *Daily Mail* who specialised in crime and security and had matched him for exclusive stories on the spy drama over the previous few months, didn't come up with a new line.

Sandy loved his job, but there were times when the pressure for exclusives became overwhelming. His news editor was more interested in scoops than good reporting and he went crazy when Sky's competitors, whether in broadcast or print journalism, managed to find an angle that no one else had. Sandy was one of the top-rated reporters on Sky News but if the *Mail* or the BBC beat him to a story his life became unbearable. Well, for twenty-four hours, at least.

This story, however, stood up well against his rivals'. He rang Rebecca. She answered this time.

"Hey, you didn't come back to me," he said.

"About what?" she replied.

"Dinner sometime this week."

"Love to, Sandy, really. But I've got stuff on, I can't."

"So you're not eating at all?"

"Very funny."

"Tomorrow night?"

"Possible; I'll let you know."

"Is everything all right?"

"Sure, just …"

"Stuff, right?"

"Yeah. But don't worry. I still fancy you rotten."

Sandy laughed. Now he felt totally different.

"That's a relief," he said.

"How about you?"

"Yeah, definitely. Even more rotten than your rotten."

She burst into laughter.

"That's all right then," she replied.

"So, dinner soon, OK?"

"OK."

Sandy clapped his hands for no good reason. Those few words from Rebecca had stirred him up. It had been a long day and he was tired, but Rebecca's voice made him feel excited. It was the same sensation he had experienced when he first met her. When he eventually found the courage to ask her out, they had spent the whole meal in a French restaurant laughing and joking. After the lunch was over, he told her he had to rush off back to the office for a breaking story. He always remembered her reply. She had just said "pity", and given him one of her now familiar quizzical looks.

The first time she came to his flat, she spent several minutes complaining about the time it had taken her to get to Isleworth where he lived and gave absolutely no indication that she was planning to do anything more than sit and chat and eat. But when he had begun preparing a pasta dish in the kitchen, she came in and put her arms around him. Her hair and perfume enveloped him. She started kissing his neck and ears. He could have just kept on taking care of the pasta. He had a pesto sauce to make. And a green salad.

In fact, at one point Rebecca had actually said, "Don't mind me, just carry on, I'm starving." But then they both giggled, and almost frogmarched each other into the bedroom, Rebecca trying unsuccessfully to lift up her sweater as they stumbled the few yards. The pasta was overcooked and the pesto sauce a little hurried, but neither cared. Food always tasted better afterwards.

Remembering that moment, Sandy was still awestruck by her passion and then her tenderness when they lay still in each other's arms. Not seeing her for several days had made him realise how much he needed that passion and tenderness. He found her intoxicating. At thirty-eight, he had fallen in love, properly, for the first time.

***

For a number of days, Gerasimov had been bringing into his office in the Kremlin a plastic lunchbox with a sandwich and fruit. He explained to the rest of the people in his office that it was his wife's idea. He joked that she had teased him about getting overweight with canteen food. The first time he arrived at the security checking point, he had displayed his wife's packed lunch and raised a hint of a smile from the normally ill-humoured guards.

Complacency was the worst weakness in a security system that should have been rigorous at all times. Gerasimov was counting on that weakness. It was a gamble, but he judged that once his lunchbox had been minutely examined on day one, day two, and possibly days three and four, the guards would become lazy.

For the first three days, the lunchbox was opened and carefully examined. Even a full colonel in the Russian intelligence world had to be treated the same as the most junior member of staff, although the early banter helped to ease the hostile security procedures. Gerasimov said nothing when the guards poked their fingers into his sandwich and then wiped their hands down their trousers as if they had touched something unpleasant.

After four days, one of the guards asked what he had brought for lunch that day but for the first time didn't follow it up by demanding to see the contents. The lunchbox still had to go through the metal-detecting machine, but by then the guards had lost interest. If their fingers had failed to find something untoward in the colonel's sandwich, the metal detector would do its job and sound the alarm.

The guards, in their dark-blue uniforms, had respect for no one. Their job was to regard each person going through the system as a potential enemy of the state. But a lunchbox? Carried by a full colonel? The initial intense interest had changed to mild curiosity and finally a wave of the hand.

Gerasimov's gamble was all about timing. He had to guess when the guards would stop opening his lunchbox and just place it directly onto the conveyor belt leading to the metal-detecting machine. If he was going to do what he was planning to do, he needed to smuggle a mini-camera in his lunchbox on a day when the guards decided against opening it first. However, Gerasimov also knew that even if on day four the guards put the lunchbox straight onto the conveyor belt, it was possible that on day five or day six they might open it and revert to the finger-poking routine.

On day five, at 7:30 a.m., Gerasimov arrived at the security gate with his normal briefcase in one hand and his lunchbox in the other. The box, plastic and white and opaque, was heavier than usual. Inside was a cheese sandwich, a banana and something wrapped in kitchen paper. Inside the kitchen paper was a hollow bone. Inside the bone was a silver-coloured Minox Riga miniature camera. The bone casing, Gerasimov hoped, would help to shield the camera when the lunchbox passed through the metal detector.

"Open the box, Colonel," one of the guards ordered.

Gerasimov laughed and replied: "You might regret it."

"Eh?"

"It's luncheon meat day."

"Luncheon meat in a sandwich?"

"'Fraid so."

The guard smirked and hesitated.

"Well," he said. "You can keep your luncheon meat. I wouldn't let my wife give me luncheon meat. Urgh."

"Wise decision," Gerasimov said and proceeded to place the lunchbox on the conveyor belt. The guard had lost interest.

No alarm bells. The box passed through without any reaction from the metal detector. Gerasimov felt sweat appearing on his forehead but tried to look calm. He walked casually through the gates, retrieved his briefcase and lunchbox, and smiled at the guards.

"Enjoy your lunch, Colonel," the guard quipped, and briefly snorted.

Gerasimov walked down the corridor towards his office. He had two things on his list for that day. He had to start recruiting for his special mission, requested by the president, and he needed to photograph two documents on his screen – the one that spelt out the contingency preparations for a tactical nuclear strike on Ukraine, and the memo ordering him to plan for the "removal" of the leadership in Kyiv. Both were marked with the classification "Of Special Importance".

Despite the huge risks involved, Gerasimov had assessed that photographing the documents on his screen was the only option that had a reasonable chance of going undetected. He would wait until everyone had gone, either for lunch or at the end of the day. He knew that security guards made regular checks and could come in at any point. Random checks from the large body of security guards, as well as the internal monitoring of workstations by the delegated member of his staff, could catch him out at any time. But he was a full colonel and a special adviser to the Secretary of the Security Council, and that carried weight with everyone else in the room. The guards at the security checkpoint might have shown him disrespect, but his colleagues treated him with a sense of awe. His seniority counted. Somehow, he had to exploit that trust if he was going to leave the office by the end of the day with photographed copies of two highly classified documents, which he knew would be viewed as golden nuggets by any Western intelligence service.

Gerasimov had realised there was no future in Russia. The war in Ukraine was a strategic, military and economic disaster, and the majority of Russians living in far-flung provinces a long way from Moscow were being kept ignorant of what was going on across the border. He had seen all the intelligence about the Ukrainian armed forces prior to the invasion and had been amazed by what appeared to be congenital naivety about their capabilities. Even the Chief of the General Staff himself had signed off on the conclusion that Ukraine's ability to defend itself against the might of the Russian army would fold rapidly once the first tanks arrived.

Gerasimov's whole life had been committed to serving the Kremlin in one way or another, principally as a member of the massive GRU military intelligence organisation. He had joined the army at the age of eighteen, with no ambitions to move into intelligence. But the promise of better prospects and a more attractive salary scale persuaded him to make the switch when he was twenty-five.

He had trained initially at the defence ministry's military academy in Moscow before moving to GRU headquarters, known as the Aquarium, at Khodinka airbase near the capital. His final progression to the elite GRU sabotage and assassination units responsible for presidential-ordered missions around the world came shortly after his thirtieth birthday. He was sent for a ten-month course at the 161st Special Purpose Specialist Training Centre in eastern Moscow, a Spetsnaz facility. He learnt all the dark arts necessary for carrying out "elimination" operations against Kremlin-perceived enemies of the state.

One thing he had learnt early on in his espionage career was that boldness generally paid off. One of his instructors put it simply: "You can knock on a door and ask to come in or just open it and walk through as if it's your right to be there." He had followed that advice in all his undercover missions. More often than he could remember, his brazenness had worked in his favour. He just wondered whether his boldness at the Kremlin meeting, when he'd dared to raise doubts about the progress of the invasion of Ukraine, had been a step too far.

One lingering thought had come into his mind. Was his selection as the leader of the GRU/Spetsnaz team to remove the Ukrainian leadership a way of eliminating him, as well as the government leaders in Kyiv? Those responsible for previous failed assassination plots in Kyiv had been captured or killed. Gerasimov felt he was a marked man.

His decision to turn against his government and change sides had one aim and one aim only: to provide such crucial intelligence to a country in the West that he would be in a position to force them to bring him and his family out of Russia for their safety.

Russian defectors had made their escape on occasion in the past and were still alive, but Gerasimov knew it was a terrible risk. If he got found out, he would be executed and his family would live a life of misery and penury for the rest of their days.

So, boldness was the key. If he was going to photograph documents on his screen, he had to do it surreptitiously but casually, and if someone entered the room when he had the camera in his hand, he needed an instant and confident reason for performing what would be interpreted as a highly suspicious act.

The first task was to convince his secretary to leave without raising suspicions. She often stayed behind to tidy up and make sure everyone in the office had shut down their computers. She wasn't obliged to do so, but it had become her routine. If Gerasimov planned to stay late, he would always mention it to her, and she would leave. But this time he felt nervous because of what he was about to do. His boldness briefly left him.

"Valentina, please feel free to go home," he said eventually. "I have one or two things still to do."

"I can stay and help," she said, remaining in her chair.

"Thank you, Valentina, but that really won't be necessary," he replied in as casual a voice as he could muster.

She hesitated. He looked away, his heart thumping. She *had* to leave.

Two or three minutes went by while Valentina rearranged the pens on her desk, as if she were pondering whether to stay or go home.

Gerasimov was on the point of insisting she leave when she stood up slowly and went to retrieve her coat. It was 7:30 p.m. He knew that at 8 p.m. every night all internal CCTV cameras were switched on. Time was running out.

She turned, wished him goodnight and was gone.

Gerasimov took the lunchbox from his briefcase and removed the bone. Having had to squeeze the Minox camera into the hollow section, when he tried to insert two fingers to get hold of the device, he couldn't get any purchase on it. It was jammed. Looking round at the closed door of the office, Gerasimov felt a surge of panic go through his body. He tried tapping one end of the bone, and with some force, but the camera didn't move. He put the bone back in the lunchbox and walked over to his secretary's desk. Three pens, a spiral-bound notebook and a thin envelope-opening knife were lying neatly on the surface. He grabbed the knife and went back to his desk. He retrieved the bone and slid the knife down the inside to ease the camera out. But again, nothing happened. He thought it had moved a little, but not enough. He tried with his fingers again but they only made the camera settle further down the bone cavity.

Valentina had been gone eight minutes. There were two CCTV cameras in his room, one on either side. They weren't on during the day, while Kremlin staff members were sitting at their desks, because the security employees manning the CCTV networks throughout the Kremlin were contract workers – they didn't have the same security clearance as Gerasimov and his staff. Monitoring from their basement room, they could potentially focus on classified documents on the computer screens, and that was judged to be a risk. More of a risk than allowing trusted members of the Kremlin apparatus to have access to top-secret communications without having a camera watching their every move. But at 8 p.m., the surveillance circuits were switched on to cover the night-time hours until 7 a.m. the following morning.

Gerasimov had twenty-two minutes left. What to do? He could break the outer bone casing and risk damaging the camera. Or jab the closed end with the knife and hope to make a hole to push the camera back through the open end. He chose the latter option. He stabbed the closed end with the knife but made little impact. Glancing frequently at the clock ahead of him, he stabbed and stabbed until, suddenly, a crack appeared. Fifteen minutes left. He stabbed a few more times until the crack widened. Then he pushed the knife through the gap and felt it hit a solid object.

He pushed hard and the camera began to emerge, like a tortoise's head from its shell. He put the knife down and pulled the Minox camera out. He had just over twelve minutes. The Minox seemed unharmed except for some scratches at one end.

He cleaned the camera with a tissue from his pocket. The first document he wanted to photograph was already on the screen. It was the "Of Special Importance" report from the commander of the defence ministry's 12 Main Directorate outlining the contingency plan for deploying and launching tactical nuclear weapons against Ukraine. It was five pages long. Gerasimov photographed each one and then found the memo, with the same classification, ordering him to put together a special forces mission to remove the Kyiv leadership. The clock said three minutes to eight o'clock.

Gerasimov had experienced every kind of combat, from full-scale infantry assaults in the wars in Chechnya to undercover sabotage and assassination operations when his life had been at risk at all times. But as the seconds ticked away, he felt more fear and panic than he had ever experienced.

The memo was a single page. Gerasimov had ninety-four seconds to photograph the page, put the Minox back into the bone cover and replace it in the lunchbox.

He was putting the bone back into the lunchbox, but doing so under his desk, when the large hand on the clock moved to the hour. Red lights appeared on both CCTV cameras in the room. Against all instincts, he refrained from glancing at the cameras. Instead, he casually placed the lunchbox in his briefcase and stood up, stretching briefly.

CHAPTER FIVE
REBECCA BEGINS TO HAVE DOUBTS

Rebecca and Sandy did manage dinner two days later. They went to Mon Plaisir in Monmouth Street, Central London. Rebecca was dying to know all about the trial.

"'Amelia' doesn't sound much like a spy sort of name," she said, when they had ordered drinks.

Sandy laughed.

"But 'Rebecca' does?" he asked her.

"Stop it, Sandy, those days are over; strictly painting now," she replied.

"Ha, we'll see," Sandy said. "I felt a tiny bit sorry for Amelia Prendergast. She didn't look like a heavy duty spy. Not like your Russian."

Rebecca kicked Sandy under the table.

"He isn't and never was my Russian," she said.

He apologised and said he was just joking.

Rebecca was happy with Sandy. They had a good relationship. It was easy-going, which was what she preferred, although she knew he was besotted with her. Maybe he was in love. He hadn't said so, but she could tell. Her feelings varied. When they were really close she loved him but it didn't mean she woke up every day yearning for him. She wasn't sure she would feel like that with anyone. She hadn't so far in her life. But she fancied him, enjoyed his company and liked the fact that he was a journalist. When they were together, it felt like a proper relationship. But Rebecca had always needed her independence. She liked waking up in the morning in her own bed and with no other body taking up space. Even when she woke up and Sandy was there, her first thought was often about who was going to use the bathroom first. Having someone always there made life more complicated. She wasn't into early-morning lovemaking, and when there was a man in her bed, she always felt there was pressure to instantly launch into a passionate embrace. No, she preferred sitting up, having a coffee and musing about her day. A man would begin to pester. But, generally speaking, not Sandy. He seemed to have cottoned on to Rebecca's morning wishes, and she appreciated that about him. Even so, she was not ready to let him move in with her, and she definitely had no great desire to move in with him.

And yet, she knew she was lucky to have met Sandy. He was, in so many ways, right for her. So what was she doing agreeing to fly to Venice to meet up with Mikhail Gerasimov? Why had she even considered his proposal? She had every reason to despise him. He had used her to carry out his nefarious crimes as a Russian spy and had lied to her from the moment he first met her.

But there were two things that made her curious. First, she had been attracted to him, though not immediately. He wasn't instantly or naturally handsome, but his eyes told her everything about him. He was a man who knew his strengths, he liked to control every situation and he never accepted refusal. She recognised his desire to dominate and accepted the challenge. She had proved more than a match for him, and it was for that reason that he moved from just exploiting her to liking her. They became a fiery couple, not just in bed, but in the way they addressed each other. Every day was different and every day was a personality skirmish. They challenged each other.

The second reason she was still curious about him was his text message. She derided him for his use of the word "need" and yet she knew he would never have contacted her again unless he had something serious on his mind. If she was honest with herself, there were a couple of other reasons. She felt excited by the intrigue and she had never been to Venice.

What she would tell Sandy when she disappeared for three days, she wasn't sure. She would have to lie. By going to Venice, she might change her relationship with Sandy forever, not just because she was going to be disloyal to him but because her reunion with Gerasimov might have consequences over which she would have no control.

The day after her dinner with Sandy, Rebecca had mulled over the reasons for not going to Venice and arrived at the conclusion that they outweighed the reasons for making the trip. She had said yes to Gerasimov but now she had changed her mind. It would be wrong. She didn't want to lie to Sandy and she had no way of predicting how it would all end. She would throw away the tickets to Venice and the booking for the gorgeous-looking hotel. She was happy with her decision. The package had been cast into the bin under the sink in the kitchen.

The following morning at 6 a.m., her phone pinged. She was awake. In fact, she had been awake half the night worrying whether she had made the right decision. She looked at the message.

"In case you're rethinking, it's vital you don't. Not for me. For Uk."

Rebecca frowned. How could it be for the UK? What was that supposed to mean?

She had a busy day ahead. Her commissioned painting was completed, and she had to take it to her customer, a branch of the Nationwide bank in New Oxford Street. She got dressed and walked into the kitchen. One cup of strong, black coffee and a plain yoghurt, and she was ready to leave. Her painting, ready to be delivered to her client, had been picked up by a courier van. As she walked down the stairs, she thought about the latest text from the Russian. There was something odd about it, but she didn't know what it was.

She was out all morning. The handover of the picture went well. There was a little ceremony as it was placed on the designated wall. Her customers were pleased, and applauded. Gratitude, as well as the £4,000 fee. Rebecca was happy, too.

Halfway through a sandwich in the café close to where she lived, her phone rang. It was Sandy. He suggested dinner out again, and she accepted. It made her feel she had, after all, made the right decision about Venice. Perhaps some other time. Maybe with Sandy.

When Sandy rang off, she had another read of the text from Gerasimov.

"In case you're rethinking, it's vital you don't. Not for me. For Uk."

Suddenly, she realised what was odd.

"Not for me. For Uk."

It wasn't for the UK, it was for *Uk*. Lower case "k".

Was that just a mistake on his part, or deliberate?

Rebecca suspected the lower case "k" was intended. From her experience of him, nothing he did was a mistake. Was it possible that he wasn't referring to the United Kingdom? Could it be, she wondered, that "Uk" was short for "Ukraine"? It was a leap of imagination, but she thought she knew how Gerasimov's mind worked.

She still had no idea what game he was playing. Why on earth did he want to meet up with her to talk about Ukraine? Since he had been deported from Britain more than a year ago, she had heard nothing from him or about him. One or two British newspapers speculated about whether Gerasimov would be punished by the Kremlin for being kicked out after failing to fulfil his mission, but none of the Russian newspapers mentioned his name. So Rebecca assumed he was still a fully-fledged spy.

If he was still a spy, why would he be contacting her? Was it part of some devious plot? Would it be dangerous for her, personally?

Now she had so many doubts that she concluded it would be reckless and irresponsible to meet up with a Russian who committed grave crimes when he was in London and was still probably working in a secret agency for the Kremlin. Why had she said yes to his text asking her to meet him in Venice? What had she been thinking?

And yet, there was a nagging feeling at the back of her mind that he had contacted her for the simple reason there was no one else in the UK whom he could approach. His name would be on MI5's blacklist. Whatever he wanted to say or offer or propose, he had chosen her to be the conduit. She would be his co-conspirator. If it hadn't been for his reference to "Uk", Rebecca might have dismissed all the thoughts going through her head. But the war in Ukraine had been going on for more than two years, and fears of an escalation to a full-scale war between Russia and the Western Alliance had grown alarmingly in recent months. Maybe Gerasimov had something important to tell her which he couldn't pass on to anyone else?

Before leaving her flat in the evening to meet Sandy at a restaurant in Notting Hill, Rebecca went to the kitchen and removed the package containing the flight tickets and hotel booking from the bin, and placed it on the table. She stared at it and then seemed to make up her mind. She took the package into the bedroom and put it on the bed.

Then she texted Gerasimov.

"Unsure worried confused."

Ten minutes later, he replied.

"Understood, but it'll be fine. Promise."

"It's not right," she texted back.

"It's OK and important."

Rebecca sat down with the phone in her hand. At that moment she couldn't actually imagine arriving at the hotel in Venice and seeing him waiting for her. It would be so weird. Three days with him in Venice. Why three days? He was obviously going to tell her something and try and persuade her to act on his behalf in some way. Was it going to be so difficult a decision that he needed three days to talk her round? She would never know the answer to those questions unless she went to Venice.

She admitted to herself that she was now dying to know what it was all about. It was a risk for her, personally, and it was deceitful to go to Venice without telling Sandy. But she could hardly tell him the truth. So …

"If I come and can't stand the sight of you I will fly straight back," she texted.

"You won't do that."

"You're cocky."

"Rebecca, just come. Enjoy Venice, if nothing else. October is a good time."

"I've taken the tickets out of the bin," she replied after a few minutes.

"Good. I'll meet you in the foyer of the hotel. A week today."

"God, is it that soon?"

"A week today."

She had nothing more to say and left the flat.

***

Exactly a week later, Rebecca arrived outside Venice Marco Polo Airport with one wheeled case and a separate canvas bag over her shoulder. She looked around for her water bus terminal. A short walk and she was sitting in the front end of the boat with the sunshine on her face. She had seen films and TV documentaries, read magazines and gazed in awe at the fine detail of the Canaletto paintings of Venice in the National Gallery in Trafalgar Square. But nothing could have prepared her for the emotions she felt as the boat took her down the Grand Canal, lined on each side by 800-year-old buildings that seemed to have been sculpted by architects with romance and love in their hearts.

Gerasimov had been right: Venice in October was perfect. The heat from the sun was warm but not oppressive. A gentle breeze made all the gondolas tied up along the way bounce up and down as if they were made of papier-mâché. Sunlight exaggerated all the colours, the reds, blues and yellows of the gondoliers, the pinkness of several of the buildings, and the canal itself, which sparkled and winked at every boat delivering tourists to their hotels. Rebecca breathed in the smells of Venice, a heady mix of saltiness rising from the water, traces of grilled fish, stewing mussels and barbecued steak in the air, and a real or imagined mustiness from the ancient buildings lining the Grand Canal.

She wished she was with Sandy. She was accustomed to his ways and felt safe with him. She had known Mikhail Gerasimov for only two weeks, and as the water bus approached the terminal nearest to Hotel Palazzo Veneziano, where she would be staying, she suddenly experienced a surge of apprehension. Now, too late, she realised she should have told someone about her trip to Venice and who she would be with. Not Sandy. But perhaps Geraldine, her friend at MI5. She had decided not to tell her of the trip because it could come to nothing, and Geraldine might have banned her from going. But now she felt alone and vulnerable. She had no reason to trust Gerasimov, despite his assurances in his texts. What were his real plans for her? If she needed help, who would she turn to?

She stepped off the boat and stood on the quayside for a few minutes as the crowds bustled past her in both directions. She saw the hotel. It looked expensive, the sort she could never afford herself. She was now just yards away from being reunited with the Russian who was an enemy to her country. Once again, she felt she might have made a mistake. But the whole atmosphere of Venice was so captivating that she started walking slowly towards the entrance of the hotel. Her heart began thumping inside her chest.

A man in beige slacks, pink shirt and aviator sunglasses, standing a few yards away to her right, next to a café parasol, watched her as she passed through the open door of the hotel and disappeared into the foyer. He made a note of the time. He then spoke briefly into his mobile phone.

"She's arrived," he said.

The man stayed where he was. At that moment, a couple, smartly dressed and laughing, entered the hotel and also disappeared into the foyer.

The couple looked to be in their thirties. The man was significantly taller than his companion. He was wearing a navy-blue jacket with brass buttons, and grey trousers. The woman was also wearing a jacket, but scarlet, and with a matching skirt; there was a multi-coloured scarf round her neck which she removed with a sweep of her right hand. They continued laughing together and strolled to the hotel reception desk. The man asked for their key. Neither of them looked round at the other people present. But instead of moving to the elevator to go to their room, they sat down in one of the sumptuous armchairs in the foyer.

Across the other side of the foyer, another couple seemed to be having an awkward moment. The man was tall and big-chested, with a square face. He appeared to be talking earnestly to the woman in front of him. She was nearly as tall as him, with shoulder-length blonde hair and an attractive face, and standing somewhat resolutely. She had a modest-sized case with wheels, and a canvas bag over her left shoulder. Mikhail Gerasimov and Rebecca Strong had met up, and it was not going well.

***

Four copies of a file marked "Operation Greengage" were positioned next to four glasses of water on a polished table in a large room on the seventh floor of MI6, the Secret Intelligence Service. The last of the four people to take a seat in the room, a woman, had only just entered. The other three acknowledged her with brief nods as she sat down at the head of the table.

Geraldine Hammer, director of counter-espionage at MI5, had walked to the MI6 HQ from Thames House on the other side of the river. It had helped to clear her head. The weather was surprisingly warm for mid-October. She had never liked the MI6 building. It was too exotically designed for a secret service. She preferred her own building, more classical in design and refurbished to house a growing workforce.

Geraldine had run the counter-espionage section for five years and felt it was nearly time to move on. Or to move up. But she was realistic. She had a black mark in her personal MI5 file. She had escaped being dismissed over the Gerasimov affair only because she was so highly regarded in the highest echelons of the Security Service, and also by the Home Office and Cabinet Office. She was forty-eight and happy in her personal life. She had two children from her former husband, and a partner, Sam Cook, whom she would probably never marry. He was a former sergeant in the SAS, a huge man with a surprisingly shy nature who adored her. They had met during the traumatic weeks when she was the target of the Russian assassination plot a year earlier. He was assigned as her bodyguard and had saved her life when Gerasimov burst into her bedroom intent on shooting her. She felt lucky. Despite her frequent absences from home, her son and daughter were remarkably well adjusted and accepted the fact that their mother had a responsible job in government, although they knew very little about it or what kept her away until late in the evenings.

For the moment, all of Geraldine's concentration was focused on the possibility of an extraordinary espionage breakthrough. Operation Greengage, the name plucked from a list of codes with no relevance to anything, had been running for months. It was about to bear fruit.

The three other people in the room on the seventh floor waited for Geraldine to speak. She wasn't in charge of Operation Greengage, but her role was probably the most important. Her deputy, Grace Redmayne, sat opposite her. The two others were from MI6. Patrick Littlefield, director of operations and assistant chief, and Freddie Stigby, Russian specialist. They formed the most exclusive and most tightly controlled joint MI6/MI5 team since the 1980s, when Oleg Gordievsky, a KGB double agent working for MI6, had to be secretly extracted from Moscow.

Geraldine cleared her throat.

"Everything is going to plan," she said. "There was a brief moment of tension, but the two are now upstairs in the room. A full transcript will be circulated by the end of the day."

As she spoke, all four opened the files in front of them. There were twenty pages. Each page was marked "Top Secret".

Operation Greengage had been running for about eleven months. Ever since the deportation of Mikhail Gerasimov from Britain, following the failed attempts to assassinate Geraldine, he had become the number one priority for the MI6 staff in Moscow. They were under orders to build up a dossier on his life, his working routines, his family, his sexual peccadilloes and, most importantly, any career moves.

The results had been sketchy, although the Moscow station succeeded in drawing up an impressive picture of his family life and work routines. The breakthrough came when Gerasimov was promoted and began travelling each day to the Kremlin. Unlike in the West, there was no announcement about his new job, but careful analysis of the structure of the Kremlin staff and previous appointments direct from GRU to Putin's inner councils suggested Gerasimov, as a full colonel, would be in a highly sensitive post with access to top security documents and meetings, and would have unique insights into the workings of the president's mind and ambitions.

The detailed file on Gerasimov had been circulated only to a very select group of people in MI6, MI5, GCHQ, the signals intelligence centre and the Cabinet Office. The file was interesting and informative but led nowhere. There was no grand plan to somehow make use of the file in a way that would benefit the United Kingdom. It was just knowledge and analysis.

Then came the text from Moscow to Rebecca Strong, in the Old Bailey.

In a meeting some months earlier with Howard Church, the new director general of MI5, Geraldine said she intuitively felt that at some point Gerasimov would try to contact Rebecca Strong. She explained she had no intelligence to back that up but was relying purely on her instincts. Church wanted to know more. So she said she had got to know Rebecca fairly well when the young artist was caught up unwittingly in the events in London the previous year. Church knew everything about Geraldine's own association with Gerasimov.

Geraldine told Church that she recognised in Rebecca a woman who had extraordinary strengths. A woman of independence who was in control of her life. And for that reason, she made the assumption that Mikhail Gerasimov would have discovered the same traits while they shared a flat for two weeks. He was the sort of individual who would normally expect to be totally in charge, and acknowledging Rebecca to be a match for him would have been attractive. Sexually attractive. A man like that might want to come back for more, whatever the risks. The director general was not convinced but he trusted Geraldine's instincts, despite the grave error she had committed in falling for Gerasimov's charms.

"So, what do you want to do with this intuition, Geraldine?" Church had asked.

"I know it's flimsy but I think we need to keep a watch on Rebecca," she had replied.

"What do you have in mind?"

"A tap on her phone, the works."

"No judge will give a warrant for that. What possible reasoning could you give?"

"I've thought of that. We need to focus the argument on Gerasimov. He was and remains a security threat to this country, and it is our duty to keep monitoring enemy agents with whom we have had dealings in the past. In his case, in the very recent past. We have reason to believe that he will try to make contact with this woman, and if he does, we will need to know, both for our interest and for hers."

Church played devil's advocate. "But the judge will say, bring me the intelligence to back this up and I will consider it. Otherwise, it's an infringement of the woman's privacy rights."

"I will remind the judge of what happened last year, how Rebecca's life was put at grave risk and how lucky she was to have survived," Geraldine said.

Church still looked doubtful.

"And sometimes precaution pays off. A breach of her rights could save her life," Geraldine persisted.

Church thought for a few minutes and then said, "OK, give it a go. Apply for the warrant yourself, don't give it to your staff."

The judge turned out to be surprisingly malleable. He read the warrant application several times, then signed it. MI5's technical department did the rest.

Although the initials "RR" at the end of the text from Moscow had initially caused confusion, Geraldine knew that it was Gerasimov. One of her brightest members of staff came up with the possible explanation.

"Rebecca was born in Redruth, in Cornwall," he said. "She might have told Gerasimov at some point. So 'RR' could be 'Redruth.'"

Geraldine had smiled and thought to herself, *Agent Redruth*.

Now, there was a broad hint in the series of texts between Gerasimov and Rebecca that the Russian, for some bizarre reason, was contemplating changing sides and using his former flat-share girlfriend as a conduit to Britain's security authorities. And the first step towards this wholly unexpected development was to take place in Venice, of all places.

Gerasimov must have some romantic blood in him, Geraldine had thought. But that didn't make her feel anything but distaste and hostility towards the Russian military intelligence officer. The growing Operation Greengage file had kept her, and her MI5 and MI6 colleagues, informed of what Gerasimov had been doing since his deportation from the UK. Now, if he was to be Agent Redruth, a turncoat working for the British, a new chapter would begin.

Patrick Littlefield, MI6 director of operations and predicted next Chief of the Secret Intelligence Service, was in charge of the new chapter of Operation Greengage. The main activities arising from this potentially spectacular espionage possibility would all take place in Moscow, which was MI6 territory.

Littlefield had an imposing presence. He was some six foot six tall, and very thin. He didn't look as if he had weight-trained ever in his life. But at fifty, he was fit. He never worried about his appearance. He preferred a jacket and roughly matching trousers to a proper suit, and always wore the same tie. It looked like a gentleman's club tie, but he disliked clubs. He had never served in Moscow during his career as an intelligence officer but his climb up the espionage ladder had included time in Ulaanbaatar in Mongolia, Warsaw, Paris and Beijing. It was his four years in China that made it a near certainty that he would become the next "C"; he spoke fluent Mandarin and Cantonese.

It was time for him to lay down the rules.

"I need hardly say," he said to the three others in the room, "that this is going to require a level of secrecy I believe none of us has experienced before in our careers. The identity of the potential new source in Moscow must remain a secret between the four of us here and, of course, head of station in Moscow. He knows nothing at this stage, and until it becomes clear exactly what we have here, he need not be informed. He will know when he needs to know and will be the only contact with the source."

The others in the room knew from experience not to interrupt when the director of operations was in full sway.

Littlefield breathed in deeply. "I believe it would be highly risky and foolishly imprudent for ministers, any ministers, and I am including the PM, to be informed of this potential development. It may all come to nothing anyway. So, just the four of us."

The other three stayed silent.

"Now we have to address the most difficult part of this exercise, and the one that may unravel everything and even cause serious embarrassment both to my service and yours, and subsequently to the government."

He turned to the woman sitting next to him. "Geraldine?"

"I'm going to put it bluntly," Geraldine said. "I plan to use Rebecca Strong to get to Gerasimov. We will be using, indeed, exploiting, a female civilian with no knowledge of our business to set the scene for us to, as it were, do our own job without us intervening or interfering. Under normal circumstances that would be totally unacceptable."

No one looked reassured.

"But for some time we have been bugging her phone and as a result we have this potential breakthrough."

"If that ever came out in the public domain, there'd be an outcry," Freddie Stigby said. "You'd lose your job. We'd all lose our jobs."

"It's a gamble," Geraldine admitted, "but I feel confident that we have taken the necessary precautions to protect Ms Strong, if that is what is required. She is merely a courier, if you like. If he has something to say or hand over, he has chosen her to be his messenger because he trusts her—"

"But why on earth didn't she come to you first, Geraldine?" Stigby interrupted. "You say you had got to know her and you had become friendly. Why didn't she make contact when she received those texts?"

"I don't know," Geraldine replied. "But I'm guessing she thought she was adult enough to make up her own mind and would come to me in due course. She is that sort of woman. I admire her for it."

"But the fact is, Geraldine," Patrick said, "if she screws this up and comes away with nothing, this is all a waste of time and we could lose out on a golden opportunity: a source high up in the Kremlin. It's all in the hands of a thirty-something painter of commercial art. It's a kind of madness."

"Not to mention the fact that we are expecting her, indeed, wanting her, to sleep with this Russian so we can listen in on their pillow talk," Stigby said rather brusquely. He was the oldest person in the room, closer to sixty.

"Come on, Freddie." Grace Redmayne laughed. "This is hardly the first time we have relied on bedroom activities to discover intelligence."

Stigby looked shocked. Patrick Littlefield smirked. Geraldine raised her eyebrows at her deputy.

"Grace is right, of course," Geraldine said quickly, "but we have a duty of care towards Ms Strong and I have made all the necessary arrangements. I have taken every possible precaution to make sure she won't come to any harm, and anyway, I don't believe Gerasimov intends her harm. I am sure that if Gerasimov has something he wants to say to us, she will cooperate with us."

"So there it is," Patrick said. "All I have to add is that while the file on Operation Greengage will remain open to those in Whitehall with the necessary classification access, any details that might or might not emerge from this Venice caper will be for our eyes only."

The three others nodded.

CHAPTER SIX
REBECCA TRIES TO FIND OUT WHAT IT'S ALL ABOUT

Rebecca and Gerasimov were still fully dressed. There had been no instant grabbing and tearing of clothes. The room was palatial, with a huge double bed taking up prominent space. But if there was a sexual charge between them, Rebecca, at least, was keeping it at bay. She wanted explanations first. They hadn't even kissed, not down in the hotel foyer and not in the bedroom once the door was closed.

It wasn't just Rebecca. Gerasimov seemed nervous, too. His first question didn't help.

"Did you tell anyone you were coming here?"

Rebecca looked at him and frowned.

"No," she replied.

"Promise?"

Rebecca didn't reply.

"OK, sorry," he said, "I believe you."

"Well, thanks."

Gerasimov moved towards her and tried to put his arms around her. She pushed him away.

"What's this about?" she asked.

"I wanted to see you."

"Sure, and that's it?"

"No, Rebecca, I have other reasons, too. I told you in the texts."

"You told me nothing."

"Well, I hinted."

"You're just playing games. Tell me properly."

"Can't we relax first? Then we can talk."

Rebecca walked to the window and looked out. She was in Venice but felt strangely homesick. She didn't want him in the same room. She didn't want him at all. She had initially felt an excited twinge in her stomach but it hadn't lasted long. All the doubts she had in London had come back. This was not a man she wanted to be with.

"You should leave, I'm tired," she said, eventually.

Gerasimov looked genuinely dismayed.

"Let me settle in and we'll see."

Gerasimov was about to protest but thought better of it and left the room without saying another word.

He walked down the corridor a few yards and took a key from his pocket. He let himself into a single room with a smaller bed and a view of a backstreet, with a glimpse of water and a bridge. Booking an extra room had been his insurance policy in case things went wrong with Rebecca.

He sat on the bed. Flying to Venice had been a gamble. A high-risk gamble. He had lied to his boss, to his staff and to his wife. He had flown from Moscow to Istanbul on a false passport, and then from Istanbul to Venice. He had told his staff he would be away on a secret mission, and covered his tracks with his overall boss by claiming he needed time off to recruit the right people for the mission he had been given by the president. He said he would be away for three or four days and hoped to have the Ukraine operation planned and ready for approval within six weeks. The Secretary to the Security Council had emphasised the urgency of drawing up a feasible plan to remove the Ukrainian leadership and questioned why it was taking so long. But Gerasimov convinced him of the need to spend sufficient time on a president-ordered project which had to succeed, to make up for all the previous failures.

Effectively dismissed by Rebecca, Gerasimov felt angry and humiliated. But he was also resolved to win her over. He hadn't planned this moment in his life to cast it aside just because a woman had resisted his advances. He knew what Rebecca liked and thought that, with time and patience, he could persuade her to relax and enjoy her three days in Venice. If he was going to succeed in achieving his ultimate goal, he needed Rebecca not only to be his ally, but also to be his willing partner. For that to be accomplished he had to persuade her of his genuine intentions to betray his country, whether that was going to involve sleeping with her or not. He thought it would be easier to win her round if they were lying in bed together with a view of Venice from the pillows. But, not for the first time, he realised that Rebecca was not like any of the women he had previously encountered in his life. Sitting on his bed in a room he had hoped he would not need to use for sleep, Gerasimov knew he was going to have to treat Rebecca with the utmost care. His priority goal in Venice was not to get Rebecca into bed, but to persuade her to become his go-between with the British intelligence services.

He waited twenty minutes and then sent her a text.

"Dinner?"

Rebecca was in the shower but heard the ping. She dried herself with a huge, blue towel and picked up her phone.

"OK." she replied. She was starving.

"Now?" he texted back.

"No, I have no clothes on. Ten minutes."

Back in London, when he was living in her flat in Notting Hill, that would have been an invitation, and he wouldn't have hesitated. But this time, despite being in Venice in a glorious hotel, Gerasimov was not going to risk making any kind of assumption. Not with Rebecca. He waited the full ten minutes and then knocked on her door.

Rebecca opened the door after three minutes, dressed for dinner in a pink, flowered dress with a dark pink belt and medium-high heels. Her hair was still damp where it curled on her shoulders. She looked sensational. He knew every curve of her body but made no move to touch her.

"Ready?" he asked unnecessarily.

"Don't I look it?"

"You do, you definitely do."

She smiled and walked past him towards the lift.

There was no sign of the man in the pink shirt. Nor of the couple who had been sitting in the foyer. But they were there, lost in the crowds, communicating with each other.

***

In London, Geraldine had been told that the reunion of Gerasimov and Rebecca had not gone according to plan. No bedroom activity, no pillow talk, no hint of what Gerasimov had in mind, and that now they were sitting in a busy, noisy restaurant with Murano glass chandeliers, overlooking the Grand Canal.

It couldn't be more romantic, Geraldine thought. But she knew Rebecca was playing a cautious game. She understood why. Despite the slightly panicky phone call she had received from Patrick Littlefield, reminding her that "this woman" could screw everything up, Geraldine was confident that the gamble she had proposed would pay off. She tried to reassure Patrick.

Geraldine recognised something of herself in Rebecca. There was a strength of character which made her question everything, especially if there was a man involved. If anyone could stand up to and challenge Mikhail Gerasimov it would be Rebecca. Geraldine had had a different experience with the Russian and she knew she had failed, both as an intelligent woman and as a senior member of MI5, trained to spot honeytraps of any kind. She still couldn't quite believe that she had been so tempted by him. He had been posing as a cultured European businessman, and she had fallen for it. She had given in to his charms for the simple reason that since her divorce from her husband she had deliberately avoided any relationship with men. No one had come her way who had shown interest, and she hadn't courted attention. Her seduction by Gerasimov had been unexpected. She gave in to a temptation she thought had been buried forever. The fact that it turned out so badly, with her rejection of his over-forceful lovemaking, just made her feel even more guilty and ashamed of her behaviour.

Now she expected Rebecca, who had been more masterful and in control when dealing with the same man, to play a role that could potentially be dangerous. Patrick was right; it could all go wrong. But Geraldine's instincts, normally sound, had won the argument. For now, much would depend on what happened after Rebecca and Gerasimov returned to their hotel from the restaurant.

The man in the pink shirt, now with a dark grey jacket, reported that "the couple" had left the restaurant and were walking back to the hotel. No physical contact could be seen. But the man whispered into his sleeve mic that when the couple arrived at the Palazzo Veneziano, Gerasimov took Rebecca's left elbow and guided her into the foyer. As he did so, Rebecca glanced at him. The man in the pink shirt provided no personal interpretation.

Rebecca and Gerasimov stood outside her room with the door open, chatting.

A tiny camera inserted into a link of the chain that held the dome-shaped light over the foot of the double bed, and an electronic bug attached to the room's WiFi router, were ready to film and record every move and every sound.

Rebecca's room number was 42. She entered the room alone. The door closed. She looked relieved and locked it. She went to the bathroom and came out wearing a long, white T-shirt, and climbed into bed. She switched off the light, settled into the pillows and closed her eyes.

Geraldine was told immediately. She had already received a poor transcript of the conversation in the restaurant. Poor, because the noise of the other diners and the never-ending sounds from the busy Grand Canal had affected the quality of the directional microphone system operated by the young couple sitting outside. But the gist of the conversation was clear. Rebecca was playing so hard to get it looked as if Gerasimov's plan, whatever it was, was not going the way he had expected. He gave no direct explanation as to why he had wanted to meet Rebecca in Venice, although he said something that gave Geraldine hope that eventually her gamble might pay off.

When they had finished their first course of mussels in Champagne sauce, Gerasimov had leant across the table and said, "Rebecca, please believe me, I have brought something with me which your friends will want to see."

He then leant back.

Rebecca replied in Rebecca fashion:

"I thought you had brought something to Venice which you only wanted me to see."

He looked at her in astonishment, then laughed. She laughed, too. The ice had been broken.

But they still slept in separate rooms.

***

The following morning, Gerasimov was up early, well before 6 a.m. He went for a brief walk along the Grand Canal and returned to the hotel half an hour later. He had arranged with Rebecca to meet for breakfast at 7:30. He spent the remaining hour sitting in the foyer. He asked for a coffee. He didn't use his phone once until around five minutes before 7:30 when he texted Rebecca to let her know where he was. She came down soon after, dressed in jeans and a light-blue shirt with the first three buttons undone, revealing creamy skin. Gerasimov stood up, kissed her on the cheek and complimented her on the way she looked. He then suggested breakfast away from the hotel.

They found a café in a back street and took a table outside. He ordered coffee and croissants without asking Rebecca what she wanted. She stayed quiet.

"You lied to me," he said suddenly.

Rebecca looked up. "Pardon?"

"You told me you spoke to no one about this trip," he said.

"I didn't," she said.

"We're being watched," he said. "Your phone is probably hacked and no doubt the room is bugged as well. I can check, if you let me into your room. I have the necessary equipment."

Rebecca laughed but stopped abruptly.

"You serious?" she asked, looking around her.

"A man in a pink shirt and the couple in the foyer," he said.

"Where? I can't see a man in a pink shirt," she replied.

"He was there last night, and this morning. I spotted him the other side of the canal, same pink shirt, he must have had to pack quickly."

"Come on, you've got to be kidding me," Rebecca said. "I promise you, I told absolutely no one. I can make up my own mind about things."

"That may be, but they know you are here. Which means they know I am here. Believe me, this is the way people in my world work. I knew it was a risk but I didn't think they would use you in this way. If they've bugged your phone, they probably did it some time ago. If that's true, they've been in on this trip since the beginning."

Rebecca shook her head. "That's illegal," she said. "They have no right to bug my phone. Why would they think of doing such a thing? What have I done wrong?"

"An insurance policy. Just in case I tried to contact you."

"So it's your fault?"

"Yes. But clever, too."

"What do you mean?"

"Your friend made a judgement call. She was right."

"She knew you would contact me?"

"No, just hoped. Intuition."

"So, now what?"

"It's all off. Too risky for me. They could grab me any time. That's what they want. To get their revenge."

"They can't do that. That's extraterrestrial or something."

"Extraordinary rendition," he corrected her. "If the Americans can do it, so can the Brits."

"So what are you telling me?"

"I'll have to leave. You can stay, it's all paid for. I had a plan, but your lot have screwed it up."

"They're not 'my lot', Mikhail," Rebecca replied, using his name for the first time. "And, by the way, you haven't told me what you wanted. You said you had brought something for me. So tell me."

"It's all irrelevant now," he said, standing up and waving his hand at the waitress.

Rebecca stood up. "This is bollocks. If you had decided to trust me with something, then trust me. But before you do, I'll make a phone call and get this sorted."

Gerasimov looked surprised. "Phone who?"

"The person who must have ordered my phone to be bugged, if you're right. I want to give her a piece of my mind and then tell her to back off."

"I do trust you but I don't trust them, and they won't trust me," Gerasimov said.

"So it's down to me, right?"

"Rebecca, the spy mastermind." He laughed.

"Piss off, Mikhail. If you want to stop this being a wasted trip, then let me make the call and we'll see what happens."

They were standing facing each other. Other people in the café were looking at them, imagining a row between lovers.

"OK," Gerasimov said.

"So let's go back to the hotel and I'll call from my room."

"It was supposed to be our room."

"Spy mastermind first, Mikhail."

"Actually, Rebecca, my room."

"What?"

"If your room is bugged by the British and by who knows who else, mine probably isn't. I booked it under another name. It was a precaution. In case you kicked me out! But it's lucky I did."

Rebecca smiled. "So my friend, as you call her, although she is fast becoming an ex-friend, was counting on me leaping into bed with you."

"Looks like it."

"And I spoilt their fun?"

"That's one way of looking at it."

Rebecca grinned.

They left the café. Still no physical contact. The man in the pink shirt noted it and spoke into his mic.

"Oh my God," Rebecca whispered to Gerasimov. She grabbed his arm. "I spotted him, the man in the pink shirt. Is that him?"

Gerasimov didn't look but just nodded. He had spotted him straightaway.

When they entered Gerasimov's room, Rebecca turned and kissed him on the lips. He tried to put his arms around her, but she pushed him away.

"Phone call," she said.

"Do you want me to leave the room?" Gerasimov asked.

"No," she replied. "I want you to hear what I'm going to say. If I can get through, that is."

She looked up Geraldine's mobile number on her contact list.

It rang for several minutes before it was answered. But not by Geraldine.

"Yes, can I help you?" a female voice said.

"This is Geraldine's number; I need to speak to her urgently," Rebecca replied.

"I'm afraid she's busy," the woman replied.

"Tell her Rebecca is here."

"And you are?"

"Just Rebecca."

"As I said, she's busy."

"Whoever you are, you better put me on to Geraldine now!"
The woman switched off.

Rebecca stared at her phone. "The bitch. I can't believe it."

Gerasimov shrugged his shoulders.

"Mikhail, I need something to get Geraldine to the phone. Tell
me something, anything."

"Just say it's something of special importance."

"But that's no good," Rebecca said.

"She'll understand," Gerasimov replied.

***

Half an hour passed. Geraldine came out of a meeting and walked
back to her office. She glanced at Vanessa who informed her that
some mad and very rude woman had phoned.

"Name?" Geraldine asked, fearing the answer.

"She called herself Rebecca. No surname."

Vanessa gripped the edge of her desk when her boss banged
her fist on the surface and stormed into her room, slamming the
door.

Geraldine grabbed her phone and dialled Rebecca's number.

It rang and rang, but Rebecca didn't pick up. Just when
Geraldine was about to switch off she heard: "Hello."

"Rebecca, it's Geraldine."

"What the hell!"

"Rebecca, I—"

"No, I mean what the hell, Geraldine!"

"Rebecca, wait a minute, this is important."

"You've been bugging my phone!"

"It was for your safety."

"Safety, bollocks."

"Rebecca, if you're going to spend this time just swearing at me, fine. But it's getting us nowhere."

Rebecca stayed quiet.

"So, Rebecca, we know what's going on. That's our business. And now I need to know what's happening next. Is there anything you should be telling me?"

Rebecca was still with Gerasimov, in his room. He nodded at her and whispered: "Tell her."

"I don't know anything, Geraldine," she said. "Except a message: 'It's something of special importance.'"

"OK, that's good," Geraldine replied. "Whatever you get, I have people there who will take it from you."

"Ha, they've been spotted. So much for your spies."

"Rebecca," said Geraldine, lowering her voice for no reason, "whose side exactly are you on?"

Rebecca didn't reply at first. She looked at Gerasimov and felt a weird sense of divided loyalties. She wasn't loyal to the Russian spy as such and certainly had no sympathy for the country that employed him and the leader who gave him his orders. She had never had reason to ponder the merits of patriotism, but she knew she was probably like most people living in the United Kingdom: she loved her country without having to express it every day of her life. So it was wrong and somehow distasteful for Geraldine to doubt her loyalties to her country. And yet, because she now suspected that Gerasimov had some bizarre plan to reverse his role and offer his services to Britain, or at least to British intelligence, she felt oddly protective towards him. If he trusted her to be his go-between, she was ready to play the part. In her mind, that included ensuring that he was given the chance to make his case and not be arrested by the man in the pink shirt.

"I'll ignore that remark, Geraldine, but please don't say it again," Rebecca replied.

"I didn't mean—"

"Yes, you did," Rebecca interrupted. "So here's the deal."

She looked at Gerasimov. He shrugged.

"The presence of your people here is causing a change of mind," she said. "I would have thought that's a bad idea. If I hand over anything, what's to say you won't get them to grab you know who and then it's all my fault? Can you trust me to do it right, and we'll see what happens?"

Geraldine sat at her desk and shook her head. She knew what Patrick Littlefield would advise: "Do not, on any account, trust this woman, Rebecca Strong, to play spy; she is out of her depth and we could lose a potential double agent working in the heart of the Kremlin."

However, Geraldine and Rebecca had one important thing in common. They had both slept with the Russian, albeit with neither of them aware of his nationality or his ulterior motive. They each had reason not to trust Gerasimov. But it was just possible that Rebecca Strong, while untrained and inexperienced in dealing with this extraordinary turn of events, might be able to judge, based on her intuition and her past intimacy with the Russian, whether he was a genuine double agent in the making or a Putin-committed spy trying to fool British intelligence.

Before she made a decision, Geraldine knew she should consult with the three others in the special Operation Greengage team: Patrick; her deputy, Grace Redmayne; and Freddie Stigby, who was the most experienced Kremlinologist in both MI6 and MI5. But Rebecca needed an answer now.

"Rebecca? OK, for the moment, that's all I can promise," Geraldine said. "But my people stay there in case of an emergency. They won't interfere, and there never was any plan to arrest him, anyway."

"So you will leave it to me?" Rebecca asked.

"For the moment. But my career is at stake here. Are you sure you're all right?"

"Yes, kind of," Rebecca replied. "Oh, and one other thing; have you done anything to my room?"

"How do you mean?"

"Are you watching and listening?"

"Rebecca, I can't comment about anything."

"If you have, that's outrageous. Watching me in bed. Who's getting kicks out of that?"

Geraldine kept quiet.

"I'm going now," Rebecca said and switched off.

CHAPTER SEVEN
ALL EARS ACROSS THE POND

The three people in the room on the twelfth floor of an office block in Tyson's Corner, Fairfax County, Virginia, north-west of Washington DC, knew everything there was to know so far. All three were alarmed and determined to put things right.

On the table in front of them were half a dozen photographs of Rebecca Strong and Mikhail Gerasimov in Venice.

"So, what are the Brits really up to?" asked Adam J. Goldstein III, assistant director of the CIA's clandestine service. He was a good-looking, well-dressed man with a bushy, brown moustache, grown relatively recently, it was claimed by his colleagues, to match the grey moustache of the director of the CIA.

"We think our cousins are falling into a trap but believe they have a Churchillian golden egg," said Walt Grolsch, referring to the famous phrase used by Winston Churchill in the Second World War when the German Enigma code covering all of Germany's military communications was broken by British cypher experts.

At thirty-nine, Grolsch was the same age as Adam Goldstein. He had a pinched face, suggesting too many hours in the office late at night, a full head of dark hair, and large spectacles. He was special assistant to the director of the National Security Agency, or NSA.

The third person was Marina Babb, high-flying assistant to the Director of National Intelligence, former CIA officer in Moscow and, at only thirty-four, the youngest in the room. She was tall, nearly six foot, and intimidating, with a strong, determined face and bright blue eyes.

"I cannot believe that Geraldine Hammer would trust this Rebecca Strong to act on her behalf," she said. "It breaks all the rules of tradecraft and makes no sense. We have to intervene."

"Wait a moment, this is too delicate for us to just barge in," Goldstein said. "We don't want to piss off the Brits."

"But we're covered, right?" asked Grolsch.

"Yes, we have three there," Goldstein replied.

"It's like an espionage circus," Babb said. "Everyone watching everyone and getting nowhere. In Venice, of all places."

"We're all on the same side," Goldstein said.

"Who knows?" she said. "Maybe Moscow knows all about it as well and have got people dotted around Venice."

"They should be easy to spot," Grolsch said.

"Most important, we need to have a strategy," Goldstein said.

"This guy's a fraud," Babb said.

"Go through the arguments, Marina," said Goldstein, who seemed to be in charge.

"Well, remember what we know about him," Babb said. "A year ago, he gave the Brits the frights. Chasing all over London, they couldn't find him. Meanwhile, he tried to assassinate Hammer in her house, failed, but got away with it. He went back to Moscow for a hero's welcome and promptly got promoted. Now he sits in an office in the Kremlin closer to Putin's lair than anyone we know. He's a favoured son. There's no way he is suddenly going to risk all that by offering his services to British intelligence. I just don't believe it. Gerasimov is on a mission but it isn't for us in the West, it's for Putin. Whatever he is offering is going to be fake. It's yet another false flag operation and we need to nip it in the bud or turn it to our advantage."

"You say we need to do this," Goldstein said, "but we don't have him, the Brits do. Or, at least, this Rebecca Strong woman does. And they won't take kindly to us getting in the way or trying to give them advice. We know from the past they'll get all huffy and protective."

"Do you think they know that we know?" Grolsch asked.

"Well, you're in the best position to know that," Babb said. "Has GCHQ mentioned anything?"

As special assistant to the director of the NSA, the worldwide signals intelligence organisation, which was bigger and better-funded than any other US spying agency, Grolsch had access to and knowledge of the vast majority of eavesdropping operations carried out by Britain's Government Communications Headquarters. The NSA and GCHQ were intimately linked. They trusted each other far more than the CIA trusted MI6 and the FBI trusted MI5. But there were still some secrets that didn't get shared.

"No, nothing," Grolsch said. "If the British intelligence services believe they have the chance to recruit a senior official inside the inner working circle of the Kremlin, they might well keep that to themselves."

"We'd probably do the same," Babb said.

They all nodded in agreement.

"I'm all for getting involved right now," Babb said, "but there is one thing that could make it tricky for us at this stage. They will want to know how the hell we know about Ms Strong's texting with Gerasimov."

"I'm not worried about that," Grolsch said. "After all, they've been bugging Ms Strong for months, so they can hardly kick up a fuss if they discover we've been doing the same."

"So, for the moment," Goldstein said, "we can take it that Ms Strong knows the Brits are listening and watching but she doesn't know about us. That gives us an advantage. I want to keep it that way. So, Marina, right now I want to hold fire. See how it goes. Anything Gerasimov does that seems out of place or likely to lead to a negative result for us, then we'll decide to act or not. At this stage, I want us to stay in the background, but we can't afford to miss anything. Most important, we have to know what Gerasimov is offering so that we can make our own judgement as to whether it's genuine or part of a devious plot to embarrass us."

"You mean embarrass the Brits," Babb said.

Goldstein smiled. "Well, quite," he said. "We wouldn't want that to happen."

***

Gerasimov had booked a gondola and decided to go ahead with the trip. With eyes and ears everywhere, he reckoned sitting in a gondola winding its way down the narrow canals was about as safe as anywhere in a city like Venice.

Rebecca had relayed her conversation with Geraldine, and although he felt relatively reassured, he knew from long experience that it was the things you didn't know that tended to ruin your day. He felt he could trust Rebecca; she had no reason, let alone the training, to be playing a double game. But Geraldine Hammer, and perhaps more importantly, her boss and the people across the other side of the Thames at MI6, might be playing a different game. He would have to be ever-watchful for anything unexpected. He wondered, too, about the Americans. Would the British have told their American counterparts about his arrival in Venice? Or did they know anyway, and if so, what action might they take?

Gerasimov had received comprehensive training about America's intelligence capabilities. He knew the NSA listened to everything. A text from Moscow to a private citizen in London? Would that have been picked up by the NSA? Just one text out of billions made each day around the globe?

The only positive he had taken from his Venice gamble was that he hadn't been immediately arrested and carted off to some dark place for interrogation. He was being watched by British intelligence agents, but they had made no move against him.

He sat back in the gondola. Rebecca was next to him. The gondolier had made a few introductory comments but now seemed more interested in hailing passing gondoliers, and ducking his head and shoulders beneath each low bridge as they progressed, than chatting to his latest customers.

"Speak to me, Mikhail," Rebecca said quietly. "I can't imagine the gondola is bugged."

They were sitting far enough away from the gondolier, resting against multi-coloured cushions, for Gerasimov to feel confident that now was the time to tell Rebecca at least the background to his big decision.

He explained his misgivings over the war in Ukraine, his fears for the future of his family and his general disillusionment about the role he had to play in Putin's regime. He told her he was prepared to give secret information to the British in return for a new life for him and his wife and children. He needed guarantees. He didn't want money; he wanted protection.

Rebecca was at first surprised that Gerasimov wanted his family to join him. That one kiss in his room in the hotel had instantly sparked a sexual reaction inside her body. For the briefest of moments she had entertained the notion that perhaps they would end up in bed after all. But she had shaken the thought from her mind. Rekindling what they had had in her flat in London was out of the question. She knew that, and not just because she was now in a serious relationship with Sandy. When Gerasimov mentioned his wife and children, she felt strangely relieved.

"And what do you want me to do exactly?" Rebecca asked, also speaking in low tones.

"Convince them," Gerasimov replied.

"Shouldn't that be your job?"

"I will give you something to help you convince them."

"I'm still doing your job for you."

"There's no other way."

"It's nothing dodgy, is it?"

"It's just a film. You can put it in your luggage."

"You could have sent it through the post," Rebecca said, "like everyone else."

"Very funny."

At that moment, Gerasimov became aware of a gondola about fifty yards away. There were two Japanese-looking tourists straining their necks to look round as their gondola eased down the canal. There were two things that disturbed the Russian: the two tourists were not relaxing against the cushions, like most occupants of gondolas, and they were both men. Each had an array of cameras around his neck, and they looked tense. Gerasimov decided they were suspicious and could be spies. He said nothing to Rebecca.

Gerasimov leant forward and spoke to the gondolier. "Could we go down that canal over there? I want to see the bridge."

The gondolier didn't look pleased but he twirled the oar to turn a sharp left and they were soon passing down a narrow channel with a very ordinary-looking bridge ahead. Three minutes later, the gondola with the two camera-laden tourists emerged at the end. *Definitely Americans*, Gerasimov thought.

"What's wrong?" Rebecca asked.

"Nothing," Gerasimov said.

"So why are you looking like that?"

"Like what?"

"Like a spy."

"How would you know?"

"Mikhail, I just know."

"OK, you're right. Two idiots in a gondola behind us."

"So what?"

"They seem to be following us."

Rebecca peered forward and saw two tourists looking round at her.

"They're not Brits."

"They could be American."

"How do you know?"

"I don't."

"And you think …"

"Probably, yes."

"Bloody hell, so now what? Everyone seems to know we're here."

"Change of plan. But don't worry, we'll finish our boat ride first. Relax."

Rebecca tried to relax but felt tense. She couldn't keep her eyes off the gondola not far behind them. She glanced at Gerasimov. He was actually sitting next to her with his eyes closed. *Plotting and planning,* she thought. He was wearing cream chino trousers and a short-sleeved, dark-blue shirt which emphasised his muscular chest and arms. She remembered how hard his chest was, something she had found attractive when she first met him. But now the circumstances were totally different. When she had left her flat in London to catch her flight to Venice, she imagined what it would be like to be next to him, gliding down the canals in a gondola. She thought then it would be impossible not to lie in his arms and surrender herself to him. But she felt nothing like that. The two "tourists", both wearing pork pie hats, were probably just waiting for the moment when she and Gerasimov kissed. She knew very little about espionage, but she didn't want to give those ridiculous men the satisfaction of taking compromising pictures of her clinching with a Russian spy. Whoever they were.

Then Gerasimov took her hand in his. But it wasn't a romantic gesture. He was passing her something.

"Put it in your bag but not straightaway," he said. "I was going to give it to you later but I want you to have it now. Just in case something goes wrong."

Rebecca felt a small, plastic container in her hand. When the camera-wielding tourists in the gondola behind were not watching, she slipped it into her small, pink handbag. She was now officially a spy. Unpaid, but definitely a spy. Back in London, she'd thought it would be fun, an exciting change in her life, but it was a responsibility. And if Gerasimov was right and the Americans were onto them, could she be arrested as soon as the gondolier returned them to the quayside by their hotel? Gerasimov told her it was a film but he gave no other details. She would probably never know what was on it. She would just hand it to Geraldine when she returned to London and that would be her brief espionage career over.

Suddenly, she missed Sandy. She wished he was there with her and not the Russian who had come back into her life unexpectedly and made everything more complicated.

Twenty minutes later, they were back in the foyer of the hotel. Rebecca's first time in a gondola had not been the experience she used to dream about. She had been with a man, but not the right one. And the enjoyment of floating down the canals with the colours and sounds of Venice around her had been ruined by the "American spies" following them. She wondered where the British spies were, the man in the two-day-old pink shirt and the laughing couple. Perhaps Geraldine had ordered them to stay in their hotels and the only problem she and her Russian companion faced was from the Americans – if Gerasimov was right about the two men in the gondola.

She noticed that when they'd stepped off their gondola there was no sign of the two men. She had looked around, as had Gerasimov, trying to spot any other lurking spies, but everyone looked busy with their own lives, strolling, chatting and gazing at the Venetian landscape. No one was looking in their direction.

Gerasimov turned to her in the foyer.

"Whatever you do, don't hide it in your room," he said. "Keep it with you always. OK?"

Rebecca nodded.

"Let's go to our separate rooms and I'll come and get you in, say, thirty minutes?"

Again, she nodded, and they went up to the fourth floor in the lift. Gerasimov put his hand on her shoulder as he stopped by his door, but she carried on walking to her room. She put the key in and opened the door.

"Hello, Rebecca."

Rebecca jumped. Sitting in an armchair by the window overlooking the Grand Canal was Geraldine Hammer.

Rebecca stood with her mouth open.

"How did you get in? And what the hell are you doing here? I thought we had a deal," she said.

Geraldine rose from the armchair. Like Rebecca, she was wearing jeans and a shirt, but with a green and blue scarf around her neck. Her auburn hair looked as if it had been recently cut.

"Calm down, Rebecca," she said. "I'm here because it's not fair on you to have this responsibility. It's my responsibility. And I need to check him out for myself."

"You checked him out once before and it didn't do you much good," Rebecca replied, and then regretted what she'd said. "Sorry, I didn't mean what that sounded like."

"It's OK," Geraldine said. "I just want to talk to him and hear for myself what he has in mind. There's a helluva lot running on this."

"He won't be happy."

"Too bad."

"So, what do you want me to do?"

"Go and get him and bring him here. I assume he is in his room?"

"Well, you obviously know all about that, don't you, Geraldine? No sex this time, sorry you missed the show."

Geraldine tightened her mouth. "That's unnecessary. And by the way, I'm very glad there's been no … sexual activity. That would have been wrong on every count, Rebecca."

Rebecca said nothing. She turned round and went to open the door.

"Has he given you anything yet?" Geraldine asked.

"You mean …"

"Anything we should be seeing."

"I'll go and get him," Rebecca replied.

Geraldine looked surprised but let her go.

Rebecca walked down the corridor. Five minutes had gone by. *He might be in the shower,* she thought.

She knocked on his door. She couldn't hear the sound of a shower.

She knocked again.

He didn't come to the door, so she knocked louder and said who she was. Still nothing.

She knocked once more and waited. At that moment, a chambermaid carrying piles of towels appeared at the end of the corridor. Rebecca explained in totally inadequate Italian that her friend in room 36 wasn't answering and she was worried. The maid looked confused and then knocked on the door.

"I told you, he's not replying," Rebecca said.

The maid put the towels down and removed some keys from the pocket of her apron. She opened the door and peered in. She turned to Rebecca and shook her head.

Rebecca pushed past her and entered the empty room. She checked the wardrobe and cupboards: nothing. Not so much as a sock in sight. Gerasimov had gone.

Rebecca ran down the corridor to her room and banged on the door. Geraldine opened it.

"He's not there," Rebecca shouted. "He's gone."

Geraldine pressed a button on her mobile phone.

"Did you see him leave the hotel?" she shouted into her phone. "Any time in the last five minutes?"

She glanced at Rebecca and shook her head.

Back on her phone, Geraldine said, "Find him."

They waited half an hour in Rebecca's room. Geraldine walked up and down, looking increasingly agitated. Rebecca sat on the bed. She was relieved Gerasimov had slipped away. It was probably for the best, especially with those gondola spies skulking around. At least she had something to hand over to Geraldine. She would be glad to get rid of it. But she hadn't told Geraldine yet. She wanted to choose her moment and she was still angry with her friend for not trusting her, and for bugging her room and phone. Just to make sure, she opened her small pink bag. It was still there, an innocent-looking black pot with a grey lid.

CHAPTER EIGHT
ALL SIXES AND SEVENS

The man formerly in the pink shirt, now replaced by a plain white one, grabbed a water taxi and headed off to the airport. There were flights to London and all over Europe. The one daily direct flight from Venice to Moscow no longer existed. As part of European Union sanctions against Russia following the invasion of Ukraine, the solitary flight had been axed.

The man in the white shirt, now sweating profusely, produced his ID card at the check-in desk, mumbling "police" and "security" in the same breath, and asked for passenger names for flights leaving in the next hour. There was no passenger with the name Gerasimov, although that didn't surprise him. He showed a picture of Gerasimov, but the previously helpful flight desk supervisor stopped being cooperative.

"I'm too busy," she said, "I don't recognise that man. You really should take it up with the airport police."

The man in the white shirt stuck around for an hour, running from one airline desk to another, hoping to catch sight of the Russian. He left the airport with nothing but bad news for his boss. Geraldine's people failed to come up with even a hint of where Gerasimov might be.

***

The 16:26 train from Stazione di Venezia Santa Lucia was ten minutes into its journey to Rome. In seat forty-three, compartment eight, sat a tough-looking man in a dark grey suit and white shirt. He had a small bag with him. Mikhail Gerasimov's eyes were closed.

⁎⁎⁎

Geraldine was steaming with frustration and anger. Her gamble had failed.

She had nothing to show for her ill-judged decisions. It wasn't Rebecca's fault, but they had just lost what could have been a critical spy in the heart of the Kremlin. With the war in Ukraine now more than two and a half years old, and the Putin regime suffering from growing domestic challenges, MI5 and MI6 could have been in a decisive position to monitor developments at the highest level in Moscow.

Geraldine turned to Rebecca with a look of total resignation. Rebecca was about to tell her what was in her handbag when her phone pinged. It was a text from Sandy.

"Where are you? I have exciting news."

"Not Gerasimov, I suppose?" Geraldine asked.

"No, Geraldine, not Gerasimov," Rebecca replied.

Normally she would have replied immediately to Sandy's text, but first, she had to tell Geraldine that her trip to Venice had not all been in vain.

"I do have something to give you," she said.

"What?" Geraldine shrieked, looking confused and expectant at the same time.

Rebecca opened her pink bag and removed the film canister. She offered it to Geraldine.

Geraldine snatched the film from Rebecca's hand.

"He gave it to me in the gondola," Rebecca said.

"Why didn't you tell me?" Geraldine demanded.

"I was going to, but we had all the trouble with the Americans, and then you just appearing in my room like that ..."

"Americans? What Americans?" Geraldine's voice was an octave higher than usual.

"We had two men dressed as tourists following us in the gondola. Gerasimov said he thought they were Americans."

"How did he know? What were they doing? What did they look like?"

"Like Japanese tourists, or South Koreans. In pork pie hats and with tons of cameras."

"But that's what tourists look like," Geraldine said, exasperated.

"They followed us down this very untouristy canal," Rebecca said.

Geraldine sat down on Rebecca's bed. If Gerasimov was right, the British espionage coup was already compromised. The Americans, she knew, would want to interfere. The whole thing was a disaster. But she had something in her hand that could make all the difference.

Geraldine stood up.

"Thank you, Rebecca, for whatever this is. You may have saved my life, or at least my career."

"Well, open it then."

"Not right now, sorry, not really appropriate."

"It's not a love letter, Geraldine, it's spy stuff, and I'm curious."

"I'm sure you are, but I am not allowed to let you see it, or anything to do with this person."

"You mean Agent Redruth."

"What! How do you know that?"

Rebecca rolled her eyes. "I guessed," she said. "It's what I would have called him."

"You will have to forget that name," Geraldine said primly.

"What, forget where I was born? Come on, Geraldine, you really can be kind of prissy sometimes."

"I'm sorry, Rebecca." Geraldine gave her an apologetic smile. "This is all secret stuff. I can't share it with you."

"Just for once, stop being all sort of superspy and treat me as an adult. I know almost as much about everything as you do, and if it wasn't for me, you wouldn't have that thing in your hand. So give me a break."

Geraldine sat back on the bed. "OK, but if it's just a film, I won't be able to show you what's on it anyway."

"There could be a note," Rebecca said. "Perhaps a farewell message for me. He's probably still hoping to you-know-what with me sometime in the future."

"Rebecca, that's not funny and you shouldn't even be thinking about it."

"I'm not, really I'm not, I was just saying."

Geraldine opened the lid of the small canister and drew out a film. A piece of paper was attached. She unfurled it and read it. Then she looked up at Rebecca.

"Was I right? Is there a message for me?"

"No," Geraldine said. "Well, not the sort of message you had in mind."

"Meaning?"

Rebecca sat down next to Geraldine and tried to peer at the piece of paper. Geraldine whisked her hand away.

"It mentions you, that's all."

"What, like how attractive I am and how I have bigger boobs than you?"

Geraldine looked shocked. "If you want to be treated like an adult, that sort of remark is pretty childish, Rebecca. This is not a game. There's a lot at stake."

"OK, I apologise, I was just trying to lighten the atmosphere. So show me. Please."

To her astonishment, Geraldine passed her the piece of paper. It was dated October eighteenth.

For Brits' eyes only. Contents very recent. Access to more, much more. All handovers to be arranged through RS. Only RS. No one in Moscow to be involved. Too risky. If RS agrees, of course.

"And you were going to keep this from me?" Rebecca blurted out.

Geraldine was shaking her head. "There is absolutely no way this arrangement is going to work. No one will agree to it. It's impossible. It has to be done professionally by our people. I don't know what he's thinking. He knows how the system works. He knows you're—"

"Just a girl?"

"Rebecca, I'm not being rude or disrespectful. But you're a civilian. If someone wanted a large, modern picture to put on their wall they wouldn't ask me to paint it. Right? It's the same here. We have highly trained officers and agents who spend their lives dealing with dangerous situations. Gerasimov will have to accept it. If he wants to work for us, he will have to do it our way."

It was Rebecca's turn to shake her head. "Normally, I'm sure you're right," she said. "But you're not in a position to dictate terms, Geraldine. He's not going to cooperate unless I'm involved. So, where will that get you? You've got this film. I've no idea what's on it but I bet it's pretty sexy stuff. Then what? No more juicy morsels from your spy in Moscow. Your lot won't be happy with that."

Rebecca then pointed upwards and around the room.

"No one's listening to us. I had it all removed before you got back from your gondola trip."

"Very thoughtful."

"Rebecca, I can't take the chance of risking your life. This is not your world, you should forget everything and just go back to your painting. I'll sort something out."

"Provided I don't have to go creeping around in the dark to meet up with him, disguised as a sheep or whatever, I would have thought it would be perfectly possible for me to meet him somewhere safer – just not in Moscow or anywhere else in Russia. And anyway, that's what he's implying in his message, right? No one in Moscow to be involved. That includes me because he knows I can't go to Moscow. So if it's somewhere else, like here, for instance, or Bognor Regis, I can play pick up and hand over."

"It'll never happen," Geraldine said.

"Well, goodbye, Agent Redruth."

Geraldine stood up.

"Rebecca, all I can say is, I will go back to London tonight, I'll tell my lot everything and see how they react. I know what they'll say."

"Use your charm, Geraldine. You know it makes sense, and you always said I would make a good spy."

Geraldine grinned. "It's true, you would."

"So ..."

Geraldine gave her a hug and started to walk towards the door. "I'll be off. What are you going to do?"

"I've got two more nights paid for. I'd be mad to leave. Is that all right?"

"Of course, enjoy yourself. But don't talk to anyone."

"Yes, boss."

Geraldine left.

Rebecca picked up her phone from the bedside table and read Sandy's message again. Two more nights with a double bed in a posh hotel in Venice on her own? Not bloody likely.

She texted back.

"Don't ask. Just get the first flight out to Venice and come to the Palazzo Veneziano Hotel. I'm waiting for you."

***

The three senior American spy officials were back in the office block in Tyson's Corner. Another display of photographs was on the table. This time, they showed Rebecca and Gerasimov in a gondola and two pictures of Geraldine Hammer entering the Palazzo Veneziano Hotel and hastily leaving it about two hours later. Another picture showed her getting into a water taxi. There was no photograph of Gerasimov leaving the hotel.

"What is Geraldine up to?" Marina Babb was the first to speak.

All three looked disgruntled. They liked things to go their way; they wanted to feel they were in control. But so far, it was not going according to plan. The whereabouts of Gerasimov was still unclear. He hadn't been spotted exiting the hotel but it was assumed he had left by a back entrance and made his getaway without anyone from either the British or the American surveillance teams being any the wiser.

The single room Gerasimov had booked hadn't been bugged. The decision had been based on the assumption that once Gerasimov and Ms Strong were in the same hotel they would share the same room and the same bed. The single room, they had concluded, was a sort of safety measure, in case Gerasimov had to do anything without the woman being a witness. But if there was going to be sex and bed talk, as fully expected, it would take place in the woman's room. So, the cameras and listening devices were duly concentrated in the room with the double bed.

Instead of bed activity, however, all Adam Goldstein and his two colleagues had seen and heard of any interest emanating from the room was Rebecca's shock at seeing Geraldine and the eventual handover of a small container with a film and a note. The camera hidden on top of the elegant wardrobe had failed to pick up the words on the piece of paper. But it was clear from the subsequent conversation between Rebecca and Geraldine that Gerasimov had made it a condition that if he was going to spy for Britain, he wanted the tall blonde with the long legs to play courier.

"Well, the Brits are not going to go for that," Walt Grolsch said. "Just like we wouldn't. It would be crazy and dangerous."

"Don't underestimate the Brits for crazy," Marina Babb said. "If there's no alternative, they will have no choice."

"And do they know about us?" Grolsch asked. "Those tourists with cameras in the gondola, behind? Were they ours, or Brits, or Russians, for God's sake?"

"Not ours," Goldstein said. "My people saw them and took photos. They checked out as regular tourists. Geraldine now suspects we know, even though the pork pie hat guys were civilians. But let's see whether she does anything about it. We can always deny it. One extraordinary lapse on their part is that they didn't sweep the bedroom for any other listening and watching devices. They removed theirs but left ours."

"Meanwhile," Babb said, "I have to report back to my director. Where is Gerasimov? Is he genuine or a fake? Do we make representations to the Brits? Should the president be told?"

Goldstein replied: "We don't know where Gerasimov is, but my bet is he is either back in Moscow or on his way. He just may be genuine, in which case we have a different ball game here altogether. We don't mix with the Brits at this stage. We bring our respective bosses up to date, but I will advise we don't need to tell the president. There's nothing to tell."

They'd started to wrap up the meeting when Marina Babb said, "One thing we've forgotten: Ms Strong's last text. She's invited her boyfriend to come and join her. Will she tell him everything or will she keep her promise not to talk to anyone? This guy is Sky News. He can't be trusted with anything. Whether Gerasimov is a fake or the genuine article, even a hint of an espionage blockbuster on Sky will bring every Tom, Dick and Walter to Venice. Sorry, Walt."

"We'll just have to watch and listen," Goldstein said. "The only saving grace is that she doesn't know what's on the film."

"Nor do we," Babb said.

"No, nor do we," Goldstein acknowledged. "That's why we've got nothing to tell the president."

"Have you got a codename for Gerasimov?" Babb asked.

"Yes: Bunyan. Better than Agent Redruth," Goldstein replied.

"John Bunyan, *The Pilgrim's Progress*, any connection?" Grolsch asked, referring to the seventeenth-century writer, Puritan preacher and author of *The Pilgrim's Progress*.

"No," Goldstein said.

***

Sandy had managed to catch the last flight from Heathrow to Venice. He was in a state of excitement and astonishment. He had begged his news editor for a couple of days off, then rushed to his flat and ordered an Uber. He didn't know what to wear in Venice in October and he didn't have time to pack anyway. So, he arrived at Marco Polo Airport in a suit and tie.

Throughout the flight he had a dozen questions in his mind: what the hell was Rebecca doing in Venice without telling him beforehand? Had she been there on her own from the beginning or was he now her second choice? Please, God, whatever she was doing there, let it have nothing to do with that bloody Russian.

He texted Rebecca to tell her he had arrived at the airport and would be with her as soon as possible. He added one more thing: *"Are you still waiting for me?"*

She replied in seconds with three thumbs-up emojis and a pink heart.

Sandy's heart began to thump like the biggest of bass drums.

***

A CIA technician with a lot of surveillance apparatus before him took note of the exchange. He was in room 29 of the Palazzo Veneziano Hotel.

"Lucky bastard," he muttered to himself.

CHAPTER NINE
SPIES DON'T TELL

When Sandy knocked on the door, hot and tired from the journey, Rebecca grabbed him and kissed him so passionately he had to beg her to let him come up for air. But as soon as she broke away from the embrace, she placed a finger on her lips and then on his.

"What—" he started to say.

"Shhh."

"But …"

"Shhh!"

She pointed up to the ceiling and then waved her arm around the room. She had searched her room before Sandy arrived and found nothing that looked like a bug or a camera. But she assumed that if the Americans had paid her a call, they would have planted something somewhere and she didn't have the know-how to spot a well-concealed eavesdropping device. She hadn't checked out the top of the wardrobe. With the arrival of Sandy in her luxury bedroom in one of the best hotels in Venice, she wasn't in the mood to delay what she had in mind by going around the room once again looking for hidden eyes and ears. But she did want to make sure Sandy said nothing that might compromise her putative new role as a spy for His Majesty's government.

So, having stopped him from saying anything further, she pushed him onto the bed and started to remove his clothes. Sandy did the same, undoing the buttons on her shirt with as much haste as was possible without wrenching them off. The first time he had seen her body unclothed he had gasped. She had laughed at the time. Now he found himself gaping at her as she removed her pink bra, bending slightly forward to reach behind to the clasp keeping her firmly in place. The bra fell to the floor at Sandy's feet. Sandy reached forward with both hands, but she pushed him back and removed the rest of his clothes.

Rebecca knew there was a risk they were being watched but she didn't care. She wasn't going to let some pervert spy, British or American, prevent her from making love with Sandy. They jumped under the sheets with a cry of excitement.

***

The CIA technician missed nothing, although the large, white cotton sheet covered up the two lovers' dignity while the movements underneath became more frantic.

***

When eventually they lay still, side by side, Rebecca stroked Sandy's face and whispered an apology.

"My God, for what?" he whispered back.

"Normally," she whispered, with a broad grin, "I would have made a lot more noise."

Sandy laughed.

"You were quieter than usual," she whispered.

"Well, you told me to shhh," he said, forgetting to whisper.

"Do you always do what you're told?"

"Only in certain circumstances," he said, this time whispering.

They lay quietly for a few minutes.

"Can I tell you something which might ruin everything?" Sandy asked.

"Probably not," she replied. "But I think I know what you're going to say."

"You do?"

"Maybe."

"But you won't know for sure unless I tell you."

"You don't need to tell me."

"But I want to."

"You can't do what you want all the time."

"Rebecca, you're maddening."

"I know."

"And I love you for it."

"There you go."

"What?"

"You've said it."

"Not really, only sort of."

"It's good enough."

"And you?"

"Obviously."

"You mean it?"

"Mean what?"

"What I said and what you said, kind of."

"You've lost me."

"God, you really are maddening."

"Cheer up, Sandy, we're in Venice. Let's go and eat."

Rebecca slid out of bed and wrapped the sheet around her body, leaving Sandy naked and uncovered, and totally visible to the CIA man down the corridor. For some reason he couldn't explain, he curled up into a ball and put his face into the pillow. He stayed like that until Rebecca emerged from the bathroom, still sheet-wrapped, and leapt onto his body.

They kissed and stroked each other.

"My God, Rebecca, whatever you're up to in Venice, I don't care. Do you really want to eat?" Sandy asked in a semi-whisper.

"Definitely. I know a place. We can talk then." This time, Rebecca spoke quite loudly, and it was Sandy's turn to say "shhh".

***

The CIA technician, who felt somewhat overwhelmed by the lovemaking scenes in the room down the corridor, took note of Rebecca's last remark and made a phone call. The restaurant by the Grand Canal with the chandeliers was, he assumed, the place Ms Strong had in mind for her tell-all to her boyfriend. The necessary listening apparatus would be set up.

***

"Tell me everything, or tell me something, or tell me what you think you can tell me," Sandy said to Rebecca.

They were sitting in a very small restaurant with no chandeliers, overlooking a fairly nondescript canal, without a gondola in sight. Rebecca had asked the hotel concierge for the name of a restaurant tucked away and not frequented by tourists. She wanted, above all, to avoid sharing her evening with two Asian-looking tourists who might be American spies. La Lanterna da Gas, a seafood and pasta restaurant located away from the normal tourist spots, seemed the ideal place. They were sitting outside on the terrace.

"Let's order first," she said. "No, wine first and then we'll order."

When the waiter delivered a bottle of Pinot Grigio in a bucket of ice and two glasses, Rebecca and Sandy helped themselves and clinked before drinking.

"Are we celebrating?" Sandy asked.

"Always," Rebecca answered.

"Anything in particular?"

"Yes, but I can't tell."

"Oh God, here we go."

"Don't spoil the evening, Sandy, especially after ..."

Sandy grinned. "OK, but I think you need to give me at least some sort of explanation. Why am I in Venice?"

"Well, charming. Don't you want to be with me in Venice?"

"Rebecca, you really can be the most annoying person sometimes. I'm supposed to be the reporter asking questions and you are supposed to answer them," he said, laughing.

Rebecca leaned across the table and kissed him on the lips.

"I know it's annoying, but I'm in a bit of a spot," she said. "There's a situation developing and I seem to be part of it and I'm not supposed to say anything to anyone. If I could tell anyone I would tell you, even though you're a TV reporter."

Sandy was about to reply when Rebecca stopped him.

"I'm so sorry, Sandy," she said, "I totally forgot to ask you, what's your exciting news? You never told me."

"I've been promoted," Sandy replied. "They've made me foreign correspondent and they want me to go to Ukraine next month after some hazardous environment training."

"That's amazing, but I don't want you going to Ukraine," Rebecca said. "Surely it's too dangerous?"

"So, you're worried about me?"

"Of course I am."

"That's nice. And I'm worried about you, too," Sandy said. "All this secrecy stuff, it's that bloody Russian, isn't it? Was he here? Was he with you in the same room where we …?"

"Yes and no," Rebecca said.

"What does that mean?"

"Yes, he was here, but no, I didn't sleep with him."

"You promise?"

"I don't need that."

"Sorry, but I had to ask."

"If you don't believe me, that's fine," Rebecca said.

Sandy heard the change in her voice.

"I'm an idiot," he said. "Of course I believe you. You drive me crazy but for all the right reasons. Most of the time."

She looked at him and grinned.

"Crazy is good," she said.

They leant across the table and kissed.

The waiter returned and they both ordered linguine with clams and prawns.

"So," Sandy said, "just tell me what you can but nothing which will put you in trouble, and forget I'm a hotshot foreign correspondent."

Both laughed.

Rebecca looked around at the other tables on the terrace. All the diners seemed engrossed in each other and their food. There were no obvious tourists, certainly none wearing pork pie hats.

"OK," Rebecca said, "I'll tell you what I think I can, although I'm pretty much a novice at this game."

"What game?"

"Spy stuff."

"Oh God, I knew it; what have they asked you to do?"

"They?"

"Whoever. MI5, I suppose. Am I right?"

"I didn't tell them I was coming to Venice, but they found out anyway," Rebecca said.

"How?"

"They knew I was going to meet the Russian, as you like to put it, but I can't tell you how."

"But what the hell's he doing in Venice? He was deported to Moscow, and that should have been it. How come he has emerged again, and here in Venice and with you?"

"That's a lot of questions. I can't tell you everything. But he contacted me for a reason other than what you probably think and persuaded me to meet him here."

"But you didn't tell anyone?"

"No."

"Why not?"

"I didn't trust them not to screw it all up."

"Screw what up?"

"Whatever he had in mind," Rebecca said. "It sounded important. I wasn't going to come and then I thought maybe I should, maybe it really was something important. And I would tell the right people at the right time. OK, it was probably stupid on my part. If I had told you, you would have tried to stop me coming, right?"

"Probably. Or else I would have come with you."

"And then what? Hello, Mikhail, I've brought my boyfriend. Mikhail, Sandy; Sandy, Mikhail."

"Very funny," Sandy said. "No, I would have been around in the background to help you. And protect you."

"That's so sweet."

"So, where is he now?"

"Gerasimov? He's gone."

The food arrived. They ate in silence for the first few mouthfuls.

"So, did you discover what was on his mind?" Sandy asked.

"I think so, but that's what I shouldn't really talk about," Rebecca replied.

"OK, but let me guess, and you can shake or nod your head. It's what I do with my best contacts. If I'm facing them, they nod or shake or smile. If it's on the phone, there is silence. It's like code."

"Sounds like what spies do."

"I guess it is. Anyway, let's have a go."

Rebecca kept on eating, twirling the linguine round her fork.

"Gerasimov, for some reason, has decided he doesn't like Putin anymore and he wants to come and live in some leafy suburb in England with his wife, kids and dog. Am I warm?"

Rebecca gave him no encouragement.

"In return, he will hand over stuff he picks up from his work, and he wants you to be his courier. If I'm right about that, it's just not going to happen. First, I know MI5 well enough to be pretty sure they wouldn't entertain such an idea, although in history they have employed some pretty sexy and attractive female spies."

Rebecca smirked.

"And second," Sandy continued, "it would be far too dangerous for you. What if you got caught in flagrante?"

Rebecca raised her eyebrows.

"Not that kind of flagrante. I meant, just caught in the act. And, by the way, where on earth is this supposed to take place? Here in Venice once a month or in Moscow or Outer Mongolia?"

"Don't be silly, Sandy. I'm never going to go to Outer Mongolia."

"Be serious, Rebecca. If I'm right, this is all totally crazy. Am I right?"

"I'm not going to nod or shake my head like your MI5 friends," Rebecca replied. "And eat your pasta. It's getting cold."

***

Patrick Littlefield was furious. Geraldine Hammer, her deputy Grace Redmayne, and Freddie Stigby were sitting in his office at MI6.

"To be honest, Geraldine, I don't know where we are right now," Patrick said. "I'm not at all comfortable with what's going on. Have we got Redruth on side or not? And what are we going to do about our cousins over the pond?"

"Well, first of all," Geraldine said adamantly, "let's see what we've got so far. We've got photographs of two documents with Russia's highest security classification. There is absolutely no doubt they are genuine. So for that reason alone we should tell our cousins. We're the same family, after all, even if they can be a pain sometimes. But I don't want them overlording us. We won't reveal our source to our CIA counterparts, although I suspect they know already, if Gerasimov's instincts are right. In fact, we must assume from now on that the Americans are somehow in the know about Redruth. But they won't, of course, know about the documents Redruth has given us. So, Langley and NATO, and Kyiv, have to be informed."

Grace Redmayne raised a finger and said, "Key to everything now is to work out how we manage Redruth. If we are to use Ms Strong as the go-between, as he insists, how do we do it? Redruth can't pop over to Europe whenever he has something to tell us. Most flights out of Moscow are subject to restrictions because of the war in Ukraine. He's a senior member of the Kremlin staff; their security people will become suspicious very quickly. As it is, the Venice trip was a big gamble on his part, especially when, as we see from the document, he has been assigned to take out the Kyiv leadership."

"Doesn't this present us with a huge moral dilemma?" Stigby asked. "If he goes ahead with this mission and either gets captured or killed, or, God forbid, succeeds, we're going to be in a mighty tricky position. We're not telling ministers, right? So then what? What if it all goes wrong and we get accused of running a dodgy agent without informing the government? Even if we could hide the fact that Agent Redruth is Mikhail Gerasimov, known assassin and would-be killer of Geraldine here, we would still be in a helluva spot. And if ministers ever discovered that Agent Redruth is the same Russian intelligence officer who was deported from the UK only last year after that mayhem in London, none of us will keep our jobs."

"Our jobs are always at stake," Patrick said. "That's the least important issue. Grace is right, we need to have a proper strategy and make sure our source follows it to the letter. The source is operating in Moscow, so it is absolutely essential that my people are involved. Every time in the past we have had high-level insiders in Moscow, our station there has played the vital role. There is no alternative. So, whatever Redruth says, there has to be a communication link between him and our Moscow station chief. What we could say is that if he manages to get out of Russia to deliver material, and it's somewhere safe, where Ms Strong can do her bit without any danger to herself or to him, then that could be an option B.

"To be honest, I am totally against it, but if we're going to keep Redruth happy we may need to concede that. But I don't see it happening, especially with the war going on in Ukraine."

"I agree," Geraldine said. "We have to get Redruth to agree to a meeting arrangement with your man in Moscow. Then we'll see how it plays if he can leave for another location out of Russia at any point."

"By the way," Stigby asked, "where is Ms Strong?"

"Still in Venice," Geraldine said, "for another day or so. It was booked, so she wanted to stay."

"She better not be with anyone else," Patrick said, "spilling the beans. Like her boyfriend. Are we keeping track of that?"

Geraldine's heart lurched. "She promised to say nothing," she said. "But the warrant for monitoring her communications has now lapsed and my team has returned from Venice. I couldn't keep them there once Gerasimov had departed."

"You mean, escaped," Patrick said.

Geraldine glowered at MI6's director of operations. But he was right, her team had let him escape.

"So," Patrick leant forward to bring the meeting to an end, "I shall instruct our chief in Moscow to make contact with Redruth. How he does that is up to him, but he knows where he lives and will soon pick up his daily life pattern. Redruth will get the message that he can't just deal with Ms Strong. I'm sure he knows that already. But we can tell him about option B, because he is obviously obsessed with Ms Strong and it will keep him sweet.

"We need to know as soon as possible when and how this Kremlin-ordered elimination of the Kyiv leadership is going to take place. When we get the details, we'll bring our cousins fully onside."

"And the nuclear deployment plan?" Stigby asked.

"That's not such a big deal," Patrick replied. "The Americans will know as soon as there's the slightest move towards putting nukes on operational alert. But, yes, we'll bring them on board.

The document we've got from Redruth is interesting but not alarming, not at this stage. The Americans are watching this sort of thing twenty-four seven. Redruth gave it to us to demonstrate what level of material he could produce. It was his marker, if you like."

As all four got up to leave, Geraldine had one more question.

"What about Rebecca?" she asked.

"Hopefully, Geraldine, she will have no future part to play, so tell her nothing," Patrick said. "In fact, tell her to get on with her life and forget all this spy stuff. It's in her own interest and it's definitely in our interest."

Geraldine sighed. Why did she feel that Rebecca Strong's role in this espionage drama was not by any means over? But she left the room without making any further comment.

CHAPTER TEN
GERASIMOV UNDER SURVEILLANCE

Gerasimov first spotted the man in the dark overcoat at around 8 p.m., when he was walking down the street parallel to the road where his apartment block was located.

He had been back in Moscow for three days. His time away from the office had raised no particular comment other than a wisecrack from one of the security guards manning the inner checkpoint down the corridor from his room. The guard said he had missed checking the colonel's lunchbox while he had been away. The only other comment came from his secretary on the first morning after his return from Venice. Valentina Orlov had welcomed him back but then made a remark that briefly sent a chill through his body.

"Colonel, it may be nothing," she said, "but the knife I use for opening letters has a strange scratch mark on the end. It's very noticeable. It looks as if someone has picked it up from my desk and stabbed something hard. There's a scratch mark there, almost a dent."

Gerasimov tried to look surprised. When he had used the knife to gouge a hole in the end of the hollow bone hiding his tiny camera, he had failed to examine it afterwards to see if he had damaged it at all. He had just replaced it on his secretary's desk.

"I told security," she went on. "They questioned everyone in the room but no one knew anything about it. It's possible they may want to ask you, too. But I'm sure you know nothing about it?"

"I've been away," Gerasimov replied. "I'm afraid I can't help."

"But, as I told security," she persisted, "I noticed the scratch the morning after I left you in the office. It was quite late, you remember, and you told me to go home. I hope that was all right."

"Absolutely," Gerasimov replied. "Don't worry, I expect there will be an explanation."

The knife conversation had rattled him. He knew from long experience that however well planned a covert operation might be, it was often the smallest thing that could unravel it. Something forgotten, something put back in the wrong place. He was trained to be meticulous but already his decision to change his life forever could have been put at risk by a scratch at the end of his secretary's paper knife. Valentina Orlov had only been his secretary for a few months and the fact that she went straight to security showed where her loyalties lay. She could so easily have kept quiet about the wretched knife. But it was something out of the ordinary and she had felt duty-bound to report it.

The man in the dark overcoat across the street had remained stationary. Gerasimov felt his heart flutter out of control. He was under surveillance. Everything he had planned was now in the balance. One small slip and his dream was over. Worse still, he knew that if he was being watched, he could be arrested at any moment.

He walked at normal pace down the street. A few more yards and he would be turning right to head for his apartment. The side street leading to his apartment block was dark. All the streetlights were out. There was no one else around. Gerasimov quickened his pace. He heard someone walking quickly behind him. He turned, expecting to be grabbed or struck.

The man in the overcoat was next to him. Gerasimov raised his right arm to defend himself.

"Colonel," the man said, "I'm a friend. We need to make contact. I'm here to help."

Gerasimov looked astonished. The spoken Russian was good but not perfect.

"Who are you?" he asked, looking around him as if expecting others to arrive.

"Call me David," the man said.

"David who?"

"Never mind about that. We need to fix how to meet, and when. We've seen the documents. We need to know when the Kyiv operation is going to take place. You can trust me."

Gerasimov stood there in a daze. This wasn't part of his plan.

"You must have known we couldn't just leave it to Ms Strong," the man called David said.

Gerasimov kept looking up and down the street. At any moment someone could emerge in the gloom and see them. Two men talking in a dark street. It would be reported.

"You've got to go," Gerasimov said.

"So, give me a location, and a time and a date to meet. It has to be soon. It will always be me, no one else will be involved," David said.

"Sivtsev Vrazhek, by the red church, six a.m., in two days," Gerasimov said. "You've got that?"

"Got it," David replied and immediately turned away and walked back down the street.

***

David Kimche, MI6 station chief in Moscow, sent a secure message an hour later to Patrick Littlefield, marked "For Your Eyes Only":

"Contact made. Meeting fixed day after tomorrow."

***

Patrick got the message at 7:15 p.m., London time. He was still in his office. He sent a secure message to Geraldine, also marked "For Your Eyes Only":

"So far, so good."

***

The "cousins", meeting in the Tyson's Corner office block, were now out of the loop for the first time. They knew nothing of the street contact made between Gerasimov and the MI6 station chief. Adam Goldstein had a dozen undercover CIA officers at his disposal working from the US embassy in Moscow but he hadn't delegated any of them to watch Gerasimov. There was a reason. He had discussed the matter with his boss, the director of the CIA's clandestine service, and been told categorically to stand back for the time being and leave the early stages of the contact arrangements with Gerasimov to the Brits.

"Too many people from too many agencies falling over each other in the same cause is neither sensible nor practical," the director had said.

Gerasimov, or Bunyan, as he had been codenamed by the Americans, could potentially be the most exciting insider human intelligence source since Oleg Gordievsky in the 1970s and '80s. And Gordievsky, a former colonel in the KGB, had been groomed as a double agent by MI6. Goldstein was told the Brits knew what they were doing. They had passed on the two documents to the CIA.

The director of the clandestine service had told Goldstein he was happy for him to continue monitoring the case and to maintain electronic surveillance on Rebecca Strong, who was regarded as an interesting and potentially valuable asset. The director's parting words were: "At some point, the Brits will tell us what's going on. For the moment, hang fire."

"We seem to be in a bit of a hiatus," Marina Babb said. "I can understand the caution about undermining the Brits, but if they screw this up that's a major opportunity lost."

"But we've still got this woman under surveillance," Walt Grolsch said. "She put on quite a show in the hotel room in Venice by all accounts. Not that I've watched it, of course."

No one smiled. Marina Babb looked disgusted but said nothing.

"Far more important than her physical exertions under the sheets," said Goldstein, who clearly *had* seen the video, "is the fact that she may have revealed to her boyfriend what the Venice trip was all about. We don't know, because we fell into her carefully laid trap. She's no fool, this lady. One moment she is whispering, so it's difficult to pick up what she is saying, and then out she comes with this bold line about knowing a good restaurant where they can talk. We put all our eggs in the one basket and got ready to eavesdrop at the same restaurant where she and Bunyan had eaten the night before, but there was no sign of them. She knew we were bugging her and deliberately laid a false trail. Yes, she's pretty smart."

"We have to assume that she told this boyfriend of hers something," Grolsch said. "And he works for Sky News. The Brits could be in for a big shock. All their plans shattered by an irresponsible reporter. It beggars belief."

Goldstein cleared his throat. "I agree, there is now a risk the whole thing could be blown sky high. Sorry for the pun. But keeping tabs on Ms Strong may now be a waste of time. I can't imagine the Brits will hang on to her. If it was us doing this we'd have our people in Moscow getting it all wrapped up. I'd be surprised if the Brits aren't doing the same right now. It's interesting they're keeping it to themselves. Not for much longer, surely?"

"Where does Ms Strong fit in now?" Babb queried. "I don't think her role in this is finished. Bunyan's too keen on her to give her up. But I can't see how they are going to get together. And as for the boyfriend, Sandy Hall, I have a feeling he will do whatever Ms Strong allows or wants him to do. I don't know her, but from what I hear so far she seems pretty clued-up about things and very much in charge of her life. If she wants to play spy, she's not going to let her boyfriend spoil the fun. I suspect he will be under orders to keep quiet. If only for her personal safety."

"Interesting assessment, Marina," Goldstein said. "You could be right. Let's hope so. In which case, keep the surveillance going. Rebecca Strong might still have a role to play at some point."

***

Rebecca certainly felt her spying days were not yet over. She was back at home after two nights in Venice with Sandy. The second night, she had made love with all the lights off in the hope that if the Americans were watching her, they would only be able to peer into the darkness. She didn't know much about thermal imaging, but it didn't enter her head that they might be able to watch her and Sandy even in the dark. It was a warm night and the sheet hadn't covered them for very long. *To hell with the Americans*, Rebecca had thought.

She waited in her flat all morning, expecting Geraldine or someone from MI5 to contact her. Gerasimov had been adamant that he wanted her to be his courier, or go-between, and she had made up her mind that she was ready to do whatever had to be done. But she needed Geraldine to lay down the ground rules. Would she, for example, have to sign the Official Secrets Act? Would she be paid? And where would she be meeting Gerasimov next?

Geraldine didn't phone. The morning went by. Rebecca sat in her kitchen drinking coffee. She wasn't motivated to start a new painting although she had several commissions. She couldn't ring Sandy because he had gone off for his week's hazardous environment course, learning how to report from a war zone without being killed and what life-saving steps to take if wounded.

By two o'clock, Rebecca had had enough. She rang Geraldine's number and, as before, got her assistant.

"It's Rebecca," she said. "Can I speak to Geraldine, please?"

"I'm sorry, I didn't catch your name."

"Rebecca."

"Rebecca who?"

"Just Rebecca."

"I think you must have the wrong number."

The phone clicked.

Rebecca was staggered and angry. She phoned back. This time the phone wasn't answered. She tried once more with the same result.

It was obvious: Geraldine had cut her off. She had been useful while she was with Gerasimov in Venice. She had handed over the film. But now she was redundant. She couldn't believe that Geraldine would be so ungrateful. Rebecca was hurt and frustrated. She also thought the assistant was a cow. She resolved to go to Thames House and demand to see Geraldine.

Then her phone rang.

"Yes?" she said in an angry voice.

"Rebecca, it's Geraldine. I'm so sorry. You've been trying to get hold of me."

Rebecca's anger left her.

"Well, I did try a few times but your charming assistant cut me off," she said.

"Yes, sorry about that," Geraldine replied.

"So, what's happening?"

"We need to meet," Geraldine said.

"OK."

"I'll text you a place and time. Will tomorrow be all right?"

"Fine."

"It'll be lunchtime. Could be squeezed for time but we can talk then."

"OK."

Geraldine rang off.

Almost immediately, Rebecca's phone pinged.

It was a text.

"Keep the faith. Don't reply. RR."

Rebecca thought she knew what he meant. It was a bit obscure, but Gerasimov didn't want her to give up the spying game. Something had happened between her leaving Venice and arriving back in London. Geraldine probably wouldn't tell her what, but whatever her spy friend said at their meeting the next day, Rebecca was determined to remain involved in some way with the Gerasimov saga. Venice, she believed, was just the beginning. In fact, Venice had achieved two things. She had played a key role in what could be the emergence of a super-secret Russian double agent operation, the likes of which she had only read about in books and sensational newspaper stories; and she had fallen for Sandy in a big way. Their romping in bed had been passionate and more intimate than her previous lovemaking with him. She knew Sandy was in love with her and she felt the same. At least, she felt it when their bodies were entwined under the sheet after their physical exertions. Now, she missed him. That was another sign.

Rebecca had every reason to go back to her former life and put Sandy at the heart of it. But her curiosity was still driving her to stay connected with the Russian to see how it all played out. She knew she was in a unique position and wanted it to stay that way. Would Geraldine allow it? She suspected it was going to be a battle, but it was one she intended to win.

***

At 6 a.m., by the red church in Sivtsev Vrazhek, a long road in the historic Arbat district of Moscow, two men met up as if by chance. Colonel Mikhail Gerasimov, wearing dark trousers, a blue windcheater and blue cap, was standing close to David Kimche, MI6 station chief in Moscow. Kimche, at forty, eight years younger than Gerasimov, was wearing a dark grey tracksuit and trainers. He had a small backpack over his left shoulder and was also wearing a blue cap.

There was quite a lot of activity in the street. Not enough vehicles to cause a traffic jam, it was too early, but vans and cars went by at regular intervals. Pedestrians hurried past buried in their thoughts or on their phones.

Gerasimov handed the British spy an envelope.

"The plan is all there. I wrote it down," he said. "No photographs, no copies. In future, everything will be written down. Security has been doubled. There's more paranoia than ever. Please tell your people. What I write down is genuine but there'll be no more photographed documents. There's no date on the plan for Kyiv, but I can tell you it has been postponed. Those above me want it to happen on the third anniversary."

"So, February twenty-fourth, next year," Kimche said.

"Yes. And the plan may change. But it will give you an idea. I'm still leading it. There are some voices raised against it."

"The president?"

"No, my namesake."

"Chief of the General Staff Gerasimov?"

"Yes."

"Why?"

"If it succeeds, he thinks it could provoke the Americans to intervene in some way."

"Thanks to you, we'll make sure it doesn't succeed. Anything else?"

"The president is going to Ukraine next week. Thursday and Friday. Itinerary still secret, but I think it will be Sevastopol."

"He's going to Crimea?"

"Yes, to rally the Black Sea Fleet."

"Thank you for that."

"What will you do with it?"

"That's not for me to decide."

"Please be careful. I'm risking everything."

"Don't worry. Nothing will ever come back to you."

"Ha, I've been in this game all my life. Things always go wrong."

"We'll look after you."

"Does that mean you'll get me and my family out?"

Kimche hesitated for a second before replying.

"If necessary," he said.

"How?"

"Leave that to us."

Gerasimov looked sceptical.

Kimche touched Gerasimov's arm. "Trust me, if we need to, we will."

A full extraction plan was already being worked out. Kimche had been ordered to make the arrangements.

"We may be lucky and have Redruth on our side for months or years," Patrick Littlefield had told him, "but it could go wrong very quickly, and we must be prepared. You can't tell him, but our priority would be to extract Redruth. Alone. Then try for the family at a later stage."

"I have to go," Gerasimov said. "Meet me same time in seven days. But not here. Leningradsky train station, platform eight, north end."

He then pressed into Kimche's hand a piece of paper with the basic details of Putin's visit to Sevastopol written in longhand.

He turned away and walked rapidly east.

CHAPTER ELEVEN
BRITISH SPIES BRING IN THEIR US COUNTERPARTS

A message marked "Top Secret For Your Eyes Only" was sent from the chief of MI6 to the director of the CIA at 9:30 a.m. Eastern Standard Time on Monday October 28th. It read:

We have been informed by an authoritative source that the Russian president will be visiting Sevastopol on Thursday October 31 and Friday November 1. While this intelligence is valid and credible, extreme caution is imperative if any action is taken, in order to preserve the safety and future usefulness of the source. I have not sent this through the Five Eyes channel. I judged it was prudent to restrict this intelligence to the UK and US only. Please advise as to your view on how we should move forward, or not, with this information.

Under normal custom and practice, the majority of secret intelligence acquired by the UK and US would be shared with the other members of the Five Eyes club: Australia, New Zealand and Canada. But ultra-sensitive intelligence was sometimes held back.

The chief of MI6, a career intelligence officer who had served three years in Washington, understood the workings of the CIA and America's plethora of other intelligence agencies better than anyone. He knew that his counterpart at the CIA in Langley, Virginia, would take the view, at least initially, that good intelligence should be acted upon. But if any action aimed at putting the Russian president in harm's way were to be taken, it would have to be approved at the highest level. The MI6 chief was pretty sure the US president would baulk at ordering anything that might look like a deliberate targeting of a nation's leader. The president had once been asked at a White House press briefing whether he would ever sanction the assassination of a Russian leader, and he had replied, without hesitation, that he would never give such an order. He said it would be unlawful and undemocratic.

However, would the US president authorise the CIA to pass the intelligence on to the government in Kyiv? And if this happened, what restrictions could the US impose on Kyiv to prevent them attempting to target the Russian leader during his trip to Crimea?

Three hours later, a message marked "Top Secret For Your Eyes Only" was sent from Langley to the MI6 chief at Vauxhall Cross on the South Embankment beside the Thames.

President reluctant to exploit intelligence but feels obliged to inform Kyiv with strict conditions. The longer-range rockets supplied by the Defense Department last month are not yet operational and in any case could not reach Sevastopol. So the means for targeting the Visitor are not available. But some form of propaganda operation might be possible. Let's keep in touch.

When Geraldine was informed of the message exchange, she immediately worried about Agent Redruth. The crucial piece of intelligence about Putin's proposed visit to Sevastopol demonstrated, beyond doubt, that Mikhail Gerasimov in his new job in the Kremlin had access to Russia's top secrets. As director of counter-espionage, she had had every reason to be suspicious of Gerasimov. He had entered the UK covertly the previous year under a false passport with a mission to target and assassinate her. The fact that he failed, deliberately, so she believed, did not make him a decent human being. On the contrary, he shot and killed two police officers sitting in their car on guard duty outside her house. As a senior member of Russia's GRU military intelligence service, he had more than proved he was a ruthless operator. But when Gerasimov failed to fire his pistol as he confronted her in her bedroom, was that even then a sign he was beginning to turn against his masters in Moscow and contemplate a new future in the West? This thought had occurred to her for the first time.

Whatever the truth was, Geraldine was a professional and all her focus now was on protecting Gerasimov as a potential agent-in-place in the heart of the Kremlin. So far, he had proved his credentials by passing over two classified documents and revealing to MI6's station chief in Moscow the vital information that Putin would be making a trip to the port of Sevastopol in Crimea in three days' time. The big question now was how the US planned to exploit the intelligence. The US president had ruled out a deliberate targeting. But what might the Ukrainians do, and would they obey Washington's wishes? It was ultimately a decision for the Ukrainians. But they didn't know that British intelligence had a new super-source inside the Kremlin, so they might not feel so hesitant about taking bold action on the day the Russian leader arrived in Crimea.

Geraldine had had her lunch with Rebecca and told her, in as gentle a way as possible, that her spying days were over. Rebecca had been angry and reminded her of the note written by Gerasimov. He wanted Rebecca to stay involved. Geraldine had tried to explain that contact with Gerasimov had to be dealt with by trained professionals. She didn't mention that a covert meeting had already taken place. Nor did she mention that the Americans had been brought on board. She liked Rebecca, but Patrick Littlefield had been right: this was no time for an amateur to be playing any kind of role, whatever Gerasimov's wishes.

However, Geraldine wasn't the only one keeping secrets. Rebecca hadn't told her that Gerasimov had texted her again. Rebecca left the restaurant with one thought in her mind. She intended to maintain contact with Gerasimov because she had an instinct that if it was all left to the "professionals" something might go seriously wrong. She couldn't get out of her mind the image of the two Asian-looking tourists in the gondola in Venice. If Gerasimov thought they were American spies, they probably were. In which case, who was really in charge of the Gerasimov case? The British or the Americans? Rebecca hadn't a clue but her instincts told her that the Americans were into everything and therefore wouldn't let Geraldine control a Russian asset of such potential importance.

**

At 4 p.m. Eastern Standard Time that same day, a phone call took place between the Chairman of the US Joint Chiefs of Staff and his counterpart in Kyiv. It lasted ten minutes. Later that day, the chairman's press spokesman issued a statement that revealed a conversation had taken place and that it had covered a broad range of topics related to the war in Ukraine. The chairman had also underlined America's continuing support for Ukraine in its defence against Russia's unprovoked invasion of the country.

What America's top military chief actually told his counterpart in Kyiv was that intelligence had been acquired that indicated Putin would be travelling to Sevastopol on Thursday. A transcript of the conversation would have read:

Chairman of US Joint Chiefs: "It is our view that this intelligence needs to be treated with care for reasons I don't need to explain."

Commander-in-Chief of the Armed Forces of Ukraine: "We have a unit on permanent standby for this sort of situation."

"I appreciate that, General, but the president is anxious no action is taken that could be interpreted as a deliberate targeting of a head of state."

"Putin has had no compunction about targeting OUR president."

"Unfortunately, General, that's different, although I agree with you."

"This information is sound, I assume?"

"We have every reason to believe so."

"We should act on it in some way, surely? I'll be guided by you, but some form of demonstration to show Putin we know where he is ..."

"That's what worries us."

"You mean the intelligence source?"

"I can't talk about that. But I started this call by asking you to treat this intel with care."

"I understand. I will discuss the matter with my president."

The Chairman of the Joint Chiefs reported the conversation to the defence secretary, his political boss. Thirty minutes later, the president's national security adviser was brought up to date.

✳✳✳

Mikhail Gerasimov, Agent Redruth to British intelligence and Agent Bunyan to the CIA, was having serious second thoughts about his decision to reveal Putin's upcoming visit to Crimea. He had passed this juicy piece of intelligence to the man who introduced himself as his future British controller in order to impress him with his access. But now he felt it had been unnecessary. The two documents he had supplied and the information about the planned assassination plot in Kyiv should have been enough to demonstrate his bona fide status in the Kremlin. But he had been told of Putin's planned trip the night before and thought it would add to his value as an agent prepared to work for the other side. Now he was worried that if the British informed the Americans, the intelligence might be acted upon in a way that would inevitably raise deep suspicions within the Kremlin about whether the president's secret trip had been compromised. Gerasimov, as one of the relatively few Kremlin staff members in the know about the Crimea trip, would be questioned.

He had no way of getting hold of his British controller. They had arranged to meet a week later, but by then, Putin would have completed his visit to Sevastopol, and if there was any action taken to target him it would have happened. Gerasimov felt powerless.

There was nothing he could do to stop it. Except ... there was one thing he could try. One person who might be able to get a message through to the Brits and to the Americans.

Rebecca Strong.

Gerasimov had received confirmation of the president's itinerary. He was due to arrive at the airport in Sevastopol at 9:30 a.m. on Thursday, to be met by the Moscow-appointed governor of Crimea and taken by limousine to the port area to meet sailors and submariners of the Black Sea Fleet. He was due to make a brief address to around three hundred Russian servicemen and women, award a medal to the commander of the Black Sea Fleet, and then hold a private meeting with the admiral and his staff on board a guided-missile frigate docked in the port. It was now unclear whether the president would stay for a second day, as previously planned. The briefing notes Gerasimov saw indicated the president wanted to return to the Kremlin on Thursday evening, although the original itinerary had included a visit on Friday morning to a nuclear-powered submarine to witness the launch of cruise missiles against targets in Kyiv. The admiral of the Black Sea Fleet had urged the Kremlin planning staff to allow Putin a second day in Crimea for the cruise missile firing, but the chief of Putin's bodyguard force had advised against the president remaining in one area for more than a day. While Sevastopol appeared to be beyond the range of any of Ukraine's Western-supplied ground-launched missiles, military attacks on Crimea, both by special operations sabotage units and by armed sea drones, had increased significantly in recent months.

So, the visit was fixed for Thursday, unless Putin changed his mind, and his departure from Sevastopol was set for 5:30 p.m. the same day. There had been discussion about sending a lookalike, but Putin had insisted he needed to be there.

Gerasimov slept badly on Monday night. He dreamed that Putin's limousine was hit by a swarm of armed drones. He woke up in the early hours waving his arms in the air as if trying to fend them off. He knew he had to get a message to Rebecca somehow. But not on his phone. The risks would be overwhelming. He got up and dressed in his normal business clothes. His wife and children were asleep. He wasn't due in the office until 8:30 a.m. He had two hours to find a way of getting a message to Rebecca without putting his life at risk.

In the end, it was simple. He went down into the Moscow Metro and joined the crowds of early risers. About ten passengers were standing closely together in the centre of his compartment. Most of them had phones in their hands, waiting for a signal. One young woman was chatting to an older man. The bag slung over her shoulder was open, and Gerasimov could see a phone lying at the top, on a red silk scarf. He moved forward quickly as the train emerged from the tunnel into a station. When the doors opened, he brushed past the young woman and slipped his hand into her bag. He grabbed the phone and left the train. She didn't notice.

***

Rebecca was asleep. She didn't see the text for a couple of hours. When she picked up her phone from the table next to the bed, she didn't recognise the number. But the message was clear and dramatic:

"URGENT. Please tell GH NOT to take action of any kind on Thursday. For my sake! RR."

It wasn't his phone but it *was* Gerasimov. Rebecca had no idea what his text meant, but she knew he wouldn't send her a message like that unless he expected her to take instant action. She leapt out of bed.

Rebecca had hoped to spend the day with Sandy. He had completed his training course and was due to travel out to Ukraine the following day for his first assignment as Sky News foreign correspondent. He expected to arrive in Kyiv by train from Poland late Wednesday evening. Sandy had told Rebecca on the phone that he was excited but deeply apprehensive. The Ukrainian capital came under almost daily attack. Although many of the missiles and drones were shot down, no air defence system was foolproof, and some rockets got through. The hotel where most foreign newspaper reporters and television crews were staying hadn't been hit. But several apartment blocks not that far away had been damaged, and civilians killed.

Rebecca was happy and scared for Sandy. She knew how thrilled he had been to be promoted to foreign correspondent, but covering wars was a world away from reporting on crime. She and Sandy had discussed it, and he had tried to explain what was expected of him. Newspapers and broadcasting organisations seemed to think that a reporter who could write about domestic issues from an office in London could just as easily be sent into a war zone and do the same while under fire. A week of training to be a reporter in a hazardous environment was all well and good, and no doubt satisfied media organisations' legal departments, but in reality, it was always down to the individual. If they could hack it and survive and deliver dramatic copy in the process, then everyone was happy. But it was a gamble every time. Sandy was sure he would be fine and told Rebecca that after his stint of four weeks in Kyiv he would return and take some time off. Perhaps, he had suggested, they could go back to Venice.

Rebecca was horrified that Gerasimov's text had mentioned Thursday. Could it be a reference to something happening in Moscow? But what if he was warning against some form of action being taken in Ukraine? Sandy would be in Kyiv on Thursday.

She decided to tell Sandy to take extra care on Thursday without revealing that Gerasimov had been in touch again. Sandy wouldn't be happy with that. But if she could at least warn him that something might happen on that day, he would be better informed than any other reporter covering the war, and alert to a potential story. But first, before she spoke to Sandy, she had to relay the message from Gerasimov to Geraldine. She forwarded the text to her friend's phone and waited for what she hoped would be a call from Geraldine.

Her phone rang three minutes later.

"Rebecca, I got the text. For heaven's sake, what's going on?" Geraldine asked.

"I've no idea," Rebecca replied. "I thought you would know what it meant."

"I can't talk about that. But sending you a text on his phone is so risky."

"It wasn't his phone."

"It wasn't?"

"No, a different number. Maybe he has a new phone."

Geraldine didn't reply at first.

"Maybe," she said eventually.

"Or what?" Rebecca asked.

"I guess he knows what he's doing. He will have taken precautions."

"Anyway, whatever, what are you going to do about it? What's supposed to be happening on Thursday and where?" Rebecca knew she wouldn't get answers to her questions.

"There's nothing I can tell you, Rebecca, you understand."

"It's all so frustrating, Geraldine, I give you tons of stuff and you tell me nothing."

"That's the way it has to be, I'm afraid, but thank you, genuinely, for sending me the text. But I'm not sure there's anything I can do."

"Oh God, what do you mean by that?"

Geraldine was angry with herself. "It's nothing, I didn't mean to say that."

"So, whatever it is, you can't stop it?"

"I didn't say that, Rebecca."

"It's not something to do with Ukraine, is it?"

"Really, Rebecca, you know I can't tell you anything."

"My boyfriend will be in Ukraine on Thursday."

"You haven't told him about the text, have you?" Geraldine sounded alarmed.

"No but—"

"No but nothing," Geraldine interrupted. "You have to keep this to yourself. There is a lot at stake."

"So, something *is* going to happen in Ukraine?"

"I didn't say that and you're not to make any such assumption."

"You know, Geraldine, the best thing would be if you actually trusted me and we worked together. Gerasimov obviously thinks it's best, and you need him, don't you? He's a big deal for you lot, I've worked that out for myself without your help."

Geraldine was silent for a moment.

"Even if I agreed with you, which I don't, my superiors would never sanction it," she said.

"I thought you were the boss."

"I'm a bossette, Rebecca," Geraldine said with a laugh. "The higher-ups on both sides of the Thames have a say in the matter. I'm sure even with your brief appearance in my world, you can appreciate that."

"It's all bureaucracy rubbish," Rebecca replied. "It's not how Hollywood paints you lot."

"Well, you're right there. James Bond was always in trouble with his bosses, disobeying orders and going his own way."

"But that's not you, right? You have to do what you're told?"

"It's not quite like that. There are rules and there are ways of doing things and we have to cooperate with each other, the different agencies, I mean."

"I get it, but surely your game is all about taking risks, too. Otherwise, if you stick to the rules all the time you'll be outsmarted by your enemies who don't play by the rules at all."

"You're learning fast, Rebecca," Geraldine said. "And you're right, in many ways. But my partners in crime decided that your time as our amateur spy was over."

"You believe that?"

"Well, perhaps not. If Gerasimov continues to contact you, you may become key to this whole thing."

"Wow, Geraldine, have you changed your mind? What are you telling me?"

"I'm going to take a big risk," Geraldine said. "I don't want you involved because it could be dangerous for you. But perhaps you could be my private, confidential source. I don't tell anyone, not my colleagues, not my boss and no one on the other side of the Thames. It will be a totally secret arrangement between you and me. But only if or when Gerasimov contacts you. You and I can then work out how to reply."

"Sounds a bit secretarial, Geraldine, not quite like parachuting me onto the roof of the Kremlin."

"All in good time," Geraldine joked. "So, do we have a deal?"

"We do. Thanks, Geraldine."

"Have to go. Stay in touch." Geraldine rang off.

***

Sandy came to Rebecca's flat later that morning. They went straight to bed and neither mentioned Ukraine.

Afterwards, Rebecca broached the subject.

"What will you do on your first day?" she asked.

Sandy smiled. "I'll be thinking of you. And this."

"Well, I should hope so," Rebecca said. "But what I meant was, what will you be reporting on your first day?"

"You mean Thursday? I'll probably spend most of the day getting my accreditation sorted out and planning stuff with my cameraman."

"So, no great heroics on the first day?"

"No; unless something happens, of course."

"Like what?"

"I've no idea."

"But you won't go rushing off to anywhere dangerous?"

"Rebecca, are you worried about me?"

"Of course, you idiot. There'll be no more of this if you go and get killed."

"I'll be fine. I'll always be careful, I promise. Just be ready for me when I come back."

Rebecca grinned. She turned away from Sandy and then asked him: "So, if something does happen on Thursday, what will you do?"

"Depends what it is and where it is. Why are you so interested?"

"Just want to know."

"Well, if it's in Kyiv and it's safe, I'll probably go to whatever has happened with my cameraman and film some stuff and do a piece to camera. Just like I do back here. But if it's anywhere else, I'll just have to find out what I can. After a few days, I'll fix to go off to spend time with one of the Ukrainian combat units. But not on day one."

"Good."

"You're weird."

"Why?"

"You always sound as if you know something I don't know, but won't tell me."

"In your dreams, Sandy Hall. I'm just a concerned friend."

"Friend? Is that all we are?"

"I don't sleep with all my friends."

"Do you sleep with any of your friends?"

"Not usually."

"That's reassuring."

Sandy snuggled up to her naked back and bottom and kissed her neck.

"Four weeks without this is going to be hard," he whispered in her ear.

"Behave yourself, Mr Foreign Correspondent. I'll be here when you get back."

"You better be."

Rebecca turned to face him and kissed him, all her curves pressed against him.

When they stopped kissing, Sandy asked: "So, Thursday is just Thursday, right?"

She moved her hand up and down his back. "Thursday is never just Thursday in Ukraine," she said.

"God, Rebecca, there you go again," he replied. "But I like what you're doing."

"I can tell," she whispered.

***

A brief communication took place between the CIA director and the MI6 chief midday on Tuesday October 29th.

We have been informed by Kyiv that there will be what they call a demonstration on Thursday 31st. No direct attempt on the Visitor but aimed at disruption. Details are being kept close to their chest, which is unusual and frankly irritating. But we've been promised no great drama. Apologies, but it's their show.

The reply from the MI6 chief followed ten minutes later.

Five has particularly requested no action. One can only hope that said demonstration is not perceived by Moscow to be as a result of special intel. Quite concerned we are in the dark about what Kyiv is planning.

When the MI6 chief told Geraldine at MI5, or "Five", as he had described the service to the CIA director, she reacted badly, even when she was assured there would be no great drama. She didn't know whether she could trust either the Americans or the Ukrainians.

On Thursday, she would have a better idea whether Operation Greengage and Agent Redruth had a future. If not, and if Gerasimov looked to be vulnerable, the emergency plan to bring him out of Moscow might have to be activated. But not with his family.

CHAPTER TWELVE
REBECCA PLAYS SOLO

Same day, 4 p.m.

Sandy had left Rebecca to return to his flat to pack for his trip to Ukraine. He rang to tell her he would be leaving for the airport at 5 a.m. the following morning. She wished him luck. He told her he loved her and would miss her. She replied, "I'll miss you too."

Five minutes later, she knew what she was about to do. The thought had been in her mind since her phone call with Geraldine. She picked up her phone from the kitchen table and scrolled down to where Gerasimov had texted her on the different phone.

She then tapped out a short message:

"Thursday can't be stopped. Sorry."

She knew Thursday was important. Gerasimov had tried to stop something, and Geraldine had told her it was too late. Now, whatever it was, it was going to happen. But at least in a roundabout way, she had warned Sandy.

Suddenly, she shivered and wrapped her arms around herself. She hadn't mentioned to Geraldine that it might be a good idea to warn Gerasimov, and Geraldine hadn't raised it. But the more she had thought about it, the more she knew she'd had to reply to his text. He had to know that her appeal to the security services had failed. If necessary, she would tell Geraldine later; after all, they had a deal that should work both ways. But in this case, Rebecca's independent spirit had taken over. Only she had Gerasimov's new number. She hadn't given it to Geraldine. So she hoped the reply text would be private, although she knew there was a risk, especially with America's all-seeing and all-listening satellites. But she convinced herself that if anything was to be done about Thursday she was the only one who could let Gerasimov know what was happening from the London end.

***

Gerasimov's reaction when he received Rebecca's text on his stolen phone was a mixture of anger and confusion.

Miraculously, the phone was still working. The girl had not yet reported it missing. But he knew it wouldn't be long before the phone was blocked and it would no longer be useable.

The phone, however, was not his main concern. If any action was taken against Putin in Sevastopol, no one in the Kremlin would believe it to be a coincidence. The Federal Security Service, the FSB, would be hot on the trail of a suspected inside leaker. Gerasimov would be drawn into the FSB's web. He had a sudden thought. If they had cause to suspect he was the traitor, they would rigorously investigate all of his known contacts. His past employers at the GRU military intelligence agency knew about Rebecca Strong. They knew he had lived for two weeks in her flat while he was carrying out his covert mission in London the previous year. They hadn't approved, but neither had they punished him for his adulterous behaviour. They had been persuaded by his argument that he had needed a safe refuge. Staying in a hotel had become too risky. Rebecca Strong had, unwittingly, provided him with a legitimate address, a safe house. One of the four GRU generals who questioned him had nodded in admiration.

So, Rebecca could be investigated if he fell under suspicion. The FSB and GRU were ruthless organisations. Gerasimov knew that Rebecca could be in grave danger. He would have to remove the battery from the stolen phone and then dump it, well away from his flat. He considered swapping his normal phone and buying a new one with a clean SIM card, but he knew that would lead to security complications. He would be asked why he had needed to change his phone. Anything out of the ordinary like that would raise suspicions. Gerasimov began to wonder whether the life of a double agent was just too fraught with danger. The only person he knew properly and could trust was Rebecca, and she wasn't in the spying game. He knew now he had been both reckless and naïve to imagine she could play a significant role in passing on secrets. The spy from the British embassy had been right: Rebecca couldn't be his go-between. So, unless he managed to get away again to Venice or some other place in Europe, he had no choice but to deal with the man from the British embassy.

Revealing Putin's Crimea trip to the British spy had been one of the worst decisions of his life. All he could hope for was that any action taken while Putin was in Sevastopol would be so minor as not to be noticed, or so far away that it wouldn't have any real impact. Bizarrely, especially in the light of his decision to betray his country, he wanted Putin back safely in the Kremlin on Thursday night.

***

Sandy arrived late Wednesday at the InterContinental Hotel in the centre of Kyiv. Turning up at a hotel packed with veteran war reporters from around the world was always a nerve-wracking moment for a new foreign correspondent. Sandy had no experience of war zones and was not expecting to recognise any of the other reporters, apart from the Sky News correspondent he was relieving. She was a veteran herself. Sandy realised he would be regarded by everyone as the new boy. But he had been crime correspondent for Sky News for more than four years, so he had a public profile, and most of the other reporters would at least know his name.

He checked in at reception. As he did so, he felt an odd sense of unreality. This was a city at war, a target for every type of Russian missile, and here he was filling in the register as if it was a hotel in Florence or Paris. There were no sounds of war as he completed the registration and took a heavy key from the receptionist. He had brought a large, Bergen-style knapsack stuffed with clothes, a heavy holdall with flak jacket and helmet, and a shoulder bag for his laptop. There was a message for him to meet his Sky News colleague in the bar as soon as he arrived. But first, he went to his room.

He sat on the bed and texted Rebecca.

"Have arrived. Wish you were here, although not really if you see what I mean. Love, S."

It was two hours earlier in London. Rebecca replied immediately.

"Stay cool. And safe. Lol, R."

Sandy wondered briefly whether she meant "lots of love" or "laugh out loud". He hoped it was the former. He texted back.

"Tomorrow's Thursday! Any further thoughts or instructions? X"

A few minutes went by.

"Sorry, no. But see earlier text. R."

Sitting in a hotel in a war-zone city, Sandy would have liked a bigger display of love or affection from the woman he had fallen for. But Rebecca, he knew, was not one for writing romantic texts. She was a strange mixture: passionate and wonderfully intimate when she was in the mood, but otherwise a little distant, as if she were worried about losing her identity and independence. Sandy didn't mind that. He had always been good at living and working on his own. But after meeting Rebecca he had found his independent spirit almost overwhelmed by her fiery character. And that was bad because now, in his hotel room in Kyiv with the prospect of venturing off to somewhere potentially dangerous the next day, all he wanted was an expression of undying love from Rebecca. But he wasn't going to get it.

He sent her one more text before going downstairs to meet his colleague in the bar.

"Thinking of you. xxx S."

When he returned to his room an hour later, there was still no reply. And Thursday had arrived, at least in Kyiv.

***

At 9:30 a.m., the president of Russia stepped out of a Mi-24 Hind helicopter at the far end of the runway at Sevastopol airport and climbed into a BTR-50 armoured personnel carrier. He was accompanied by the Chief of the General Staff, General Valery Gerasimov, three bodyguards and an air force officer carrying a heavy briefcase.

The Soviet-era armoured vehicle moved rapidly along the direct route from the airport to the port, where Putin was to address Black Sea Fleet sailors.

Forty minutes later, dressed in a dark-blue suit and red tie, the Russian leader was greeted with thunderous cheers from the sailors, who raised their hats in the air. He told them they were fighting for the safety and security of the Russian motherland and thanked them for their courage and victorious actions.

Following a brief ceremony in which Putin pinned a medal to the naval uniform of the admiral of the Black Sea Fleet, whose jacket was already covered in medals, the Russian leader was escorted by his bodyguards to the gangplank leading up to the guided-missile frigate *Admiral Essen*.

It was now 10:25 a.m. The meeting with the admiral and his staff on board *Admiral Essen* had been fixed in Moscow for 10:30 a.m. and was to last an hour. Russian soldiers guarded the quayside, standing no more than two feet from each other. Crowds had gathered for the address to the sailors, amazed to see Putin in their midst without any prior notice. But most of them had left the port.

Exactly thirty minutes after Putin boarded the frigate, there was an ear-splitting explosion on the warship. The few people left gawping on the quayside, hoping to see Putin re-emerge from the frigate, screamed and held their hands to their ears. Some of them ran off in panic. About half a dozen people who stayed behind, still holding their heads, were rewarded with a second sighting of the president.

Putin emerged from *Admiral Essen* surrounded by his bodyguards, who were frogmarching him down the gangplank, accelerating as they went. The armoured vehicle that had brought Putin to the port shunted forward, and the Russian leader was almost hurled into the back. His bodyguards piled in and someone shouted in Russian, "Go go go!" The Russian air force officer with the heavy briefcase was left behind in the rush to extract the president from any further risk of attack.

The briefcase contained the top-secret codes for the presidential launch of a nuclear attack.

As the armoured vehicle disappeared into the city of Sevastopol, black smoke was pouring out of the stern of the guided-missile frigate.

***

In war, nothing goes to plan. The apparent deliberate targeting of President Putin was no such thing. The special Ukrainian security unit given the task of carrying out a demonstration attack during Putin's visit to Sevastopol had been given clear instructions: Putin himself was not to be targeted. He was to come to no harm. The objective was to send a message to him that whenever or if ever he dared to visit troops in Russian-occupied parts of Ukraine – and that included Crimea, annexed by Moscow in 2014 – he needed to be aware of the risks.

The intelligence supplied by their Western partners had been good but not precise. The known facts of his itinerary were that

Putin would be arriving at Sevastopol at 9:30 a.m., that he would speak to sailors, carry out a medal award and then go on board a warship for a meeting with the commander of the Black Sea Fleet. Apart from the arrival time at the airport, there were no specific times for the rest of Putin's visit. Nor was there any intelligence supplied regarding on which warship Putin would be holding his meeting.

The Ukrainian security unit included naval specialists. The plan, approved by the Kyiv leadership but not passed on to the Americans, was to launch a long-range underwater drone from Odesa, with the nose packed with high explosives. It was to be a journey of around two hundred miles, well within the range of the latest naval drone that had been designed and developed by the Ukrainian defence industry.

The target would be one of the Russian warships in the port of Sevastopol. There were half a dozen to choose from. The frigate *Admiral Essen* was selected because of where it was docked; according to images provided by an American commercial satellite company, it was more isolated than the other warships.

The commander of the Ukrainian unit estimated that the twenty-foot-long drone would take around three hours to reach its target. Launching it from the port of Odesa at 7 a.m. meant it would hit the guided-missile frigate at about 10 a.m. Judging by the limited intelligence at his disposal, the commander believed Putin at that time would still be addressing sailors on the quayside. The explosion would interrupt his speech but would not endanger his life. A perfect demonstration.

However, there was a last-minute hitch. Ukraine's leader, President Volodymyr Zelensky, wanted to be reassured that Putin would not be in danger. He knew that Putin had no compunction about trying to assassinate him and his cabinet – Moscow had tried at least once at the beginning of the invasion – but Zelensky insisted on maintaining the moral high ground. He didn't want to be accused of trying to kill his hated enemy, and he knew that

President Biden was adamantly opposed to state assassinations. So, for half an hour on the phone, the Ukrainian leader went over again with the commander of the special security unit how "the demonstration" was going to play out.

It was just before 7:30 a.m. when the underwater drone was finally released. It should have reached the warship target between 10:15 a.m. and 10:30 a.m., but unexpected strong cross-currents en route hampered its journey. The drone arrived at 11:03 a.m., undetected by Russian sonar devices or by a team of dolphins trained to pinpoint hostile objects approaching Sevastopol underwater. The drone hit the stern of *Admiral Essen*, with Putin and the admiral in the wardroom at the other end of the ship.

***

Within an hour, the Telegram messaging service reported on the drama.

"A large explosion has been heard on a warship in Sevastopol. Early reports suggest a hostile attack. No announcement about casualties so far."

Initially, there was no mention of Putin being present in the city. Foreign reporters in Kyiv, all devoted readers of Telegram because of its reputation for breaking reports or rumours to do with the war in Ukraine, began making inquiries. Sandy Hall didn't have the same contacts, but the reporter he replaced had provided him with the basic numbers for the Ukrainian defence ministry and presidential palace. Over the next half an hour, a potentially huge story began to emerge. Reporters were informed that an explosion on an unidentified warship had taken place around 11 a.m. No details were added. Indeed, there was no confirmation that the explosion had been caused by Ukrainian military action. However, the one detail that was provided was that President Putin had been visiting Sevastopol at the time of the explosion. Reporters rushed to their laptops and phones.

Putin's Kremlin spokesman put out a brief statement which downplayed the incident:

A minor explosion occurred this morning on the guided-missile frigate Admiral Essen. *The cause is being investigated, but it appears to be linked to an overheated boiler. President Putin was on a visit to Sevastopol to meet and congratulate crews of the Black Sea Fleet. But the president was not in the vicinity of the incident.*

Sandy was mesmerised by the reports. It was Thursday. Rebecca had told him to watch out for Thursday. He had no idea why she had said it, but he knew it wasn't just because Thursday was to be his first full day in Ukraine as Sky News's new foreign correspondent. Sandy's reporting instincts were going wild. A boiler explosion on a key warship was not a great story. A boiler explosion on a key warship when Putin was in town was a better story. But a mystery explosion on a warship caused by a covert Ukrainian military unit to coincide with the arrival of Putin for a visit dedicated to applauding the Black Sea Fleet, whose home was in the port of Sevastopol? That was a potentially huge story. Had the Kyiv government known that Putin was coming? Was this an attempt on the Russian president's life? Sandy got increasingly excited the more he thought of all the story options. And it was only his first day.

The Kremlin continued to try and smother the story with meaningless comments about the state of boilers on some of the Black Sea Fleet's older warships. But images of black smoke pouring from the stern of *Admiral Essen* and a picture of Putin addressing hundreds of sailors only half an hour before the explosion generated rampant rumours on social media. As so often since the war began, the Ukrainian defence ministry did not confirm any military involvement. Without any proof that Ukrainian saboteurs had been responsible, early reports of the incident put out by news agencies focused on Putin's surprise visit to Sevastopol and the mystery surrounding the explosion.

Sandy's first report on Sky News played it safe. He emphasised the intriguing coincidence of the Russian president being in Sevastopol at the time of the explosion but stuck strictly to the official statements from the Kyiv defence ministry and the Kremlin. The BBC and all of the US broadcasters followed a similar line. The story could have died, but late in the afternoon, a woman in Sevastopol was interviewed by a Russian state television station. She said she had witnessed the explosion and seen Putin emerge from the warship after the black smoke began to rise into the air. She said the president was surrounded by others and seemed to be in a great hurry. The report on the state-run TV station broadcast around 5:30 p.m., but by 6 p.m. the story was no longer running. The Kremlin had stepped in to scotch the eye-witness report. But the cat was out of the bag: Putin had been on board the warship when the explosion occurred!

Sandy and all the other reporters besieged the Kyiv defence ministry with questions, but they were told there would be no further statements that day. The Kremlin spokesman dismissed the story on Russian state television and denied that Putin had been in any danger at any time during his visit to Sevastopol.

At 10 p.m., warships from the Black Sea Fleet off Sevastopol fired twenty cruise missiles at targets in Kyiv. Nineteen of them were shot down by US-supplied Patriot surface-to-air missiles. One landed near the Ukrainian defence ministry, and debris from the nineteen shot down fell onto three apartment blocks. Two adults and three children, all from the same family, were killed.

For Sandy, it was his first experience of coming under fire in a war. He and the other reporters in his hotel ran down the stairs to the basement as soon as the air-raid alerts sounded. They were joined by the few guests staying at the hotel, all Ukrainians. Sandy looked around, frightened and excited at the same time. He turned to a fellow reporter and pointed at the Ukrainians, who were sitting calmly. A child with his mother was playing with a toy soldier.

"They're used to it," the reporter whispered. "You're a new boy. These people come down here to the basement almost every day. It's kind of routine."

Sandy was amazed.

When the explosions outside stopped and they were allowed to leave, Sandy sent a late report to Sky News summing up the day's events and highlighting the cruise missile attacks. The foreign editor told him to get some sleep but to file an early morning piece to camera, outlining his views and conclusions about what happened in Sevastopol.

Sandy sent a text to Rebecca:

"Quite a first day. I'm OK, if you're worried. xxx S."

She replied:

"Please take care. X."

The kiss was welcome after his long day. He went to sleep with a smile on his face.

He woke early and rang his cameraman. He would be ready to do his piece in an hour. He then put all his thoughts together to come up with something new about the Sevastopol incident. A number of papers in the UK and US had ventured to suggest that the explosion on the frigate might have been as a result of a Ukrainian military strike. But only one report, in the *Daily Express*, claimed a Ukrainian source had hinted that a naval underwater or surface drone had hit the guided-missile frigate. The paper went on to report that similar drones had been used in the past to attack the twelve-mile-long Kerch Strait Bridge linking the Crimean peninsula to the mainland.

Sandy's first thought was that the firing of twenty cruise missiles at 10 p.m., which had forced all the reporters into the basement of the hotel, seemed like a deliberate retaliatory strike. But retaliation for what? Not for an explosion on a warship in Sevastopol caused by a faulty boiler! When, as the *Daily Express* reported, the Kerch Bridge was hit by naval drones, Moscow responded with missile strikes on Kyiv and Odesa. So, the latest barrage was surely because the Kremlin wanted to seek revenge on Ukraine. Was this Moscow's indirect way of admitting Putin had been targeted? If so, it made sense to report that the explosion was probably caused by a deliberate Ukrainian military strike on the warship and timed for when Putin was on board. One more tantalising question had to be asked: was Kyiv tipped off that Putin was going to Sevastopol? Which led on to: was the tip from US intelligence? And if it was, did that mean President Biden had sanctioned the attempted assassination of the Russian leader?

Sandy's head was filled with all the potential huge implications of his questions. But how hard should he go with this story? At the forefront of his mind was the bizarre warning, or apparent warning, by Rebecca. Had she been told by her new spy friends that something was going to happen on Thursday? Sandy knew that he had to treat this implied piece of intelligence with the greatest care. He decided the best way to deal with all the information and speculation was to raise questions rather than provide definitive answers. It was too early to ring the Ukrainian defence ministry, and anyway, he didn't expect its press office to oblige with answers. So, his first piece for Sky News that morning would have more questions than answers, but it could still be pretty dramatic.

He worried about upsetting Rebecca but he was sure his rivals would be coming to all the same conclusions. If he didn't get in early, every other newspaper and broadcaster would beat him to it. The *Daily Express* had already scooped everyone, even though its story was not based on official confirmation of a Ukrainian military strike on the Russian warship.

At 7 a.m., Sandy's special report from Kyiv was leading the news. It was a sensational report even though Sandy tried his best to put forward his analysis while emphasising he had been unable to persuade any official in the Kyiv government to confirm his conclusions.

Geraldine had arrived early in her office and was reading through overnight intelligence reports. She looked up to see the 7 a.m. news on Sky and turned up the volume.

Sandy was dressed in jeans and a blue anorak. He looked tired and, Geraldine thought, vulnerable. She felt sorry for him. Spies took danger for granted, but the average employee in her care had been nowhere near a war zone. Yet here was a reporter, not that long ago crime correspondent for Sky, now thrown into a war and having to report back in a calm and controlled voice. She admired him for that.

"The explosion that rocked a Russian guided-missile frigate in the Crimean port of Sevastopol at eleven a.m. yesterday may have been a deliberate attempt to kill or injure President Putin."

"Oh God!" Geraldine bellowed.

"The Russian president was on board the warship, Admiral Essen, at the time of the explosion, holding a meeting, probably in the wardroom. This has been confirmed by a witness who saw President Putin being rushed out of the warship within minutes of the explosion. The witness, a young woman who had been standing on the quayside, was interviewed on Russian state television, although the interview was later erased from news bulletins."

"You bet it was," Geraldine said. There was no one else in her office to hear her outbursts.

"No other Russian media outlet mentioned the presence of the Russian leader on the warship. The spokesman for the Kremlin claimed that the explosion was caused by a faulty boiler, but the force of the blast and the pungent black smoke that poured out of the ship indicated it was more likely to have been caused by some form of military strike.

"Ukraine has previously used sea drones, on the surface and underwater, to hit key Russian targets. The Kerch Bridge linking Crimea to the mainland has been hit several times by long-range naval drones. If it was a drone that struck the warship, it raises three questions: was Ukraine tipped off that President Putin would

be on board the targeted warship on that day and at that time? If so, was the strike intended to assassinate the Russian leader? And, thirdly, who could have provided such intelligence: would it have come from Ukraine's own intelligence-gathering capabilities or could it have been passed to Kyiv by the US or some other Western partner? Or, indeed, might it have been provided by a source within Russia? The heads of both the CIA and MI6 have in the past called on Russians to pass on intelligence to the West if they were opposed to the war in Ukraine and the Russian leadership's decision to invade the country.

"At this stage, these questions are speculative. However, the fact is Mr Putin survived whatever was intended. It is also a fact that within hours of the explosion on board Admiral Essen, *Russian warships in the Black Sea launched twenty cruise missiles against Kyiv. That suggests that the Kremlin at least believed there had been a deliberate targeting of Mr Putin.*

"Sandy Hall, Sky News in Kyiv."

Sandy's report might have emphasised that it was speculative, but the reaction from certain quarters was immediate and explosive. By the time Sandy had finished, the expression on Geraldine Hammer's face had changed dramatically. She was the first to pick up her phone.

She rang Patrick Littlefield, who was sitting in the back of his government Jaguar on his way to Vauxhall Cross.

"Patrick, it's Geraldine; have you seen Sky News?" she asked.

He hadn't.

"When you get to the office, watch it, and tell me whether we should be worried about Redruth," she said.

"Are you?" Patrick asked.

"Yes," she replied.

"Then let's meet," he said. "In an hour, my office. Bring Grace."

Geraldine hesitated before making the other phone call. But then she dialled the number.

A very sleepy voice answered.

"Rebecca, it's Geraldine. Your boyfriend seems to know a lot more than anyone else reporting from Kyiv. Did you tell him anything?"

Rebecca sat up in bed and dropped the phone as she did. By the time she retrieved it she could hear Geraldine asking the question again.

"Sorry, I dropped the phone," Rebecca said. "I don't know what you're talking about. I was asleep."

"He was on Sky. What he reported made me wonder whether he was party to confidential information. Something only you outside my normal secret circle knew about."

"Like what?" Rebecca said. "I haven't seen Sky."

"I'm not going to go into detail on the phone," Geraldine replied. "But watch Sky and you will see what I mean. I have to go. I will ring you later."

Geraldine rang off.

Rebecca switched on Sky News but had to wait forty minutes to see Sandy's report. When she saw him reporting from the roof of his hotel in Kyiv, her whole body began to shiver. Her heart began beating at what seemed like double speed.

She snatched her phone from the bedclothes and sent a text.

"WTF!!!!!"

CHAPTER THIRTEEN
AGENT REDRUTH GETS A FRIGHT

Friday morning.

Within thirty minutes of his arrival at his office in the Kremlin, Colonel Mikhail Gerasimov received a summons. He was to see his boss, the Secretary of the Security Council, immediately.

Gerasimov didn't jump up immediately from his desk. He knew nothing about the Sky News report but he had received the overnight intelligence summing-up of the events in Sevastopol the day before. The judgement of the FSB hierarchy was that the president's life had been deliberately put in harm's way. There was confirmation that the guided-missile frigate that had hosted Putin's meeting with the admiral of the Black Sea Fleet had been struck by an underwater drone. This discovery was to remain top secret for the foreseeable future.

The other highly embarrassing incident, which would always be kept secret, was the separation of the president from the air force officer carrying the briefcase with the nuclear codes. Putin was so angry when he realised what had happened that he ordered the hapless officer to be replaced immediately. The officer was picked up by helicopter and brought back to Moscow in disgrace. As a precaution, the nuclear codes were changed. Putin ordered a total news blackout and not a word appeared in the Russian newspapers or on social media.

The FSB, heading the investigation into the Sevastopol explosion, warned that there was a serious possibility the president's itinerary had been leaked. Three options were listed: it could have come from within the relatively small number of Kremlin staff in the know about the president's planned visit, or from the private staff of General Gerasimov, Russia's most senior military chief, or from the selected personnel of the Black Sea Fleet who had been told to prepare for the arrival of their commander-in-chief.

Gerasimov didn't panic. He concluded that if he was the main suspect for whatever reason he would have been arrested by now and marched off to the FSB basement cells in Lubyanka Square. But he knew that he was probably more vulnerable than most of the forty or so people who would be on the FSB interrogation list; his file would give the FSB ammunition. It would include the fact that he had come up against the British intelligence and security services during his aborted covert mission in London a year earlier and that he stayed for two weeks in a flat rented by a woman called Rebecca Strong, who appeared to have connections with MI5's director of counter-espionage. Someone in the FSB could be asking the question: has Gerasimov been turned by the British? Then there was the small matter of the three days he had taken off recently and his unexplained return after only two days. Being a trusted senior member of the Kremlin staff, no questions had been asked at the time when he explained he needed to be away from the office to start planning his Kyiv mission.

Gerasimov stood up and left the room. He walked quickly down the corridor and up one flight of stairs to the inner Kremlin sanctum. He knocked on the door bearing the nameplate "Secretary of the Security Council", engraved in gold lettering. He entered without waiting for a response. An officer in uniform greeted him and pointed to the open door across the other side of the room.

The Secretary of the Security Council was an imposing figure, tall, gaunt, and with a high forehead. His most remarkable feature was his eyes, which were dark brown, almost black. He was not a man with any known sense of humour. He had supported Gerasimov's promotion and attachment to his private office but he hadn't gone out of his way to be particularly friendly. The secretary, who was a man with a multitude of burdensome responsibilities, had no time for pleasantries. He didn't invite Gerasimov to take a seat.

Gerasimov steeled himself for a grilling, although if he really was suspected of being a traitor he was fairly sure it wouldn't be the secretary confronting him.

The secretary finished initialling a document and raised his eyes. "Your Ukraine mission has been brought forward."

As soon as he said these words, Gerasimov felt an overwhelming surge of relief.

"Mr Secretary?" he replied.

"After yesterday's outrage, there has to be retribution."

"I thought the cruise missile attacks were retaliation for Sevastopol," Gerasimov replied.

"Yes, yes," the secretary muttered. "But this is personal. The president is adamant. He wants like for like. The whole Kyiv gang must go. Are you ready?"

Gerasimov was put on the spot. He had written out a rough plan for launching a covert targeting operation against the Ukrainian president, but there were few details. Gerasimov had hoped the president would scrap the whole idea. He was faced with the worst possible kind of catch-22 situation. He had no choice but to obey the order given to him, but at the same time he had to engineer it so the mission failed in its objective without him being accused of incompetence, or worse still, wilful obstruction. He would pass on his plan to his British controller so that Kyiv would be warned, but what if something went seriously wrong? What if he and his whole team were captured or killed? Could the British intelligence service provide him with a guarantee of survival if he was captured and, if so, how would that be interpreted in Moscow?

Gerasimov felt there was no winning option. But he had to convince his superiors that he was ready to carry out this seemingly suicidal mission. At least it might cast doubt in the minds of the FSB investigating the suspected leak of highly classified information that he was responsible. His name might even be crossed off the list of suspects. So, Gerasimov was robust in his reply to the secretary.

"I will need more time, Mr Secretary, to train and equip for the mission. But I will be ready," he said.

The secretary nodded. "Provide me with the full plan by the end of next week," he said. "The president wants it put into action as quickly as possible. There is no excuse for delay or postponement. So, on my desk in seven days."

Gerasimov turned round and left the room. His next meeting with his British controller was in four days. He resolved to complete the detailed planning for the Kyiv mission by then. David Kimche only had a rough outline of the plan and would have to be told the timing had suddenly changed.

***

Adam Goldstein had gathered his team together. Not at Tyson's Corner, where the CIA had offices, but at the headquarters in Langley, Virginia. Goldstein had been summoned to the HQ to meet with the director of the CIA and he'd arranged for the two others to join him in an office on the third floor. Walt Grolsch had arrived in a hire car from NSA headquarters at Fort Meade in Maryland. Marina Babb had come from her office in McLean, Virginia.

When they were seated, Goldstein got to the point.

"We have a situation; it needs sorting," he said brusquely. "This woman, Rebecca Strong, is a liability. She has placed Bunyan in grave danger. He is going to be chief suspect for this leak. The FSB are not fools; they'll have him at the top of their list. The Brits seem strangely calm about it. But if we are going to have Gerasimov, sorry, Bunyan, as an insider for any length of time – and we need him more than ever – we've got to come up with a fancy solution to save him from the FSB."

"But he's not our agent, Adam," Marina Babb pointed out.

"He will be soon if I have anything to do with it," Goldstein replied. "The Brits have screwed up big tine. Trusting this bloody woman, Strong, was stupid from the start. I mean, her boyfriend for God's sake. Do we know anything about this Sandy Hall individual?"

"We know what we know," Grolsch said. "We're monitoring everything between him and her. Like that warning she gave about Thursday."

"She didn't actually tell him what was going to happen," Babb interjected, "it was more like a 'please take care on Thursday' sort of message."

"Marina, for God's sake, this is a reporter here," Goldstein said. "He knew she had something she couldn't tell him. She didn't know what was going to happen on Thursday but she knew something was going to happen. And her boyfriend put two and two together."

Marina Babb looked down at her hands. She hated it when Goldstein patronised her.

"All I'm saying is that she didn't really break a confidence," she said quietly. "It didn't make any difference to what happened in Sevastopol."

"Of course not," Goldstein replied, "but it's what's happening now, after the incident, that concerns me and should concern you. Will the FSB link the leak to Bunyan? Putin will want blood, and the list of suspects can't be that long."

No one responded. Babb was seething. She clenched her fists under the table and looked at Grolsch as if for support. But Grolsch said nothing. He didn't want to antagonise Goldstein.

Goldstein looked at his two colleagues. "I'm going to ring Geraldine and find out what she's doing about it," he said.

"Don't tell her we're bugging the woman's phone," Grolsch said.

Goldstein looked at Grolsch in exasperation but didn't respond.

"I'll send you both a note after I've spoken to her," he said.

***

Geraldine received a phone call twenty minutes later. She didn't know Goldstein very well. They had communicated before but their paths hadn't crossed on any previous intelligence operation.

"Geraldine," he said, without a hello first, "what news, if any, from Moscow?"

"We've heard nothing directly from our source," she replied. "Communication, as you can imagine, is difficult. But if he is under any sort of suspicion, we'll know about it soon enough."

"Not very reassuring, if I may say so," Goldstein said.

Geraldine bristled.

"Well, I have to say," she responded, "what happened in Sevastopol was a direct consequence of your decision to inform Kyiv of the intelligence we received. As you know, I did warn against anything that could be interpreted in Moscow as intelligence-sourced information. I was led to believe that Kyiv would just carry out a demonstration of some sort. I didn't know what that meant but I sure as hell didn't imagine it would be a direct attempt to target Putin when he was on the ship."

Goldstein, at the other end of the line, cleared his throat.

"That was unfortunate, I agree," he said eventually. "Kyiv has since told us that had not been the intention. It was all bad luck. But clearly Putin is now going to be steaming for retribution, and your source better look out."

"We'll handle it," Geraldine told him.

"I think, to be honest and frank with you, Geraldine," he replied, "we should take him over; we have far more resources in Moscow. If we're going to get anything more out of him in the future, he will need huge backup."

Geraldine snorted. "There is no way, Adam, that we're going to drop our source," she said as firmly as she could, "just as we wouldn't ever expect you to hand over one of your sources."

"So, what about this woman, Rebecca Strong?" Goldstein threw back. "What are you going to do about her?"

His question stopped Geraldine in her tracks. So the CIA *did* know about Rebecca and Gerasimov. They *had* been in Venice. But how did they catch on? She had never mentioned to the Americans the connection between Rebecca and "the source" in Moscow. It was basic espionage rules that even between the closest of allies, primary sources and their links to others who could be classed as secondary or tertiary sources remained totally confidential. Sources or agents relied, for their very lives, on the discreet and professional management of their controllers. Bandying their names around among different intelligence agencies, even those within the magic circle of the Five Eyes club, was taboo. But Goldstein had known about Rebecca from early on and clearly knew that the British intelligence source was none other than Mikhail Gerasimov.

"Might I ask, Adam, what you mean by that?" she asked, not wanting to give him the satisfaction of hearing her confirm Rebecca's name.

"Come on, Geraldine, we're not born yesterday," he replied pompously.

"Again, what exactly are you trying to say?" Geraldine persisted.

"Plain facts, Geraldine," he said, in a voice that made her want to slap his face. "This whole charade was caused by this woman revealing all to her boyfriend. If this is the way you're protecting your asset in Moscow, God help him."

Geraldine was furious but tried to keep her temper. "I can only surmise," she said, "that for reasons which would seem to me to be wholly unjustified and somewhat underhand, you have been bugging a British citizen without authorisation."

Geraldine knew that she now probably sounded pompous. But what the CIA was doing was against the rules. It was also insulting. She suddenly felt desperately sorry for Rebecca. The poor girl had already been bugged by Geraldine's agency, though for perfectly good reasons, in her view. How long, she wondered, had the CIA and NSA been monitoring Rebecca? And were they still doing it?

"I'm not going to go into anything we might or might not be doing, Geraldine," Goldstein replied. "I'm just making the point that this source you have is now vulnerable. Which is a pity, because right now we need the best intelligence we can lay our hands on if we're going to shunt Putin to one side."

Goldstein's choice of words – "shunt Putin to one side" – took Geraldine by surprise. What exactly was Washington planning? It made her think that perhaps the Sevastopol incident was far more sinister and calculated than the Americans were trying to make out. Had they recommended Kyiv should seize the opportunity to eliminate Putin, and was all the talk about a "demonstration" a bluff?

Geraldine was a senior member of the British security and intelligence services and benefited from the amazing depth of secret information provided by the US agencies through the Five Eyes club. But ultimately, she knew that at the highest levels of strategic decision-making in Washington, the Brits were not always party to everything. The special relationship between the US and UK was historically important but, at Geraldine's level, she could never be one hundred per cent positive that they were telling her everything. Again, Geraldine asked herself, could the Sevastopol explosion actually have been a real attempt on Putin's life, sanctioned by Washington? She couldn't ask Goldstein, and even if she did, he wouldn't give her an answer or he would deny it.

"Adam, I can assure you we will take care of our source," Geraldine said. "We have the experience and the right people. So, please, with the greatest respect, back off."

"It's your funeral," Goldstein replied bluntly and cut off the call.

Geraldine stared at her phone as if she had just been stabbed in the face. Goldstein might have reached the heights in his intelligence career but in her view he was an oaf and unpleasant and a bully. She rang Patrick Littlefield to tell him of their conversation.

"He totally overstepped the mark," Geraldine said, "and he was pompous as hell. I think you should speak to Langley and get him off my back. Redruth is our responsibility, but he just wants to take over."

"Don't worry, Geraldine," Patrick replied. "I know Goldstein of old. It's the way he is, pushy and blunt and, yes, pompous. But this is our operation and I'll make sure it stays that way."

Before Geraldine put the phone down, Patrick reassured her about the Sevastopol incident. "I don't believe for one moment that the US administration would sanction an attempt on Putin's life. Absolutely not."

***

Sandy was overwhelmed with work. His Sky News report had set off multiple follow-ups from other newspapers and TV broadcasters. Several of the US channels, including CNN and ABC, had wrongly suggested that his report was probably based on British intelligence sources. Sandy was mortified. He had hinted at a possible Russian inside source for the leak about Putin's visit to Sevastopol, but he had not claimed any official or unofficial sourcing. When he was questioned by the Sky News foreign editor, Sandy openly admitted it was pure speculation but that he had judged it as a legitimate question to be raised.

What worried him more than anything was the text from Rebecca. He anguished over it. Was she just having fun? She loved sending brief, mysterious texts that took time to decipher. Or was she berating him for his Sky News report? Had he gone too far in his surmising? He hadn't breached any confidences as such but he knew that his speculation about a possible inside source had only been included because of what Rebecca had told him. He had to admit it to himself, the implied warning about something happening on Thursday had been too tempting to resist. And this must have been why Rebecca had texted him: "*WTF!!!!!*"

He had been asked to do a follow-up, but so far he had nothing to add other than a second burst of Russian cruise missiles again hitting targets in Kyiv and Odesa. With thirty minutes left to file a new report, he grabbed his phone and texted Rebecca.

"*Are you angry with me? S xx*"

She replied instantly.

"*What do you think?*"

Oh God, Sandy thought.

"*My report was speculation. X*"

Three agonising minutes went by. Then his phone pinged. He dreaded the reply.

"*Informed speculation!*"

He looked at his watch. Time was slipping away. He had to find the right words to make Rebecca less angry and still love him.

"*Really sorry if I went too far but it was kind of the obvious thing to speculate. I'll be more careful next time. I love you! S xx*"

He had to wait five minutes for her reply.

"*You're history.*"

CHAPTER FOURTEEN
UNWELCOME VISITORS

Rebecca had been out all morning. She had had no hesitation in ending her relationship with Sandy - she had trusted him and he had betrayed her for the sake of a scoop. She needed to get out of her flat. She walked nowhere in particular, and was angry for most of it. More than anything she felt she had let down Geraldine. She was also worried about Gerasimov, although not because she had any romantic or emotional attachment to him. Whatever she had felt for him when they briefly lived together in her flat, that was all gone. But she still felt responsible for him. For his survival. In reality, there was nothing she could do to stop anyone harming him, but if Sandy's story on Sky had put him in danger, she blamed herself. She could have told Sandy nothing, just wished him good luck in Ukraine. But her conversation with Geraldine had alarmed her and she'd wanted to warn him. It was an act of love on her part, and he had betrayed her love.

She returned home at around 2 p.m.

She opened the door of her flat and immediately jumped back. One brief look had revealed a devastating sight. Her flat had been trashed and there were thick red stripes and blotches across the walls. No shape or design to them. Just a wild splatter of red paint. She pushed the door fully open and stared at the destruction in front of her. The large canvas on her easel had been ripped into four pieces. There was red paint everywhere, not just on the walls. She walked slowly into her bedroom. Above her bed, in the same red paint, there were four words in capitals:

WE ARE WATCHING YOU.

Rebecca checked the kitchen. Every plate, cup, glass and bowl had been smashed. The fridge door had been wrenched open and everything inside thrown out across the floor.

Rebecca screamed in anger and bewilderment and slumped to the floor. She knew she was being given a warning. But by whom? Was it the Russians, or the Americans trying to blame the Russians ... not the Brits, surely? If it was the Russians, it meant they must have concluded Gerasimov was the Kremlin leaker and traitor, in which case he was probably already in prison or executed. Her life was also in danger.

That thought made her jump up. She took her mobile and photographed the whole flat, and sent a dozen images to Geraldine's private phone. She captioned the pictures: MY FLAT! Despite having dumped Sandy, she wished he was there with her.

Rebecca wondered whether any of her neighbours had heard or seen the intruders. The noise of breaking crockery must have been horrendous. But it seemed no one had called the police.

She had to wait an hour for a reply from Geraldine, who texted:

"Don't move. Sending a team."

Her doorbell rang forty minutes later. The MI5 team consisted of four heavyweight blokes in dark-blue boiler suits. They told Rebecca to sit in the kitchen while they examined every aspect of the flat and took their own pictures. But they were not police officers. They weren't interested in solving a crime. So there was no dusting for prints or questions about CCTV systems in the building that might have caught a snapshot of Rebecca's visitors. Clearly under instructions from Geraldine, they methodically returned the flat to a passing resemblance of normality. They scrubbed the walls and flooring clean of the splashes of red paint, brushed all the broken crockery into a pile and emptied it into a large, black plastic bin liner. One of them also made her a cup of tea and lightly patted her on the shoulder.

The gesture made her suddenly feel tearful. It had been a shock. It had also made her feel vulnerable. The tears poured down her cheeks. All four MI5 guys gathered round her and tried to cheer her up. But when she asked if it was the Russians, none of them replied.

"You'll get another visit soon," one of them said. "You can ask questions then."

"Shouldn't I ring the police?" Rebecca asked. "But you've cleared everything up."

"Wait for your visitor," she was told.

They spent five more minutes tidying up. One of them picked up the torn bits of canvas and tried to put them back into some shape on the easel. It was a sorry mess, but he said he liked it, which brought a smile to her face.

"At least the front door isn't broken," the same bloke said. "You'll be all right till madam gets here. "

"Madam?" Rebecca asked.

"Our boss," he said.

At that moment her doorbell rang. It was Geraldine.

Her team left and Geraldine sat in the kitchen opposite Rebecca.

"I'm sorry for all this," Geraldine said.

"So am I," Rebecca replied, "but who did it?"

"I don't know, Rebecca," Geraldine said, although she had already come to a conclusion. She didn't think it was the Russians. She was convinced it was the Americans but didn't want to tell Rebecca. She suspected it was Goldstein's way of trying to remove Rebecca from the Redruth operation.

"I suppose you won't tell me anything anyway because you don't trust me anymore, right?" Rebecca said.

"You told Sandy stuff you should have kept to yourself. I know why you did it and I can understand that, but the fact is his broadcast set a helluva ball rolling," Geraldine replied.

"Ha! I doubt Sandy's story made much difference. The KGB or whatever they're called these days would have jumped to the same conclusions a long time before Sandy did."

"Are you now backing him up for what he did?"

"No, I've dumped him because he let me down. But it was pretty obvious there must have been a leak about Putin's trip and therefore it could have come from one of his own people, right? That's all Sandy said. It doesn't let him off the hook as far as I'm concerned but the more I think about it, the more I believe it wasn't that big a deal. And what about Gerasimov? Is he all right? Have you been in touch with him?"

Geraldine said nothing.

"Yeah, yeah, you can't tell me," Rebecca said. "But someone came and destroyed my flat. They haven't taken anything. There wasn't anything worth taking. But it wasn't some delinquent trashing my flat for kicks. This was someone telling me to shut up or the next time they'll come for me. Am I right?"

"Rebecca, I don't know, I'm sorry," Geraldine said. "I agree you weren't selected randomly. This was deliberate. But whether it was the Russians or—"

"Americans? Do you seriously think it could have been our side that did this?"

"Our side?"

"The bloody Americans. The CIA or whatever. Why would they? Doesn't make sense. Don't you guys all work together?"

Geraldine shrugged. "Yes, of course we do," she said.

"There's a 'but' there, isn't there?"

"No, not really, Rebecca, but there are sometimes different sensitivities depending on which side of the ocean you are on."

"I don't know what that means, Geraldine, but at least you're talking to me. So you haven't rejected the possibility that it might have been your friends over the water who did this to my flat?"

"I don't know."

"That tells me a lot," Rebecca said. "I told you Gerasimov said there were American spooks watching us in Venice. So, what's it about? Do they want Gerasimov for themselves?"

"I always said you were astute, Rebecca," Geraldine replied obtusely.

"But why go for me?"

"I'm not saying it's the Americans. All I'm saying is that there are differences of view, not just about our mutual acquaintance—"

"Gerasimov, his name's Gerasimov," Rebecca interrupted.

"Well, quite," said Geraldine.

"So, not just him; what else or who else?"

Geraldine hesitated.

"You mean me, right? They don't like me," Rebecca said.

"That would probably sum it up quite neatly."

"And this is what they do when they don't like someone?" Rebecca asked, waving her arm around the kitchen.

"I've said too much already, Rebecca," Geraldine replied. "You'll have to leave it with me. If it was the Russians I will know soon enough."

"You mean you'll never hear from Gerasimov again?"

"We'll see."

"Will you let me know?"

"I doubt that will be possible," Geraldine said, standing up to leave.

Rebecca stood up too. They briefly embraced.

"Who's going to pay for all my broken kitchen stuff? And I'll have to repaint all the walls, is anyone going to pay for that?" Rebecca asked.

"I'm really sorry for all the damage," Geraldine replied, "but I don't think my lot will agree to pay up. In fact, I know they won't. It would have to be recorded and then the parliamentary committee that oversights us will spot the bill and ask awkward questions."

"Bloody hell, you spies are useless! Couldn't you just bury it in the small print somewhere?"

"This particular committee is very good at the small print."

"If I'd known, I would have phoned the police and then claimed off insurance, but your boys have now cleared everything up. I'm screwed."

"Please don't inform the police," Geraldine said quickly. "It would make things even more complicated."

"Thanks, Geraldine, for nothing."

Geraldine muttered an apology and left the flat.

Rebecca went to her bedroom and sat on the bed. She knew, more than ever before, that what she was about to do was risky. If Geraldine believed the Americans were the ones who invaded her flat, then they would still be watching her and eavesdropping. She suddenly realised she should have asked Geraldine to get her team to sweep the flat for hidden electronic devices. She hadn't thought of it. Nor had the MI5 clean-up team. And what about her phone? Should she replace it with a new one with a different SIM card? She liked her phone and decided she couldn't be bothered to go through all the hassle of swapping it for another one just because bloody spies were trying to ruin her life.

"I'm not going to let these people dictate my life," she said out loud.

She hesitated for a few more moments and then texted Gerasimov.

"You OK?"

She spent the rest of the day waiting for a reply.

It never came.

*****

Two days later, at 5:55 a.m., David Kimche, MI6 station chief in Moscow, stood at the north end of platform eight at Leningradsky railway station. He was engrossed in reading a newspaper. He didn't look at his watch once. About twenty others were on the same platform. No one seemed to be interested in the tall man in the dark grey raincoat with a satchel over his left shoulder. The next train was due in fifteen minutes. If Agent Redruth was going to turn up, it had to be soon. Kimche had already decided he would board the train and go to the first stop. Agent Redruth, he knew, would have devised his own plan to leave the station without arousing suspicion. He had a Kremlin security pass, so he could come and go without having to buy a ticket or answer questions from insolent railway staff.

With eight minutes to go before the train was due to arrive, Kimche was aware of someone standing a few feet behind him. There were now double the number of people on the platform.

The train approached slowly. Kimche didn't turn round but kept his nose buried in the newspaper. Three other people pressed forward close to him as commuter passengers stepped out of the train in a rush of noise and elbowing. As Kimche raised his right leg to step into the train, he felt a movement in the pocket of his raincoat. He didn't look round but carried on into the compartment and looked for a seat by the window. Only then did he glance out of the window. But there was no sign of Agent Redruth. Kimche shoved his hand into his pocket and felt a thick envelope.

The first stop was the Kurskiy Vokzal station in the outskirts of Moscow, only twelve minutes away. Knowing that the FSB tried to follow his every move, Kimche had taken elaborate precautions to reach Leningradsky station. As far as he was aware, he had not been followed, but he would take equally elaborate precautions to make his return to the embassy without a shadowy FSB escort.

Kimche arrived back at the embassy without being confronted by Russian security officers. He went straight to the "citadel", the heavily structured room in the basement which was safe from Russian eavesdropping. He closed and locked the door behind him and removed the envelope from his raincoat pocket. There were five sheets of A4 paper, all covered in neat handwriting. Headed "The Plan", the pages detailed Gerasimov's proposed "elimination" of the Kyiv leadership. Kimche read it through three times. His impression after the first four pages was that while the plan appeared well drafted, it relied on intelligence that could change every day. President Zelensky's whereabouts could never be guaranteed, but Gerasimov's mission outline depended on the Ukrainian leader's presence within the massively guarded presidential compound.

Six Russian GRU Spetsnaz commandos, led by Gerasimov, were to be involved in the operation. Dressed in Ukrainian military fatigues, they were to cross the border from Belarus at 3 a.m. in a captured Ukrainian armoured personnel carrier. It was identical to a model of armoured vehicle designed by the Soviet Union, but the Ukrainian military had added a .50-calibre Browning machine gun supplied by the British. The armoured vehicle would be flying the Ukrainian flag. As part of a decoy strategy, Russian special forces would cross the Belarusian border into Ukraine about half a mile south of where Gerasimov and his team were to drive across the frontier. The provocation, effectively an invitation to engage in a firefight with the Ukrainian border forces, was intended to divert attention away from Gerasimov's armoured vehicle.

If all went to plan, Gerasimov and his six commandos would take between four and five hours to travel the 143 miles to the outskirts of Kyiv. At 10 a.m., there would be a cruise missile attack from two warships in the Black Sea, combined with a swarm of Iranian-supplied kamikaze drones, all aimed at the capital, to provide diversionary cover.

The date for the operation to eliminate Zelensky and other Kyiv government officials was Wednesday, November 13th.

What took Kimche's breath away was a paragraph at the beginning of the fifth page. It read:

Source Z has been primed to arrange access to the presidential compound via the north-east entrance. Z will know the itinerary for the day and will inform of the precise whereabouts of the targets. Any changes to expected presence of key individuals will be prior-noted to allow for a switch in timetable. Operation password is POBEDA.

"*Pobeda*" was the Russian word for "victory". The remainder of the elimination plan seemed to Kimche to be suicidal. Once access had been gained to the inner sanctum of the presidential building, the commandos would be expected to act swiftly. They had a three-minute timespan. Zelensky had a rotational bodyguard force of twenty soldiers who would never allow their president to be approached, let alone shot. But, again, there was an alarming paragraph:

Source Z has devised a ploy to divert presidential bodyguards.

Exit for the commandos would be via the same door. Provided the mission was successful and the commandos managed to escape, a signal was to be sent to Moscow with a coded message. Twenty minutes later, more cruise missiles and armed drones would target the presidential compound. Gerasimov and his commandos would return to the armoured vehicle beyond the security ring around the palace and head back to the Belarusian border. They would be protected overhead by two Sukhoi Su-27 fighter jets. As a precaution, a Mi-8 Hip transport helicopter would be on standby across the border in Belarus to fly into Ukraine to evacuate the mission team if the armoured vehicle ran into trouble.

Kimche had never served in the forces, but he realised what the Russians were up to. They hoped a lone Ukrainian-flagged armoured vehicle travelling down the road from the Belarusian border would be far less suspicious – and thus the journey more survivable – than the sudden arrival of a Russian helicopter flying towards Kyiv.

Kimche thought that was it, but then he saw on the back of the fifth A4 sheet there was a brief personal message from Gerasimov:

I don't have a name for Source Z. It's known to only two people. But he's a key official, non-military, in Zelensky's private office. The password is the only means I have for identification on the day.

No one has yet accused me over the suspected leak re Putin/ Sevastopol. But there is heightened security and wild rumours, and I have had to explain my movements in a long Q and A form. The FSB has already dragged in dozens of suspects.

I fear for my safety.

In brackets at the bottom, he'd added:

(I need half a dozen burner phones. Impossible to buy here. Meet me in three days at east end of Danilovsky Market, furthest away from Tulskaya Metro Station. Noon.)

CHAPTER FIFTEEN
REBECCA RELENTS A LITTLE

Sandy had been in a state of despair ever since getting Rebecca's dismissive text. He couldn't believe he had ruined his relationship with her. She was the first woman he had genuinely fallen for. He had had plenty of interested girlfriends but none of them had awakened that intense desire for another person's body as Rebecca had. She didn't flaunt her body. In fact, in some ways she took it for granted that Sandy would like it. She wasn't shameless when naked, just natural. It made him wild with desire and passion. And now he had lost her. Sandy was feeling so depressed he couldn't even bear to read the emails from his office congratulating him on his first assignment as a foreign correspondent. All he could think of was Rebecca in Venice and how they had gorged on each other's bodies. He sent half a dozen texts begging her to forgive him, but she ignored him. It was over.

Late on his second day in Kyiv, the Kremlin in Moscow put out a short statement that forced Sandy to forget his misery. The statement read:

The Ukrainian Nazis will be held responsible for the direct assassination attempt on President Vladimir Putin. All retaliatory measures will be considered as fully justified.

The Sky News foreign desk rang Sandy and told him to do a report as rapidly as possible on what the Kremlin message meant and what sort of retaliatory measures Putin might take. It was the usual sort of instant demand every foreign correspondent received when reporting from the frontline. The correspondent was supposed to be an expert analyst based on very little, and in Sandy's case, extremely limited experience of this kind of major story. Sandy rushed to the Sky office in the hotel, which was the bedroom next door to his. He told his cameraman to get set up on the roof and said he would join him in twenty minutes.

In the event, it took forty minutes, because Sandy worried about being too sensational. He knew the foreign desk would expect him to say that Putin was hinting at a nuclear strike. But would the Russian president really resort to using nuclear weapons when he surely knew that such action could bring a massive response from the US and NATO? Washington had warned enough times that if Putin ordered a nuclear strike on Ukraine it would have catastrophic consequences. Sandy was also reluctant to put the threat of a nuclear attack in the intro to his report for all kinds of reasons, one of which was that he was in the centre of Kyiv, not that far from the presidential stronghold, and the thought of trying to continue operating as a correspondent under nuclear attack was so far from any sense of reality that it physically made him shudder.

In the end, he decided to take a cautious line that informed but without alarming everyone who might watch his report on Sky:

The Kremlin tonight issued a bellicose threat to Kyiv after claiming that the sea drone attack on the guided-missile frigate Admiral Essen *in Sevastopol, was an attempt to assassinate President Putin. Ukraine has still not accepted responsibility for the attack. The Kremlin statement gave no details about the kind of retaliation it had in mind, but there have been fears voiced in the past that Moscow might turn to nuclear weapons. Russian military doctrine dictates that if Russia should face an existential threat, the use of nuclear weapons would be both lawful and justified. An alleged attempt on Putin's life might be considered equivalent to an existential threat.*

Russia launched cruise missile and armed drone attacks on Kyiv and Odesa after the Admiral Essen *was hit. But this evening's statement from the Kremlin was the first time Moscow has accused Kyiv of deliberately targeting the Russian president. An eye witness in the port at Sevastopol confirmed that Putin had been on board the frigate when the explosion occurred.*

A nuclear strike would still seem to be an unlikely option to be favoured by Putin. Apart from the US and NATO, China, a strong ally of Russia, has also warned Moscow against resorting to nuclear weapons in the war in Ukraine.

It is possible that Moscow might order a like-for-like retaliatory strike, targeting the Kyiv leadership itself. Ukraine's President Zelensky goes nowhere without a heavy presence of bodyguards, but he does like to get out to meet with the troops in the frontlines. It's likely that security will be stepped up even further.

There are many questions still to be answered about the Sevastopol strike, not least whether the planned attack by a sea drone was notified to the Americans before it took place, and whether Washington knew an attempt was to be made against Putin himself. The Kremlin undoubtedly has been asking the same questions since the sea drone attack.

Sandy Hall, reporting from Kyiv.

***

Rebecca saw Sandy's report while sitting in bed. The sight of him on the rooftop made her realise how much she missed him. But could she ever forgive him for breaching the confidence she had shared with him? She picked up her phone and texted:

"Please be careful. R"

She contemplated adding a kiss but decided against it. She was still angry with him for betraying her confidence. She missed him but couldn't forgive him. Not yet, at least. She didn't tell him her flat had been trashed. She wasn't convinced the CIA would stoop to such outrageous measures. She was sure the Russians were behind it.

*∗∗

Gerasimov had presented his assassination plan to his boss, who took it without comment. He seemed surlier than usual. Gerasimov wondered whether it had anything to do with the embarrassment over the separation of the officer with the nuclear codes and the presidential party. Putin's inner circle, including Gerasimov's boss, had all received an almighty bollocking. Putin had warned that if it ever became public knowledge, he would sack everyone. Gerasimov was in the know because he had seen the emergency signal ordering a helicopter to pick up the officer and his nuclear-codes briefcase.

Gerasimov had not passed this intelligence titbit on to David Kimche. He concluded it was too great a risk and, anyway, the drama was over.

Meanwhile, the hunt for the Sevastopol leaker had been going on for three days and there were already grim stories of people being whisked away to the FSB interrogation basement and not returning to their offices or homes. Gerasimov had been asked to fill in a questionnaire itemising everything he had done in the days leading up to the attack in Sevastopol. The FSB wanted to know to whom he had spoken, where he had been, and why. He was told it was routine, but nothing was routine with the FSB. It was clear he was on their list, not necessarily as a prime suspect, but just being on the list posed potential life-ending danger.

Gerasimov had been on an FSB list of persons of interest once before. He had been serving as a middle-ranking GRU intelligence officer in south-east Syria. Concern had been expressed that liaison between Russian forces and the government of President Bashar Assad had shown signs of a breakdown in communication. On one occasion, a 1,000lb bomb had been dropped in error by a Russian Su-27 on a group of men on the outskirts of Damascus. Intelligence had claimed they were members of the Isis Islamic group attempting to infiltrate the city. But the intelligence, provided by the Russians, had been inaccurate. The men, all of whom were killed, were members of the Palestinian group PFLP-GC, which was allied to Assad.

As one of the many GRU officers serving in Syria and responsible for analysing intelligence, Gerasimov was questioned at length by a visiting FSB team. The interrogation had been brutal, but he had survived when it became clear that one of his superiors had made the fatal conclusion that an Isis hit squad had entered Damascus. The superior, a GRU colonel, was shipped back to Moscow and never heard of again.

When Gerasimov completed the FSB questionnaire about his movements prior to the attack on Putin in Sevastopol, he took the grave risk of lying at least a dozen times. If he was subjected to a lie-detector test he would fail. But he had one unique advantage over all the other names on the FSB suspect list; he had been selected by the president to plan and carry out a covert assassination mission against Moscow's enemies in Kyiv. Not even the FSB would dare to arrest and detain the person chosen for a task of such importance to the safety and security of the motherland. Gerasimov knew that if his lies were uncovered, if his Venice trip was exposed, his Kyiv mission would not save him. But he hoped that the mission would persuade the FSB to hold back on any rigorous investigation into his work and private life, at least until after the Kyiv operation had been completed, successfully or otherwise. If so, it might mean his returned questionnaire would be at the bottom of the pile.

Whatever happened in Kyiv, Gerasimov knew that his chances of remaining a trusted senior member of the Kremlin staff were looking shaky at the very least. He needed to warn his British controller that the time could be approaching for him and his family to be evacuated. He was no fool; he knew that the British intelligence service would want him to stay in post for as long as possible, handing over secrets on a regular basis – he was their dream double agent – but he could feel the FSB's tentacles closing around him. The British would surely recognise the risks he was taking and reward him by extracting him, as well as his wife and kids. He tried to convince himself he had already done enough to deserve a new life in the West.

He planned to test the wind when he saw his controller, David Kimche. Key to everything was going to be the choreography for the mission in Kyiv. He had to make it look like a genuine plot to kill Zelensky, without actually carrying it out. He must also survive, but without it looking like he had put his personal safety before the mission or that he was a traitor and had sacrificed the lives of his fellow commandos. Being already on the FSB list as a potential suspect in the Sevastopol leak investigation, his life would be over. However clever the British might be, they would not be able to rescue him once he was in the clutches of the FSB.

The closer he got to the planned meeting with David Kimche, the more panicky Gerasimov became. He hardly knew the man and wasn't sure whether he could be trusted. Bizarre though it might seem, he wished it were Rebecca meeting him at the designated spot in the Danilovsky Market. She had every reason not to trust him and not to help him, and yet he knew for certain that she would play her role perhaps better than a trained spy. She was an extraordinarily strong character, as her surname implied, and he felt comfortable with her.

Right now, he didn't know whether the British would be able to guarantee the sort of choreographed scenario that would be required during his mission in Kyiv if he was to survive. He had drawn up the plan for the Kremlin mission but it would be down to MI6 and, he assumed, the Americans, to coordinate with the Kyiv security authorities to ensure it failed. He knew Zelensky would be told of the planned attempt on his life and hoped all the necessary precautions would be taken. But Gerasimov would be leading the six Spetsnaz commandos into a trap and had to trust the Ukrainians to organise it so that he wasn't killed in the process. As a Russian, he had been trained to view Ukraine as the enemy. Now, he had to rely on Zelensky's bodyguards to keep him alive. Could he trust them to do that?

He knew it was ridiculous to imagine that Rebecca could do anything to help but if he could, through her, get some firm assurances from the British intelligence people, notably from Geraldine Hammer, that they would back him all the way, he wouldn't need to rely solely on the promises of the spy from the embassy whom he had only met twice.

***

Two days later. 11:15 a.m.
David Kimche arrived at the Danilovsky Market forty-five minutes before noon. It was normally a five-minute walk from the Tulskaya Metro but there were so many people on the pavement and spilling onto the road that it took him twice the time. But he was still early enough to carry out a thorough reconnaissance of the market and surrounding area. He was wearing casual clothes, jeans, a heavy woollen jacket and boots. He had a large shopping bag over his shoulder. As he walked around the stalls laid out with fruit and vegetables of every kind, he selected small quantities of apples, lemons and pomegranates and put them into his bag. The food market was circular and packed with people. Outside the market were cafés of every variety offering food from around the regions, including Armenian, Georgian and Moroccan. The smells from the cafés were so enticing Kimche found himself breathing more deeply to try and distinguish the different flavours emanating from the crowded tables.

From his long career as a spy, Kimche was trained and skilled at noticing anything that appeared out of the ordinary. It could be an extra-long glance across the food stalls or a shopper wearing clothes that seemed out of place or a man in dark glasses when there was no sun. Kimche wandered round the market several times and added to his bag a punnet of strawberries from Israel. At 11:45, he spotted a woman a few yards away in a long purple dress, down to her ankles, engrossed in a conversation with a stallholder selling the biggest aubergines he had ever seen. She was wearing a black shawl that covered her head and shoulders. There was something odd about her. It wasn't just her size, which was large, it was the way she thrust her chest forward as if she was trying to make a point. Perhaps she was complaining about the price. She bought three aubergines and put them into a canvas bag. She turned away from where Kimche was watching but for the briefest of moments she looked in his direction and then walked off slowly. The woman was Colonel Mikhail Gerasimov, Agent Redruth.

It was now noon.

Kimche followed and stopped close by when they reached a stall selling charcuterie.

The MI6 man was the first to speak.

"Everything is arranged," he said quietly. "We've been in touch with Kyiv and passed them your plan. They know what to expect and have made the necessary arrangements to ease your journey into the capital. You'll get unobstructed access on the main route into Kyiv. It's absolutely crucial you identify Source Z. You'll be wearing body cameras? It's all set up to look realistic. You must wear something distinctive for identification purposes."

Agent Redruth pointed to a ham on the bone and asked for four slices.

"We'll all be in Ukrainian combat gear but they'll be wearing light olive berets. Mine will be grey," he replied. "You've told the Americans?"

"Yes, of course," Kimche replied.

"It could all go wrong."

Kimche said nothing.

"The set-up has to be very good," Gerasimov said. "If I survive and all my team are killed there will be some explaining to do when I get back."

"We've done everything we can to make it work," Kimche replied.

"Can you promise to get me and my family out if it does all go wrong?"

Kimche nodded. But Gerasimov wasn't reassured.

Kimche slipped six burner phones into Gerasimov's shopping bag, and turned away. He started to walk towards the metro station and didn't look back.

***

The day before Operation Pobeda was due for lift-off, a secure conference call was held between London and Langley. Theoretically, MI6's Patrick Littlefield was chairing the meeting. This was, after all, a British-led double-agent operation. However, the Americans had done most of the groundwork with the Ukrainian security authorities to ensure that the fake Russian assassination attempt on Zelensky was properly orchestrated.

When Kyiv was told of the Russian plot, Zelensky's bodyguard commander protested. The veteran military officer wasn't told the full story, but it was made clear to him that every detail of the Russian plot was already well known and that if the counter-plan was followed, nothing would go wrong. It was explained to him that it was vital for the Russian plot to go ahead in order to identify a traitor working in the president's private office. No mention was made about the secret source in the Kremlin. The Ukrainian commander had expressed his view that even in the most minutely planned missions, things generally went wrong.

However, Zelensky had been informed in confidence by the director of the CIA of the presence of a Kremlin source as part of the Russian commandos whose survival was crucial, and the president had personally given his blessing to the operation. At one point, he had even asked if he was expected to pretend that he had been hit by gunfire and wanted to know if he should fall to the floor and cry out. But the CIA director told him that his presence would not be required. He said the Kremlin source would be wearing an identifiable beret to ensure his survival. The others had to be killed.

At the start of the conference call, Patrick outlined the British plan for how things would progress once the assassination attempt had been foiled.

"Our source will be arrested and Kyiv will make much of the fact that all the Russian assassins except one have been killed and their leader detained. We've suggested that Zelensky's government could say he was injured in the firefight and was receiving treatment in hospital," Patrick said.

"The world will be shocked that Moscow has nearly succeeded in killing the Ukrainian president. No mention, by the way, should be made of the betrayal of Source Z. Let the Russians keep guessing about what might have happened to him. He will be dead or arrested, but the Ukrainians could pretend that he is still functioning as a Russian spy and feed the Kremlin false information."

"And what then happens to your source?" Marina Babb asked outright.

"He will recover in hospital from his supposed wounds," Patrick said. "Kyiv could make one announcement about his state of health but then nothing further. Let Moscow stew, wondering whether he really is alive, and if they are desperate to get him back, talks eventually could begin to swap him for a senior Ukrainian figure currently in Russian hands.

"It could take some time, and at first Kyiv must be absolutely opposed to releasing the man who led a team to kill the president, but in due course there will be an exchange and our source will be returned to Moscow. Hopefully as a hero. Perhaps he'll get a promotion and move even closer to Putin."

As if to demonstrate that, in his view, this was an American show, Adam Goldstein chipped in as soon as Patrick Littlefield had stopped speaking.

"Just need to say that it might be tricky, if not impossible, to save the life of your source," he said in a matter-of-fact voice. "Obviously, it would be to the benefit of us all if he were to return safely to Moscow and carry on with his job in the Kremlin. But life is life. The whole operation depends on too many people playing their part, and personally, I think the risks are too great."

Patrick looked exasperated. So did Geraldine.

"The question is, what choice did we have?" Patrick said. "Our source comes up with an assassination plot against Zelensky. We could hardly do nothing. Our source needs our help to keep Zelensky safe. Of course there is a risk something could go wrong. But whatever happens, Zelensky will not be in danger; we will have played our part in safeguarding his life and, with luck and good fortune, our source will remain a key asset."

Goldstein wasn't satisfied. "OK, it's a great opportunity, potentially," he said. "He has already provided excellent material. But let's be honest. What are his expectations of surviving once he is back in Moscow, if he gets back there? The only one to return, and the rest of the team dead? What does he tell his bosses? More specifically, what will he say to the FSB? Will he return a hero or a traitor? When Zelensky appears in public after the event and declares he is alive and well, no thanks to the Russians, then what? Your source will be a dead man."

There was total silence on both sides of the Atlantic. Every single person in the conference call had asked the same questions over and over again in their respective offices.

Goldstein jumped in again. "The Kremlin will never go for a prisoner exchange," he said.

MI6's longstanding Russian expert, Freddie Stigby, spoke for the first time.

"But they just might," he said. "They will never believe that the man chosen by Putin's inner circle to lead the assassination mission in Kyiv is a traitor. Even if someone high up did suspect it, he would never reveal his suspicions to Putin. It would be far too embarrassing and humiliating. So, I think they might believe there was a genuine firefight in the heart of the presidential stronghold in Kyiv and that every effort was made to kill Zelensky. The fact that our man ultimately fails in his mission and gets injured and captured in the process will not please Putin. But I believe he will come round. Putin is more likely to give him a medal than hand him over to the FSB."

"It might work, Adam," Walt Grolsch said.

Goldstein seemed reluctant to offer his support. But secretly, he admired the British plan and wished he had come up with it himself.

"OK," he agreed. "But will you tell your source everything?"

Geraldine knew there were no plans for Gerasimov to meet his MI6 controller in Moscow again before leaving for Belarus. The final details of how Gerasimov might be returned to Moscow had not been passed on to him, so he couldn't be informed about the whole British plan before he left for the mission. Unless he used one of his burner phones to ring David Kimche, there was no way of getting a message to him. Or unless, for some bizarre reason, Gerasimov contacted Rebecca. If he did, out of the blue, which had been his habit in the past, she could be used to relay the expectation that he would eventually return to Moscow to carry on as a double agent. Geraldine suspected Gerasimov would demand to be evacuated from Kyiv, and his family from Moscow.

"No," Geraldine replied to Goldstein.

"Well, maybe that's for the best," he said. "Let's have a conference call after it's all over."

Goldstein stood up to indicate the meeting was over.

CHAPTER SIXTEEN
AGENT REDRUTH'S BIG GAMBLE

"Wish me luck!"

Rebecca received the text late afternoon.

She had arranged to meet a friend for the evening. But she knew Gerasimov only texted when he had a good reason. He was trying to tell her something. It was a different phone number – he was using one of the burner phones supplied by David Kimche – but Rebecca knew it was him.

She rang Geraldine's private phone. Instead of her protective secretary answering, this time it was Geraldine's voice.

"Rebecca, are you all right?" Geraldine asked.

"Fine. I've heard from, you know," Rebecca replied.

"Saying?"

"'Wish me luck.' That's it. What do I do?"

Geraldine thought for a moment and then said, "Tell him: we're still working on future plans for returning to Moscow. Don't mention my name, obviously, but he'll know it's from me."

"What's it all about?" Rebecca asked.

"Can't say, sorry."

"Will he be all right?"

"Yes."

"Any hint?"

"No."

"So I do what you want but I get nothing in return."

"It has to be that way, Rebecca. You know how it works by now."

"Yeah, I sure do."

"All I can say is that it will become clear to you in due course."

"Great."

"Bye, Rebecca, and thanks."

Rebecca immediately texted Gerasimov:

"I'm told to tell you future plans are still being worked on for your return to Moscow."

Gerasimov was at home. He had been out of the office all day, making final preparations for the Kyiv mission. He texted back:

"?"

Rebecca replied:

"Sorry, no clue. R."

That was it. Nothing more from Gerasimov. But Rebecca rang her friend to cancel meeting up, just in case Gerasimov needed to contact her again. It made her realise how her secret spying role had taken over her life, although she knew in reality she was playing the most minor of parts. Geraldine never took her fully into her confidence and yet she expected Rebecca to continue the contact with Gerasimov. After her call with Geraldine, she was once again in the position where she had hints of something about to happen but no idea what it might entail. But the one thing she had learnt from Gerasimov's brief text exchange was that he was obviously still a free man. Sandy's Sky News report had not led to him being carted off to some dungeon for interrogation and torture. That was a huge relief. But why was he asking her to wish him luck? And what was Geraldine's message about? It was clear from Gerasimov's question mark text that he hadn't any idea either. Rebecca thought it was a bizarre way of handling a double agent, keeping him in the dark, especially if he was about to embark on some dangerous mission. *What could it be?* Rebecca wondered.

As she sat in her flat feeling deflated and frustrated, she thought of Sandy. He had sent several texts after she had urged him to take care, but she hadn't replied. Now she wanted to hear from him; although it was two hours later in Kyiv, she texted:

"Are you OK? Sorry about before! Missing you. Big event possible! R x"

Sandy was in bed in his hotel, nearly asleep, when he heard his phone ping. He knew it would be Rebecca. He texted back:

"So I'm not history after all?! I was going to jump off the roof!!!"

"Crazy bitch."

"That's what you do to me."

"Never jump."

"What big event?"

"It's only possible."

"Like what?"

"Don't know. Really."

"Here we go again."

"Lol."

"I'm not laughing."

"Crazy bitch."

"Can't wait to see you!! S xx"

"Me too. X"

***

Shortly after 3 a.m. on Wednesday, November 13th.

The first thing that went wrong in Operation Pobeda was that Captain Stanislav Kravchenko, a Ukrainian engineer and commander of a huge underground communications and surveillance bunker, close to the border with Belarus, had not had time to read his latest orders from Kyiv. He knew nothing about an imminent approach across the border of an armoured personnel carrier equipped with a .50 calibre Browning machine gun, let alone the bizarre decision to leave it alone and unharmed as it began its journey to Kyiv. He was watching the giant TV screens in the bunker's command centre when he saw the vehicle and ordered an instant attack. The vehicle was flying a Ukrainian flag, but Captain Kravchenko wasn't fooled.

Inside the vehicle, crammed together in silence, sat Gerasimov, six GRU Spetsnaz commandos and a crew of three: the driver, a gunner and the commander. The area on either side of the highway was thickly forested, and when a Ukrainian armed drone launched an attack, the driver veered off the road and headed into the woods. The explosion damaged one end of the tracked vehicle, but the driver found he still had sufficient control to steer between the trees, although he had to slow right down.

Gerasimov shouted to the commander of the armoured vehicle: "What's going on?"

The commander, who was peering through the thermal-imaging camera system, trying to direct the driver, shouted back, "Drone! Keep your heads down."

The woods provided cover from further drone attacks, but Gerasimov knew at any moment they could be surrounded by Ukrainian troops and the mission would be over. So much for the promise by the British embassy spy that he would be given a free run to Kyiv.

Miraculously, or so it seemed to Gerasimov and his fellow commandos, they were not surrounded by hundreds of Ukrainian troops. Nor were there any further attacks. The driver, a special operations veteran who had served for three years during the brutal wars in Chechnya, struggled to control the vehicle as he swerved left and right through the trees. Gerasimov ordered the crew commander to head back to the highway. It appeared to the commander to be a suicidal decision, but Gerasimov wanted to take one more gamble to see if the British and Americans had the clout to clear his path to the Ukrainian capital.

He didn't know that after the launch of the armed drone, Captain Kravchenko had received an urgent signal from command headquarters in Kyiv. It was only then he read the orders that had been buried in a long list of confidential emails on his laptop in the command centre since midnight. He also had to deal with a new emergency which stopped him from questioning the bizarre orders from Kyiv. Russian special forces had launched an attack across the Belarusian border.

The Soviet-era armoured personnel carrier bounced out of the woods having travelled just four miles from the Belarusian border. There were another 139 miles or so to go and already the highway was filled with both military and civilian traffic. The Ukrainian flag attached to the vehicle and the occasional wave by the crew commander standing up in the open turret appeared to fool Ukrainian drivers going in both directions. The drone attack had only caused minor damage to the vehicle tracks, and the driver was able to manoeuvre it without too much difficulty.

Gerasimov's Spetsnaz comrades were grumbling. They had been thrown around inside the armoured personnel carrier and spent the whole time, while ploughing through the trees, swearing at the driver. Now on the highway, it was like switching from choppy seas to a millpond. But that concerned them, too. One asked Gerasimov why they seemed to be progressing up a highway without hindrance. He and his fellow commandos knew just from reading the basic intelligence that the Ukrainians had built massive defences between Kyiv and the border with Belarus in order to deter Russian troops from entering Ukraine across the frontier.

Gerasimov ignored the question.

When they were stopped at a checkpoint, the plan was for the crew commander to handle the situation. He spoke enough Ukrainian to get by and had memorised a full explanation for why the vehicle was travelling on the highway on its own. He was to say they were part of the State Border Guard Service and were headed for Kyiv for a week of rest and recreation. The story prepared back in Moscow now had an extra ingredient, which Gerasimov hoped would add a little combat flavour to impress those manning the checkpoints. The commander would point to the damaged track at the front of the vehicle and sound off about how the bloody Russians had attacked them with a drone.

It was a gamble. But the whole mission was a gamble. Gerasimov had no guarantees that they would even reach the presidential compound in Kyiv, let alone gain entrance without being fired on. How many people had had to be told that a fake assassination operation was due to take place in the capital later that morning? And how many would react in the way they were supposed to react according to the script? For security purposes, the fewer who knew, the better. But in order for him to survive, he would rather everyone knew!

The first major checkpoint was about a mile outside the city. Concrete blocks, dugouts, trenches and at least thirty soldiers loomed into view as the armoured vehicle bearing Gerasimov and his team approached. Unknown to Gerasimov, none of the checkpoint troops were in the loop about the arrival of an armoured vehicle filled with Russian assassins. A particularly large Ukrainian soldier with an AK-74 Kalashnikov held across his chest stood in front of the vehicle and began examining the damaged track. He looked up at the crew commander and asked what happened. Gerasimov, straining his ears to listen to the commander's response, thought the question from the checkpoint soldier was a good sign. He seemed more interested in how the vehicle had been damaged than why a lone personnel carrier was on the road.

"Came out of nowhere," the crew commander said. "Bloody lucky it wasn't a kamikaze. My driver saved our lives."

The big soldier nodded. "Where you going? Give me your papers."

Gerasimov had arranged for false documents to be supplied to the whole team. But he needed the Ukrainian to be sufficiently satisfied with the crew commander's papers and not demand to see everyone's documents. If the soldier insisted on the rear door being opened up, the non-Ukrainian speakers huddled in the back would give the game away.

"Passengers?" the soldier asked.

"Yeah," the commander replied. "Full up and fed up."

The Ukrainian soldier laughed.

Gerasimov was going to give the commander a medal. So far, very good.

"OK, on your way," the soldier said. "Let the poor buggers out when you can."

The commander laughed and waved as the driver moved slowly forward.

They passed through two more checkpoints without a problem. Perhaps, Gerasimov hoped, this was because the orders from Kyiv to let his vehicle head to the capital unchecked had at last been received.

Source Z had provided explicit instructions about where to park the vehicle, on a street with apartment blocks a few hundred yards from the heavily guarded presidential compound. They were then to make their way on foot to the north-eastern entrance, where Source Z would meet them. Unknown to Gerasimov, the senior Ukrainian official codenamed Source Z, who was working undercover for Moscow, had warned the troops at the gate that seven border guard soldiers would be arriving for an awards ceremony at the compound. President Zelensky himself was to present medals to the seven men for their bravery and devotion to duty. The official would personally lead them into the presence of the president. Source Z was a powerful figure, feared and respected by all the compound staff, including the president's bodyguards. His orders always had to be obeyed.

The crew of the armoured personnel carrier stayed with the vehicle as Gerasimov and the Spetsnaz commandos set off for the presidential compound. It was 9:20 a.m. The roads were filled with traffic and the pavements were busy with people. No one seemed interested in or curious about the seven men in Ukrainian combat uniforms pushing their way through the crowds. Gerasimov led the way. They reached the designated gate at 9:30 a.m. and saw a tall man with broad shoulders in a dark grey suit standing chatting to a group of Ukrainian security guards.

Something was wrong. The tall man, who Gerasimov assumed was Source Z, was now arguing with the security guards. But he was clearly losing the argument. Despite his authority, the security guards were all shaking their heads. Gerasimov suddenly realised what it was about: they were going to be disarmed before they were let into the compound. The Russian assassination team would be entering the presidential compound without their assault weapons. Before he left Moscow for Belarus, Gerasimov had been assured that Source Z was so influential a figure that he could fix it for them to carry their weapons into the compound. He'd thought at the time it seemed highly unlikely that they would be allowed to go fully armed into the most tightly secured building in the Ukrainian capital, but the assurances had been given.

However, as a precaution, he had instructed each member of his team to carry a concealed pistol strapped to an ankle.

Suddenly, the city was filled with the wailing sound of an air-raid warning. The tall man shouted at the guards: "Take cover. Leave me with the soldiers. We're going to be late for the ceremony."

With that, the tall man herded Gerasimov and the six commandos away from the security checkpoint and urged them to run to the presidential compound. They still had their weapons. The guards didn't stop them.

The tall man looked at Gerasimov as they ran to the side entrance of the compound. "*Podeba*," he said.

Gerasimov nodded.

Source Z glanced at his watch. "Two minutes," he said.

CHAPTER SEVENTEEN
SANDY GETS A SCOOP

Source Z pointed to a door down a corridor and then vanished. Gerasimov had a plan in his head but there was no time to think it through. He and the six Spetsnaz commandos, all carrying their Kalashnikovs, burst through the door and instantly scattered into a V formation, with Gerasimov the furthest back.

Facing them was a bizarre sight. It took their breath away and, for a few seconds, they had no idea what to do or how to react. In front of them were three cardboard cut-out life-size figures of President Zelensky. He was looking at them from three angles with his arms folded. No one else was in the room. The six commandos stared at the figures then looked back at Gerasimov.

Then, without warning, six Ukrainian soldiers jumped out from where they had been hiding behind screens on either side of the room and pointed their assault rifles at the Russians. Gerasimov was the first to react. He hurled himself to the floor and threw his Kalashnikov across the room. The six Spetsnaz commandos were so shocked they hesitated for the briefest of moments.

The Ukrainian bodyguards opened fire, raking high-velocity rounds into the Russian commandos. The bursts of gunfire filled the room with a tsunami of noise and anguished cries. All six Russian commandos were hurled backwards, collapsing in a heap on the floor where their leader was still lying prostrate, petrified but uninjured.

More Ukrainian soldiers charged into the room, their rifles pointing forwards. They looked confused and uncertain how to react when Gerasimov slowly got to his feet and put his hands in the air above his head. At that moment a Ukrainian officer of the same rank as Gerasimov came into the room and walked towards him. He motioned to him to put his hands down and stood in front of him.

"Come with me," he said.

He took Gerasimov's arm and led him out of the room. The Ukrainian soldiers stood aside.

The colonel took Gerasimov to his office in the compound.

"I'm afraid, Colonel, for the sake of authenticity, we are going to have to shoot you," he said.

Gerasimov looked astonished and then realised what he was saying.

"Yes, of course," he said, "for when I get back to Moscow, if I ever do."

The colonel removed his pistol from its holster and fired one shot, angled to enter the fleshy part above Gerasimov's right hip.

Gerasimov winced with pain and looked down at the blood seeping through his combat jacket. "Thank you, Colonel," he said.

"You're welcome," his Ukrainian counterpart replied, with a smile.

Three hours later, after hundreds of calls from journalists asking about the sound of gunfire from within the presidential compound, the defence ministry in Kyiv released a statement.

Earlier this morning, Russian saboteurs gained access to the presidential compound with the intent of assassinating President Zelensky. The president was not present when there was an exchange of fire between the saboteurs and Ukrainian soldiers. Six of the seven Russian invaders were killed. The seventh, believed to be their leader, was wounded and is in detention. A full investigation will be held into how the failed Russian assassins managed to gain entry into the compound.

The statement left many questions unanswered, but every journalist in Kyiv reporting the breaking story speculated wildly about the latest attempt to assassinate the president. There had been claims of previous attempts, especially during the first days of the Russian invasion. In one assassination operation, Russian troops had parachuted into Kyiv but none of them had survived.

The statement made no mention of how the Russian soldiers had arrived in Kyiv. Nor was there any mention of an armoured vehicle and its crew of three Russians. But there were eye witnesses who said they had seen a lone armoured personnel carrier parked in a side street about three hundred yards from the compound. Several people came forward to tell the media they had seen seven soldiers in Ukrainian combat uniforms pushing their way through the crowded pavements en route to the presidential compound.

Sandy Hall had little time to gather enough information to send a first report back to Sky News, but after several days of working at full stretch in his new role as foreign correspondent, he had grown in confidence and enjoyed filling all the gaps in his story with intelligent analysis and background material. He sent a three-minute report raising a number of key questions that needed to be answered: who let the Russians into the compound? Had they entered Ukraine via Russia or Belarus? How were they allowed to enter the compound with weapons? Was there a traitor in Zelensky's inner sanctum? Who was the Russian leader of the assassination team, and where was he now?

Shortly after Sky News carried Sandy's report, the pre-arranged secure conference call between London and Langley began, with opening remarks by Patrick Littlefield. He, Geraldine, Grace and Freddie were sitting in his office at MI6.

Patrick said that under the circumstances, the events in Kyiv had gone according to plan and he felt everyone should be congratulated. But now, decisions had to be made about what to do next. The choreography for the fake assassination had worked well and the British intelligence asset was safe. Patrick refused to use either the real name or the codename for Gerasimov even though his American colleagues had made it clear they knew who he was. He invited everyone to give their views.

Grace Redmayne, surprisingly, chipped in first.

"The most important thing is our asset," she said. "While he stays in Ukrainian hands, and obviously that's key to the whole concocted story, he can't be sitting at his desk in the Kremlin providing us with unrivalled intelligence of Putin's next moves in the war. So we should think of a way of getting him back to Moscow as rapidly as possible, without him falling under suspicion. The FSB will be more than anxious to talk to him, not just about the failed assassination but also how he managed to survive. And there's still the other business hanging over him, the leak about Putin's trip to Sevastopol. There are a lot of potential hazards ahead."

Adam Goldstein had been itching to interrupt.

"Personally, I think you've landed your asset with a shitload of problems," he said. "I don't see how he can just return to Moscow and be welcomed back to his old job. Putin isn't going to want a failure sitting down the corridor from him."

"You seemed happy to go along with this prisoner-exchange plan when we discussed it before," Patrick said.

Goldstein rolled his eyes at Walt Grolsch and Marina Babb, who both nodded in agreement. It seemed they were having second thoughts.

However, MI6 Russian expert Freddie Stigby demurred. "I think it's more complicated for Putin," he said. "As I said before, it's in his interest to paint as positive a picture as possible about the assassination attempt. OK, it didn't work, but six of his people sacrificed their lives to try and rid him of his number one enemy. He might want to show some gratitude, if only for the families of the dead soldiers. It would be bad psychology and bad messaging from the Kremlin for our asset to be hung, drawn and quartered as soon as he arrived back in Moscow. Unless, of course, the FSB produce evidence he is a traitor. That's always going to be the risk."

"Geraldine?" Patrick turned to her.

"You probably won't like this," Geraldine said, focusing her eyes on Goldstein, "but I think we have to be very bold in this situation. I've been going over in my mind what proactive thing we could do to help our asset and fool Putin."

"Go on," Patrick said.

"Well, in my view, we need to get the name 'Colonel Mikhail Gerasimov' out into the open," she said. It was the first time she had mentioned the name of the Kremlin source to the Americans.

Goldstein literally snorted.

Geraldine ignored him. "The media is going mad about this story, so let's help them along. Let's get the Ukrainians to reveal who the leader of the Russian assassination team is and then we can make a big play to Kyiv about how we want Gerasimov back in the UK to face charges for what he did in London last year. He murdered two police officers, remember, and got away with it. The Met Police now have the evidence. So let's make a big fuss about getting him extradited. We'll have to tell ministers, but not everything."

"Sorry, I've lost the plot, how does that help your … Gerasimov?" Goldstein asked.

"Putin will never allow Kyiv to extradite him to the UK and will move heaven and earth to get him swapped for a Ukrainian prisoner and returned to Moscow," Geraldine continued. "Kyiv will play ball once we've explained to Zelensky what's going on."

"And how do you propose to let the media know that the sole survivor of the assassination attempt is Colonel Mikhail Gerasimov? Hold a press conference?" Goldstein asked in a voice that dripped with sarcasm.

"No, of course not," she replied brusquely. "I think we should provide as much information as we think fit, in a confidential way, to the Sky News reporter Sandy Hall, who is in Kyiv. And – and this is the bit you won't like – we should use Rebecca Strong to tell him what we want to tell him."

"Ha!" bellowed Goldstein. "More amateur spying!"

"Amateur but practical," Geraldine responded.

"So, you're going to ask her to give this Sandy Hall a ring and tip him off?" Goldstein asked, looking increasingly exasperated.

"No, I'm going to put her on a flight to Poland, if she agrees, of course, and arrange for her to meet her boyfriend on the Ukraine border. No telephone call, no bits of paper. Just two people meeting for a chat. Good old-fashioned tradecraft."

Marina Babb was looking intrigued.

"I sort of like the idea," she said, "but how are you going to persuade this reporter to leave Kyiv and go on a long train ride to the Polish border? Your Rebecca woman will have to call or text him, and that could get picked up by the wrong people."

Geraldine glanced at her deputy.

"Grace has a contact in Sky News, high up," she said. "She will ask him to tell Sandy Hall to get to the border as rapidly as possible for a meeting with a secret source who has a blockbuster story. He'll be on that train before you can say Bob's your aunty."

The conference call was about to end when Geraldine cleared her throat and said she had something to add. Goldstein had already stood up to leave. He turned round reluctantly.

"I'm not accusing anyone," Geraldine said, "but I want to make something absolutely clear. Rebecca Strong is an asset to my organisation. Her flat was invaded and trashed, and a message put on the wall of her bedroom in red paint. 'You are being watched,' it said. I feel confident you will agree, especially now she is to play a not insignificant part in safeguarding our asset's future, that nothing of this nature should ever happen again."

Goldstein looked uncomfortable but said nothing.

"It was probably the Russians," Marina Babb said.

"I think not," Geraldine replied.

Patrick brought the conference call to a close.

***

Rebecca was in a window seat in economy class on a British Airways flight from Heathrow to Warsaw, which had left at 9:05 a.m.

She had been given explicit instructions by Geraldine: there was to be nothing in writing. Geraldine had given her all the details of the story she wanted Rebecca to pass on to Sandy, but she had to memorise them. MI5 had booked her return flight and a return rail ticket from Warsaw to Medyka in south-east Poland, the busiest crossing-point for train and bus trips into Ukraine.

Rebecca had had no hesitation in agreeing to Geraldine's proposal. It meant she would see Sandy. Geraldine had arranged for them to stay one night at the Hotel Marko. She told Rebecca that Sandy had been instructed by Sky News to meet a contact at the hotel for a big story, but he had been given no information about the man or woman he was to meet. He had been told the contact would know what he looked like. When Rebecca heard this, she burst out laughing.

"This is going to be fun," she said to Geraldine.

"Fun, yes, but you're going for a very important reason and you've got to persuade Sandy to run this story," Geraldine said.

"Is it true?" Rebecca asked with her familiar quizzical look.

"Of course, Rebecca," Geraldine said quickly. "I wouldn't ask you to do something that was either dishonest or untrue."

"But why do you want Sandy to mention Gerasimov's name? Won't that put him in danger?"

"We're hoping it will do the opposite. It's complicated."

"It's unbelievable that he was the leader of the group that tried to kill Zelensky."

"As I said, it's complicated. The end result, we hope, is that he will be returned to Moscow and continue working for us. But that's absolutely secret, totally, totally. You understand, don't you?"

"Yes, don't worry. I'm not an idiot."

"We may have to ask you to sign the Official Secrets Act."

"So, you don't trust me?"

"It's not that, Rebecca, it's just, well, that's the way we have to do business in our world."

"If I do sign the Official Secrets Act does that mean you'll tell me more stuff?"

"It's possible, but the normal rule is you are told only what you need to know."

"I need to know everything."

Geraldine laughed.

"In that case," she said, "you'll have to join MI5. If you're accepted, it will mean training for two years, and vetting alone will take nine months. Do you want to be vetted so we know everything about you?"

"You already do, pretty much."

Geraldine laughed again.

"It'd be fun having you in the service, Rebecca, but let's not get ahead of ourselves. First, the Poland trip. It will all be arranged and paid for, and your safety is guaranteed. If you have any doubts, please say so now."

"Ha! You're paying for me to spend a night with my boyfriend in a nice hotel. Why would I have doubts?"

For a moment, Geraldine looked almost shocked. Then she burst out laughing. "Sex on the service. Lucky you," she said, with a huge grin.

Thinking about the conversation now, in her window seat, Rebecca smiled. She was looking forward to giving Sandy the surprise of his life. She imagined the look on his face when he saw her in the lobby of the hotel. It was definitely going to be fun.

After landing, she went through passport control without any problem. She had almost expected to be greeted by an official and taken as a VIP past all the ordinary passengers. *Please, madam, come this way, we are honoured to greet a representative of His Majesty's government.* Rebecca giggled. She knew she had to take this special mission seriously but there was no reason why she shouldn't enjoy every moment.

Her train to Medyka on the Polish border was due to leave at 2:20 p.m. She had time to buy some food and drink before climbing on board for the six-hour journey. She expected to be in the hotel to meet Sandy at around 9 p.m.

Rebecca intended to read the paperback she had bought at Heathrow – *Lessons*, by Ian McEwan – but after an hour she felt sleepy, and she slept for the next two hours. When she woke, she looked out at the Polish countryside. Poland was beautiful. She didn't know why she had imagined otherwise but she realised that her preconceived view of the country was entirely tainted by all the grim images of Poland that had filled the pages of newspapers and history books over eight decades: invasion by Hitler's Nazis, incarceration of the Jewish people, ghettoes, and now mass migration of Ukrainians escaping the war, poor families camping in the streets and parks in Polish cities, and the constant fear of Russian aggression across its borders. But from the train, she saw a different country: countryside as beautiful as anywhere else in the world, smart-looking houses, traditional villages and an impression of wealth and prosperity. Rebecca, the quasi-spy, was learning. She felt confident in herself. She was also excited that she was going to be involved in something out of the ordinary, something bold and important.

In Venice, she had played her part in being a go-between with Gerasimov. But with the British and American intelligence services apparently watching her every move and listening in to her bedroom activities, she had felt somehow cheated. She wasn't being treated like a grown-up. She was being used and not properly respected. Now, as she travelled alone to the Polish border with Geraldine's script in her head to pass on to Sandy, she felt good. They needed her. Geraldine needed her. Perhaps even the Americans needed her. She had a proper role. Yes, that felt good.

She ate the whole baguette stuffed with cheese and ham that she had bought at Warsaw airport and started to feel excited about what lay ahead. Another two hours and she would be in the lobby of the hotel waiting for Sandy.

However, Sandy was in the foyer of Hotel Marko before Rebecca arrived. He had been waiting for an hour and was beginning to wonder whether the whole thing was some sort of joke. He felt he should have stayed in Kyiv to continue reporting on the assassination plot. He had no idea who he was supposed to be meeting. His foreign editor had contacted him with the news that he was to get to the Polish border town of Medyka and wait for a contact who had a big story to reveal. Sandy was highly sceptical, partly because his foreign editor also had no idea what it was all about. He told Sandy some executive had rung and given orders.

By 9:30 p.m., Sandy had been waiting for nearly two hours, and was getting frustrated and angry. He was about to ring the Sky News foreign desk when he got the shock of his life.

A tall, blonde woman came through the revolving doors and started running towards him with the biggest grin on her face.

"Rebecca!! What the hell are you doing here?" Sandy shouted, as he leapt up from the very uncomfortable armchair and flung his arms around her. They hugged and kissed like they hadn't seen each other for months.

When they eventually separated, Rebecca apologised for being late. Sandy looked so confused she had to laugh.

"I'm your contact, silly," she said.

"You mean, I've come all this way to see you?" he asked, incredulously.

"Yes, sorry, would you have preferred some bloke in a Homburg and dark glasses?"

"God, no, but I never expected you would be the one."

"So, a nice surprise then?"

Sandy took hold of her hand and hurried her across the foyer to the lift.

"You're in a rush, Mr Hall; are you that keen to see what I've got?" Rebecca asked, with that big grin again.

"I want to see everything you've got," Sandy replied as they stepped into the lift. They grabbed each other and kissed like wild teenagers as the doors closed.

When they got to their room, still enveloped in each other's arms, he struggled to open the door, which made Rebecca giggle. They both fell into the room and started to pull at each other's clothes.

"Careful, Sandy, it's a new blouse," Rebecca said, as he began to wrench at the buttons.

"My God, Rebecca, I've missed you," he whispered, undoing the last button and pulling off her pale green blouse with her help. Just like he did the first time he saw her in a state of undress, he gazed at the breasts spilling out of her bra.

She managed to remove Sandy's shirt, trousers and pants while he struggled with her bra. They leapt onto the bed. Sandy was still wearing his socks.

Later as they lay in bed, Sandy gently stroking Rebecca's hair, he asked: "So tell me, what great secrets have you brought for me?"

But after her long journey and energetic lovemaking, Rebecca had fallen asleep.

"Great," Sandy whispered, but then closed his eyes. The secrets could wait, although he was dying to know whether he had a scoop on his hands.

Rebecca woke before him and kissed him on the lips. He stirred and opened his eyes. He had to remind himself where he was. Not that many hours ago he had been in Kyiv and there had been a warning of a Russian airstrike as he left for the train station. He should have taken cover but he'd had less than thirty minutes to make the train. Now, here he was, lying in bed with Rebecca and feeling her blonde hair covering his face as she kissed him. He had no idea what time it was, but before he could ask her again about why she had flown from London to see him, she was lying on top of him and rubbing her body against his.

"Rebecca Strong," he whispered into her ear, "you are incorrigible and edible and I want every bit of you."

"Good," she whispered back, "because I want the same."

She reached down and he uttered a high-pitched yelp.

It was only afterwards he glanced at his watch. It was nearly midnight.

They ordered sandwiches and wine from room service and when it arrived, they both sat on the bed, naked. Only then did Sandy turn to Rebecca and ask the same question he had put to her two hours earlier.

"I'll tell you everything as long as you stroke my back and anything else that takes your fancy," she replied.

"Rebecca, I'm beginning to think I'm never going to hear what it is you have come all this way to tell me," Sandy said, but started to stroke her breasts and shoulders.

"Don't stop," she said. "Listen carefully, but you can't take notes. Nothing in writing."

"I can't take notes while I'm doing this," he replied, and leant forward to kiss her. She opened her mouth and let him explore her with his tongue. But then she gently pushed him away.

"Time to be professional," she said, "but keep stroking."

She told him everything. Sandy was incredulous.

"This is amazing stuff, Rebecca," he said, "but won't it put your Russian in danger?"

"I've told you, please don't call him 'my Russian', Sandy," she said. "This has all been thought through, and he's going to be OK, provided everything works out as planned."

"Sorry, Rebecca, I won't call him that again. But one crucial thing; how am I supposed to source this? Can I say 'British intelligence sources', or 'Western intelligence sources' or what?"

"Absolutely not British sources, Sandy, that would immediately raise suspicions in Moscow. I said, don't stop stroking me. Geraldine told me to tell you to be very careful how you source it but no connection can be made with the Brits."

"But I have to source it. It's too sensational. If I don't source it all I can do is speculate and that would be meaningless."

"She wants it to come from Kyiv."

"But I can't say it's a Ukrainian source when it's not. I can't do that."

"I've left the best bit to last," Rebecca said, with a smug look on her face. "There's a colonel in the Ukrainian intelligence service who is prepared to tell you, on the record, who the leader of the assassination squad is. He's called Colonel Andriy Bilyk and he's waiting for your call tomorrow."

"Bloody hell, you're kidding," Sandy gasped. "And I suppose you have his phone number in your head?"

"As it happens, I do."

"And do I have to remember it or can I write it down?"

"You can write it down."

Rebecca was now moving her body from side to side as Sandy continued stroking her. In between sighs she told him the mobile number for Colonel Bilyk. He did his best to stroke her with his left hand while he wrote down the number on a napkin with his right.

"My God, Rebecca, are you really sure he will answer my call?"

"Geraldine or someone in her weird world has fixed it."

"What a scoop, and all thanks to you."

"So thank me properly, Sandy Hall," Rebecca said, and kissed him passionately.

As Sandy became enveloped in Rebecca's arms, he thanked God she had allowed him to write down the Ukrainian colonel's mobile number. He would never have remembered it.

CHAPTER EIGHTEEN

REBECCA JOINS UP

Sandy's report appeared at 8 a.m., three days after the failed assassination in Kyiv:

Sky News can exclusively reveal that the leader of the Russian assassination unit that failed to kill President Zelensky at his compound in Kyiv three days ago was Colonel Mikhail Gerasimov. This is the same Colonel Gerasimov who attempted to assassinate MI5's female director of counter-espionage in London just over a year ago and shot dead two police officers guarding her house. Colonel Gerasimov, a senior officer of the Russian GRU military intelligence service, was deported after insufficient evidence was found by the police to put him on trial.

Confirmation that he was behind the assassination plot in Kyiv has been provided to Sky News by Colonel Andriy Bilyk of the Ukrainian intelligence service. Colonel Bilyk told me that Gerasimov was seriously wounded in the shoot-out inside the presidential compound and is currently receiving hospital treatment under secure conditions. Colonel Bilyk said Gerasimov was refusing to cooperate but his identity had been confirmed by the Ukrainian intelligence service.

Sky News has also been told that Gerasimov and the six other members of the assassination unit entered Ukraine from Belarus in an armoured personnel carrier sporting the Ukrainian national flag, and that the assassins were all wearing Ukrainian combat uniforms. A full investigation is underway into how the vehicle travelled from Belarus to Kyiv, a journey of some 140 miles, without being stopped.

The armoured vehicle, with three Russian crew on board, was found parked in a street a few hundred yards from the presidential compound. The three Russians were arrested and are being questioned.

In a further development, I understand the British government has asked Kyiv to extradite Gerasimov to the UK to face charges of murder and conspiracy to murder. Since his deportation, the Metropolitan Police serious crime squad has uncovered vital material evidence which was not available when he was arrested last year. A government source said there was every expectation that Kyiv would agree to extradite Gerasimov.

Sandy Hall, Sky News, Kyiv.

There was total silence from Moscow. Putin's spokesman was questioned by Moscow-based reporters but he declined to make any comment about the Sky News report. The Foreign Office in London also refused to make any comment, but later in the day, the Home Office put out a statement that confirmed initial steps had been taken to seek the extradition of a senior Russian intelligence officer. Annoyingly for Sandy, the Home Office didn't name the Russian. But every media outlet leapt on the story and named Mikhail Gerasimov as the Russian the Home Office wished extradited to the UK. A Home Office press officer had informed the media off the record that the Sky News claim was accurate.

Rebecca arrived back at Heathrow on the day Sandy's scoop broke. When she came through Arrivals she was surprised to see a man in a dark-blue suit standing a few yards away, holding up a large piece of cardboard with her name on it. She walked towards him and said who she was.

"I didn't order a car," she said.

He showed her his identity card. "I've come from Thames House, Ms Strong. They want to see you, if that's all right."

She looked surprised but followed him to the carpark. Her life really had changed. Ten minutes later, she was sitting in the back of a black Range Rover heading down the M4.

She was dropped outside Thames House on Millbank, and Geraldine herself was in the foyer waiting to welcome her. But she was standing the other side of the glass security barrier which consisted of several rows of revolving doors.

"Pick up your pass from reception," she said.

Rebecca was handed a visitor's pass and told to wear it at all times while she was in the building. Her bag was passed through the metal-detecting machine and she had to leave her phone at reception. A security guard came with her and swiped his card through the system to open one of the circular doors. As she entered, the glass door behind her shut and the one in front of her opened.

Geraldine greeted her and they went up in the lift to Geraldine's office. It wasn't Rebecca's first visit to MI5 headquarters and once again, she was impressed by the number of people her age or younger in the building, most of whom didn't even glance in her direction. Geraldine led her into her private office and asked if she would like a coffee. Rebecca declined.

"First of all," Geraldine said, once they had sat down opposite each other, "congratulations on completing your mission so successfully."

"My second mission," Rebecca said. "I should get paid for working for His Majesty's government."

"Actually, that's one of the reasons I wanted to see you," Geraldine replied. "It's unusual and I've had a fight on my hands to get clearance, but I'd like to put you on a more formal basis, a sort of part-time paid contract. We have plenty of private contractors who work for us, and we still have links with a number of former and retired staff, whom we can turn to if necessary. So, in that sense, what I want for you is not out of the ordinary. What *is* different is that you are a special case. We need you for as long as we retain Mikhail Gerasimov as an asset. So it could be a very short contract or, hopefully, if all goes to plan, quite a long one. Are you prepared for that? Indeed, are you interested in joining us in that capacity?"

Rebecca pondered for a moment.

"Of course I am," she answered. "I don't know what I'll tell my parents and friends but I guess I can sort that out. My painting assignments can carry on, right?"

"Rebecca, the first and most important thing is that you can tell no one what you're doing for us. OK, Sandy has a very good idea, obviously, but even he mustn't be told that you are actually going to work for us on a proper basis. Do you understand that?"

"I do, but it might be tricky sometimes, especially if you want me to fly off somewhere at short notice."

"That probably won't be necessary again, but I can't rule it out. As for not telling your loved ones, that's the way it is for all of us here. It's what you have to accept in the intelligence world. Sorry about that."

"OK, fine. So what's next?"

"First, I will have to get you to sign the Official Secrets Act. You don't need a lawyer or anything. I'll arrange it and witness it. What it does is regulate on a statutory basis your understanding of the importance of keeping secrets to yourself and the obligations you will now be under, and of course, the penalties for breaching any section of the act. It sounds a bit forbidding but it's common sense, and I have absolutely no doubt you will be a brilliant and trustworthy asset for my service."

"So I'm not officially a spy then? I'm an asset."

"It's just the terminology. You can think of yourself as a spying asset if you like but since you can't tell anyone, it doesn't make much difference what you call yourself."

Rebecca grinned.

"It's all quite exciting really," she said. "So, when do I sign up, and what is King Charles going to pay me?"

Geraldine smiled and then drew out a sheaf of papers from her desk drawer.

"Have a thorough read through this lot," Geraldine said. "It's the Official Secrets Act, which you need to initial on each page, and then you sign at the end of the last page. There's a separate document which outlines in only a general sense what your role will be. You'll find the payment agreement there, too."

"Do I take it away to read or do you want me to sign up now, here in your office?" Rebecca asked.

"Do it now, please, if you don't mind. I know you've had a long journey back from your Polish trip, but I'd like to get it all signed and sealed today. I've set aside a room for you to peruse the documents carefully. My assistant will take you there and when you're ready to sign, just give her a ring on her extension, which is 3395, and she will bring you back to me to witness the signature."

"In that case, I will have a coffee after all," Rebecca said. "And can I leave my bag with you or shall I take it with me?"

"Just leave it here, that's fine," Geraldine said. "By the way, how was the hotel?"

"Very nice," Rebecca replied. "How's your sex life, Geraldine?"

Geraldine laughed out loud. "I can't tell you that, it's an official secret."

They gave each other a hug, and Geraldine buzzed her assistant to take Rebecca and the Official Secrets Act to the room booked for her.

***

The Russians were the last to find out about Rebecca Strong.

The team of investigators from the Federal Security Service – the feared FSB – examining the long list of suspects in the Sevastopol leak inquiry had already cleared all the sailors who had taken part in the welcome party for Vladimir Putin's visit. None of them had been briefed about who was coming to see them on that particular day. They frequently received VIP visitors and one visit was the same as the next. The senior officers of the Black Sea Fleet had also been cleared.

The FSB turned their attention to the Ministry of Defence, which had organised Putin's trip. Secretaries who had typed out the itinerary and ordered cars had been closely questioned. The hierarchy at the ministry, including General Valery Gerasimov, Chief of the General Staff, were all subjected to questions. No one was above suspicion in the eyes of the FSB. By the time the investigators had finished questioning the Black Sea Fleet personnel and those in the know at the defence ministry, there were only fourteen more names on their list. All of them worked at the Kremlin. Among the names was Colonel Mikhail Gerasimov.

After his dramatic survival and capture by Zelensky's bodyguards, Gerasimov was left until last for the simple reason he was not going to be available for questioning in the foreseeable future, possibly ever. But the FSB team began deep background checks on his whereabouts for every day in the three months leading up to Putin's Sevastopol visit. They turned up at Gerasimov's flat by prior arrangement and spent an hour interrogating his wife.

No matter how many times the two FSB officers tried to reassure Natasha Gerasimov this was just a routine procedure, she was terrified. In her mind, and with good reason, the FSB was the KGB in new clothes. She remembered how, as a child, her parents had always warned her to be a good girl or the KGB would come and take her away. Now she had to face two of them, in her own flat and without her husband to protect her. And where was her husband? No one had officially told her about his mission in Kyiv and his detention in a hospital. Ever since neighbours had visited her to commiserate, passing on what social media reports were saying about her husband, she had been in a state of panic. There was little on the news about what happened in Kyiv. She only watched Russian channels on her television and they hadn't mentioned her husband's name.

Natasha was both proud and relieved to have a husband who had served in military intelligence and was now working in the Kremlin. It made her feel safer. She trusted Mikhail to look after her and their two children and protect them from harm, whether from the state or from the criminals who ruled so much of Moscow. She loved him for that reason and always longed for him to return home after his many trips overseas. After fifteen years of marriage, she also felt protective towards him, especially now that he was in a senior and sensitive job in the Kremlin. She knew little about his work but she believed everything she heard from her gossipy relations, namely that the Kremlin was a scary place. Now that Mikhail was some 500 miles away, stuck in a war zone and lying injured in a hospital, she felt she was entitled to be told what was happening and when her husband would be coming home.

But the FSB officers now sitting in her front room with the tatty carpet were not interested in the Kyiv drama. They said their only concern was what her husband had been up to in the months leading up to the much-publicised attempt on Putin's life in Sevastopol.

Natasha was horrified.

"What did my husband have to do with that?" she demanded. "He's spent all his working life serving our country."

The two FSB officers ignored her protestations and took it in turns to question her.

"So, Mrs Gerasimov, are you happily married?" one asked.

Natasha looked startled. "Of course," she replied.

"Would you lie for him?" the other one asked.

Natasha had no idea how to answer. "I don't know what you mean," she said.

"If you knew he had done something bad, would you tell us?"

"He hasn't done anything bad," she replied stoically.

"But what if he had?"

"I really don't know," she said, beginning to feel tearful. "I'm sure he hasn't, but he probably wouldn't tell me anyway."

"So, he doesn't trust you?"

"That's not what I meant. You men are all the same, you don't tell your wives what you do at work, and Mikhail keeps it all to himself. But he works in the Kremlin, you know that, so he can't tell me anyway." Natasha sounded a little bolder.

"What did he tell you when he disappeared for a few days in October?"

Natasha remembered he had been away. He'd said he had a mission to prepare.

"As I said, he never told me anything about his work and that includes when he goes away," she said, determined not to be browbeaten by her unwelcome visitors.

They continued to ask her what she thought were pointless questions, and then stood up to leave. When they had gone she went into the kitchen and burst into tears.

Valentina Orlov, Gerasimov's secretary, wasn't questioned at home. She was taken to FSB headquarters in Lubyanka Square and given a hard time. She was informed that her job was at stake. They accused her of covering up for her boss and demanded to know where he had gone during his time away from the office. Her interrogators said it was her responsibility and duty to know where her boss was at all times.

Valentina was thirty-one and unmarried. She had little social life. She lived in a one-room apartment on the outskirts of Moscow and admitted to only one friend, a secretary in the defence ministry whom she had known since schooldays. But she liked her job.

She had never had a reason to be in FSB headquarters at any time in her career. Like Natasha Gerasimov, she was petrified.

Valentina had to face three FSB interrogators. They told her they knew that Gerasimov had been away from the office in October. They wanted her version of why he was away.

"He didn't tell me," she said in a quiet voice. She was sitting, they were all standing. The room had very bright strip lighting which made her screw her eyes up. There was only one piece of furniture, the hard wooden chair on which she was sitting, her hands tightly clasped in her lap.

"What did you write in your office diary when he was away?" she was asked.

"I just wrote the dates down, nothing else," she said, her voice trembling.

"Which were?"

"It was October 18th to 21st."

"So, three days?"

"Yes, returning to the office on October 22nd, except ..." Her voice trailed off.

"Except?"

"He came back a day early," she replied.

The tallest of the three FSB interrogators, a man in his forties with a pockmarked face and heavy shoulders, walked round her three or four times and then asked her: "Did he explain why he returned early?"

"No," she replied.

"Are you lying to us?"

"No, please no," Valentina said very quietly. "He never told me where he was going and I didn't feel it was my place to ask him."

"Had he taken time off before without telling you what he would be doing?" the same FSB interrogator asked.

"I ... I ... I don't remember," she faltered. "It's possible. He has a very important job and I'm just a secretary. I'm not expected to ask him what he is up to during his time away from the office."

The FSB man leapt on her answer. "So you're telling me he was up to something?"

"No, I didn't mean that, not in that way, anyway," she said quickly.

"What way, exactly?" one of the other FSB interrogators asked.

"I don't know what you mean," she said, looking confused and scared.

"Ms Orlov, do you know something you're not telling us?" the same man asked.

"No, not at all. I don't know where he went. All I know is, he came back a day earlier than planned, which I thought was odd, but he never explained to me why."

"OK, OK," the third FSB interrogator chipped in. "We just want the truth, that's all. Don't worry, you have no reason to be concerned about your job unless you are deliberately hiding something."

"I'm not," she protested. "Although, there was one thing …"

The three FSB men were, at that point, all standing in front of her, the tall one with the pockmarked face only about a foot away from her trembling knees. They said nothing, waiting for her to carry on.

"It was nothing," she said in a timid voice, "but I did raise it with security at the time."

She then told them about her scratched and dented paper knife and Gerasimov's lack of interest when she told him about it the following day.

All three FSB men looked bewildered.

"What's that got to do with anything?" the pockmarked one asked her, a sneer on his face.

"Well, it's just that he stayed late that day, and when I left the office no one else was there but him. The others had all gone home. And the paper knife was definitely fine when I left. I was the first in the next day and immediately noticed the scratches and dent."

"Did you ever find out what had happened to your paper knife?" the tall one asked, still sounding disinterested.

"No," she said.

The two others showed no interest in her story either, and they wrapped up the interrogation without having achieved anything. The mystery over the missing days remained unexplained.

A decision was taken to re-question Gerasimov's wife about her husband's time away from the office. If that produced nothing, then a full-scale investigation would be launched to uncover where Gerasimov had gone and whether he had met anyone. The senior of the three FSB interrogators, the man who had spoken last to Valentina, said all flight manifests for those days would need to be checked.

When Valentina Orlov had been allowed to leave, the pockmark-faced FSB interrogator, whose name was Major Pavel Kozlov, delegated himself to carry out the flight checks. He went straight to his office on the second floor of the FSB headquarters and fed the relevant codes and passwords into his computer to gain access to all the departure and arrival information for every airline using the Sheremetyevo Alexander S. Pushkin International Airport, the busiest of Moscow's four airports. He inserted the dates he was interested in and then put "Mikhail Gerasimov" into the manifest search queue. Nothing came up. He tried the name and same dates for the three other airports. Again, there was nothing.

He didn't give up. The FSB computer had a vast database with images of every passenger using the Moscow airports over the previous ten years. Kozlov acquired Gerasimov's image from a GRU staffing website and transferred it into the FSB database. A two-year-old photo of Gerasimov when he was a lieutenant-colonel appeared on a passenger manifest for a 5:05 a.m. flight from Sheremetyevo Airport to Istanbul on Turkish Airlines TK2335. The name under the photo for the five-hour flight was Konstantin Smirnov.

"Ha!" bellowed Major Kozlov.

Then he had another thought. He wondered whether Gerasimov had flown to Istanbul for his planned three-day trip or whether the Turkish airport was just a transit point. If he was trying to reach somewhere without leaving an easy trace, he might have moved on elsewhere, especially if Gerasimov's flight from Moscow involved something devious or sinister. Kozlov was now totally focused. He rang a contact at Sheremetyevo and asked him to see if a passenger called Konstantin Smirnov, who left for Istanbul on October 18, had booked an onward flight. It took a few minutes.

"Passenger Konstantin Smirnov took an onward flight to Venice," Kozlov's contact told him.

Kozlov sat back in his chair and whistled. "What the hell's this all about it?" he asked out loud.

He wrote down on a pad four questions: 1. Why did he go to Venice? 2. Who was he meeting? 3. Where did he stay? 4. Why did he leave early?

He didn't know Colonel Mikhail Gerasimov personally, but he had read his file; he knew everything about his career in the GRU intelligence agency, his extraordinary abortive mission in London the previous year, his deportation, and now, the drama of the failed assassination operation in Kyiv. His name was all over the Western press, following the British government's reported interest in having him extradited from Kyiv to the UK to stand trial.

Kozlov realised he had a highly sensitive case on his hands. It was his job to discover whether Gerasimov had leaked the details of Putin's visit to Sevastopol and, if so, to whom and why. Could he possibly be a traitor? He had led the mission to assassinate Zelensky but the Ukrainian president was alive and well, and Gerasimov had survived. He was the only survivor. Could this be some giant conspiracy? Kozlov was only a major but he was forty-four and had more than twenty years of intelligence work behind him. He had a reputation for ruthless obstinacy.

He made a list of the top ten best hotels in Venice and started ringing them. He spoke no Italian but his English was good after studies at the FSB Academy in Michurinsky Prospekt in Moscow.

In each case, he told the hotel reception his name was Chief Inspector Frederic Baptiste and that he worked for Interpol in

Geneva. He explained that he had the onerous task of trying to trace an individual who was on a wanted list and was known to have stayed in a hotel in Venice between October 18th and 21st. He gave the name of Konstantin Smirnov. If the receptionist could possibly check the register to confirm the individual had stayed there during that period, he would be eternally grateful.

All of the hotels he rang over the next hour raised data protection issues and refused to give any information over the phone. Kozlov oozed charm and said he had selected their particular hotel because he knew it was by reputation the best one in Venice. He said the request was a matter of international security. The individual in question, he said, was a Russian. Nine of the hotels still declined to cooperate.

The last hotel on his list was the Palazzo Veneziano.

He went through the same script.

"I need to tell you that the gentleman I am ringing about is a Russian," he said. "And, as you know, there are European Union restrictions on Russians travelling anywhere in Europe because of the war in Ukraine, and that obviously includes Venice. I think it's very much in your interest as well as mine for you to cooperate. This man is dangerous."

The receptionist, a man, didn't reply for a few minutes. Kozlov thought he might have rung off. Then, suddenly, he spoke.

"October 18th, you say?"

"Yes, that's correct," Kozlov replied, holding his breath.

"And Konstantin Smirnov?"

"Yes."

"A Russian?"

"Yes."

"Ah. Those poor Ukrainians. Terrible what's going on. With the Russians, I mean."

"Yes, terrible."

"The war has to end."

"Quite."

"So, let me see. October 16, 17, 18. Yes, here we are. There was a double and a single room booked under the name of Konstantin Smirnov."

Kozlov slapped his right thigh and felt a surge of excitement going through his body.

"Two rooms?" he questioned.

"Yes, a double and a single."

"And was any other name given, by any chance, seeing as how there were two rooms?"

The male receptionist hesitated for a few seconds.

"Yes, there is another name, she was given the double room."

"She?"

"Strong. Rebecca Strong."

CHAPTER NINETEEN
THE RUSSIANS GET ACTIVE

Adam Goldstein had fixed another secure conference call. He and the head of Ukrainian intelligence had been on the phone about Mikhail Gerasimov. Goldstein never referred to Gerasimov as "Agent Bunyan" except when he was talking to his two colleagues, Walt Grolsch and Marina Babb.

At 10 a.m. Eastern Standard Time, 3 p.m. in London, the seven people most closely involved in the "Kremlin asset" case were sitting facing each other across the Atlantic. Patrick Littlefield would normally expect to open the proceedings but this time he waited for Goldstein to start the meeting.

"Morning, everyone," Goldstein said, in a more amicable voice than usual.

Most of the others just nodded. Geraldine replied with a "good afternoon" and looked at her watch at the same time.

"I would say we are in a pretty good situation, so far," Goldstein said. "I've had a couple of sessions with Kyiv on the phone and can give you an update on how things are playing vis-à-vis Gerasimov."

No one responded.

"So," Goldstein went on, "Gerasimov is currently being held, sorry, *looked after*, at a safe house in the southern suburbs of the capital. I am informed he is well, and getting impatient. But this is a long game, as you know. The Kyiv government has placed a blanket ban on anything emerging in the media about either his whereabouts or his state of health, given that he is supposed to be lying in a hospital somewhere with grievous injuries."

Again, no one said anything. Goldstein carried on.

"The media are obviously showing a lot of daily interest in what's happened to this Russian. 'The mystery of the Russian assassin' seems to be a favourite headline in the local Ukrainian papers and on all the radio stations. Social media has gone mad. But the Kyiv shutters are down. Amazingly, since the Sky News report naming him as Mikhail Gerasimov, nothing else has been leaked. And this is what I wanted to raise today. The only leaks we can allow must come via us, and only us. Kyiv has compartmentalised very well so far; only a few people are aware of the full story. They had to know in order for us to choreograph this whole thing to get the asset back where he belongs and still functioning for our joint benefit."

Everyone nodded.

"Kyiv has yet to decide what to do about the senior official in Zelensky's office, codenamed Z. He was grabbed as soon as the Russians had entered Zelensky's inner office and has been under wraps ever since. We're leaving it to Zelensky to decide what to do with him, but it looks like he's going to be publicly identified and put on trial as a traitor. Zelensky wants to get across the message to Moscow that if they think they can have one of their spies operating inside the presidential compound, they will fail. He has dismissed the option of keeping the official detained somewhere and using someone else to feed false information to the Russians in his name. Source Z is finished and Zelensky wants that shoved down Putin's throat."

Goldstein cleared his throat and sipped some water from the glass in front of him.

"The war is not going well for Putin," he said. "Russians, in Moscow at least, are showing more and more distaste for what's going on. Putin needs something to distract them. So, getting Gerasimov back as a hero could just swing things for him, although I remain sceptical. My betting is that he will make a move about a prisoner swap in the next few weeks, perhaps even earlier, and then we will have to make a judgement about whether it's safe for Gerasimov to return to Moscow. Could we literally be handing him over to be executed or will Putin go along with the heroism angle and make as much of it as he can to bolster support and admiration for his leadership? It's going to be a gamble. We don't know, for example, where the FSB has got to in their investigation into the Sevastopol leak. If they pinpoint Gerasimov as the most likely suspect, he'll be done for, and we will have handed him over to his executioners. I know I was initially doubtful about the whole scheme and I still have worries, but so far it has worked. Any thoughts?"

Patrick looked at his colleagues in his office at MI6. Geraldine gestured to him to reply.

"We have reason to believe," Patrick said slowly, "that someone from the FSB has begun making inquiries into our asset's whereabouts in the weeks leading up to Putin's visit to Sevastopol."

"WHAT!" Goldstein shouted. "What evidence have you got?"

"It's still low-level stuff, nothing concrete," Patrick said quickly, "but we've heard that certain inquiries have been made."

Marina Babb looked confused. "You mean somewhere other than Moscow? Like, overseas?"

"Yes, overseas," Geraldine stepped in.

"Where?" Walt Grolsch asked.

"We'll let you know more when we have collected further information," Geraldine replied.

"Geraldine, cut the crap," Goldstein said, exasperated. "We're all in the same family here. Which part of this universe is some bastard FSB guy making inquiries?"

Geraldine glanced at Patrick, who nodded slightly.

"Venice," Geraldine replied.

Goldstein exploded. "In person?" he shouted.

"No, on the phone, ringing round all the top hotels," Patrick said. "One of my chaps in Rome got a call from a source."

"And did he find the hotel where Gerasimov stayed?" Marina Babb asked.

There was no longer any secrecy between the British and American spies about Venice. The British knew the CIA had had agents there monitoring Rebecca and Gerasimov, and the Americans knew the British knew. It didn't have to be spelt out.

"We don't know yet," Geraldine replied. "The source worked at one of the hotels that received the call, but it wasn't the right one. He checked with two other hotels and they all received the same call. Someone calling himself Chief Inspector Frederic Baptiste from Interpol. He asked whether a Russian he named as Konstantin Smirnov had stayed there on the dates we know Gerasimov was in Venice. Gerasimov had travelled to Venice under that name. We've checked on this Chief Inspector Baptiste and he doesn't exist."

There was silence both sides of the Atlantic for a few seconds. Freddie Stigby spoke first.

"The FSB may have had a lucky break," he said, "but surely no hotel would give up information about anyone staying at their place. Even if they have managed to track down the hotel, what would it mean? Gerasimov spent a few days with a blonde woman in a hotel in Venice. The FSB will need a helluva lot more than that to go to Putin and say they have found the traitor. It will be tricky for our asset, no question, but he's been in the business for a long time, he'll know how to explain it away once he gets back to Moscow, if the prisoner swap goes ahead. Meantime, we will do what we can to find out who has been asking questions at hotels in Venice and work out what he might do next."

Before the meeting ended, Grace Redmayne reminded her colleagues about a planned next step for deceiving Putin into offering a prisoner swap.

"Yes, thank you, Grace," Geraldine said. "We're talking to Kyiv about a possible leak concerning a future prisoner swap. Our asset is supposed to be having hospital treatment but there's no reason why the UK government shouldn't be pushing hard for his extradition. The harder we push, the more likely Putin will intervene to try and stop it happening."

"So where will the leak come from, Kyiv or London?" Goldstein asked.

"We think it should be in Kyiv," Geraldine replied.

"OK, we'll leave that to you," Goldstein said, and ended the call.

Patrick, Grace and Freddie looked astonished; Goldstein had actually agreed not to interfere.

**

Rebecca had reverted to her other job for a few days and was busy painting a landscape for a boutique hotel in West London.

Her phone rang shortly after lunch. She didn't recognise the number.

"Hello?"

"Is that Rebecca Strong?" The voice was male with a slightly harsh accent. Not British.

"Who's speaking?" she asked.

"I'm sorry to bother you. My name is Andrew Bellows. I represent a lot of international clients and I gather from Google that you are an artist and often paint pictures for commercial buildings. Am I right?"

Rebecca had her own website with all her contact details and frequently had phone calls from potential customers for her paintings. This was not an unusual call. But strangely, ever since playing spy on behalf of His Majesty's government, she was much more wary of any kind of approach, even though she welcomed all the commissions she could get. Among the wad of papers she had signed at Thames House, one of the documents had laid out what and how she was going to be paid for her services. Apart from expenses, she was to get a monthly retainer of £1,400. Part-time spying wasn't going to make her rich, so she still needed painting commissions.

She answered her caller cautiously.

"Yes, I do, but I'm afraid I'm very busy at the moment," she said.

"Of course, of course, I understand. It's just that a lot of my clients run big businesses and they have asked me to organise the purchase of modern paintings, large ones, for their various establishments, private as well as public. I'm talking about multiple commissions, if they are satisfied with your particular talents," the man said.

Normally, Rebecca would have leapt at the opportunity, but it all seemed too good to be true. Multiple commissions from rich businessmen? Why didn't they just buy from an auction or go to their local art gallery?

"And what do you know about my 'particular talents', as you put it?" Rebecca asked.

"Well, it's not my appreciation of your work, you understand," the man called Andrew Bellows said. "My clients have referred me to commercial artists such as yourself and I have the task of selecting paintings on their behalf. So it would be very helpful if we could meet up and then I can have a look at some of your work. Do you think that would be possible?"

Rebecca decided she didn't like the man's voice. There was something oddly sinister about it. He didn't sound like some hot-shot representing international companies.

"You say you're called Andrew Bellows?" she asked.

"That's correct."

"Do you have contact details? I'll be in touch when I've had time to consider your proposal."

"Of course, I can give you my phone numbers and email address," he said. "Just one thing before I do – do you think there would be any chance of you painting a series of landscapes of Venice?"

Rebecca's heart jumped.

"Venice?" she asked and felt her voice trembling.

"Yes, Venice. My clients are particularly keen to have paintings of scenes in Venice. You have been there, I presume?"

Rebecca said "yes" before she could stop herself.

"Such a lovely city, don't you think?" the man asked. "Perhaps we can talk again in the very near future. I know where you are, so there will be no difficulty. I'll be in touch soon, Ms Strong. So nice to talk to you. Goodbye."

Major Pavel Kozlov, FSB investigator, put the phone down and smiled.

Kozlov had taken only a day to confirm that the Rebecca Strong staying in a double bedroom booked by Konstantin Smirnov, aka Mikhail Gerasimov, in a posh hotel in Venice in October was the same Rebecca Strong whom Gerasimov had lived with for two weeks in a flat in London during the failed assassination attempt of one of Britain's top spies.

One thing had been missing from Gerasimov's file: a photograph of Rebecca Strong. Kozlov had contacted GRU headquarters and requested to speak to Gerasimov's former department chiefs. He was put in touch with a General Igor Sidorov, who agreed to hand over a photograph of the woman; they arranged to meet at his office. Kozlov thanked him. Later, when he saw the picture of Rebecca Strong, which was now in Gerasimov's file, Kozlov sighed and said under his breath: "You old goat."

Kozlov called his two co-investigators and they sat down in his office to discuss the latest discoveries and to decide what to do next.

"What we have here," Kozlov's senior FSB colleague, Colonel Boris Gusev, said, "is not necessarily evidence of betrayal. Gerasimov has a propensity for attractive women. It seems this is why he didn't shoot the woman, Hammer, at her house in London last year when he had the chance. That's a big negative but it didn't seem to damage his career for some reason. As for this other woman, Rebecca Strong, he clearly took a fancy to her and then thought he could exploit her by using her flat for cover. Nothing wrong with that, in my view. But now, let's bring it forward to the Venice encounter. Kozlov, give us your take on it."

"On the face of it," Kozlov said, "it's just a good old-fashioned case of adultery. Gerasimov wanted to see this Rebecca Strong again, fixed for her to meet up in Venice, spent two days and nights enjoying himself, then felt guilty perhaps and left a day earlier than planned. End of story."

"But?" Colonel Gusev queried.

"Well, there are several 'buts' and a lot of questions," Kozlov replied.

"Go on," said Gusev.

"First, why did he book a double room and a single room? An adulterer needs a double room. What's the single room all about? Was there some reason other than sex in his mind when he made the booking? Did he think she might not want to sleep with him, so he booked the single room as backup? But if that was the case, why did this woman agree to fly out to Venice to meet him? Surely, after their smooching at her flat in London a year ago, she definitely had sex in mind. This is Venice, right?"

"She's a looker, too," the third FSB man, Major Anton Lebedev, said with a grin.

The other two ignored him.

"So?" Gusev asked.

"Leaving aside the bedroom situation for the moment," Kozlov went on, "what worries me most is the timing. Why did Gerasimov leave Moscow for Istanbul under an assumed name, and then go on to Venice, when he was supposed to be finalising details of the secret mission in Kyiv? It should have been his top priority and yet he felt he could fly to Venice, of all places, for a few days with a woman who comes from a country effectively at war with Russia. The UK is our enemy, propping up the bloody Ukrainians with all their fancy weapons. What on earth is a senior Russian official doing consorting with the enemy? If it was just sex, that's still a crime when our country is suffering from the West's support of Ukraine. But what if it was more than sex?"

"Such as?" Gusev asked.

"Maybe Gerasimov fancied chucking in his wife and kids and going to live with Rebecca Strong," Kozlov replied.

"Don't see it," Gusev said. "Not a man like Gerasimov. OK, he likes women, but he's not going to throw everything away. And we'd find him, he knows that."

"I agree," Kozlov said. "So there has to be something else. Who is Rebecca Strong? She's a commercial artist, but is that a cover? Could she be working for the UK government?"

"Go on," Gusev said.

"Maybe Gerasimov was offering his services to the British," Kozlov surmised. "I've checked him out thoroughly and at a meeting with the Security Council he indicated he wasn't impressed with the way the war was being handled in Ukraine. Maybe he has become disillusioned and decided to put out feelers to the West and chose Rebecca Strong to be his go-between? This could be pushing it too far. I could be totally wrong, but in many ways it all fits."

Colonel Gusev thanked Kozlov for his thoughts and summed up what should be done next.

"Let's get this Rebecca Strong in our clutches," he said.

***

Rebecca rang Geraldine about the phone call from Andrew Bellows.

Geraldine was instantly alarmed.

"Did he threaten you?" she asked.

"Not in so many words," Rebecca replied. "But the way he said he knew where I was, I found that threatening."

"I fear your instincts are right," Geraldine replied. "I'll send round a protection officer to be with you for a few days, just to make sure you don't get an uninvited visitor."

"No, please don't bother," Rebecca said. "I'll be OK. I'll ring you if he phones again."

"OK, but we'll check out the phone number he used," Geraldine said.

The next day, Andrew Bellows was forgotten when Geraldine phoned and asked Rebecca if she wouldn't mind going to Poland for a second time and meeting up with Sandy again. There was another story she wanted to appear on Sky News.

"Of course I will," Rebecca replied. "Although, isn't it a long way round to get Sandy to run a news story?"

"It's the way we want to do it," Geraldine replied. "While he's in Kyiv, it's useful for us."

"I doubt Sandy would want to be known as being useful to MI5," Rebecca said. "He's a journalist, not a spy, or 'asset' as you like to call me."

"Rebecca, I didn't mean to make it sound like we're using Sandy," Geraldine quickly replied. "It's just that there's a good story about to break and we thought it would be in his interests to hear about it first. Another scoop for him."

"OK, that sounds a bit better," Rebecca said. "He gets a bit precious if he feels he's being fed stuff for other reasons."

"The one and only reason, Rebecca, is the protection of our asset, Agent Redruth. If it wasn't for you he would never have been called that, as you know. So if Sandy can play a role to keep Redruth alive and functioning for us, then it's justified, don't you think?"

"Yes."

Geraldine told Rebecca her tickets and onward rail booking had all been arranged. It was to be the same hotel in the same Polish border town. She then outlined what she wanted her to tell Sandy.

Two days later, Rebecca took an Uber to Heathrow for her flight to Warsaw. When she boarded the plane, she settled into an aisle seat and prepared to do very little for the next two hours.

Ten rows behind her, also sitting in an aisle seat, was a tall man with heavy shoulders and a pockmarked face. Andrew Bellows, aka Major Pavel Kozlov, was on the case.

He had flown immediately from Moscow to Heathrow via Istanbul under the name of Andrew Bellows following his phone call to Rebecca. He had planned to follow her whenever she left the flat. It was a sheer stroke of luck that almost as soon as he took up station across the road from her building, early in the morning, two days later, Rebecca Strong emerged with a case in her hand and climbed into a waiting car. He'd hailed a taxi and followed.

CHAPTER TWENTY
KOZLOV BEGINS TO PUT TWO AND TWO TOGETHER

Major Kozlov's boss had ordered him not to let Rebecca Strong out of his sight. They had agreed that whatever conclusions they eventually drew about Gerasimov, now the number one suspect in their Sevastopol leak investigation, the tall blonde woman was somehow at the heart of it all. She would lead them to the answer they were looking for. What they didn't know at this stage was whether "the looker", as their colleague, Major Anton Lebedev, had described her, was a fully paid-up member of Britain's Security Service, or whether she was being exploited and used as some sort of courier because of her past relationship with Gerasimov. Kozlov and Colonel Boris Gusev thought MI5 had probably blackmailed her into cooperating and would dump her as soon as she had outlasted her usefulness. Lebedev, unwittingly astute on this occasion, felt Rebecca Strong could probably make up her own mind about what she did and that if she was cooperating with MI5 she was doing so willingly and rather enjoying herself. Kozlov and Gusev had stared at Lebedev, perhaps thinking that maybe he wasn't just a sex-obsessed idiot after all. In fact, the more Kozlov studied Ms Strong, the more he realised how apposite her surname was. Little did he know that Gerasimov had come to exactly the same conclusion after he had spent a few days with her the first time he met her, more than a year ago.

So, while watching the top of her head on the plane for more than two hours, Kozlov made a decision: he wouldn't underestimate the capabilities of this woman. Twenty minutes before the flight was due to land in Warsaw, Rebecca got up from her seat and walked towards him to go to the bathroom. As she approached his aisle seat, the plane shuddered slightly in thick cloud and she put her right hand on the seat in front of him to steady herself. She caught him looking at her. She smiled and apologised for no reason. He replied, "No problem." She then moved on and was gone for five minutes.

When the plane landed at Warsaw, Kozlov waited for Rebecca to go past him before he got up, retrieved his bag from the overhead locker, and followed her, keeping his distance.

Kozlov enjoyed his job and hoped that if he could prove this woman making her way down the stairs to the waiting bus was a covert spy working for British intelligence, it might persuade his superiors to give him the promotion he had been after for a year or so. He was more interested in the upgraded salary he would get than the higher rank itself. Kozlov was single and he had had little success with women. When he read Gerasimov's file, he had been envious of his obvious attraction to women. But he knew it was also his weakness, and if Gerasimov was going to be pinpointed as the traitor in the Kremlin, it was more than likely that a woman would unwittingly play a big part. That woman, Kozlov was convinced, would be Rebecca Strong. Wherever she went, he would follow her. He was sure the reason she was in Poland was somehow linked to Gerasimov, and he intended to find out what she was up to.

Seven hours later, Rebecca Strong walked into the Hotel Marko in the border town of Medyka and leapt into the arms of an excited-looking man with longish hair. Kozlov was standing by a large plant set in a multi-coloured jardinière. He surreptitiously lifted a small camera up to chest level and took half a dozen pictures. He then turned round to face the window before examining the photos. Two of them showed the man's full face. The other four were a blur of half his face and a mass of

Rebecca's blonde hair. Kozlov was satisfied. He sent the pictures to his colleagues back at FSB headquarters and asked them to identify the male as rapidly as possible. The answer came almost immediately.

Sandy Hall, foreign correspondent of Sky News.

For Kozlov, that was another strike against Gerasimov in his potential downfall. Sandy Hall, he recalled, was the reporter who broke the news about Gerasimov being the leader of the Russian assassination team in Kyiv. Who was the reporter's source? Supposedly, it was a senior figure in the Ukrainian intelligence service. But, Kozlov asked himself, why would the Ukrainian intelligence service select Sky News for this scoop? Why not the local TV service or the *New York Times* or the BBC? Perhaps there was more to it. Perhaps there was some link-up with the British intelligence services to get Gerasimov's name into the public domain? If so, why? And, as Sandy Hall was the reporter, did that mean Rebecca Strong had played a role too? Kozlov vowed to get hold of the hotel register, in case the couple still hugging each other in the foyer had been in Hotel Marko on a previous occasion. Kozlov felt the myriad pieces of the jigsaw were very slowly coming together.

The couple had now disentangled and were heading with unseemly haste to the lift. Kozlov decided there was no point in following them. They would be busy for at least an hour. Meanwhile, he could better use his time by checking the hotel register.

He walked to the reception desk and flashed his FSB security pass at one of the young female receptionists. She didn't even glance at it, let alone register that it was a Russian FSB identity card. But when she heard the mumbled word "security" and saw a man in front of her who looked like someone who was used to being obeyed instantly, she didn't question him. Kozlov pointed to the computer screen and used his hands to show he wanted her to swivel it round. She did, without hesitation. He saw that a double room for one night had been booked in the name of Rebecca Strong. He then scrolled down to the day before the Sky News scoop was broadcast about the failed assassination plot. He saw nothing of interest at first but then he found it: a double room booked for one night in the name of Rebecca Strong.

Kozlov was now certain that once the couple had finished whatever they were doing in the bedroom up on the fourth floor, another Sky News scoop was going to emerge.

Kozlov knew what this meant. Rebecca Strong was definitely a courier of messages from the British intelligence service, feeding secrets to the Sky News reporter, selected for his dual role: a purveyor of news on a successful television station and Rebecca's boyfriend. It was perfect. Kozlov decided to keep his conclusions to himself. He wanted to be absolutely sure, and he also needed to come to a view about what this arrangement meant vis-à-vis Colonel Mikhail Gerasimov.

At the moment it was circumstantial. But the more he thought about it, the more convinced he became that Rebecca Strong, Sandy Hall and Gerasimov were all tied in together. A conspiracy of treachery against the Russian Federation. Gerasimov wasn't a hero who should be brought home from Kyiv and honoured by the president. He should be dragged home in handcuffs and delivered to the interrogation cells in the basement of FSB headquarters. And Rebecca Strong, as a party to the betrayal, should be eliminated. All these thoughts went through Kozlov's mind.

Then one more thought came to him: if the British government was supposedly so keen to get Gerasimov extradited to the UK, what were they going to do with him? Not put him on trial, not if he was supposed to be working secretly as a double agent for them in Moscow. What game were the British playing?

Kozlov felt the only conclusion that could be drawn was that the British were publicly fighting to have Gerasimov extradited as a scam to fool Putin into putting in a bid for a prisoner swap with Kyiv to get him back to Moscow. And if Kyiv agreed, and refused to extradite him to the UK, Gerasimov would return to his job in the Kremlin and carry on serving the interest of the British government as a secret spy. So it was all a double bluff! *My God*, Kozlov thought, *it's brilliant*. If he was right, then the Kyiv government was part of the plot. Kyiv would agree a prisoner swap with Moscow – Gerasimov in return for Ukrainian soldiers captured by the Russians in the war – in order to help the British with their dastardly scheme to maintain their secret asset in the heart of the Kremlin. It was a scam on a huge scale, and only he, Major Kozlov of the FSB, knew, or thought he knew, what was going on.

***

The next morning, Sandy Hall left at 5 a.m. to get the train back to Kyiv. He had a great story to write and wanted to be back in the Ukrainian capital as quickly as he could. Kozlov, staying at the same hotel, was up an hour later and missed the departure of the Sky News reporter. But his focus was on Rebecca Strong, and she didn't appear for breakfast until nine o'clock. Kozlov watched her from the other side of the dining room.

Rebecca seemed to be in a different world; she had a mesmerised look on her face. Kozlov guessed she was thinking about her boyfriend. More than ever, Kozlov felt it was his duty to bring her treacherous game to an end.

Rebecca was drinking her first cup of coffee of the day and began looking around the room at the other guests eating their breakfast. There were about twenty people in the room, split between couples and individuals. None of the couples were talking. She noticed one man on the far side of the room who looked away as soon as she glanced at him. The hasty movement, turning his face towards the wall, made her stop and think. Was there something familiar about him? She continued to watch him until he turned his face round and started drinking his coffee. That was it! It was the pockmarked face. It was the same man who had been sitting in an aisle seat on the plane from Heathrow to Warsaw. The same man she apologised to when she stumbled on her way to the bathroom. She was sure it was him. So, was it just an extraordinary coincidence that he should be in the same hotel as her in southern Poland or was there something more sinister? Was he following her?

The man with the pockmarked face was studiously avoiding looking in her direction.

Rebecca's train back to Warsaw was due to leave in an hour. She got up from the table and left the room without a backward glance. She went to her room, packed her bag, and went down in the lift to reception. The room had already been paid for, but she handed over the key and asked for a taxi. She waited in the lobby for ten minutes, sitting in an armchair which had a good view of the lift and stairs. When her taxi arrived, she got up immediately. Before she left she turned round to wave at the receptionist, who had been friendly to her, and saw the man with the pockmarked face standing by the reception desk. He wasn't looking at her.

At the railway station, she bought a coffee and sat waiting for the train. She didn't see the man enter the station, and when the train arrived, she looked up and down the platform before getting on board. But again, there was no sign of him. She began to have doubts. Perhaps it was a coincidence after all. She slept most of the journey but woke up with a start after five hours. She stood up and stretched and made her way to the tiny toilet. As she went, she looked out for the pockmarked face but saw no one. She had woken feeling tense but now tried to calm her nerves. If he was somewhere on the train, she had a plan for how to deal with him. But she hoped it wouldn't be necessary.

The train drew into Warsaw station just under seven hours after leaving Medyka. She queued for a taxi for the airport. She looked everywhere but didn't spot the man. She started to feel more relaxed. Once at the airport, she checked in straightaway. She only had hand luggage, and took forty minutes going through security. She still had just over an hour before her flight was due to leave.

As soon as she sat down to wait for the boarding announcement, she saw him. He was standing at the back of a short queue in front of a coffee stand. She only caught the side of his face but it was unmistakable. It seemed she would need to carry out her plan after all.

She saw two Polish police officers with guns and walked quickly up to them. She asked if they spoke English. They smiled at her and nodded.

"Please, I need your help," Rebecca said, sounding a little out of breath. "A man tried to grab me. He put his hands on my ..." – she pointed to her breasts – "and then tried to kiss me."

The police officers reacted immediately.

"He assaulted you?" one asked.

"Yes," Rebecca replied, raising her voice. "He's still there."

"Where?" both asked at once.

"There, the man in the queue by the coffee stand." Rebecca pointed in the man's direction.

"Come with us," one of the officers said. Both gripped the guns in their holsters with their right hands as they moved smartly towards the coffee stand.

As Rebecca pointed again at her assailant, Kozlov turned his head and saw the two police officers hurrying towards him. He saw Rebecca behind them. For a brief moment he looked stunned, as if he knew what was about to happen.

Both police officers grabbed him and held his arms tight to his sides.

"Sir, you have to come with us," one of the officers said.

"What's this all about?" Kozlov asked.

"Sir, you have been accused of a sexual assault," the officer said.

Kozlov stared at them and then at Rebecca Strong, who was standing close by. He knew if he was arrested, she would have beaten him at his own game. He had, after all, underestimated her.

He wrenched himself free and hurled himself at Rebecca, knocking her backwards. Her head hit the floor with a loud thud and she lay semi-conscious as other people close by screamed and ran off, falling into each other in the panic.

Kozlov began to run, but one of the police officers had his gun in his hand. He shouted at the top of his voice, in Polish: "STOP, OR I SHOOT!"

Before he could carry out his threat, a large man with a baby in a papoose on his chest stuck out his foot and Kozlov crashed to the floor. The officer pointed his gun as he struggled to get up. The officer shouted for the second time: "STAY ON THE FLOOR OR I SHOOT!"

The second officer joined his colleague, also with his gun pointing downwards. He pulled Kozlov's arms behind his back and handcuffed him.

Rebecca was slowly recovering. People had gathered round her, and a paramedic in red overalls was running towards her. She looked over at the scene a few yards away and saw the man with the pockmarked face being dragged to his feet. Six other police officers had appeared, all with guns drawn.

The young paramedic shone a torch in both her eyes and felt behind her head, asking if it was painful.

"Just a bit tender," she replied. "I think I'll be OK."

"You really should go to hospital for a check-up, you might have mild concussion," the paramedic said.

"I'll be fine, honestly, but thank you," she said.

One of the police officers returned and asked for her name.

"Ms Strong, you will have to make a full statement," he said. "Down at the police station."

"But I have a flight in thirty minutes," she replied, looking alarmed at the thought of being stuck in Warsaw for days. She hadn't taken that into account when she thought up her scheme to get the pockmarked stalker arrested.

"That's out of the question, Ms Strong. We will need a statement from you if we are to press charges," the officer said.

The police officer said he would arrange a hotel room for her at the airport and advised her that they would pick her up at eight o'clock the next morning to be taken to the police HQ.

***

Rebecca was ready for them the following morning and she was driven into the city. She was escorted to the main interview room, where a female police officer and a senior male detective were present to take her statement.

Rebecca regretted what she had thought was a clever ruse to get the man she assumed was a Russian detained by police. She had been naïve. If she put her false story in writing she could end up in jail herself. She felt rising panic and wondered if she should try and ring Geraldine to get her out of the clutches of the Warsaw police.

"I have been thinking about this overnight," she told the officers, "and I have decided I really don't want to press charges. The man was rude and a bit scary but I may have overreacted when he seemed to be grabbing me. I know he then pushed me over, but he was probably angry at being arrested and blamed me. So I don't want you to charge him."

The woman police officer and detective looked surprised and then angry.

"Ms Strong," the detective said, "you made a serious accusation and you can't just drop it. That's not the way it works here. The man has been read his rights and has been in a cell overnight, while you were in a nice hotel."

Rebecca was astonished by what sounded like a very sexist remark. The female police officer nodded her head as if agreeing with her colleague.

She decided to be contrite.

"I am so sorry, it all happened very quickly, but after a lot of thought I want to go home," she said, trying to sound tearful. "If I make a statement, I'll have to appear in court, right? I don't want to face him again."

"We could charge you with wasting police time," the detective said in a surly voice.

The female police officer said nothing but just nodded again.

"Are you going to change your mind?" the detective asked.

"I apologise, but no, if that's all right," Rebecca replied. She just wanted to leave Warsaw as quickly as possible. If the Russian was freed, at least she would be on her way back to London.

The detective and police officer looked at each other and then stood up.

"Ms Strong, you won't be charged, but you'll have to pay us back for the one night in the hotel," the detective said bluntly. "My colleague will deal with that. Please don't come back to Warsaw."

"I really am sorry," Rebecca replied meekly, as relief surged through her body. "Will the man now be released?"

Neither replied. But when she went with the female officer to the reception area to pay for her one night's stay, the woman said something quietly.

"He's not going to be freed."

Rebecca looked at with her eyebrows raised.

"It turned out he wasn't who he said he was," the officer replied. She declined to say anything more.

Rebecca thanked her and left the police station. Her plan, it seemed, had worked after all.

***

Sandy's latest scoop was broadcast on a Sky News bulletin while Rebecca was still in the hotel in Warsaw.

Sky News can reveal exclusively that the Kyiv government has now approved the request from London to extradite Colonel Mikhail Gerasimov, the alleged leader of the Russian assassination squad sent by Moscow to kill President Zelensky. Gerasimov was injured during the failed attempt to kill the Ukrainian leader and has been receiving treatment for his wounds in an unidentified hospital. I am told that Gerasimov has recovered well from his injuries and could be ready to be extradited to the UK within the next four to five weeks. He is facing charges in London of double murder, attempted murder, conspiracy to cause terrorism, illegal possession of an assault weapon, and being in possession of a number of false passports. The British government is eager to have him back in London so that he can face what promises to be another sensational spy trial. Last month, Amelia Prendergast, a Russian mole inside MI5, was sentenced to thirteen years in prison in a trial related to the alleged crimes committed by Gerasimov, a senior member of the Russian GRU military intelligence service.

Having such a senior officer of the Russian military intelligence service in the dock at the Old Bailey will be deeply embarrassing for President Putin, especially after the failed attempt to assassinate President Zelensky. I understand that although the Kyiv government wanted to put Gerasimov on trial here in Ukraine, President Zelensky personally intervened as a favour to the British government, which has been in the forefront of Western allies providing weapons and military assistance since the Russian invasion. No word has yet come from Moscow about the agreement between Kyiv and London to have Gerasimov deported to the UK. A spokesman for the Kyiv government told Sky News that Moscow deserved to be humiliated by having one of their top intelligence officials appearing on trial.

Sandy Hall, Sky News in Kyiv.

CHAPTER TWENTY-ONE
OPERATION GREENGAGE AT CRISIS POINT

A week had passed. There was still no hint of a move by the Kremlin to intervene over the British/Ukrainian agreement to extradite Mikhail Gerasimov to the UK for trial.

David Kimche, MI6 station chief, had been working hard to glean information from his limited circle of agents operating in Moscow. Recruiting Russians to pass on information had always been one of the toughest assignments for MI6 officers based in Moscow, although since the invasion of Ukraine, the numbers had increased significantly. None of the Russians recruited by David Kimche, however, were employed in the most sensitive ministries. Half a dozen had come forward since the invasion because of their disillusionment with the Putin regime but three worked in the Ministry of Economic Development, two had political staff jobs in the Duma, the Russian parliament, and one was a clerk in the ministry of transport. While their inside information was always valuable, they were far removed from the inner workings of the Kremlin. Kimche had been supplied with rumours and speculation by his agents.

This was why the extraordinary offer from Colonel Mikhail Gerasimov to work for British intelligence was priceless. He had inside information that would always be top secret, although even at his senior level in the Kremlin he would never be able to say to his British controller that he knew for certain what was going on in Putin's mind. No one did. But Agent Redruth was still a unique asset and, without him, Kimche's job was harder than ever. The agents he did have had no insight into whether Putin was going to offer a deal to Kyiv or swap Gerasimov for Ukrainian soldiers captured in the first months of the war. More than a hundred were being held in detention centres in Belgorod Oblast, about twenty-five miles north of the border with Ukraine.

There had been an editorial on a Russian military website which had called on Putin to bring Gerasimov back to Moscow. But there had been no reaction from the Kremlin. A Russian reporter had raised the issue during a press conference with Putin's spokesman, following the reports from Sky News and other Western broadcasters, but he had refused to make any comment.

Operation Greengage, the secret British codename for Agent Redruth's mission in Moscow, was at a turning point. The future of the mission depended on Putin. Geraldine was still fairly convinced that he would make a move to get Gerasimov back to Moscow. But now the whole gamble was at serious risk because of the information Rebecca had brought back from her trip to Poland.

Patrick Littlefield sent coded orders to David Kimche to tap every source he had to see if there was a sign that the FSB investigation into the Sevastopol leak was reaching any sort of conclusion. Kimche had one agent who was a male secretary in the FSB headquarters. He could meet him only about once a month and always at grave risk both to himself and to his agent. The Russian, in his thirties, spied for MI6 for money to help pay for a wedding he was planning with his fiancée, an exotic dancer he had met in a bar in St Petersburg. Without the extra cash from MI6, he couldn't afford either the wedding or a future life with his betrothed.

The Russian had been promised double the normal payment if he could come up with anything about the Sevastopol leak investigation. To Kimche's amazement, the agent delivered spectacular intelligence, scribbled on an FSB-headed, A4-sized sheet of paper and left in the hollow of a tree in Yekaterininskiy Park in central Moscow. Kimche sent the crucial intelligence in a top secret memo for the eyes only of Patrick Littlefield, director of operations (DO).

To DO from Kimche, Moscow,

A primary source, credible and authoritative, has revealed a blow-up inside the FSB over the Sevastopol leak investigation. Three FSB officers were delegated to investigate Redruth. My source names them as Colonel Boris Gusev, Major Anton Lebedev and Major Pavel Kozlov. The last name is key. Kozlov went to Warsaw as part of the investigation. He apparently sent a message with a photo attached for his FSB colleagues to check out. He asked for the identity of someone he photographed at a hotel on the border with Ukraine. My source didn't know what that was about. But it provides added confirmation for us, following R. Strong's experience, that Kozlov has been following her and must have witnessed her meeting up with the Sky News reporter.

Kozlov's arrest in Warsaw caused panic and bewilderment at FSB HQ. My source says at the heart of the panic is that Kozlov failed to make a full report back to FSB HQ before his arrest at Warsaw airport. My source says Warsaw has informed Moscow that a suspected FSB officer has been detained and is facing a charge of entering Poland on a false passport.

My source says Colonel Gusev has been suspended from duty for failing to keep in constant contact with Kozlov, who has a reputation for acting on his own initiative. So far, because of Kozlov's failure to make a report before he was detained, there appears to be no direct link being made to Redruth, even though Kozlov went to Warsaw to investigate R. Strong's connections to him. In fact, the FSB leadership is so angry with Gusev that his suspicions that Redruth is a traitor have been largely dismissed. The source says the FSB has sent two investigators to Poland to try and pick up where Kozlov left off, and to attempt to gain access to Kozlov. They know where he is being held. If they get access to Kozlov, Redruth could be in serious trouble.

The Kimche memo was sent to Geraldine, who immediately summoned Grace, her deputy.

"What do you think?" Geraldine asked Grace when she had read the memo.

"The question is, how much of this turmoil inside the FSB is being sent up the chain to the Kremlin and, indeed, to Putin himself?" Grace queried. "The FSB hierarchy might have dismissed suspicions about our man for the moment, but Putin is a different beast. He is suspicious of everyone. If he knows what has been going on – if he, for example, has been told about Kozlov's arrest while following leads in Poland – he will surely begin to have his doubts about our asset. This is potentially very dangerous. We might have to call off Operation Greengage and get him back here."

Geraldine frowned. Operation Greengage was her baby. She knew Grace's summing-up was sensible but she felt her deputy was being too cautious. Her view was that it was too early to give up on Agent Redruth. There was still a chance that the plan to entice Putin to go for a prisoner swap and return Gerasimov to his job in the Kremlin could work. That chance, she thought, was worth taking.

"Grace, you're right," Geraldine replied, "but I'm not going to pull Operation Greengage yet. I'll talk to Goldstein and co and see what they think. But let's wait and see what Putin does. Redruth is going to be staying in Kyiv for another few weeks. I'm counting on Putin going for the scam. He will want Gerasimov back in Moscow, I'm sure of that. Provided the FSB doesn't come up with startling new evidence against our man, it could still work in our favour. We, and I mean all of us, the West, NATO, the coalition, need Agent Redruth in place inside the Kremlin. Whatever happens in Ukraine over the next few months, it's going to be absolutely vital to have our intelligence asset up close and personal. So, Operation Greengage stays."

Grace looked worried.

"Tell me, what's on your mind?" Geraldine asked.

"First of all, I share your enthusiasm for hanging on to Agent Redruth for as long as we can," Grace replied. "But we are, I think, at a critical point. We know that Kozlov has probably uncovered our scheme and is maybe the only Russian on the planet who can in one stroke destroy Operation Greengage and expose Gerasimov as a double agent and, therefore, guarantee his execution."

Grace waited for some reaction but Geraldine waved her on.

"What worries me is the unexpected," Grace went on. "Even if the FSB officers sent to Warsaw are denied access to Kozlov in jail, what if Kozlov somehow manages to get a message back to Moscow from his prison cell? I'm playing devil's advocate here, but these sorts of questions need to be addressed, don't you think?"

"Of course," Geraldine said, "and I have gone over all these possibilities in my mind. But in our business, we have to take risks and we have to weigh up what those risks are. We can't cancel Operation Greengage because one FSB officer, currently sitting in jail, might have come to certain conclusions and could blow the whistle on the whole plot."

"I agree, mostly," Grace said. "But we're talking here about someone's life. Redruth has entrusted us with his life and we must take every precaution to ensure that he doesn't end up hanging by the neck or thrown from a top-storey window."

Geraldine nodded in agreement.

"So, what do you suggest?" Geraldine asked her.

"We have to do something about Kozlov," Grace said. "We can't just let the Polish authorities deal with him in the normal legal fashion."

"What do you want to do, kidnap him from prison?" Geraldine asked with a laugh.

Grace didn't look amused. "No, but for as long as possible, we need Kozlov held under wraps, and no access granted. We have good relations with our counterparts in Warsaw, so why don't we get our chief to ring their chief for a little chat?"

"OK," Geraldine said, "but that won't solve our problem long-term, and it still leaves the risk that other FSB investigators will reach the same conclusions that Kozlov appears to have reached."

"Well, one step at a time," Grace said. "If you're determined to keep Operation Greengage alive, let's get Kozlov dealt with, even if it's only for a few months, and by then we will know whether Putin is going to take the bait and try for a prisoner swap to get Gerasimov back to Moscow. If he does, then we can make further decisions, always keeping in mind that his safety is our paramount concern."

Geraldine nodded in agreement and thanked her assistant for her usual insightful advice. But when Grace had left her office, Geraldine sat back in her chair and tried to work out what was going on in her head. There was something she had to admit to herself. There was no question Operation Greengage could generate vital intelligence if Agent Redruth was able to return to his post and continue providing an insight into Kremlin thinking about the war in Ukraine. Human intelligence on the ground, rather than secret information scooped up by satellites 350 miles up in space, sometimes provided the most valuable inside information. More than anyone, Geraldine wanted Gerasimov back in the Kremlin. But a tiny thought in the back of her mind reminded her that of the small number of people involved in Operation Greengage, she was the only one who had personal reasons for disliking Gerasimov. So, if he got caught as a traitor, would she really mind?

Professionally, she had leapt at the chance of having such a key asset inside the Kremlin, but personally, she wished it were anyone but Colonel Mikhail Gerasimov. So, if he was exposed as a traitor, at least she would get her revenge. That was the tiny thought at the back of her mind.

Geraldine shook her head as if to blow away such thoughts. She knew, as her deputy had wisely pointed out, that it was her professional duty to safeguard Agent Redruth as their prize asset and to do everything she could to keep him in post while being ready to whisk him out of Moscow at the first sign of the FSB closing in on him as the main suspect for the Sevastopol leak. It was vital for Britain's intelligence services to have a reputation for protecting their secret agents, men and women who were prepared to betray their own countries at great risk to their lives.

***

Midnight in London, seven o'clock in the evening in Langley, Virginia, and 2 a.m. the following day in Kyiv, Adam Goldstein received a call. Colonel Andriy Bilyk, head of the Ukrainian intelligence service, was on the line.

"Colonel Bilyk, what's up?" Goldstein asked, looking at his watch. He was due out for dinner with his wife and next-door neighbours at eight o'clock.

"We have a situation here," the colonel replied, sounding out of breath as if he had run to the phone. "Your man is making life difficult. He is making certain demands and we're not sure of the best course of action."

"My man?" Goldstein asked, not immediately grasping who he meant.

Colonel Bilyk didn't reply. He let Goldstein work it out for himself.

"Oh, sorry, Colonel, of course … my man," Goldstein replied after a few seconds had passed. "We're on a secure line but let's refer to said man as 'MG'."

"Well," Bilyk said, "MG is not happy being cooped up in a safe house here in Kyiv and is desperately worried that the longer he is away from his place of work, if you see what I'm getting at, the less likely he will be able to return. He has a plan in his head but he doesn't trust us, and to be honest, we don't trust him. As you know, we are where we are with him because we are doing you a favour. He won't talk to us about his plan until he has spoken to a representative of your service. Actually, that's not strictly accurate. He wants to talk face-to-face with someone from your British counterparts."

"Have you spoken to the British?" Goldstein asked.

"I will do, but I wanted to test the waters with you first," the colonel said.

"So what exactly is he saying?" Goldstein queried.

"I have only spoken briefly to him," Bilyk said, "but he was adamant he feels he is in danger staying here and waiting for word from Moscow about a potential prisoner swap. He is worried Putin won't bite and will leave him to rot, although I hasten to add he is being well looked after, three meals a day, but obviously he can't leave the safe house, and he is getting frustrated and angry. We can't let this go on for months. If Putin makes no offer, the press here will start asking questions about what we're doing with him. They will want to know why we aren't extraditing him to the UK, as agreed with London. We can put off the press, but how will this be interpreted in Moscow? They will start to get suspicious, don't you think?"

"What's his plan, then?" Goldstein asked.

"He won't say until he has spoken to the British," Bilyk said. "To be frank with you, we want him off our hands, and the sooner the better. So I'm going to ask the British to send someone to us and we'll arrange a meet. As I said, the sooner the better. I assume you go along with this?"

"Yes. Ring Geraldine Hammer, although it's late in London," Goldstein replied.

It was well after midnight in London when Geraldine's mobile rang. She answered after two rings.

Colonel Bilyk told her of his problem.

Geraldine thanked him. She then rang Patrick Littlefield and received his approval for her proposal.

Forty-five minutes after midnight, Geraldine made a call to MI5's newest part-time recruit.

Having been fast asleep in her flat, Rebecca answered the phone with an expletive.

"Rebecca, it's Geraldine; sorry for the late hour but I have another job for you."

CHAPTER TWENTY-TWO
REBECCA'S MOST DARING MISSION

Grace Redmayne went straight to Geraldine the following morning.

"Geraldine, I strongly advise against sending Rebecca to Kyiv," she said. "What this mission needs is an experienced intelligence officer who knows how to operate in a dangerous environment. Rebecca, I agree, has some excellent qualities, but she is not trained for this sort of mission. It would be too risky for her and could be disastrous for our Redruth operation."

Geraldine had been expecting her deputy to be opposed.

"Look, I know you are not a fan of Rebecca's, or at least not much of a fan," Geraldine said, "but for this mission, I firmly believe she is the only one Redruth will want to see. She has good intuition and common sense, and Redruth trusts her."

Grace wasn't convinced. "But she cannot be expected to make decisions on the hoof, like a properly trained intelligence officer. I think it's foolhardy."

"I've discussed it with Patrick, and he has approved," Geraldine said.

Grace looked astonished. "Surely he raised all the same reservations?"

"Yes, he did," Geraldine said, "but I persuaded him, just as I hope to persuade you, to back me. Rebecca won't be required to make operational decisions. She'll listen to what Redruth has to say and return to London. All decisions will be made in London, in collaboration with Langley."

Before Grace could answer, Geraldine said, "There's one other thing I haven't told you. I have asked Sam to go with her to be her bodyguard."

Sam Cook had all the qualities Grace had been talking about for a mission of this type. *His years in the SAS, serving all over the world, make him the ideal person to protect Rebecca*, Grace admitted to herself. It was an inspired choice, even though on the surface Grace thought it seemed somewhat irregular for the director of counter-espionage to recruit the man she was having a relationship with to participate in the secret mission.

Sam Cook's qualifications for the job were unrivalled. During his twenty years in the SAS, he had been the personal bodyguard to one of the Special Air Service's most renowned directors of special forces.

He also knew Rebecca and Gerasimov. He had been attached to a paramilitary force used by the government during the crazy few weeks the previous year when Gerasimov caused mayhem in London. Sam and his colleagues provided protection for Rebecca in the final days of the drama.

Grace stood up to leave Geraldine's office. "I guess that's your masterstroke, Geraldine," she said, not very graciously. "Is that why Patrick approved?"

"It certainly seemed to help," Geraldine replied. "Don't be angry with me, Grace. I know it's unusual but my instincts tell me this is the right thing to do."

"Well, I just hope she comes to no harm," Grace said. "Kyiv is not Venice."

Grace left the room.

***

Rebecca was excited but apprehensive. When she was told Sam would be with her at all times, most of her nerves left her. He was a lovable giant and she knew she could trust him to be her protector, whatever happened in Kyiv. She had wondered whether she would be allowed to see Sandy while she was there, but Geraldine had warned her that the mission was highly sensitive and top secret. There would be no time or opportunity for seeking out her boyfriend.

"So, I'm going to Kyiv with your boyfriend but I can't see mine," Rebecca had quipped when Geraldine outlined her mission.

Geraldine had snorted. "Your boyfriend is a TV reporter. You even hint at what you're doing in Kyiv and he won't be able to resist doing a story," she said.

***

Rebecca and her bodyguard were on the night train from Warsaw to Kyiv. She couldn't believe she was back in Poland so soon after the Warsaw detective had warned her not to return.

She and Sam were sharing sleeping quarters, at his insistence. Rebecca was tempted to make a joke about seeking Geraldine's permission but decided against it. This was a crucial assignment and Sam had made it clear he didn't want her ever to be out of his sight. Rebecca had brought pyjamas but decided to sleep in her clothes. Sam did the same. The journey went without mishap.

Rebecca loved the romance of overnight sleeper trains. As she tried to sleep, she thought about planning a trip with Sandy when he returned from Ukraine, although she realised that her life was no longer her own, or at least, not as it used to be. She had always relished her independence and even with a permanent boyfriend she had felt she was in control of her life. Sandy was crazy about her and generally agreed to anything she suggested. But now, Geraldine could ring her late at night and order her to catch a train to Kyiv at short notice. The disruption to her normal life had been unexpected and exciting, and she had grabbed the opportunity to be a part-time secret agent. But as she lay in her top bunk, dressed in jeans and a blue jumper, she still couldn't quite register how her life had been so dramatically transformed.

A sudden gurgling snore from the bunk underneath jolted her from her drowsiness. In a few hours, she would be arriving in Kyiv. She hadn't even had time to google the Ukrainian city. Nor had she had time to think of the potential danger she might face in Kyiv. Above all, she didn't look forward to meeting Mikhail Gerasimov again. She had hoped her trip to Venice with him would be the last time they had to meet face-to-face. As her eyes closed again, she thought of Venice and the gondola ride with Gerasimov. It seemed a long time ago. Now here she was, hours away from meeting up with him once again, but in very different circumstances.

Rebecca and Sam emerged from Kyiv-Pasazhyrskyi railway station at 6:40 a.m., each carrying a knapsack. Rebecca looked around, expecting to see a devastated city, but none of the buildings in front of her were damaged and she could see a golden spire in the distance. It was a city at war, but also a city alive with people going about their normal business. Rebecca was confused but relieved. Sam looked at her and knew what she was thinking.

"It's often like this, war zones," he said. "There'll be parts of the city that have suffered shell and missile strikes, but life goes on. That's the way it is."

Two black SUVs were waiting for them. The lead car flashed its lights. Sam took Rebecca's elbow and guided her towards the vehicles. They both climbed into the back of the first car and it moved off immediately. The second followed close behind. As they drove quickly through the streets of the city, Rebecca peered through the darkened windows, hoping she might catch sight of Sandy.

She would have loved to have tipped him off that she was coming to Kyiv. She missed him. It seemed crazy that she couldn't spend just a few hours with him. It was a golden opportunity. But then she realised she would have to tell Sam, and he would insist on being by her side at all times. This trip was to be strictly professional.

As the driver took them out of the centre of Kyiv, Rebecca gave up looking for Sandy but continued staring out of the window, spotting more and more damaged buildings. Round one corner, there were three fire engines with their crews hosing down the smoking ruins of a six-storey office block. The driver said there had been a Russian cruise missile attack overnight. For reasons he couldn't explain, the city's air defence systems had failed to bring it down. The driver said the building was empty and had no military value.

They drove for forty-five minutes, by which time they were on the outskirts of the city. It was a residential area. The driver said they were in a district formerly used by heads of diplomatic missions. Many of the residences were empty. There was little sign of war damage. The two-car convoy stopped outside a residence with high steel gates. The driver made a phone call and the gates began to open slowly. The two vehicles swept through and drove up to a large house with wisteria vines creeping across the front. Rebecca and Sam got out of their car and were ushered by the driver through the front door, which had been opened as soon as they arrived at the gate. They were told to wait in the hall.

"This is so weird," Rebecca said.

"Being here, or seeing Gerasimov again?" Sam asked.

"Both, I guess," Rebecca replied. "Are you going to sit with me when I see him?"

"Yes," Sam said. "As I told you, I'm not letting you out of my sight."

"How sweet," she replied.

"That's my orders."

"Oh, so not so sweet."

Sam laughed.

"I'm here to protect you, Rebecca, sweet or not."

"Are you armed?"

"Not as such."

"What does that mean?"

"If I need to be armed, I will be."

"Gerasimov's not going to hurt me."

"No, which is why I'm not currently armed."

"I'm glad you're with me, Sam."

"My pleasure."

"Really?"

"Of course."

The driver came back into the hall. He was now carrying an Uzi machine pistol.

"Follow me," he said.

They walked round behind the stairs to a room at the back of the house. The driver opened the door and beckoned them in.

Gerasimov was standing by a window overlooking a long stretch of lawn. He turned and smiled when he saw Rebecca and nodded at Sam. The last and only time he had seen Sam was when he and his Russian accomplice had been escorted under arrest by three SAS soldiers out of Geraldine's home in London. Sam, a fluent Russian speaker, had been the crisis negotiator. The big man was unforgettable.

Gerasimov came forward to give Rebecca a brief embrace. He shook Sam's hand.

"So, Rebecca, I asked for someone from British intelligence and I get you," he said with a smile. "Have you given up painting for spying?"

Rebecca stepped away from him. He had lost weight. His face, always so square-shaped and prominent, seemed thinner. He was wearing casual, dark-blue trousers and a sweater with a zip down the front.

"You look wonderful, as ever," he said.

"I'm just a messenger," Rebecca replied after a few moments. "You look thin. Aren't they feeding you?"

"I'm eating fine, thank you." Gerasimov laughed. "So, this is like Venice, right? I tell you what I want and you take the message back to London?"

"Something like that," Rebecca replied.

Sam intervened. "Colonel, I don't want to interrupt but we are here for a very short time. We need to get down to business and then we're out of here."

"What, you're not staying the night? A quiet evening over dinner?" Gerasimov said, smiling sarcastically.

"Mikhail, I'm afraid Sam's right," Rebecca said. "Where can we go to talk? Is this room secure?"

"I see your boyfriend is in Kyiv, causing quite a fuss with his scoops," Gerasimov went on, ignoring Rebecca's questions.

"Colonel, shall we?" Sam said, looking at his watch. It was 8 a.m. He wanted to leave the house in two hours.

The driver with the Uzi had left the room and closed the door. Gerasimov pointed to two armchairs in the right-hand corner of the room and raised his eyebrows at Rebecca. As they sat down, Sam remained standing.

Rebecca started. "As I said, I'm only a messenger, but I've been told enough to understand that you're not happy with being stuck here and waiting for Moscow to react. If you have an alternative idea, I promise I will take it back with me and let them know."

"But will you be my advocate, as well as my messenger?" Gerasimov asked.

Rebecca thought for a few seconds. "That depends on what you tell me."

"Very good answer," Gerasimov said. "You will make a good spy, Rebecca."

"So, tell me, and we will do our best to meet your request," Rebecca said and immediately felt embarrassed. She saw Gerasimov look at her with a smile on his face.

"Just a messenger, eh?" he said. "Sounds like you're in charge, Rebecca."

"Sorry, I spoke a bit out of turn," Rebecca replied. "What I meant was that you can trust me to explain what you need when I get back to London."

Gerasimov laughed. "Don't worry, Rebecca, I was just joking," he said. "But let's get down to it."

He glanced at Sam, towering over the two of them.

"Just ignore me, Colonel," Sam said. "I'll stay here, if that's all right with you. I don't have any role other than protecting Rebecca."

Gerasimov nodded and then turned back to Rebecca.

"The problem with the grand plan your people have come up with is that it depends on Putin playing ball, and I'm pretty sure he won't," he said. "If I have to stay here for much longer, it's going to drive me mad, but it would also lay me open to other dangers. I'm told by my Ukrainian protectors that the local media are pestering the government to say where I am and what's going to happen to me. I'm also worried about where the FSB are with their investigation into the Sevastopol incident."

Gerasimov knew nothing about Major Kozlov and his pursuit of Rebecca. Geraldine had told Rebecca to say nothing about it, so she kept quiet when he started referring to the potential risks ahead. Geraldine had warned her that if he knew an FSB officer had been arrested in Poland while investigating links between her and Gerasimov, she might as well axe Operation Greengage and give up any idea of having an intelligence asset inside the Kremlin because he would demand to be flown straight to the UK for his own safety.

After signing the Official Secrets Act, Rebecca had been brought up to date with everything she needed to know about Operation Greengage. She knew that it was Gerasimov, Agent Redruth, who had tipped off the British about Putin's planned trip to Sevastopol. Rebecca realised that she was one of only a few people who had been given this information, although Sandy had speculated about a Kremlin leak in his story from Kyiv. It made her shudder to think what Kozlov might have done to her to extract this secret if she hadn't engineered his arrest at Warsaw airport before he could get his hands on her.

"All my training has been about taking bold decisions," Gerasimov continued, "so rather than waiting around here for something to happen in Moscow, I need to confront the situation. It needs to be me who makes the first move."

"Like what?" Rebecca asked him.

"I need to get out of here and make my way to Russian-occupied territory in eastern Ukraine and present myself as the hero who carried out a sensational escape," Gerasimov said. "Any doubts about me in the FSB will be brushed aside."

"Smart, but risky," Sam said quietly.

"Haven't you done smart-but-risky in your career?" Gerasimov asked him.

"Sure, many times," Sam said.

"But how on earth are you going to escape from here and get to where you need to be? Won't it be impossible to go through all the Ukrainian lines and reach the Russian side?" Rebecca asked. "I shall get asked the same questions in London. What do I tell them?"

"My plan is to get to Zaporizhzhia in the south-east," Gerasimov said. "It's about five hundred and fifty kilometres. I know the area; I was there in 2018 for a GRU operation. To get from here to there, I will need help. Your help."

"We've got no one here," Sam said. "A few special forces guys at the embassy, but they can't be taken away from their duties. A few vehicles, and that's about it. The Americans have more personnel, a lot more, but they won't want to risk putting any of them out in the field. The White House would never approve. The Brits would be the same."

"That's why I said I will need *your* help," Gerasimov said bluntly.

Sam looked confused.

"What, Sam and me, you mean?" Rebecca asked. "There's nothing we can do, is there?"

Gerasimov stood up.

"You may be early in your new career, Rebecca, but in our business we do what we have to do, when we have to do it," he said.

"Seriously, Colonel," Sam interrupted, "we've just come to hear what you're worried about and then we go back to London. There's nothing we can do here, and I certainly don't want to involve Rebecca in anything dangerous."

Gerasimov looked down at Rebecca. "And I always thought you were a tough cookie, as you like to say in the UK," he said, without a hint of humour. "Well, I'm afraid you have no choice. I've made up my mind. I'm getting out of here in the next forty-eight hours, with or without your help. I've done little else but plan for this over the last few weeks. But there are certain things I can't do, which is why I need your help."

Rebecca and Sam were shocked at the way Gerasimov's voice had suddenly changed. He was no longer the man Rebecca had shared a gondola and a bed with. This was Colonel Mikhail Gerasimov, ruthless GRU intelligence officer. But also the man prepared to be a long-term, risk-taking double agent working secretly for British intelligence from inside the Kremlin.

Rebecca knew how much Geraldine wanted her prize asset to take up his secret assignment once again, but Gerasimov's ultimatum potentially would put all that at risk. Geraldine wanted him to wait until Putin officially requested a prisoner swap. So how was she going to react when she heard of his crazy new plan?

Rebecca was a novice. She had no idea how to meet this challenge. She knew she couldn't just ring Geraldine on her mobile and tell her what Gerasimov had said. But if she didn't let Geraldine know about the dramatically changed circumstances, she would never be forgiven. In fact, her brief espionage career would come to an abrupt end.

Sam asked Gerasimov exactly what he had in mind. Gerasimov sat down again.

"I will have the Russian end sorted out," he replied, "so when I'm near Russian defence lines, they will come and get me. That won't be a problem. But this end is where I need your help. I have to physically break out of here, which won't be too much of a challenge because I'm not a prisoner. But I need you to contact Colonel Bilyk, the head of Ukrainian intelligence who arranged for me to be here. He has to smooth my path from Kyiv to the Russian frontline."

Sam looked exasperated. He had no idea how to get in touch with this Colonel Bilyk and was about to say as much when Gerasimov continued.

"I want to break out of here, but I need Colonel Bilyk to know that I'm doing it and why," he said. "Provided he goes along with it, and I think he will, then he can make sure we don't get stopped on the road to the Russian defence lines."

"We?" Sam asked.

"Yes, you're coming with me," Gerasimov said, "to guarantee my survival. Kyiv will have a lot of explaining to do if two British nationals, one of them a woman, get killed."

Rebecca jumped up. "Mikhail, I always thought deep down you were a total bastard. There's no way Sam and I are going to go with you to the bloody Russian frontline," she shouted.

"Calm down, calm down," Gerasimov said. "You won't have to go that far. I will fix it so that you can drop me off at night within a mile or so of the Russian defences, and they will be waiting for me. You can then turn around and head back to Kyiv."

"I've done some crazy stuff in my life, Colonel," Sam said, "but this plan is full of holes. And it's far too risky, and not just for us. This Colonel Bilyk may be head of intelligence but he doesn't command the troops fighting your lot out there. And where are you going to get a vehicle?"

"That's another of your tasks," Gerasimov said.

Sam stood in front of him. "Spell it out, Colonel, so we know the full package of demands you're making."

"OK, so we will need a vehicle, hired for two days," Gerasimov said. "Plus, I need a phone and a strong torch. You have less than two days to get it done. Tell Colonel Bilyk I'll be out of here at 10 p.m. in two days, that's Friday. You will need to bring the vehicle somewhere close to the gates by or before that time and wait for me. As long as everything goes to plan, you could be back in Kyiv by late afternoon Saturday. You should bring food and water, but don't worry about me."

"What if we fail to get hold of Colonel Bilyk?" Sam asked. "It's a long way and we could run into all sorts of trouble. I can't put Rebecca into that sort of crazy danger."

"I think we might be able to fix the Bilyk end of things," Rebecca said.

Sam looked surprised. Gerasimov smiled.

"You see, she *is* going to make a good spy. Positive and bold, that's what you need to be." Gerasimov stood up again. "Let's not waste any more time. You have two days to sort everything out and I'll see you outside the gates at 10 p.m. Friday."

"Just so you know," Sam said, "there's very little likelihood we'll get authority from London to be involved in this caper of yours. We can't just say, OK, fine. We will have to consult London, and if they say no, you're on your own."

"If they say no, then I say no to working for your intelligence services," Gerasimov said. "It's as simple as that."

He went to give Rebecca a hug, but she turned away. She and Sam left the room and went to look for the driver. Instead of the original plan, which was to be driven straight back to the railway station for the long journey home, they now potentially had to find a hotel for two nights, hunt down Colonel Bilyk and rent a vehicle, but most importantly they had to inform Geraldine of what was going on. Both Sam and Rebecca were sure Geraldine would never give her authority for the crazy plan.

They found two rooms in the Sophia Hotel in Sofiivska Street, in the old part of Kyiv, and asked the driver to drop them off there.

Sam said they had to ring Geraldine.

"We can't do it on our phones, it's not secure," he said. "We'll go to the British embassy."

Fortunately, Rebecca had been issued with a temporary Security Service pass for the assignment. Sam had a military pass, as a reservist with the SAS. The embassy had no idea they were in Kyiv, but Sam hoped their official passes would be sufficient for them to be granted access to the core area of the building, from where they could make a secure call to London.

It was less than a mile to the embassy, situated at number 9 Desyatynna Street, right opposite the Ukrainian ministry of foreign affairs.

They had decided to walk, although Rebecca was petrified at the thought of bumping into Sandy – the possibility of a Russian missile strike as they walked didn't even enter her head. When they left the hotel, there were plenty of people on the street, but Rebecca noticed all of them seemed to be in a hurry.

The embassy was an imposing building, painted in lime green which had faded over the years. Security barriers were set up outside the entrance and piles of sandbags, some of which looked as if they needed to be replaced, rested against the walls and around the front door.

Their security passes worked, but when the ambassador himself came through to speak to them he expressed astonishment that he had not been warned of their trip to Kyiv. Jeremy Brigstock looked harassed and weather-beaten. He was quite short, with tufts of greying hair on either side of a bald head, and seemed overwhelmed by the combination of the tall, sexy-looking blonde with an MI5 pass and the hugely built man from the SAS. When they asked to make a call to London from the secure communications room, he took them there personally. His questions about their reasons for being in Kyiv were answered with polite but vacuous replies.

The ambassador lingered in the room when Rebecca began dialling Geraldine's number, and Sam had to ask him to leave. He looked put out but left the room with a heavy sigh.

It took ten minutes to make contact with Geraldine. Her assistant had to get her out of a meeting.

After Rebecca had outlined Agent Redruth's demands, with the speaker on so Sam could hear, Geraldine was apoplectic. She admitted she was concerned that Putin had still made no move to negotiate Gerasimov's transfer to Moscow, but escaping from Kyiv and expecting to be met with open arms when he arrived back in Russia seemed to Geraldine to be too much of a stretch. It was bold and daring, but hopelessly unrealistic.

"And furthermore, you are hardly out of your nappies in this espionage business, Rebecca, if you don't mind me saying so, and this whole scheme is wildly dangerous," Geraldine said. "I would never forgive myself if you were to get hurt. And Sam too, of course."

Rebecca looked at Sam, who was sitting next to her. He took the phone. As they'd walked together to the embassy, they had both begun to wonder whether Gerasimov's plan might, after all, be possible. Rebecca had reminded Sam of Gerasimov's final threat: help him escape or give up any idea of having a secret double agent in the Kremlin.

"I agree with everything you said, Geraldine," Sam said now. "Hello, by the way. But hear me out."

"Hello, Sam. Please don't try to change my mind, I don't want to be responsible for sending you into harm's way," Geraldine replied. "You'll have to tell Redruth he must be patient. Putin could still come up trumps."

"Geraldine, I'm used to being in harm's way and I can look after myself, and Rebecca," he said in a soft voice. "I have to tell you he is adamant about leaving, with or without us, but he argued he has a better chance of success with us. Provided we get the sureties from Colonel Bilyk, and Gerasimov gets the same from his Russian pals, the risks will be significantly reduced. As for the other end, that's entirely up to Gerasimov. If he thinks there's a good chance he will be welcomed back and treated as a hero, then we all win. Of course there's a risk it could all go wrong. No one knows what Putin is thinking from day to day. He might welcome him, then lock him up. At least by making a heroic escape from his Ukrainian captors, Gerasimov might lengthen the odds of him being detained and put on trial, or worse."

There was silence at the other end. Rebecca grabbed the phone.

"I agree with Sam," she said. "With Sam looking after me, I'm prepared to go ahead with it. It could work, so it's worth trying, right?"

Rebecca and Sam waited for Geraldine to reply. A full two minutes went by.

"I can't see our cousins over the water agreeing to any of this," she said eventually. "To be honest with you, Rebecca, they've been highly sceptical of your role from the very beginning. But this is our operation, so I could ring Bilyk and see what he says."

"Remember, Geraldine, you gave me Bilyk's number when you arranged for Sandy to interview him over the assassination plot in Kyiv," Rebecca said, "so I could ring him myself. He presumably has been told of your plan to send me and Sam to Kyiv, so it won't be a surprise if I ring him."

"Yes, he knows," Geraldine replied, "but that was before this ridiculous plan of Redruth's to escape back to Moscow."

"But if I get hold of Bilyk and he agrees, then will you let us go for the escape plan?"

"With huge reluctance," Geraldine replied.

Rebecca gave a thumbs up to Sam, and they both grinned.

When they got back to their hotel, Rebecca and Sam went to her room. She found Colonel Bilyk's number in her contacts and rang.

He answered immediately.

They spoke for five minutes.

When the conversation was finished, Rebecca turned to Sam, who was standing the other side of the bed, and nodded.

"He was charming," Rebecca said. "He said it would be a relief to be rid of the Russian and wished me good luck."

"Right, well done, let's go get us a vehicle," Sam said.

CHAPTER TWENTY-THREE
THE ESCAPE BEGINS

With the help of the hotel concierge, Sam was given the address of a garage in a district on the left bank of the Dnieper River, which ran through the centre of the capital. They took a taxi and found the garage, whose name, roughly translated from Ukrainian, was "Mixed Motors". It was squeezed between a laundrette and a flower shop. Sam and Rebecca walked into the premises. No one was around, so Rebecca called out. A young man in overalls that seemed too big for him, with spiky fair hair and bright blue eyes, appeared. He looked at his two visitors with astonishment and said something in Ukrainian.

"Sorry, we're English," Rebecca said.

The young man grinned.

"Well, I didn't think you were locals," he said, in English with an American accent.

"Bloody hell," said Rebecca, "so you're not a local either?"

He laughed and put out his hand. Rebecca and then Sam did likewise.

"I'm James McShaffer Junior, but everyone calls me Pinenut," he replied. "Mum's Ukrainian and lives with me here, and my dad's from Texas. He skipped off some years ago."

"Nice to meet you, James," Rebecca said.

"Pinenut, please," he said and then laughed again. "Funny, your first two words to me were also my first two words to you."

"Sorry?"

"Bloody hell."

"You said bloody hell in Ukrainian?"

"Yep, when you two walked in like off a Hollywood film set."

They all laughed.

"Anyway, what can I do for you?" Pinenut asked.

Sam said, "We need a vehicle, a strong one, maybe a Land Rover type or something like that."

"Where you off to?" Pinenut asked.

"It's just for a couple of days," Sam said, without answering his question.

"I don't want to pry," Pinenut said, "but since the war, very few people come in here to hire a vehicle for a couple of days just to drive around the city. If you're planning on being more adventurous, like going out beyond the city limits, you're not going to get far, Hollywood glamour couple though you may be."

Rebecca glanced at Sam, who shook his head. But her intuition was working overtime. She liked the guy called Pinenut.

"We're planning on driving quite a long way out of the city, Pinenut," Rebecca said. "Why are you called 'Pinenut', by the way?"

"As a child, that's all I ate," he replied.

They all laughed again.

"Look, you don't know me and you have no reason to trust me," Pinenut said, "but, basically, I'm a Texan at heart and I also love this country. So I'm an odd combination, just like you two are. Oh, and one thing you should know is that I get around a lot and anyone who is anyone in this city knows me."

Rebecca looked at Sam again; he didn't shake his head this time.

"Pinenut, to be honest with you, we need a vehicle to go several hundred miles out of the city, towards the Russian lines but not as far as that," Rebecca said.

"What are you, reporters or something?" Pinenut asked.

"More something than reporters," Rebecca said.

Pinenut cackled.

"Goldilocks and the Big Bear," he said and burst out laughing. Rebecca and Sam both roared with laughter.

"Seriously though, Goldilocks," Pinenut said, "I can give you a good vehicle, but between here and wherever you're going there will be dozens of checkpoints. Your good looks will get you through some of them but there are plenty of bastards, sorry for the language, who will demand a helluva lot more than a pretty smile."

Sam stepped forward. "What are you suggesting?"

"I'll come with you. I'll drive," Pinenut replied.

Both Sam and Rebecca were about to say "thank you, but no" when he quickly added: "I assume neither of you speaks the language, so you'll need me. I can scam us through the checkpoints. Most of them will know me anyway."

Neither Sam nor Rebecca could come up with an answer. Each knew it was out of the question, but on the other hand it seemed like an invitation that couldn't be turned down. Even with Colonel Bilyk's pledge to ensure them a safe passage, they had no idea whether he had the power to make their trip to the Russian defensive lines safe for them. Nor did they know for sure whether he would actually do anything at all to help them. They might find that at the first checkpoint they would be stopped and prevented from going any further. The worst scenario would be if they came across a hostile Ukrainian checkpoint where the guards insisted on interrogating all the passengers. Gerasimov's presence would be instantly suspicious. Bilyk was one of the very limited number of people connected to the Kyiv government who knew about the Russian, who he really was and the double role he had played in the assassination attempt on Zelensky. There was no way any military checkpoint could have been warned of the sensitivities surrounding his presence in Kyiv. So, if Gerasimov was discovered and questioned, it would be bad news for all of them. Could a wisecracking Ukrainian/Texan called Pinenut make the difference between success and disastrous failure?

"Unless, of course, you're planning to do something illegal or criminal?" Pinenut said, as his two visitors stumbled over how to react to his offer to be their driver.

"No, no," Rebecca replied, aware she sounded unconvincing.

"I think we'll have to think about your kind offer," Sam intervened. "Perhaps if you show us a suitable vehicle, we'll decide one way or the other."

Pinenut grinned and pointed to a car in the far corner of the garage. It was a dark grey, five-seater Skoda station wagon.

"I don't have any Land Rovers, but wherever you're going, this is a strong car, and reliable," Pinenut said, "and I love driving it."

Rebecca smiled. She really liked this guy. He was determined to be their driver and she knew he would be good company.

They went to look at the Skoda. Sam behaved like he was going to buy it, examining the tyres and checking the upholstery.

"You can have it for twelve thousand dollars," Pinenut said with a laugh. "Renting for two days, it will be two hundred dollars cash, plus the diesel. I'll arrange insurance, that'll be another hundred dollars if you're driving, but nothing if I drive."

Rebecca had made up her mind even if Sam hadn't. She wanted Pinenut in the driving seat. She was in a tricky situation with Sam. They were working together but technically she was acting as the lead, assigned by Geraldine as the official MI5 representative, while Sam was there to protect her and keep her out of danger. He didn't work for MI5, but as a retired and legendary member of the SAS he had all the security clearances required. She was thirty-eight and an artist. He was fifty-one and a veteran of scores of highly classified special forces missions around the world. But Rebecca knew that Geraldine trusted her intuition. And Pinenut seemed to her to be a godsend.

However, how were they going to explain to Pinenut that they needed first to drive to a Ukrainian government safe house in the diplomatic district, wait there for a large man to climb over the wall, take him 340 miles or so down the road leading to the

Russian lines, drop him off, turn around and head back to Kyiv? She had promised there would be nothing illegal, but pretty much everything they planned to do could be described as dodgy – extremely dodgy.

Rebecca nodded to Sam. He had the cash.

He handed Pinenut three hundred dollars. "We'll take the Skoda, thanks," he said.

"So you want insurance?" Pinenut asked.

"We'll need to share the driving; it's quite a long way," Sam said.

"Come into the office and I'll get you to sign the paperwork," Pinenut said. "Do you want it straightaway?"

"No, two days' time," Sam replied.

"And we'll pay you to be our driver for part of the journey," Rebecca said, raising her eyebrows at Sam.

"Don't worry about that," Pinenut replied. "It sounds like an adventure and it gets me away from doing not a lot here."

Sam signed the papers and, after seeming to hesitate, went ahead with telling their new friend what had been worrying them.

"Pinenut, you're a good guy, and finding a bloke from Texas right here in Kyiv is a bloody miracle," Sam said. "But we have to warn you that what we're planning to do with your vehicle is somewhat out of the ordinary."

"Well, I guessed as much," Pinenut said, grinning all over his face. "Anyway, there's a war on, nothing is ordinary here, so if I can help, that's good with me."

"And, just so you know," Sam went on, "we'll be picking up another person for the trip."

Pinenut shrugged. "There's plenty of room for four in the Skoda," he said, "provided he or she is not as big as you."

They all laughed.

"He's not as skinny as you, Pinenut, if you don't mind me saying so," Sam said, "but he'll fit in fine, and no, he's not as big as me."

"No one is," Rebecca chipped in.

Pinenut snorted. He asked them what time they wanted the car in two days.

"Could you pick us up at the Sophia Hotel at 9 p.m. on Friday?" Sam replied.

"I'll be there," Pinenut said. "And back the following day? If so, you only need to hire the car for twenty-four hours."

"Hiring for the two days is fine, thank you," Sam said. "Gives us leeway."

"In case something goes wrong," Pinenut said. It wasn't a question.

"Just to be on the safe side," Sam said.

They all shook hands. Sam and Rebecca started to leave, but Rebecca turned back and gave Pinenut a hug.

"Bloody hell, Goldilocks," Pinenut spluttered.

Rebecca laughed and waved goodbye.

***

Friday, 9:30 p.m.

The Skoda station wagon was parked down the road from the large residence with the high front gate. From where they were parked, neither the house nor the front gate was visible. There was no sign of the moon because of thick cloud. With few lights on in the city, there was an intense darkness. There was a light on in the house, but the passengers in the Skoda couldn't see it. There was also total silence inside the car. Rebecca felt incredibly tense and nervous, but when she looked at Sam, sitting in the front passenger seat, he appeared to be calm. Pinenut kept glancing in the mirror at Rebecca. Otherwise, he too seemed relaxed, even though he had no idea who the fourth passenger was going to be and where he was coming from.

As the time approached the ten o'clock deadline, Rebecca was so anxious she leant forward and whispered into Sam's ear, "I have to pee."

"Go for it, there's no one around," he whispered back.

Pinenut heard and grinned. "Go pee, Goldilocks," he said.

Rebecca looked at her watch: there were three minutes to go. She slipped out of the car and ran to the back. She looked around. No one was visible. She was back in the car just before ten o'clock. They had another ten minutes to wait. Then suddenly Gerasimov was walking towards them. Sam told Pinenut to flash the lights once. Gerasimov opened the rear door and climbed in next to Rebecca without saying a word.

"Michael, hi," Rebecca said quietly, deliberately avoiding using the Russian pronunciation of the name. "Meet Pinenut."

Pinenut swivelled round and nodded at Gerasimov. Then he put the car in gear and drove off.

Rebecca and Sam had spent the previous twenty-four hours finalising the escape plan. They bought a phone and torch for Gerasimov, and food for the journey there and back. Most importantly, Rebecca rang Colonel Bilyk again and gave him the make of car and registration and asked him to provide a signed document that they could show at checkpoints. Bilyk had begun by calling her "Ms Strong" but by the end of the conversation he became quite chatty and referred to her as "Rebecca". He had warmed to her and suggested at one point that if she ever wanted a tour of the intelligence ministry she should give him a call. She promised she would. The smitten colonel said he would have the document she needed delivered to her hotel within the hour.

Rebecca had given the intelligence service document to Pinenut. He had looked impressed.

The presence of Pinenut in the driver's seat and the Bilyk document certainly impressed the first checkpoint they reached on the outskirts of Kyiv. The soldier who demanded to know where they were going at such a late hour and shone his torch inside the car softened his voice when he saw Pinenut.

Pinenut gave the explanation he had rehearsed with Sam: they were driving towards the frontline town of Orikhiv in the Zaporizhzhia region; Rebecca Strong, in the back, was a journalist with the *Financial Times* of London and was covering a story about families living near the Russian-occupied Zaporizhzhia nuclear power plant; the two other passengers were her bodyguards; they were travelling overnight, hoping to avoid Russian artillery strikes. The guard at the first checkpoint wished them luck and waved them on.

"Well done, Pinenut," Sam said, "worked well."

Gerasimov was busy with the phone he had been given. As the car left the capital, he sent a text to General Ivan Golubev, deputy commander of the GRU military intelligence service, whom he had known and worked under for many years before he moved to the new appointment at the Kremlin.

"General, I have escaped from my hated captors and am making my way to Zaporizhzhia. Provided there are no problems, I should be within a mile of the Russian frontline in about seven hours. As a special favour, could you arrange for me to be picked up at around 6 a.m. tomorrow (Saturday). By then I'll be close to the frontlines. I shall flash my torch five times every half hour. I will keep my phone on for tracking. I will be alone, no vehicle, and concealed. Gerasimov."

"Any second thoughts before it's too late?" Rebecca asked him.

"No," he replied.

But he sounded tense. He was taking a huge gamble. He hadn't spoken to General Golubev for a long time and had no way of knowing whether he bothered to check his texts late in the evening or whether he would order a Spetsnaz team to rescue him. He was also thinking of Natasha and his kids. He was desperate to know whether they were all right. Even if it all went ahead as he hoped, he had no idea how he would be received if he made it back to Moscow. Or, indeed, whether he would ever be given back his job working for the Security Council in the Kremlin. It was more likely that he would be the shortest-lived British intelligence double agent in the history of espionage.

To relieve the tension in the car, Pinenut started to chat about his life since the Russians invaded Ukraine. He said nothing compared with the first few days of the invasion when Russian troops attempted but failed to seize control of Kyiv.

"My mother was petrified, she knows how brutal Russian soldiers can be when they are in occupying mood, and for that I will never forgive them."

Rebecca peered at Gerasimov, but either he wasn't listening or he chose not to react. As Pinenut prattled on, there was a ping from Gerasimov's pocket. He took out his phone and looked at the message on the screen.

"Arranged. Golubev."

Gerasimov had hoped for more from his former superior commander, something to indicate how his text for help had been received in Moscow. But the one-word message from the general was reassuring. Provided the annoyingly talkative driver succeeded in getting them through all the checkpoints, Gerasimov felt he had a reasonable chance of reaching the Russian-occupied zone. He felt fairly confident that as long as they got to within a mile or so of the Russian lines by car, without being fired on or detained at a checkpoint, he would be able to use the cover of darkness to walk the final stretch before being picked up. But that would be the most dangerous phase of his escape. Heavily defended Ukrainian frontlines would be his main obstacle. If the designated Spetsnaz commandos had to venture too far out of the Russian lines, they would never reach him, and by daylight he would be an easy target. Rebecca had told him about the authorisation signed by Colonel Bilyk and it was clear from Pinenut's exchanges with checkpoint guards so far that the document was like a passport to travel. But Gerasimov feared that the further away they were from Kyiv, the less likely the Bilyk document would guarantee them safe passage.

After three hours on the road and five checkpoints negotiated, Sam insisted on taking over the driving to give Pinenut a rest. Pinenut objected but didn't argue for long with the man who was twice his size. Rebecca had fallen asleep with her head resting on

Gerasimov's shoulder. Gerasimov remained wide awake. Pinenut stayed awake for an hour in the front passenger seat but then nodded off. They had 150 miles to go before the drop-off point.

At 4:30 a.m., the Skoda braked to a sharp stop. The rear tyres screeched. Pinenut and Rebecca woke and lurched forward at the same time. Standing a few feet from the front of the car were three soldiers, pointing guns at the windscreen and shouting.

Pinenut climbed out quickly with his hands raised and greeted the soldiers. Sam, Rebecca and Gerasimov peered through the windscreen, trying to work out what was going on. With the headlights fully on, they could see the soldiers gesticulating and pointing at the car. Pinenut came back to the car, reached inside and grabbed the authorisation document. He returned to the soldiers and handed it to them. They seemed satisfied but continued talking to Pinenut. The three others saw Pinenut shake each of their hands and turn back to the car. The three soldiers left the road.

"Let's go before they change their minds," Pinenut said. "I'll drive."

He and Sam swapped seats.

"What was all that about?" Gerasimov asked, addressing Pinenut for the first time since the journey had begun.

"They warned me there had been some Russian artillery fire fifty kilometres up the road, about an hour ago," Pinenut said.

"Do we keep going?" Rebecca asked. She knew the answer but couldn't stop herself asking the question.

"We keep going," Gerasimov replied. "We can't go back, or I can't go back, so let's move it."

It was the first time Pinenut realised he was going to lose one of the passengers. He didn't want to know what Sam and Rebecca were up to but he was happy it was the morose man in the back who was planning to leave them.

The atmosphere in the car had changed. Rebecca was getting nervous and frightened; Sam seemed extra alert and kept on leaning forward to peer through the windscreen. Pinenut remained relaxed but looked in the mirror at Gerasimov every few minutes. He knew nothing about him, but he knew he wasn't Ukrainian or a citizen of Kyiv. Everyone he met in Kyiv always chatted to him about the war and the barbaric Russian soldiers. The man in the back had hardly spoken and when he did, it was in English. Pinenut wondered whether he was Russian.

The Skoda was the only car on the road in either direction. It was nearly 5 a.m. Rebecca had fallen asleep again, but Sam and Gerasimov were wide awake.

The road curved to the right. Suddenly, a blinding light flashed in the sky and a huge explosion lifted the Skoda off the road and hurled it towards the woods that lined the highway. The Skoda rolled over and over four times and came to a halt on its wheels. For a few minutes, there was total silence, except for the ominous sound of dripping diesel. Smoke was pouring from the shattered bonnet.

Gerasimov was the first to move. He checked his arms and legs and chest. Nothing was broken. He felt as if he had been brutally assaulted but he had survived relatively unscathed. Rebecca lay against him, motionless, blood pouring from a head wound. Sam was slumped forward against the windscreen. Pinenut, like the other two, was unconscious. The smell of leaking diesel was getting overpowering.

The door next to Gerasimov was jammed and the window frame was twisted. He undid his seatbelt and climbed over Rebecca. Blood was still pouring down her face. He reached the other door and tried to open it. It gave a little but was also jammed. He turned to face the door and leant back against Rebecca, then slammed both his feet against it. The door burst open. He quickly clambered out and then reached in, removed Rebecca's seatbelt and pulled her body gently across the back seat and out of the door. He carried her into the woods and set her down carefully, propped against a tree. He took a handkerchief from his pocket and pressed it against her head wound. The handkerchief stuck to the blood and he left it there.

Gerasimov ran back to the car and wrenched open the front passenger door. He removed the seatbelt around Sam and heaved him out of the seat. Sam also had a head wound, although it didn't look as bad as Rebecca's. He wrapped his arms around Sam's chest and dragged him across the grass into the woods, placing him next to Rebecca. Sam had started to groan, but Rebecca remained comatose. Gerasimov felt for a pulse. She was alive and breathing.

He ran back for Pinenut, who was still unconscious. He had no head wound but one of his arms was broken. He was half the weight of Sam, and Gerasimov managed to drag him out of the car after pulling open the door, which was hanging on the bottom hinge. He carried him to where the other two were lying and placed him down. Pinenut had a pulse but his broken arm looked serious. A splintered bone had broken through his sweater.

Sam was now stirring. He opened his eyes and saw Gerasimov tending to Pinenut, and Rebecca lying against the tree next to him, a bloody handkerchief stuck to her head.

Gerasimov swivelled round when Sam started to get up. At that moment, Pinenut also came to. They all spoke at once but their words were lost in a gigantic explosion as the Skoda blew up and sent a fireball into the dawn sky.

They stared at the burning car.

"You saved our lives, Colonel," Sam said, and then started examining Rebecca's head wound.

The water they had brought with them in the car was gone, along with all the other provisions they had bought for the journey. Rebecca was still unconscious. The wound needed to be cleaned but they had no way of helping her.

Pinenut had got over his initial shock of emerging from his unconscious state and began to whimper with pain. Gerasimov strapped his arm to his side with a belt, but the badly broken bone made it impossible to insert a splint. The biggest concern was for

Rebecca, whose face was now deathly white with splodges of blood down one side. But the blood flow had eased.

"I have to go," Gerasimov said. "I have less than an hour to get to my pick-up point." He looked at Pinenut. "Do you have a phone?"

Pinenut pointed to his trouser pocket. Gerasimov extracted it and dialled 112, the emergency number. He held the phone to Pinenut's ear.

"Ambulance!" Pinenut shouted into the phone. He told the emergency service roughly where they were and said there were three injured, one of them, a woman, seriously and still unconscious. He was told to leave his phone on. When he was asked if another vehicle was involved in the crash, Pinenut looked confused and said he thought not.

"What did happen?" he asked, when he called off.

Both Sam and Gerasimov answered. They had been hit by artillery fire.

Gerasimov wished them luck and turned to go. "Take care of Rebecca," he said.

"Thank you again, Colonel," Sam said. "I hope it all works out."

Gerasimov nodded and headed off as the morning light began to fill the sky. The darkness he had planned to use as cover to complete the final part of his escape was disappearing. He had more than a mile to go.

CHAPTER TWENTY-FOUR
UNCERTAINTY OVER AGENT REDRUTH'S WHEREABOUTS

Rebecca woke two days later. Her eyes only half opened, and then closed again. She realised she was lying in a bed and that someone who looked like Sandy was sitting in a chair next to her. She opened her eyes fully and blinked a few times. Sandy was smiling and took her hand.

"Rebecca, thank God," he said, leaning forward and kissing her on her forehead.

"What's going on, where is this, why are you here? You're not supposed to know I'm here," Rebecca mumbled.

Her head hurt. She lifted her free hand and felt a bandage wrapped round her head. It was difficult to move her arm because the wrist was attached to two tubes. She and Sandy were alone in the room. A huge vase of flowers was on her bedside table.

"Aah, thank you," she said.

"They're not from me, sorry," Sandy replied. "I rushed here as soon as I heard. The flowers are from your new boss."

He leant forward and read out the note attached to the lilies and freesias.

"Rebecca, please get well and forgive me. Grace and I, and the cousins across the water, all send love. You're a star. Geraldine."

"She's not really my boss, Sandy, it's just a temporary thing," Rebecca said.

"Yeah, right," Sandy said.

"Who told you I was in hospital here?"

"Your boss," he said. "That was a first, MI5 ringing *me*. Are you all right? You look pale … but still gorgeous. How did you get hurt and what the hell are you doing in Kyiv? And not telling me!"

Rebecca remembered very little of what had happened to her. She remembered the long drive out of Kyiv, the brilliance of her new friend, Pinenut, in getting through checkpoints, and then sudden oblivion.

"Oh my God, how are Sam and Pinenut and Gerasimov?" she cried out.

Sandy looked confused. "I don't know anything," he said. "Nobody has told me. Who's Pinenut? And why did you say 'Gerasimov'? What's he got to do with anything? Isn't he in a hospital under guard here in Kyiv? And what Sam are you talking about? Not big Sam?"

Sandy had been the only reporter present outside Geraldine's house in South London in the early hours when Gerasimov and his Russian GRU colleague had been brought out by the SAS over a year ago. He had witnessed this huge man standing outside the house negotiating in Russian on the phone with the two Russians inside. It was only weeks later when he had gone for lunch with Rebecca to a brasserie in Covent Garden that he saw the big man again, sitting at a table in the same restaurant. His lunch companion was Geraldine Hammer, who had been standing close to Sam throughout the drama at her house.

Rebecca went quiet. "Sorry, Sandy, I'm not allowed to tell you anything. I shouldn't have mentioned those names. I'm hopeless. I'll never make a spy, not with you around, anyway."

"So you want to get rid of me?" Sandy asked, withdrawing his hand from hers.

She grabbed his hand back. "No, never," she whispered.

"So, tell me, tell me something, anything. Is it the Sam I met before?" Sandy asked.

"Yes. Please ask someone if he's here. Sam Cook."

"And Pinenut?"

"Yes, him too, although I can't remember his real name."

"That's helpful. And Gerasimov?"

"No, not him. Don't ask anyone about him. Please."

"OK, OK."

A nurse entered the room and told Sandy he had to leave. He gave Rebecca a gentle kiss on the lips and said he would be back in the evening.

"Is there anything I can write about this?" he asked.

"No, nothing. Not one word," she replied and blew him a kiss.

***

The CIA was the first to hear about the disaster on the road just over a mile from the Russian frontline. Colonel Bilyk rang Adam Goldstein to tell him that the grand escape plan for Colonel Mikhail Gerasimov had ended in failure. He told Goldstein a man speaking in Ukrainian had called the emergency services and told them three people had been injured in an accident, one of them seriously. Bilyk said he had checked with the military in the area and received confirmation of a Russian artillery strike about fifteen minutes before the emergency call. When an ambulance arrived, three people were found lying in the woods. Their car was a mass of smoking metal. One of the three, a man who gave his name as Sam Cook, told the ambulance crew there had been a fourth passenger but he had been trapped in the car and had died in the explosion. He said his body would have been incinerated. Bilyk told Goldstein that must have been Gerasimov, and he offered his condolences.

Goldstein immediately rang Patrick Littlefield to relay the news that the British gamble had not been successful and that the whole escape idea had been doomed from the beginning.

His last words to MI6's director of operations were succinct. "I'm afraid Geraldine's obsession with this Rebecca Strong woman was a huge mistake. Your asset had great potential but it's a lesson to us all. It was too ambitious from the start."

Patrick felt like a schoolboy being ticked off by his headmaster. For ten minutes he sat in his office, going over in his mind whether Goldstein was right. Gerasimov had offered his services, and it could have been a brilliant success story for both MI5 and MI6. And it was because of his previous liaison with Rebecca Strong that the whole Agent Redruth saga had begun. So Patrick felt Goldstein had been churlish and unreasonable in dismissing Rebecca as a mistake. But it had to be said, the death of Agent Redruth was both a tragedy and a disaster for British intelligence.

He dreaded having to make the call to Geraldine. But at least Rebecca had survived, albeit seriously wounded.

After another five minutes of thought, he picked up the phone and rang her.

"Geraldine, Patrick, I have some very bad news," he said.

"Oh God, tell me," she said.

He told her everything Goldstein had said, although he left out the critical comments.

Geraldine laughed. She actually laughed.

"What the hell—" Patrick began.

"I've just had a call from Sam," she said. "Redruth is very much alive. At present, we have no idea where he is nor whether he was rescued by Russian special forces as he had planned. But not only did he survive the artillery strike on their car, he pulled the other three to safety before the car exploded, and saved their lives. He was last seen heading off towards the Russian lines."

"My God, Geraldine, I didn't want to make this call and now you've turned it all upside down. Amazing news," Patrick said, his body flooding with relief.

Geraldine told him Sam was fine and in good spirits, but was worried about Rebecca. At that stage she was still unconscious in hospital but the doctors said they were hopeful she would come round soon. There were no internal injuries. Sam had spent a few hours in hospital but had been released and was back in the hotel. Their Ukrainian driver, whom Sam didn't name, had undergone an emergency operation on a badly broken arm and was recuperating.

"Goldstein was convinced the whole thing was a disaster," Patrick said.

"I have very little time for Goldstein," Geraldine said. "I get the feeling he wanted this project to fail just because we were running it and not them. Now there's a glimmer of hope Operation Greengage might have a future, but no thanks to him."

"My feelings, too, Geraldine, but we can't afford to let our personal views get in the way. We have to keep Goldstein and co on board, but this will remain our show. If it works, then Langley will benefit as much as we will and Goldstein might even end up being appreciative," Patrick said.

"I don't think being appreciative is in his nature, Patrick, but I agree, of course, we must keep them informed. It might be better though if you tell Goldstein the good news. I might be tempted to crow a bit," Geraldine said.

Patrick said he would contact Goldstein straightaway.

***

Gerasimov was sitting in a bunker close to the command centre of the Russian military unit that controlled the Zaporizhzhia region. He was exhausted. The previous six hours had been traumatic.

After leaving Rebecca, Sam and Pinenut, he had set off along the side of the road heading for Zaporizhzhia. Apart from the one-word text from General Golubev, he had no firm assurances that he would be rescued. He didn't even know whether Spetsnaz teams operated in the Zaporizhzhia region. The regular forces were mostly made up of reluctant conscripts, and Gerasimov had no confidence they would have either the capability or the motivation to risk their lives for just one Russian emerging out of the blue on the Ukrainian side of the war zone.

Gerasimov had had to use all the skills he had learnt as a GRU officer and a combat veteran to get sufficiently close to the Russian lines to make a rescue attempt at least feasible. He had been forced to crawl like an animal through forests by the side of the road when he spotted Ukrainian landmines scattered along the highway. Military patrols were also out in force. Gerasimov knew that booby-trap wires would have been placed in areas in the woods, which was why he reverted to crawling, rather than running, while searching for concealed traps. After discovering one wire stretching from the roadside into the trees, he had to give the area a wide berth, adding half an hour to his journey. He looked at his watch and realised he was never going to make his 6 a.m. deadline to be picked up. There were also too many Ukrainian soldiers around for him to flash his torch as he had promised in his text to General Golubev. But he hoped someone would have been delegated to keep track of his mobile phone. Gerasimov had little faith in the Russian army, but if ordered by a GRU four-star general to perform a set task, even a bolshie conscript would probably do as he was bid.

Covered in scratches and desperate for water, Gerasimov had emerged an hour late for his rescue near the Russian lines. He lay concealed in a ditch, with a large branch he had picked up from the woods covering his body. He waited, breathing heavily, for twenty minutes, when the air was filled with a cacophonous burst of artillery fire. Gerasimov could hear the shells going over his head. He covered his ears and closed his eyes, which was why he was unaware of the presence of four soldiers standing above him and calling his name. One of the soldiers reached down and shook the branch covering Gerasimov's body. He jerked up and opened his eyes.

"Colonel Gerasimov?" the soldier shouted, as more artillery shells screamed over their heads.

"Yes!" Gerasimov shouted back.

He clambered out of the ditch. The four soldiers, their faces wrapped round with combat scarves, saluted him and then pointed towards two armoured patrol vehicles.

"Let's go, Colonel," one of the soldiers shouted. "You're in the lead vehicle, sir."

Gerasimov was pushed into the back of the armoured vehicle. With a roar of the engine it set off towards the Russian lines. Artillery shells continued to fly over them.

***

Gerasimov had been in the Russian command bunker for twenty minutes. It was surprisingly spacious and had been fitted out with personal touches, including internal polished wooden doors with elaborate carvings. The room where Gerasimov was sitting had two armchairs with dark purple coverings. The operations centre was next door and he could hear a buzz of activity. It was Russian-occupied Ukrainian territory, but the bunker had a definite air of permanence about it, Gerasimov thought.

He had been given a plate of meat and rice, and bottled water. He devoured both. The Russian soldiers, members of an elite Spetsnaz hostage-rescue force, had been respectful and friendly. But as soon as they handed him over to the local military commander, also a colonel, the mood seemed to change. Gerasimov was regarded as a stranger, almost a nuisance for disrupting the daily routines of the commander, who treated his unexpected visitor with neither respect nor admiration.

"Well, Gerasimov, I have to say, your sudden arrival is all a bit strange," the colonel said. "I don't really want to know what you've been up to but you lost all your men in Kyiv. That's bad news."

Gerasimov was going to say something but decided against it.

"My role, it seems, is to ship you back to Moscow as quickly as possible," the colonel said.

"Thank you," said Gerasimov.

"Don't thank me, thank your General Golubev who rang me last night," he said. "It was quite a night. I got another call much later on from Moscow. The FSB want to interrogate you."

The colonel gave that piece of unwelcome news with a smirk on his face.

Gerasimov didn't react to the colonel's sneering comment. He didn't believe a commander so far from Moscow would be in the know about how the FSB investigation into the Sevastopol leak was developing. He concluded he was just irritated at having a fellow colonel in his bunker.

"You're to stay here for the moment," the commander said. "A helicopter is coming for you in an hour to take you to Melitopol air base. Then you're booked on an overnight transport flight to Moscow this evening."

The commander didn't wish him luck. "I'm tied up all day, so I won't see you before you leave," he said. With that, he left the room.

In less than twenty-four hours, Gerasimov would be in Moscow facing his interrogators. Sam and Rebecca, if she had recovered, would tell London he was alive, but his new secret employers would have no knowledge of his current whereabouts. Nor would they be in a position to come to his rescue if the FSB had uncovered new evidence against him and he disappeared into the bowels of the Federal Security Service's notorious basement interrogation centre.

Gerasimov thought again of his wife and two children, trying to carry on their daily lives without knowing where he was and whether he would ever return to them. Since the failed assassination mission in Kyiv against Zelensky, he doubted his family would have received any sympathetic visits from the FSB. The Russian newspapers and state broadcasters had raised questions about the mission, why it had failed, why the leader of the assassination team had survived, and whether he would be put on trial in Ukraine or swapped in a prisoner exchange. After weeks went by without news of Gerasimov's fate, interest had switched back to the war in Ukraine and the continuing attritional battles going on in the south and east. The Kremlin remained silent about Gerasimov, never confirming his identity.

However, there remained considerable interest, in the Russian and Western media, in the Sevastopol story and the hunt for the leaker. But the FSB had refused to offer a running commentary on the investigation. While Gerasimov was staying in the safe house in the diplomatic area of Kyiv, he had been kept informed of news from Moscow. It had helped him make up his mind to plan for his escape, news of which had yet to break. But he knew it couldn't be long. He suspected the story would emerge first from Kyiv.

He was wrong. The news broke in Moscow, on Telegram, the popular Russian social media platform.

The rumours and speculation were passed on to Gerasimov by one of the Spetsnaz soldiers who had rescued him from his ditch on the wrong side of the Russian frontlines.

"So, Colonel; you are in the news," the soldier said. He had come in to ask if Gerasimov needed anything.

It was a speculative report, but Gerasimov suspected someone from the unit he was with must have contacted Telegram. There were few details. It didn't specify whether he was safely back in Russian hands. It merely stated that "according to sources", Colonel Mikhail Gerasimov, "believed to be" the sole survivor of the mission to eliminate the Ukrainian leader, had made a dramatic escape and was no longer in Ukraine. It had set off a maelstrom of news stories, all of them based on unofficial sources who claimed to be in the know.

"Nothing official?" Gerasimov asked.

"No, all rumours, but pretty accurate, right?" the soldier replied.

"Did Sandy Hall of Britain's Sky News report anything different to the others?"

"No, the British media all ran exactly the same stories."

Gerasimov nodded.

"They don't know you're here. None of us would contact Telegram, Colonel."

Gerasimov smiled. He wondered whether the unfriendly commander himself had tipped off Telegram.

As Gerasimov waited for the helicopter to fly him to Melitopol in Russian-annexed Ukraine, he wished he could find out how Rebecca was. He owed her a lot but he would probably never see her again. Either he was going to be executed for treason or he would be living a dangerous undercover role as a double agent, with every day a potential last day in his life. He didn't imagine there would be an opportunity for him to get together with Rebecca. It made him think back to the two weeks he had spent with her in her flat in London.

"Awesome woman," he muttered out loud.

***

Major Pavel Kozlov, prisoner number 3654, was angry. He was an inmate of Mokotów Prison in Warsaw, awaiting trial but with no date for his case to be heard. He had been given a local lawyer who had shown little interest in his claim that he had been framed by a tall blonde English woman called Rebecca Strong. He had been charged with being in possession of a false passport and conspiracy to commit espionage. The lawyer warned him he could be facing ten years.

The lawyer knew nothing of the phone call that had taken place between the director general of MI5 and his counterpart, the head of the MCS secret service in Warsaw, in which it had been agreed that Kozlov's real identity and role would be kept confidential for the time being. He had been charged under the name on his false passport, Pavlo Kuzma.

The lawyer said if there were any mitigating circumstances he should reveal them now. Kozlov told the lawyer he had been refused access to a phone and demanded he speak with the prison authorities to grant him this right. As the days went by, Kozlov had become more and more frustrated that he had been unable to call the FSB in Moscow to tell his colleagues what he had found out.

As he sat in his single-unit cell, he had become increasingly convinced that Gerasimov was a traitor. When the news broke, unconfirmed by Moscow, that Gerasimov had escaped from his captors in Kyiv, all his instincts as a longstanding FSB officer told him that both the assassination attempt and Gerasimov's "escape" were fake. He had no proof, everything he had in his head was circumstantial, but he had learnt over the years that the larger picture became more credible when little details began to multiply and form a consistent pattern. Rebecca Strong was one of the big details. She had met Gerasimov in London during another of his failed missions, she had been present in Venice when he travelled there covertly, and she had been with her boyfriend from Sky News in Poland shortly before the breaking news that Gerasimov was the leader of the assassination attempt against Zelensky and had mysteriously survived while the rest of his team had been killed. In his view, everything pointed to one giant conspiracy, involving the British, the Ukrainians, the Poles and probably the Americans.

His lawyer asked for him to be granted one phone call, but the governor of the prison rejected the request, citing national security.

The lawyer pushed Kozlov to tell him what it was all about, but his client claimed ignorance. If the Poles were going to play this game, Kozlov decided he would have to find another way of getting a message out to his FSB colleagues in Moscow.

For the next few days, during the brief recreation time he was granted, he began to make friends with fellow prisoners. All of them were either awaiting trial or sentence. Kozlov spoke reasonable Polish. He had always been good at languages. One prisoner in particular was chatty. He said he had been convicted for stealing a number of mobile phones from a shop and being in possession of a knife, but had been assured by his lawyer that he would get a short sentence and would be released, having already served two months in prison on remand. The date for his sentencing was due at any time.

Kozlov spoke very generally about his reasons for being in Mokotów Prison and said he, too, hoped to be released soon. He told the prisoner that it was always a difficult time when first released from prison. He claimed he had spent eighteen months in jail some years before. He suggested it would be nice to meet up when they were both free.

The prisoner appeared doubtful at first but began to warm to Kozlov, who then had one more suggestion. Kozlov asked if he could give the man a phone number to ring so that when he was released, he would be met outside the prison, and they could all arrange to meet up for a drink. The prisoner thought that would be all right. Kozlov said he would write the phone number and the message he wanted passed on to his friend on a slip of paper.

"Let me know when you are off for your sentencing and I'll give you the bit of paper then," he told his fellow inmate.

Kozlov returned to his cell and tore a blank page from the back of a novel he had been reading. Using a pencil, he wrote in Polish:

Ring 007495663724 and say: Hello, hope to be free soon, come and meet me and please congratulate Rebecca and Mikhail for brilliant partnership. Tell everyone MG is a DA, PK.

Kozlov slipped the piece of paper into his new friend's hand when he left the following morning for his sentencing. Everything now depended on the prisoner's lawyer being right about a short sentence and the prisoner himself bothering to make the phone call.

Kozlov knew there was a risk the former prisoner would be suspicious about the first three digits – "007" was the international dialling code for Russia – and the following "495" indicated it was a Moscow telephone number. The other risk was the message. The man would be confused and his suspicions might be increased by Kozlov's use of initials. A Russian voice answering the call might also persuade him to switch off immediately. He probably didn't speak any Russian and he might be instantly put off by the unfamiliar language at the other end of the phone.

Kozlov thought his chances of getting the message to his superior FSB officer, Colonel Boris Gusev, were about fifty-fifty. If Gusev answered the phone, or perhaps Major Anton Lebedev, the other FSB officer involved in the hunt for the Sevastopol leaker, Kozlov hoped they would realise what his coded message meant: Mikhail Gerasimov is a double agent, Pavel Kozlov.

CHAPTER TWENTY-FIVE
AGENT REDRUTH FACES TOUGH INTERROGATION

The following morning, within minutes of arriving in an Antonov AN-72 military transport aircraft at Kubinka air base, near Moscow, Gerasimov was bundled into a Tigr 4x4 military vehicle and driven quickly to the capital. Gerasimov asked the driver where they were going but received no answer.

No one of any importance had been at the airport to welcome him home. There were no reporters or TV camera crews lined up to interview him. It was like Moscow wanted him out of the way as quickly as possible. He had expected at least someone from his office to be there. The only comfort was that he wasn't arrested by the FSB as soon as his foot touched the tarmac. But he soon realised it wouldn't be long before he was to endure the company of the FSB. His driver dropped him off outside the FSB headquarters in Lubyanka Square, in downtown Moscow. So, a debriefing by the general staff, which he thought would come first, was taking second place. *That is ominous*, Gerasimov thought.

"They're expecting you," the driver said, unnecessarily. It was 8 a.m.

Gerasimov walked up the steps into the building that used to house the old KGB and approached the glass-fronted security check-in desk.

"Colonel Gerasimov," he said to a security guard in uniform behind the glass. "I'm expected, apparently."

The guard checked his register, a large leather-bound book, and then double-checked on the computer to his right.

"Yes, Colonel," the guard replied. "Please, take a seat."

Gerasimov looked round and spotted an empty seat. Three other men were waiting, all of them carrying briefcases. They didn't look as if they were preparing to be interrogated. They stared at Gerasimov and noted his lack of a briefcase.

Also unlike the other visitors, Gerasimov wasn't wearing a suit. He was dressed in the clothes he had worn during his escape from Kyiv. The trousers had dirt on the knees and his weatherproof jacket had a rip at the side. His shoes were muddy. The three other men looked away, disapprovingly.

Gerasimov had to wait an hour before a woman in a grey dress came towards him and asked if he was Colonel Gerasimov. She told him to follow her. Gerasimov was surprised he wasn't given a visitor's label to attach to his jacket. They walked along a series of corridors and then the woman stopped at the top of a flight of stairs.

"Go down and through the first set of doors, and you'll be met there," she said, pointing, and immediately went on her way.

For a brief moment, Gerasimov considered running back down the corridor and out of the building. But then he straightened his shoulders and took the first step down. When he walked through the first set of doors there was a man in a black suit standing a few feet away.

"Colonel Gerasimov, welcome back," he said. "I'm Major Anton Lebedev. My colonel would have been here to meet you but he has been detained elsewhere."

Colonel Boris Gusev, the FSB officer in charge of the Sevastopol leak investigation, was still suspended from duty following the disappearance of Major Kozlov. But Gerasimov had no knowledge of what had been going on at FSB headquarters. He knew nothing about Major Pavel Kozlov. He was taken aback by Major Lebedev's friendly and respectful tone.

Lebedev invited Gerasimov to follow him down the corridor. When they reached a door on the left, Lebedev swiped his security pass through the electronic system, opened the door and beckoned Gerasimov in.

There were three other men already in the room, sitting on metal chairs close to each other behind a table laden with green files. Gerasimov was told to sit on a chair in front of them, and Lebedev stood to the right of the table.

For all his experience as a combat soldier and intelligence officer, Gerasimov felt instantly intimidated. The room was bare. The three men sitting down all looked hostile. The green files were ominous. To make matters worse for him, he was exhausted after his escape from Ukraine, he had slept badly in the Russian bunker, and his clothes were dirty and smelly. He didn't think they were about to treat him with the respect he was due as a full colonel with a senior position in the Kremlin.

Lebedev opened the proceedings.

"First of all, Colonel," he said, "we are glad you are back safely. You are here purely to help us with our various inquiries."

Gerasimov was amazed. That was not what he was expecting.

"Of course," Gerasimov replied, trying to sound relaxed.

"Major Alekseev has some initial questions for you," Lebedev said, pointing to the short FSB officer sitting in the middle chair of the three.

Major Alekseev opened one of the green files and said, "We have reason to believe, Colonel, that the leak about the president's visit to Sevastopol came from your office. Do you know anything about this?"

It was like being hit by a thunderbolt. The first question was effectively accusing him of being the leaker and traitor.

"No," Gerasimov replied. He had decided to keep his answers as short and as firm as possible.

"We have interviewed everyone in your office, except you, of course."

Gerasimov said nothing.

"Did you leak this secret information to a third party?"

"No."

"Are you a secret agent for a foreign power?"

"No."

"Do you support the president and his special military operation in Ukraine?"

"Yes."

Major Alekseev rifled through the pages of the file in front of him.

"This says you raised doubts about the way it was going."

"If I recall, there was just one occasion when I registered certain concerns."

"You were critical of the president's operation."

"No, I was merely offering my opinion."

Major Lebedev moved closer to Gerasimov and suddenly intervened.

"Have you met with Rebecca Strong recently?" he asked.

The question totally floored Gerasimov.

"Er, no."

"Why the hesitancy?"

"I wasn't sure what you meant."

"But you know whom I'm referring to?"

"Yes."

"Is she a British spy?"

"As far as I know, she is an artist. I met her in London during last year's GRU mission."

"You had sex with her," one of the other FSB officers said.

"Yes."

"Have you had sex with her recently?" the same officer asked.

"No."

"You're lying," Major Lebedev said, "on two counts. First of all, we know you met with this woman in October in a hotel in Venice. You booked a double room. You had sex with her."

"I didn't," Gerasimov replied.

"So you admit you were in Venice with her," Lebedev persisted, "but deny having carnal relations?"

"Yes; forgive me for not telling you about Venice, but it was strictly a personal matter," Gerasimov replied, a feeling of panic building in his stomach. "She wanted to revive the relationship we had had in London and insisted on meeting up in Venice. I agreed, against my better judgement, but only because I wanted to make it clear to her that I had no interest in us having a relationship. That's all it was; it was nothing sinister."

"So you took time away from your work when you were supposed to be planning an important mission in Kyiv, and told no one where you were going," Lebedev said.

"All of this is enough to finish your career for good," Major Alekseev said. "Adultery, being absent without authority, consorting with a British woman, and lying to the FSB. Why should we believe anything you tell us?"

Gerasimov leaned forward and looked straight at Alekseev. "I am a dedicated, loyal patriot. I have served my country honourably, and at risk to my life on numerous occasions. OK, I have a weakness for beautiful women, but my former bosses at GRU know I shacked up with this Rebecca Strong woman in London and understood my reasons for doing so. They said it was justified. So, when she started pressing me to meet up, I felt it was my duty and responsibility to see her face-to-face and end it all for good. If you checked out my booking in the Venice hotel you will know that I booked two rooms, a double for her and a single for me. There was no sex, and when I had made my position clear to her, I left Venice immediately and returned to Moscow."

"But you used subterfuge to get to Venice and to return to Moscow," Lebedev said, "a false passport and going via Istanbul. We checked, so you can't deny it."

"Of course I did," Gerasimov replied. "I'm a senior Russian intelligence officer, I can't go anywhere in my real name, you know that. And there's a war on; Russians of any kind are not exactly persona grata anywhere in Europe. As for travelling to Istanbul first, it's the only airport in Europe you can fly to from Moscow, as you will know."

"You have all the answers," Lebedev said.

"Yes, I do, because it's the truth. I'm sorry if it doesn't fit in with your preconceived notion that I'm the leaker you are looking for, but I'm giving you honest replies."

For the first time, Gerasimov had raised his voice.

He added: "If you're finished, I'd like to get to my wife and family. I was rushed straight here and haven't seen them."

All four FSB officers looked startled. Alekseev recovered the quickest.

"No, we haven't finished with you yet," he said, "and we're certainly not going to take your answers as the truth. So, I ask again, are you in league with this woman, Rebecca Strong?"

"No."

The FSB officer who hadn't spoken so far opened another file on the table.

"Do you know Rebecca Strong's boyfriend?" he asked.

"No."

"So you don't know he works for Sky television?"

"No."

"And that Sky television seems to know more about you than any other broadcaster?"

"No, I don't."

"Why do you think that is?"

"I don't know."

Alekseev waved a finger in the air, indicating he was tired of the questions that were getting nowhere.

"Tell me about the assassination plot that went wrong," he said.

Gerasimov was briefly thrown by the change in questioning.

"What do you want to know?" he asked, as he rapidly thought about what strategy he should adopt to thwart their questions.

"Why did it fail?" Alekseev demanded.

"It failed," Gerasimov said, "because I and my team were betrayed."

Alekseev looked surprised. "How exactly?"

"Someone leaked it," Gerasimov replied.

Alekseev looked around at his colleagues.

"Go on," he said.

"We walked into a trap. Everything had gone to plan; we had gained entrance to the presidential compound and we were ready to fulfil the mission entrusted to me by the president."

Major Lebedev walked around to stand behind his three sitting colleagues.

"What are you saying?" he asked.

"Whoever leaked our secret mission must have also leaked the date of the president's visit to Sevastopol. That's the only thing that makes sense to me. The president, thank God, wasn't hurt, but I lost all six of my men."

"Why weren't you killed?" Lebedev asked.

"When we entered the room where Zelensky was supposed to be, I knew immediately it was a trap. There were cardboard images of Zelensky. It was like we were being taunted. I screamed to my men to drop to the floor and open fire, which is what I did. But they didn't react fast enough and were gunned down by soldiers who suddenly emerged from behind screens. It was a total set-up, an ambush. We had no chance. They knew we were coming. My men lost their lives because we were betrayed. I was just lucky. I was hit, and they could have finished me off, but they must have thought having a prisoner would give them something they could exploit."

Gerasimov's dramatic explanation seemed to make all four interrogators hesitate.

After a minute or so, Lebedev switched the questioning again. "How come you so easily managed to escape?" he asked.

Gerasimov was ready for this one.

"I escaped because I knew it was my duty to do so and I'm an experienced GRU officer. Using initiative and boldness were two golden rules I was taught as part of my training. And no, it wasn't easy, as you suggest. I had to use daring and cunning to escape from the hospital where I was being treated, and was nearly killed when the vehicle I had commandeered was struck by artillery shells fired by my own comrades. I am here because of the brilliance of the guys who risked their lives to grab me from Ukrainian-held territory."

There was silence from the four FSB officers. Eventually Alekseev stood up.

"We will need a full report from you about the mission in Kyiv that failed, and every detail about your escape," he said. "You will be asked the same questions by the general staff, who you will be taken to next. But we need your report as quickly as possible. We may need you to come back for further questioning once you have sent us your report."

"You may go, for the moment," Major Lebedev said.

Gerasimov stood up, thanked them and left the room. The four interrogators stayed behind. Gerasimov could hear them all talking at once.

***

Sandy was back at the hospital, holding Rebecca's hand. She seemed drowsy. He was dying to ask her more about why she was in hospital and where Gerasimov was, but he held back.

Rebecca had received another visitor earlier. Sam Cook had walked in without her being warned beforehand. He passed on messages from London but had no news about Gerasimov. He also told her about Pinenut. His operation had been successful and he was now recuperating in a room down the corridor. Sam told Rebecca he was as cheerful as ever and didn't appear to hold a grudge against them for concealing what they had been up to. On the contrary, despite the broken arm, he had no regrets about being involved in the adventure, as he called it. But he told Sam he was confused about the presence of a Russian in the car, whom he now knew from news reports to be Colonel Mikhail Gerasimov.

"What did you tell him?" Rebecca asked Sam.

"Nothing, absolutely nothing," Sam replied. "But I did reassure him we were the good guys and had our reasons. He seemed to accept that. Before we go back to London we should take him out for a meal and thank him properly for what he did for us."

Twenty minutes after Sam left, Sandy had walked in.

After asking how she felt and when she might be allowed out of hospital, Sandy could hold back no longer.

"Rebecca, the whole world now knows that Gerasimov escaped from custody in Kyiv, although how he did is a mystery to me and every other reporter here," he said.

Rebecca just smiled.

"I rang Colonel Bilyk, who is now my best contact in the Kyiv government," Sandy went on, "but he told me nothing. In fact, he gave the impression he wasn't sure how he escaped either, which I don't believe for a moment."

"I can't tell you anything, lover boy," Rebecca replied, "because if I did it might put my life in danger."

"Bloody hell, Rebecca," Sandy exploded. "There you go again. You say nothing and then hint something major went on and that you were involved, and probably Sam, and maybe this Pinenut fellow. Who is Pinenut?"

"You'd like him, he's a helluva guy," she replied, pulling Sandy forward to kiss him on the lips.

"Kissing me like that won't stop me asking you questions," he said with a grin, "although I guess if you carry on kissing me I won't be able to ..."

She put her arms around his neck and kissed him hard. He reached down and felt her breasts, covered only by a thin hospital gown.

"Hmmmm, I like the gown," he mumbled, as he continued to kiss her and caress her.

"Naughty boy," she mumbled back, "taking advantage of me like that, but don't stop."

A nurse entered the room, carrying a tray with several medicine bottles on it, and they broke apart.

The nurse grinned. "That's probably the best medicine," she said, "but I'm afraid I have your other medicine here. It's time."

Sandy stood up. "I better go," he said, "I've got stuff to do."

"Killjoy," Rebecca muttered.

Sandy turned to blow a kiss as he opened the door.

"Come back tomorrow morning," Rebecca said. "I'll wear the same gown if you like."

The nurse looked at Sandy and laughed. Sandy's face went pink.

***

In room 47 on the fourth floor of FSB headquarters in Moscow, a phone began to ring. The room was empty. The nameplate on the door read "Colonel Boris Gusev".

After eight rings, the phone beeped. A brief message in Russian followed.

A faint, hesitant voice could then be heard. The language spoken was Polish.

"Shit, is that Russian? Hello? Hello? I don't know whose phone this is but I have a message from Pavlo Kuzma. We met in Mokotów Prison in Warsaw. I've just been released. His message is … where is it, bugger, sorry, he wrote it down on a bit of paper, I had it just a moment ago … oh, there it is. This is his message. Hello,

hope to be free soon, come and meet me and please congratulate Rebecca and Mikhail for the brilliant partnership. Tell everyone MG is a—"

The messaging time ran out.

CHAPTER TWENTY-SIX
MI6 STATION CHIEF MAKES A MOVE

While Gerasimov was in Kyiv, his future prospects as a Russian double agent in the balance, David Kimche was under orders to lay the groundwork for his return to Russia. If Gerasimov was accepted back at his old job in the Kremlin, it would be up to Kimche to mastermind the tradecraft to ensure a flow of secret information courtesy of Agent Redruth. The trickiest challenge for Kimche, veteran spymaster though he was, would be to arrange the first meeting after Gerasimov's return to Moscow. Kimche knew that Gerasimov might be unable to make any sort of contact with him. It would be too risky. But the message from London was that Operation Greengage was top priority, and every effort was to be made to keep it going.

Kimche had thought of travelling to Ukraine to try and meet up with Gerasimov at his safe house in Kyiv, but Patrick Littlefield had ruled that out, having decided it would be too dangerous. Not physically, for his man in Moscow, but because of the risk of a leak in Kyiv. The arrival of a senior British spy in the Ukrainian capital, if leaked, would set off a hundred questions, none of which would be welcomed at Number 10. Patrick told Kimche to come up with another scheme for contacting Gerasimov if he managed to get back to Moscow.

Kimche was still meeting irregularly with the male secretary he had recruited from the FSB headquarters. The information he had provided about the FSB investigation into the Sevastopol leak had been invaluable, but now Kimche decided he had to persuade his FSB source to become a more active agent. The codename for the source was "Treasure". His real name was Nikolai Lukin. He was due to marry his exotic dancer fiancée in a year's time and hoped to have the money he would need by then to arrange the wedding and set her up in a flat that would keep her happy. Agent Treasure was desperately anxious that someone with better prospects and a more affluent family would snatch her from him. So, as he constantly reminded his British controller, the more money he could make from his extracurricular activities, the better chance he had of hanging on to her. With that in mind, Kimche thought it wouldn't be too difficult to persuade him to take on a riskier, more burdensome role as a secret agent for MI6. He would simply offer him a substantial bonus for the task he was going to give him.

The last time they had met, a week earlier near a children's playground at a housing estate in the Moscow suburbs, Agent Treasure had informed Kimche that Colonel Gerasimov remained at the top of the FSB suspect list and that if he returned in a prisoner swap, he would be taken straight to Lubyanka Square for interrogation.

Kimche had been informed of Redruth's determination to leave Kyiv. He had a plan that was simple but dangerous both for Agent Redruth and Agent Treasure. He intended to give Agent Treasure written instructions to be passed to Gerasimov when he arrived back in Moscow.

The timing would be crucial. Agent Treasure, of course, had no knowledge of Gerasimov's secret escape plan. But Kimche had told him to go to a certain food truck not far from Lubyanka Square every day at 11 a.m. to buy his lunch. Kimche said he would be there on one of the days.

The same day Gerasimov was rescued by Russian special forces after his escape from Kyiv, Kimche went to the street food truck just before 11 a.m. He spotted Agent Treasure in the queue.

They each separately gave their food orders and then stood back to wait. There were about thirty other people either queuing or waiting. Nikolai Lukin was wearing a raincoat with large pockets. Kimche, standing behind him, slipped an envelope into the right-hand pocket, and another one into his left-hand pocket.

He then whispered: "Please follow the instructions in the envelope in your right pocket. If you succeed, you will get a bonus of five thousand dollars. Just nod your head if you agree."

Agent Treasure nodded his head and then walked to the truck to collect his food.

***

Later that day, Nikolai Lukin, Agent Treasure, learned that Gerasimov had miraculously escaped from his captors in Ukraine and would be flown to Kubinka and taken straight to Lubyanka Square the following morning. To earn his five thousand dollars, Lukin had to take the greatest risk of his life. Somehow, he had to bump into Gerasimov before or after he left the FSB headquarters. Catching him before he entered the building would be impractical. He would have no idea of the precise timing and might well be escorted into the building. It had to be after he left. But what if he was detained for days, or arrested and moved to the FSB cells? Lukin knew if that happened he would never get his money.

However, he had a stroke of luck. He was in his office at FSB HQ when he got a call from a fellow secretary who had seen a crumpled-looking man in dirty clothes being taken downstairs into the basement. The rumour, she said, was that it was Colonel Gerasimov. Lukin looked at his watch. It was nine o'clock in the morning. He decided to wait two hours and then leave the building, ostensibly to buy his lunch.

Lukin was hovering the other side of the square with his sandwich when he suddenly spotted the man he recognised as Colonel Gerasimov coming out of the building.

Lukin moved quickly across the square, his heart thumping.

Gerasimov left Lubyanka Square and had just turned a corner when he heard someone calling his name. He looked round warily and saw a man hurrying towards him. He looked to be in his thirties or early forties. He didn't recognise him.

"Colonel Gerasimov," the man called again, out of breath.

Gerasimov considered ignoring him and hurrying off but the man caught up with him and had a big smile on his face. The man then held out his hand and, as Gerasimov hesitantly shook it, he felt something being passed to him. It was a rolled-up envelope.

"I just wanted to say welcome back to Moscow and well done for escaping," Lukin said.

Gerasimov looked bemused.

"Have a nice day," Lukin said, and then walked away quickly.

Agent Treasure had completed his mission. He was also now in possession of something so secret that the future of Operation Greengage depended on his silence: he knew Colonel Gerasimov was also working secretly for British intelligence. But Agent Treasure's whole life plan was built around his future wedding and the money he would receive from his British handler to pay for it. That was infinitely more important to him than his secret knowledge of Colonel Gerasimov's loyalty to his country. After all, they were traitors together. David Kimche had counted on this reasoning when he took the huge risk of involving Agent Treasure in making contact with Gerasimov.

Gerasimov continued walking rapidly down the street to the nearest Metro station. He put the envelope into the inside pocket of his windproof jacket, looking around him as he did. He couldn't spot any obvious surveillance but he knew there was a good chance his every move would be followed now that the FSB had formally questioned him. He entered Lubyanka Metro and immediately stood to one side behind a pillar. A man came hurrying into the Metro, looking around from left to right. He didn't seem to spot Gerasimov but he suddenly waved. A woman across the other side waved back. They kissed and hugged each other and walked hand in hand towards the escalator. Gerasimov waited another five minutes before emerging from behind the pillar. He couldn't see anyone who looked interested as he appeared. He was surprised but relieved.

***

Another conference call between London and Langley had been set up for the same day Gerasimov arrived back in Moscow. It took place several hours after Nikolai Lukin had passed the envelope to Gerasimov.

As far as British intelligence were aware, Agent Redruth's whereabouts were uncertain. Kimche had reported that, according to his sources, Gerasimov would be taken straight to FSB headquarters and that he had arranged for an agent to make contact with him. But he had no confirmation as yet that contact had taken place. Geraldine had wanted to postpone the conference call until more was known about Gerasimov's status, but Langley insisted they needed to talk.

The usual suspects were seated when the call began: Goldstein was with his two colleagues, Walt Grolsch and Marina Babb, and Patrick Littlefield sat alongside Geraldine, Grace Redmayne and Freddie Stigby. They all looked tired. What had begun as an exciting espionage coup, the recruitment of a high-ranking Russian intelligence official with a job in the Kremlin, had turned into weeks of stress and nervous tension, and an overwhelming sense that it could all end up in failure or, much worse, the execution of their agent. Goldstein had made a number of calls to both Geraldine and Patrick, emphasising the danger of continuing with Operation Greengage. The exposure and death of such an important asset, he argued, would be a disaster for British intelligence and humiliating for the West in general. He said it would give a huge boost to Putin, whose reputation as the man of steel had been dealt severe blows by the continuing failures of the Russian military in Ukraine.

Now, Goldstein asked the MI6 director of operations to bring everyone up to date.

"I wish it could be right up to date," Patrick said, "but as of now we're not sure where our asset is. We know he is back in Moscow. Our man there has ensured that if and when he is taken to Lubyanka Square and, hopefully, released, a note will be passed to him detailing instructions for future contacts. But, of course, this all depends on our asset getting his old job back and continuing to have access to the sort of document classification that has been so revealing up to this point."

"This is why I called this conference call," Goldstein said, in his usual abrupt manner. "Does your asset have any value right now or, indeed, will he have any in the future? It seems to me his chances of getting his job back and providing us all with top-grade intelligence are, at best, close to zero. I'm not saying pull out straightaway, but the way things are going, this asset could become a liability."

"Well, we'll decide when or whether to 'pull out', as you say, Adam," Geraldine replied testily. "But right now, our asset deserves all the attention and protection we can give, considering what he has gone through for our benefit. We know the FSB is after him, but he's trained to deal with these bullies, and I have every expectation that he will successfully endure their interrogations."

She looked at Goldstein. He didn't seem convinced.

"As for whether our asset will return to his Kremlin job, we have no idea at this stage," Geraldine went on. "But, obviously, that is the whole point of this exercise, so we'll just have to wait and see."

Patrick concurred with Geraldine's summing-up and promised to inform Langley of any developments.

Marina Babb leaned slightly forward in her chair. "To be honest, if I was working in the top echelons of the Kremlin, would I want Gerasimov back in harness, receiving classified documents and briefings when he is currently at the top of the FSB's suspect list for the Sevastopol leak? And also, of course, after the failure of the assassination mission in Kyiv."

"I agree," Walt Grolsch said. "Why take the risk? I'm afraid your asset's future is screwed. He's going to be spending months on gardening leave while the FSB digs up every aspect of his life. You said before that you thought Putin would welcome him back as a hero for escaping from his Ukrainian captors. But there's no evidence of that, is there? If there was, it would be all over state television. Putin is going to leave the FSB to do their dirty work. Gerasimov is finished, whether he's exonerated or not."

Goldstein was nodding his head in agreement.

In London, there were sombre faces. Their American cousins were probably right, although neither Geraldine nor Patrick wanted to admit it.

MI6's Freddie Stigby, however, agreed that Putin was unlikely to allow Gerasimov back into the Kremlin fold unless there was a very good reason for doing so.

Goldstein, as he always did, stood up and brought the conference call to a close.

***

While Colonel Boris Gusev was on enforced leave, his secretary was supposed to go to his office to check for any messages and report back to him. She hadn't been for a few days but turned up one morning, early, and unlocked his room. His desk contained two trays but they were both empty. It was as if he didn't exist.

The secretary, a middle-aged woman, sat down and pressed the rewind button on his message system. There were a few internal calls, nothing of any consequence. Then her eyebrows raised when a hesitant voice speaking in a foreign language that sounded to her like Polish, left a message which was clearly too long because it ended abruptly. She had no idea whether it was important or not but she realised that whoever had left the message must have been given Colonel Gusev's phone number for a reason, and whoever asked him to call her boss must have been in the privileged position of knowing his private office number. That, she concluded, was reason enough for her to consult with Colonel Gusev's colleagues on the Sevastopol leak investigation team.

She opened the door and walked down the corridor to the room where Major Kozlov and Major Lebedev worked. She knocked on the door but there was no reply. Major Kozlov, she knew, was in Warsaw and out of contact. She hadn't been told the reason. She had seen Major Lebedev the day before. She decided to go back to Colonel Gusev's office and write a note, which she would slip under the door of Major Lebedev's room. She kept the note short and simple. It merely stated that there was a strange message in a foreign language she thought was Polish on the colonel's phone and she could play it back for him whenever it was convenient. The secretary was old-fashioned. She didn't like emails. She preferred a note under the door every time.

∗∗∗

Gerasimov was at home. Natasha had come to the door when she heard the key and had burst into tears.

They hugged for a few moments.

"Mikhail, what is going on? Where have you been?" Natasha cried.

"Not now, Natasha," he replied.

"You look terrible. All the neighbours have been saying you were wounded in combat. Are you all right?"

"Don't worry, I'm fine," he said.

Natasha started crying again. "The children have been missing you. Shall I get them out of school?"

"No," he replied. "I've missed you all, too. But I have things I must do."

He extracted himself from his wife's embrace and went to the bathroom, where he opened the envelope. It contained detailed instructions about where he was to meet his British controller, and there was a list of six dead-drop locations where he could leave messages. The note from David Kimche emphasised that meetings in future should be kept to a minimum because of the high risk of being subjected to an FSB surveillance operation.

Suddenly his landline rang in the hall. It was the head of personnel and human resources in the Kremlin.

"Colonel Gerasimov, you are to report to your office at 8 a.m. tomorrow. You have an appointment at 8:15 a.m. with the Secretary of the Security Council," the official said.

Gerasimov had assumed his first appointment after his visit to Lubyanka Square would be at the defence ministry, where he was due to be debriefed on every aspect of the failed assassination operation, his detention by the Ukrainian authorities and his escape. While he was not looking forward to it, he hoped his reception at the ministry and questioning by some senior officer on the general staff might be more sympathetic towards him than the FSB. But an appointment with his Kremlin boss sounded more ominous. Gerasimov wondered whether his boss had initiated the session for tomorrow or whether the president himself had demanded he be questioned.

***

The following morning, Major Lebedev opened the door to his office and saw the piece of paper lying on the floor. He picked it up, read the message from Colonel Gusev's secretary, and ran down the corridor. She was always in early, and opened the door for him when he knocked loudly.

"Get me the message," he said rudely.

She walked back to the desk and switched on the recording system. Lebedev didn't speak Polish but there were four words that required no translation: Mokotów, Warsaw, Rebecca, and Mikhail. Lebedev suspected immediately it was a message from Kozlov. The two FSB officers sent to Warsaw to try and speak to him had been blocked by the Polish authorities. They had discovered he was in Mokotów Prison but had been refused access.

The last two words made Lebedev react physically, as if he had suffered a sharp electric shock. He used the colonel's phone to ring personnel.

"Who do we have in the building who speaks Polish? I need someone now," he said, in a loud voice.

He was given a name and an extension and rang immediately. The phone was answered. Within four minutes there was a knock on the door. A young man was standing there, looking nervous.

"Right," Lebedev said. "Listen to this tape and tell me what it says."

The secretary rewound the taped message and played it back. The young FSB linguist took notes as he listened to the message.

"Well?" Lebedev almost shouted.

The young man read out his notes.

"Shit, is that Russian? Hello? Hello? I don't know whose phone this is but I have a message from Pavlo Kuzma. We met in Mokotów Prison in Warsaw. I've just been released. His message is … where is it, bugger, sorry, he wrote it down on a bit of paper, I had it just a moment ago … oh, there it is. This is his message. Hello, hope to be free soon, come and meet me and please congratulate Rebecca and Mikhail for the brilliant partnership. Tell everyone MG is a—"

"MG is a what?" Lebedev shouted.

The young linguist looked startled.

"It doesn't say, that's it, it stops in mid-sentence," he said.

"What!" Lebedev exploded. He told the interpreter to leave.

Lebedev asked the secretary to ring Colonel Gusev at home. He was forbidden to contact him while he was suspended, but this was an emergency. When she got through to her boss, Lebedev grabbed the phone.

"Colonel, Lebedev here, we have a development," he said, his voice only slightly calmer. "You've got a message on the answerphone in your office, which infuriatingly is cut short, but it's a message from Kozlov."

The colonel must have interrupted with a question.

"About Rebecca Strong and Colonel Gerasimov," Lebedev replied. "The message is a bit cryptic but in my view it's clear what he is telling us. Gerasimov is our man. He's back now. We need to arrest him."

There was a brief silence from Lebedev while Colonel Gusev spoke.

"But Colonel, this is of huge national importance, you're needed here," Lebedev said.

After a few more minutes of talking to his boss, Lebedev put the phone down and turned to the secretary, who was looking enquiringly at him.

"He said it was up to me," Lebedev said. "Poor Kozlov, locked away in prison. No proof, that's what the colonel said. No proof he is our leaker. A flimsy case based on circumstantial evidence. But I know Kozlov is right. So, if it's up to me, I've got to do something."

The secretary looked sympathetic.

"Could you please find me the contact number for Mokotów Prison in Warsaw and email it to me," he said to her.

Lebedev returned to his office and rang the extension for the young Polish-speaking interpreter. He asked him to come to his room as soon as he could.

The young man knocked on the door ten minutes later. He introduced himself for the first time as Ivan Morozov.

"Well, Ivan," Lebedev said, "I have a task for you. I want you to ring up Mokotów Prison in Warsaw and say you represent a prisoner named Pavlo Kuzma and would like to arrange to speak with him as soon as possible. Can you do that?"

The young man looked surprised but nodded his head. Lebedev gave him the number to ring.

Morozov rang and waited a full five minutes before the phone was answered. He relayed the message.

He then used his initiative.

"We are very concerned that Mr Kuzma has been imprisoned for no justified reason and we are anxious to hear from him," he said.

There was silence for a moment. Morozov looked at Lebedev with a questioning expression on his face.

Eventually, Morozov replied to a question.

"I am representing the legal authorities here in Moscow," he said. "I have been asked to ensure that one of our citizens is being treated properly and to find out if he is to be charged and with what offence."

There was another period of silence.

"What are they saying?" Lebedev shouted.

"They are checking for me, Major," Morozov replied, covering the phone with his hand.

After another few minutes, in which he seemed to be listening intently, he called off.

"Well?" Lebedev asked, trying to sound less manic.

"The woman said she had no authority to release any information about any prisoners but then added something I don't understand."

"Go on."

"She said, technically, there wasn't a prisoner called Pavlo Kuzma registered at Mokotów."

"They know who he is," Lebedev said quietly.

***

Unbeknown to Lebedev, a Russian Black Sea Fleet guided-missile destroyer was at that moment preparing to fire a barrage of cruise missiles at Kyiv. Four missiles were fired, three of which hit a weapons depot on the outskirts of the city. The fourth one missed its target after a navigation defect altered the missile's course. It landed with a huge explosion on the roof of Kyiv's City Hospital, No. 6 in Liubomyra Huzara Avenue.

Rebecca Strong was out of bed and getting dressed to leave the hospital when the ceiling in her room caved in. She was struck by a large piece of plasterboard and covered by a shower of dust and splintered wood, and fell heavily to the floor. For the second time since her arrival in Ukraine, she lay unconscious.

CHAPTER TWENTY-SEVEN
GERASIMOV GETS A BIG SURPRISE

Rebecca came to after about ten minutes. She felt as if she had been battered over the head with a baseball bat. When she opened her eyes, nothing she saw made sense. Her bed was effectively cut in half, there was a gaping hole in the ceiling, the floor was covered in plaster and bent pipes and broken glass, and the air was so filled with dust she immediately had to close her eyes again. She stayed where she was on the floor and started feeling every part of her body. The jumper she had put on only seconds before the missile had hit the hospital was torn, and as she peered through semi-closed eyes, she thought she could see blood seeping through the wool. She tentatively put her right hand over her stomach and her fingers came away with blood on the tips. But she found nothing else obviously damaged, apart from her head, which was thumping with pain. She could move her legs and arms. The bloody patch on her stomach worried her, but she decided to try and stand up in order to grab a sheet or towel to press onto the wound. She got up slowly and walked, bent double, to where a towel was still miraculously hanging from a rail. She shook dust from the towel, folded it over and pressed the clean side to her stomach. She suddenly felt she was going to faint, so sat down quickly on the floor and prayed someone would come to her rescue. She could hear screams and shouting from different parts of the hospital, but no one came to see her.

Rebecca sat on the floor for twenty minutes, blood seeping from her wound and turning the white towel red. She no longer felt faint. Her head, however, was causing such pain that she tried to keep as still as possible. Amidst all the screams and sounds of panic, she thought she heard someone running down the corridor outside her room. She called out. Suddenly the door, which was hanging on one hinge, was thrust open and a very large man burst into the room. It was Sam Cook.

He took one look at Rebecca's bleeding stomach, lifted her up and ran down the corridor to where other injured patients and hospital workers were being treated by half a dozen doctors and nurses. One doctor saw the blood on Rebecca's jumper and the red-stained towel and pointed Sam to a trolley bed. Sam gently laid her down.

"Sam, my head, it's hurting," Rebecca whispered.

Sam pointed to her head, and the doctor nodded.

Half an hour later, Rebecca had received fifteen stitches in her stomach wound and was on a morphine drip. She was able to smile at Sam. She was lying in a bed in a room undamaged by the missile attack.

"Thank you," she said, just above a whisper. "I'm getting used to being blown up. Can we please get the hell out of this country."

Sam was about to reply when a distraught-looking Sandy appeared. He rushed towards Rebecca, but Sam held him back.

"Steady, steady," he said.

Sandy wrestled himself free and went to kiss Rebecca on her forehead. She flinched but stroked his face.

"I didn't know your hospital had been hit until someone told me," Sandy cried. "You could have died and I wasn't here for you."

"Well, I didn't, so don't worry," Rebecca said. "Sam saved me."

Sandy looked daggers at Sam but then his shoulders dropped. "Thank you, Sam, that's twice you've saved her," he said.

"First time wasn't me," Sam said, "it was—"

He just stopped in time. He had been on the point of saying it was Gerasimov who had saved her life.

Sam's phone rang. He left the room to answer it. When he returned, he told Rebecca: "That was Geraldine, she wants you out of here as soon as possible. She has made arrangements for you to see specialists in Warsaw, to make sure the doctors here have done a good job."

"Bless her," Rebecca said, holding on to Sandy's hand.

"When are you going to Warsaw?" Sandy sounded alarmed. "She needs rest."

"I'm all right, Sandy, don't fret." Rebecca smiled.

Sam said it wouldn't be for a couple of days. First, she would rest in the hotel and be seen by a doctor from the British embassy.

"I could come with you to Warsaw," Sandy said. "My time is up here. I'm being replaced in two days' time. Would that be OK?"

Rebecca glanced at Sam. "Of course," she said. "But there'll be no hanky panky in Warsaw."

Sandy grinned. Sam looked shocked.

At that moment, Rebecca received another visitor.

"Pinenut!" she cried out.

He came forward with a big grin on his face. His right arm was encased in a huge cast and resting in a sling.

"I'd get you to kiss me but my boyfriend might get jealous," she said.

Pinenut introduced himself to Sandy.

They were interrupted when a doctor and two nurses came in to examine Rebecca. Sam, Sandy and Pinenut were ushered out.

***

On the day Gerasimov was due for his 8:15 a.m. appointment in the Kremlin, a meeting took place an hour earlier in the Presidential Executive Office. Present around a huge marble table were President Putin; General Valery Gerasimov, Chief of the

General Staff; Alexander Bortnikov, Director of the FSB; Sergey Lavrov, Minister of Foreign Affairs; and Nikolai Patrushev, Secretary of the Security Council of the Russian Federation, and Gerasimov's boss.

Putin spoke.

"The meeting in Warsaw is to take place in ten days," he said. "I have every confidence it will lead to a settlement of some kind, a settlement that will give us victory and honour, and deliver to the Kyiv comedian a bloody nose, and to his Western partners-in-crime, humiliation and ruin."

Everyone around the table nodded in agreement.

"It is imperative," Putin went on, "that this be conducted in the strictest secrecy. All the necessary arrangements have been made."

Each individual around the table had received the same document the night before. It described in detail the secret negotiations that had been going on with the newly elected right-wing Polish government. The new Polish prime minister had agreed with the Moscow envoy sent by Putin that the war in Ukraine had to be brought to an end as rapidly as possible. A battlefield stalemate had been in existence for more than nine months. Neither side was making much progress. But the Russian invasion force had hung on to most of the Ukrainian territory it had seized and Putin had decided that was sufficient to claim victory. The election of the new Polish leader who had campaigned to end the war and return the two million Ukrainian refugees back to their country had given Putin the opportunity he had been looking for. He hoped that Poland, under a different regime, would be in a position to put pressure on Washington and other European leaders to reach consensus for a ceasefire and a war-ending deal. There was already division within the US-led coalition over the huge cost of backing and arming Ukraine for another year.

Final negotiations before Poland was to come out and publicly reveal a breakthrough with Moscow were due to take place on Saturday November 30th. A small Russian delegation led by Sergey Lavrov would be flown in a private plane to Poland. The delegation was to include senior representatives from the general staff, the FSB and the Kremlin.

Putin had more to say.

"I will be adding a few more select people to the delegation."

Lavrov, who normally tried to keep his lugubrious facial expression constant so as not to indicate any personal differences with the president, raised one eyebrow, but without looking straight at Putin. Only the FSB director, sitting next to him, noticed.

Nobody asked whom Putin had in mind but, much to the surprise of everyone except General Gerasimov, he volunteered their names.

"I have included two GRU officers, Majors Belov and Zarubin, after consultation with the Chief of the General Staff, plus Colonel Gerasimov from the staff of the Security Council," the president said.

Nikolai Patrushev couldn't hide his astonishment. Gerasimov was due in his office in less than forty minutes to be told his Kremlin days were over. Irrespective of whether he was the leaker and therefore a traitor, his performance in Kyiv as leader of the failed assassination mission was judged by his boss to have been both unsatisfactory and highly suspect. Gerasimov was to be suspended until the FSB investigation had been completed and he was to remain at home until further notice. Now Patrushev had no idea what he was supposed to do. He was also angry with Putin for not consulting with him.

"You look troubled, Nikolai Platonovich," Putin said, addressing him by his first and middle names.

"I am speaking with Gerasimov in my office later this morning, Mr President, but I had a different conversation in mind," he replied.

"Well, it's fortunate you are seeing him," Putin said. "You can tell him about his new assignment."

"Mr President, Colonel Gerasimov is still under investigation," Alexander Bortnikov, FSB director, said. "Is it wise to …?"

He stopped when he saw Putin's eyes almost closing. It was the sign that the president was displeased.

"Should I tell him what the assignment is, exactly, Mr President?" Patrushev asked tentatively. He had missed the warning sign. "Can he be trusted when he is a suspect for the leaking of your visit to Sevastopol?"

Putin opened his eyes fully for a moment but then squinted.

"All is not as it may seem," he said. "Gerasimov is to be told nothing other than he is to depart in a week's time with the delegation. He is not to be informed where the delegation is going or what the purpose of the delegation is. The Chief of the General Staff is fully cognisant of why I want Gerasimov on the trip."

Both Patrushev and Bortnikov looked swiftly in General Gerasimov's direction. But the general's face remained impassive.

Putin had one more thing to say: "I will address the nation once the new Polish leader makes the announcement."

The meeting came to an end. Everyone left except the Chief of the General Staff and the president.

"Bortnikov is on thin ice for not telling me about Major Kozlov," Putin said. "Lavrov, too. He must have known one of our people had been arrested in Warsaw. Nobody told me. It's only thanks to Major Lebedev that I'm kept informed of the investigation."

"Bortnikov always plays his own game, Mr President," General Gerasimov replied.

"Perhaps for not much longer," Putin said, and stood up.

"All has been arranged for Warsaw," the general said.

Putin nodded and they walked together out of the Presidential Executive Office.

***

Rebecca recovered quickly from her stomach and head injuries. She left the hospital, or what remained of it after the cruise missile strike, and was taken to see the doctor at the British embassy. He never asked what she was doing in Kyiv but suggested it would be wise to leave the country as soon as was practicable. He agreed it would be sensible to spend two days resting at her hotel, and said she would need to have the stitches in her stomach checked after seven or eight days.

That evening, Rebecca sat down for dinner at her hotel in the company of Sandy, Sam and Pinenut, who now considered himself part of the family. He had come up with an idea. He said he would like to drive them all to Warsaw in a new car he had acquired. It would be a journey of some ten hours, but once over the border he knew of places to stay in Poland which would help Rebecca to get plenty of rest. He also said it would be fun.

"I haven't been out of Ukraine for two years and I'm sick of being bombed every night," he told them.

Sandy said he was owed time off after his assignment in Ukraine. Sam said he had spoken to London and had been ordered to protect Rebecca at all costs. Getting out of Ukraine was the obvious option, and a car ride sounded a great idea. They all looked at Rebecca.

"Pinenut, you really are a star, I'd love it," she said. "But there's no way you can drive with your arm in concrete. Sam and Sandy can share the driving."

Pinenut, who was clearly infatuated with Rebecca, grinned and agreed it might be best for someone else to drive. He told them he would get everything ready for the journey, including stocking up with food and drink. It was now Thursday November 21st. They would leave Kyiv on Monday morning and expect to be across the border in Poland by late evening. Pinenut said he would book two nights in a hotel near the border.

Sam said he would arrange with London for rooms in a hotel in Warsaw for two nights from November 27th, and flights back to the UK on Friday evening, November 29th. That would give time for Rebecca to be seen at the hospital.

"You're all spoiling me," Rebecca said.

***

Gerasimov had been sitting in front of Nikolai Patrushev for two minutes and he was already astonished. He had gone over every possible scenario in his mind before he had knocked on the door for his 8:15 a.m. appointment. He thought there was a good chance he would be fired or suspended, or worse, exiled to some administrative post in Siberia. What he didn't expect was a new assignment. But Patrushev had opened his remarks not with a dressing down, but with a job he was to be told nothing about. All Patrushev would say was that he had been selected by the president himself to be part of an important delegation. He didn't say where it was going or what precisely Gerasimov's role would be.

"It's an honour, Colonel," Patrushev said.

Gerasimov was told the delegation would be leaving early in the morning on Saturday November 30th, and led by the foreign minister. A flight of around two hours would be involved.

"In the meantime, you are to report to your office each day," Patrushev went on.

Gerasimov couldn't believe his ears. *Surely*, he thought to himself, *something sinister is happening.*

Was the destination for the two-hour flight within Russia? If so, where could it possibly be going? If it was going beyond Russia to another country, it couldn't be anywhere in Europe because of the war in Ukraine. Every country in Europe was a member of NATO, although not all were as committed to Ukraine's defeat of Russia. The leader of Hungary kept calling for a ceasefire, and the new government in Poland appeared to be pushing for a fresh initiative to bring the war to an end.

Gerasimov thought of other possible destinations. Minsk, capital of Belarus, was only an hour and a half away. Flight time to Astana, capital of Kazakhstan, was certainly more than three hours, and anyway, Gerasimov couldn't think of a reason why a high-level delegation would be going there at this time.

"Am I to be briefed at any point about the purpose of the delegation and where it is going?" Gerasimov asked.

"It is a matter of extreme national security and there will be no details provided until you are on board the aircraft," Patrushev replied.

Gerasimov tried not to look amazed by the reply. What on earth was going on?

As he listened to Patrushev explaining the importance of telling no one, either in his office or at home, about the November 30th flight, Gerasimov could only think of one thing: should he inform his British controller by leaving a note in one of the dead drops he had been given? He knew the risks would be immense; he would have to use the most painstaking and complex counter-surveillance techniques to avoid FSB watchers. But if Putin was plotting some mysterious, no doubt devious, mission, his controller should be told. Gerasimov's heart began to beat at twice the normal rate at the thought of what he would have to do in the time he had left before the November 30th deadline.

***

David Kimche had already checked the first dead drop on the list he had given Gerasimov. Despite all the advances in technology available to spies, dead drops were more often than not still the favoured basic tradecraft method for exchanging secret information. The stump of a tree, a lamp post with a broken plate at the bottom, a wall with crumbling mortar, a fixed litter bin with a chink in the concrete standing, anywhere classified information provided by an agent could be concealed. For a period, British spies in Moscow had favoured using fake rocks as cover for secret documents, but the FSB had got wise to this technique and fake rocks were abandoned.

Kimche preferred using the simplest form of dead-drop location. He had three golden rules: they had to be easy to spot but not too obvious, they should be used only once by the agent, and nothing left should ever be visible to a passer-by. The chosen spot at the top of the list of dead drops handed by Agent Treasure to Gerasimov was a hole in the brickwork behind a newsagent stand outside Savyolovskaya railway station in the northern district of Maryina Roshcha.

Kimche had taken a free newspaper from the stand and then dropped it to check behind. He spotted the hole in the wall. The station, inside and outside, was busy, and Kimche judged that Redruth would be able to slip a piece of paper into the brickwork without causing interest from the flow of people, especially at peak times each day. The station served suburban areas and was busiest between 8 a.m. and 9 a.m., and later in the day between 5 p.m. and 6:30 p.m.

Kimche knew there was a risk if he made too many checks on the dead drop. As MI6 station chief, he had to use elaborate methods to throw off his FSB watchers. He also knew that it was most likely Redruth would be unable to leave anything behind the news stand so soon after returning from Ukraine.

However, Kimche was under strict instructions from his boss, Patrick Littlefield, to make every effort and to take every risk to maintain communications with Redruth.

Kimche waited three days before making his second journey to the dead drop outside Savyolovskaya station. He planned to take four different taxis and two Metro trains. He immediately spotted two FSB watchers when he took the first taxi and knew he had failed to shake them off when he was sitting in the back of the third taxi. A scooter, which he had seen before, was following close behind. When he climbed out of the fourth taxi, he walked straight into a large department store and headed up the escalator. He spent ten minutes in the store observing everyone. He thought he spotted an FSB watcher but the suspect moved away and didn't look round.

Kimche knew, after researching every aspect of his route to Savyolovskaya station, that the department store had a basement where parcels and packages for collection were lined up along the walls. There was a door to an outside pick-up area. He made his way casually to the basement, using the back stairs. No one followed him. He ignored staff members who stared curiously at him and walked with his head held high towards the exit. The door was stiff but unlocked. He opened it and breathed a sigh of relief. In the paved area facing him were a handful of parked cars and vans, but no sign of anyone either waiting or watching. He walked away from the store and back to the main street, and within four minutes was inside Mayakovskaya underground station. Last stop for him was Savyolovskaya on the Metro and then up the escalator into the railway station.

He had taken an hour. He came out of the station and headed for the news stand, which was located to the left of the entrance. He took out his phone and gave the impression to anyone looking that he was busily sending a text. In fact, the phone was dead. The SIM card and battery were sitting in a drawer in his desk at the embassy. He went to the news stand and took one of the free papers. He tucked it under his arm but then dropped his phone. He reached down to pick it up and peered behind. Something was stuffed into the hole in the brickwork. He removed it and stood up, hiding the crumpled paper behind his mobile. He then walked quickly back into the station and down the escalator into the Metro. He emerged ten minutes later and caught a taxi to central Moscow.

He was a longstanding intelligence officer and had run agents not just in Moscow, but also in places as far afield as Beirut and Ulaanbaatar. But he still felt almost overwhelming excitement at the thought of what might be written on the screwed-up piece of paper in his coat pocket.

Kimche arrived back at the embassy just before lunch and went straight to the citadel, the special bunker room in the basement of the embassy where the MI6 station was based. He took off his coat, threw it on his desk and sat down heavily in his swing chair. His heart was beating fast. He reached to the coat and drew out the piece of paper. He read it out aloud to himself.

"Something extraordinary is going on. A special delegation headed by Lavrov is flying from Moscow on November 30th, early morning. I have been ordered to be part of it. Whatever the mission is, it's so secret I haven't been told where it's going or what it's about. But the flight will take about two hours. I have been told Putin personally selected me for the delegation! That's all I know, but my instinct is it's to do with Ukraine, and the flight destination is not, repeat not, within Russia. My own participation in this secret mission fills me with foreboding. I fear Kremlin has plans for my demise. R."

CHAPTER TWENTY-EIGHT
DEADLINE TO UNCOVER PUTIN'S SECRET MISSION

David Kimche's secret cable to MI6's director of operations set off instant alarm bells. Redruth had come up with a devastating but frustrating piece of intelligence from within the Kremlin. Patrick Littlefield's first thought was that Redruth may have been deliberately fed disinformation to see whether he leaked it. It would be his death sentence. But then he thought, *why go to such lengths to prove Redruth is a traitor?*

Patrick decided to hold a meeting with Geraldine, Grace Redmayne and Freddie Stigby before informing the Americans of the latest development. He wanted to get clear in his mind what the British consensus judgement was before involving the increasingly sceptical American cousins.

Patrick had kept the cable from his station chief in Moscow to himself. He would break the news when the rest of the Operation Greengage team arrived.

They all turned up on time for the noon meeting on the sixth floor of MI6's Vauxhall Cross headquarters. As soon as they were assembled, he handed the cable to Geraldine and asked her to pass it round.

Freddie's immediate reaction was the same as Patrick's.

"This feels like a typical disinformation ploy by Moscow," he said.

"That was my initial instinct," Patrick replied. "Geraldine? Grace?"

Grace was tapping something on her mobile.

Geraldine looked at her and frowned and then responded to Patrick.

"I wonder," she said. "The message from Redruth is infuriatingly short on detail but potentially could mean something big is happening. Let's look at it first as a genuine piece of intelligence. The first question is, why is Redruth involved at all? Why would Putin want him as part of this supposed delegation? We have to assume the FSB will have briefed Putin on the list of suspects for the Sevastopol leak, so he will know Redruth is the top suspect. No one can read Putin's mind, but if he has personally ordered Redruth to be on this flight it probably has nothing to do with the delegation, if there is a delegation."

"Meaning?" Patrick asked.

"It's a way of getting him out of the country and then disappearing him," she replied.

"But why bother?" Freddie asked. "Why not just take him to a tall building and open a window?"

There was silence for a moment.

Then Grace looked up from her phone. "Looking at it as a genuine piece of intelligence, in other words, making the judgement that a delegation led by Sergey Lavrov is actually going to happen on November 30th, where could they be going?" she said.

Before anyone could answer, she continued: "I've checked on my phone to see where they could reach within a two-hour flight time. Just for the sake of argument, it takes four or five hours to fly from Moscow to, say, Siberia, and anyway, why on earth would a special, secret delegation go to Siberia, or come to that, anywhere in Russia?"

Everyone was focused on Grace.

"So, let's assume the delegation is heading somewhere outside Russia," she said. "The obvious place would be Minsk in Belarus because of Putin's strong alliance with that madman Aleksandr

Lukashenko. But flight time is only an hour and a half. And again, why would Putin send a delegation to Minsk right now? They are already on side, and Putin only has to pick up the phone."

Grace looked around the table and saw she still had everyone's attention.

"So, where would Putin want to send a delegation on a highly secret mission?" she asked rhetorically. "A mission so secret that Redruth was told he would not be informed until he was on the plane, and, who knows, perhaps not until the plane arrived at the destination."

No one spoke.

"The only place that makes any sort of sense is Warsaw," she said.

"Warsaw!" Freddie blurted out.

"Warsaw is just over two hours' flight time from Moscow," she said. "If there is any place in Europe where Putin might think he has leverage right now over the war in Ukraine it would be Warsaw. The new prime minister campaigned on bringing the war to an end, which would be music to Putin's ears, because dividing NATO is what he has been after ever since the war began."

"Grace, that's brilliant," Geraldine said, "but it still doesn't address why Redruth is included on this secret mission, if it's genuine."

"I fear you got it right, Geraldine," Grace replied. "Redruth is to be dispatched. For some reason we can't fathom, it may have been decided his death would be better orchestrated beyond Russia's shores rather than, as Freddie put it, arranged via a sixth-floor open window in Moscow."

Patrick turned to Freddie. "Freddie, what's your reading about Redruth?"

"Well, first of all, Putin always does what he wants, the way he wants it," Freddie said. "So, to us Westerners, it might seem totally bizarre that he should put Redruth on a plane to wherever, let's say Warsaw, when he must know that he has been interrogated by the FSB as a suspected traitor to Russia. But Putin thinks differently. It's possible that he wants the man who supposedly escaped from his Ukrainian captors to be dealt with as far away from Moscow as possible. And without his fingerprints on the gun, as it were."

Geraldine shook her head. "I suspect we're missing something here," she said. "There has to be another reason why he would send Redruth out of the country. I agree with you about Putin perhaps wanting to keep at arm's length from the Gerasimov case, although he hasn't been shy about this sort of thing in the past. But I feel there has to be more to it, though for the life of me I can't think what it might be."

Patrick looked worried. "Potentially, we have a major development here. If Grace's analysis is correct, there is a plot going on between Moscow and Warsaw that could disrupt the whole alliance and fatally divide the pro-Ukraine coalition, which Washington has been so assiduous in assembling. If someone of influence, such as the new Polish prime minister, albeit a newcomer to the scene, comes out and claims to have reached an historic deal with Moscow, that coalition could crumble very quickly. There are enough doubters in the camp already, especially in the Republican Party in Congress. Or, and I have to say this, sorry Grace, what if it *is* just a piece of disinformation to expose our asset as a traitor? If we take it seriously and launch pre-emptive action to stop a Moscow/Warsaw alliance, Redruth is a dead man."

Before anyone could respond, Patrick went on: "The other thing is, should we tell our respective ministers, or perhaps go straight to the PM, and let our political masters make the big decision? After all, if this ends badly and embarrasses the government, we're going to get it in the neck for keeping ministers out of the loop."

"I know what my minister will say," said Geraldine. "She will demand to know the source of the intelligence and will be outraged that she hadn't been told before about a secret asset in Moscow. If I were to tell her who the asset is, which of course I never would while he remains a viable agent for us, she would literally blow up."

Nobody laughed. Privately, they knew Geraldine was right. The relatively new home secretary, Veronica Greenwood, had a reputation for losing her temper and was generally dismissive about the role of intelligence in the business of government. She had political responsibility for MI5 but had made it plain from the beginning that she was sceptical about the value and affordability of the security service.

The foreign secretary, James Blandford-Smith, would be less confrontational, but Patrick said his political master would immediately want to sound the alarm in Washington and the European capitals.

"That would be fine and the responsible thing to do, but only if the intelligence is genuine and Grace's very helpful assessment is on the ball," Patrick said.

"So you're saying we should keep this to ourselves for the moment, until we know for sure it's Warsaw?" Geraldine asked.

"It's a risk, but yes," Patrick said.

"And our cousins?" Geraldine asked.

"If we tell Langley, our hands will no longer be on the tiller," replied Patrick. "Everyone would rush in with their views and take over. We have to stay in control because of Redruth. We owe it to him to treat this piece of intelligence with discretion. He may be facing a death sentence and it's up to us to do something about it. With the whole circus involved, his fate might get pushed aside."

Geraldine looked admiringly at Patrick. She totally agreed with him.

"There is one thing, of course," Freddie said. "If the delegation is real and it goes to Warsaw and Redruth is on it, that'll be the end of Operation Greengage."

Everyone in the room knew that was true but had been reluctant to admit it. If the latest intelligence from Redruth was accurate, that would be his final offering as a Kremlin insider. The focus from now on would be on rescuing him from the murderous clutches of the Russian state.

"So we're agreed," Patrick said. "For now, we keep this between us until we can uncover more intelligence. I'll get our Moscow and Warsaw stations to prioritise this. If we get confirmation that this Putin delegation is heading for Warsaw we will alert everyone. In the meantime, we need a new plan to rescue Redruth. But until we know for sure about Warsaw, that's going to be quite a challenge. The only saving grace is that a rescue in Warsaw should be less perilous than an evacuation from Moscow. Any thoughts?"

"By wonderful coincidence, we will have our intrepid team, Sam and Rebecca, in Warsaw around this time," Geraldine said. "And before you say anything that will make you sound like Adam Goldstein, these two have been amazing so far. But I'm going to send one of my top guys to Warsaw to meet up with them. He will work out a plan of action. Rebecca has been injured twice in the line of duty and it's probably best she stays out of it, but Sam, with all his experience, and my man from here, Jack Swift, will be ready to grab Redruth if this delegation does turn up at Warsaw airport on November 30th."

Patrick was dubious. "I'm sure they are both capable of carrying it off," he said. "I know Jack, he's the best. But, and this is all theoretical of course at this stage, we can't have a major incident taking place in public view at the airport, especially if it goes wrong. Even a successful snatch job could lead to an international incident. Lavrov, if it is to be him arriving in Warsaw, will have armed bodyguards with him. Can you imagine if there's a shoot-out and people get killed? Our people. I'm assuming neither Sam nor Jack will be armed."

"I can arrange for them to have personal weapons," Geraldine said, "but you're right, snatching Redruth at the airport could lead to unpredictable consequences. Jack will work out the best way of doing it."

"I want one of my people there, too," Patrick said. "I have someone in mind, ex-military. He's been in Warsaw for two years and was in Moscow before then. George Gardiner."

"I expect Sam knows him," Geraldine said. "So yes, that would make a good team."

"So that's decided," Patrick said. "But we mustn't get ahead of ourselves. The key thing is to pin down Warsaw. Fingers crossed Redruth will learn more before November 30th and let us know, although it sounds unlikely."

***

Gerasimov's first day back in the office was one of the most uncomfortable in his career. His secretary was dutiful but looked at him like he was an alien from outer space. No one welcomed him back. One asked whether he had recovered from his wounds, a question that threw him for a few seconds until he remembered. The flesh wound he had received at the hands of the Ukrainian colonel had fortunately helped him when he was obliged to have a medical examination. There was a jagged scar where the bullet had entered his side.

None of the people in his office knew anything about the president's plan for a special delegation leaving Moscow on November 30th. He had hoped to pick up at least some gossip about the trip, which he could have passed on to his British controller. But he spent a week in the office with very little to do, and realised early on that he would no longer have access to either top secret communications or documents stamped "Of Special Importance". His security clearance had been downgraded. If ever he needed proof that he remained high on the list of suspects for the Sevastopol leak, that was it. As each day went by, he became more and more convinced he was being set up for a Kremlinauthorised revenge hit, and that his presence on the delegation was just a way of getting him out of the country.

Since becoming a double agent for MI6, Gerasimov knew that if he ever considered he was in extreme danger, he had the right to call on his British handlers to arrange his escape from Moscow. The instructions passed to him by David Kimche's agent inside the FSB had included a section on the proposed escape plan in the event of an emergency. The plan was codenamed "Operation Lion". But if he was going to be dispatched after the two-hour flight from Moscow, Operation Lion would be irrelevant.

He knew he had to activate Operation Lion before he was put on the plane with the delegation. He felt he had done enough already as a double agent to persuade the British to extract him now that his life was in danger. But he feared for his family. Operation Lion only mentioned one individual: Agent Redruth. He vowed to take this up with his British controller as soon as possible.

The first part of Operation Lion sounded like a chapter from a spy novel in the 1960s. He was to place a potted plant of any variety in the window of his third-floor kitchen, which overlooked the side street. The plant should be big enough to be easily visible to a passer-by. If this failed to generate the immediate activation of Operation Lion, there were two fallbacks. The first was a note with the word "LION" written on it in capital letters, which was to be placed in an empty jar inside a fallen tree trunk in Neskuchny Garden in central Moscow. The second fallback was only to be used in the gravest emergency, a coded message to MI6's twenty-four-hour duty phone: "Sorry the visit to the zoo had to be abandoned."

Gerasimov hadn't been told exactly how he would be spirited out of Moscow, but according to the instructions, twenty hours after placing the potted plant in his kitchen window he was to go to Park Kultury Metro station, across the river from Gorky Park, and look out for a taxi with the registration Y799YA. He was to get in and tell the driver he wanted to go to the south entrance of Gorky Park, in Bolshaya Sadovaya Street. He would be met there and would transfer to a Transit van. That was as far as the instructions went.

At eight o'clock in the evening on Tuesday November 26th, Gerasimov placed a potted chrysanthemum on the window ledge in his kitchen and told his wife it was a gift from him as thanks for all she had been put through in recent weeks, with his long absence in Ukraine and the interrogation she had had to endure by the FSB. He had no idea how his British controller kept an eye out for the plant signal but he assumed regular checks were made, probably by different people so as to avoid suspicion from any watching FSB surveillance teams. Because he put the chrysanthemum in the window when it was dark outside, Gerasimov decided he would go to Neskuchny Garden the following evening and leave the note with "LION" written on it in the jar inside the fallen tree trunk as backup. By then, he would be less than four days away from being picked up to join the mystery two-hour flight as part of Putin's special delegation.

Although the Operation Lion instructions had been explicit, there appeared, in Gerasimov's view, to be one fundamental weakness. He wouldn't know for sure whether his cry for help had registered with the British spies until he was standing outside Park Kultury Metro station waiting for the taxi with the particular registration to arrive. If neither the plant nor the message in the jar were spotted, he faced the prospect of standing outside the Metro station looking like a lost soul. Lost souls in Moscow, especially ones on a list of FSB suspects, were likely to be unceremoniously grabbed and taken off for questioning.

Gerasimov decided that when he went to Park Kultury Metro station, he would stay for no more than ten minutes and would then return home. He would do the same the following evening, knowing there would be a grave risk of being spotted and arrested by FSB watchers. If there was still no taxi, he would make the coded call on the way back home. Phoning was a huge risk because of the fear of being traced, but at that point, with less than two days before leaving for the airport on Saturday morning, he would be desperate. The other weakness in the escape plan, he felt, was that he didn't know whether the call would be answered by his controller or one of his colleagues, or whether he would just be expected to leave the coded message.

Gerasimov went to bed full of trepidation. What he didn't realise was that his wife had forgotten his request not to close the curtains. He had specifically told her to leave the curtains open and had given a somewhat bizarre reason. He said the shop where he had bought the plant had advised maximum natural light for the first few days. Not only did she close them but, before clearing up after he had gone to bed, she removed the potted chrysanthemum from the windowsill. She put it on the table and stood admiring it for a few seconds. Her husband was not in the habit of buying her flowers.

**

Days earlier, in London, Patrick had sent a priority cable to the stations in Moscow, Warsaw, Budapest, Sofia, Bucharest and the capitals of the three Baltic countries: Estonia, Latvia and Lithuania. The cable was marked "Top Secret" and sent to the individual station chiefs. It said:

Most Urgent. Every attempt must be made to find out whether a Russian delegation led by Sergey Lavrov is expected in the region on November 30th, Warsaw deemed the most likely. Please tap all your sources. Any rumours, theories, thoughts welcome. But confirmation is the Holy Grail. Respond by the end of today GMT. Patrick Littlefield (DO).

Five hours later, Patrick received multiple cables. They were all exclusively filled with theories and thoughts, but no rumours, not even a hint, and definitely no confirmation. The station chiefs in the Baltic countries all said the same: they didn't believe that any NATO nation, even Poland with its new leader, would dare to defy Washington and host a secret visit of a Russian delegation. The Budapest, Bucharest and Sofia stations merely stated that there had been no hint or indication of the arrival of a Russian delegation in the region. The station chief in Budapest had used his gumption and checked all incoming flights to Eastern Europe from Moscow on November 30th. There were none.

The station chief in Warsaw was the only one to produce a small but intriguing nugget of intelligence, although for a reason Patrick failed to understand, he left the piece of information until the end of a long and detailed analysis about why the new Polish leader might be tempted to forge a secret backchannel with Moscow, following his openly sceptical view about the way the war in Ukraine was going and his doubts about whether it was any longer in Western interests to plough so much money and arms into the conflict. The analysis was sound, but Patrick skipped through it, looking for something, anything, that might back up Agent Redruth's tip-off.

The last paragraph made Patrick sit up sharply.

Unconnected but curious: a Russian FSB officer, Major Pavel Kozlov, who was detained by the Polish authorities after arriving in Warsaw on a false passport, was due to appear in court next week on several charges. I'm informed by sources in the justice system that the case has been withdrawn and that it is likely Kozlov will be released and deported.

Patrick rang Geraldine.

"Got it," he told her, when she answered the phone.

"Confirmation?" she replied.

"No, but something else," he said.

He read out the Warsaw station chief's last paragraph.

"My God," cried Geraldine, "there is a deal, isn't there? This is all part of a dirty backstairs plot between Moscow and Warsaw?"

"Looks like it," Patrick said.

"And do you think this is why Redruth has been included in this delegation?" Geraldine queried. "So that Kozlov can formally denounce him? Weird, and not what you'd expect from Putin, but who knows? Perhaps even Putin wants final proof in this case before accepting he has had a double agent working in the Kremlin."

"Maybe," Patrick said. "But now what do we do? Redruth's life is in serious danger once he gets on that plane. Can we risk that? And if we do, how sure are we that we can follow him wherever he is taken and rescue him?"

"Have you heard from Redruth in the last twenty-four hours?" Geraldine asked.

"No, nothing. David Kimche has been watching out and checking each day, but no sign of panic on Redruth's part," Patrick said. "But even if he's happy to risk taking the flight, we still have to make a decision at our end."

"Of course," said Geraldine. "We also have to decide whether we now need to blow the whole Moscow/Warsaw thing and warn off the Poles."

"We can't do that until the delegation touches down in Warsaw, right?" Patrick said. "We still don't have proof it's going to happen. The Kozlov ingredient looks pretty conclusive but if we move now, Moscow will just deny everything, as they always do. Warsaw might deny it, too, so we end up with nothing."

"Except Warsaw will get the message loud and clear that underhand deals with Moscow are a betrayal of the alliance," Geraldine said.

"I still think we need to catch the Russians red-handed," Patrick said. "That will be humiliating for Moscow and also put maximum pressure on the new leader in Warsaw to dance to the alliance's tune and not go rogue."

"OK, agreed," Geraldine replied, "but as soon as we get a sighting of Lavrov's delegation on Polish soil, we will have to alert everyone, especially Washington. They will be furious with us for keeping quiet, but in the end, Lavrov will be forced to turn back and return to Moscow and our Polish friends will have to answer to Washington. All those Abrams tanks and F-16s being shipped to Poland to boost their defence forces could suddenly not arrive. Yes, they'll get the message all right."

"Timing is going to be crucial," Patrick said. "If we delay too long in warning everyone, there'll be an almighty row. It will all depend on our team in Warsaw. They will have two missions: to identify Lavrov beyond any doubt, and at the same time watch for anything that suggests Redruth is going to be taken off somewhere separately."

"Who do you want in charge?" Geraldine asked.

"My guy in Warsaw, George Gardiner, if that's OK with you," Patrick said. "He knows the ground and I've brought him up to scratch with Operation Greengage. There was no other way. I know we wanted to keep Greengage really tight, but he had to be told."

"That's fine," said Geraldine. "That means George, Sam and Rebecca are in the know. I think we will have to tell Jack Swift as well. He can't be the only one operating in the dark."

"Agreed," Patrick said. "And anyway, we're no longer talking about running a high-level asset in the Kremlin where secrecy is paramount. To rescue Redruth we need every team member to understand the responsibility we are giving them."

"Quite," said Geraldine.

All that was left was for them to decide on a codename for the dual mission in Warsaw. They consulted the long list of codewords that had been picked randomly by computer. Geraldine spotted "Limehouse" and chose that. She had once rented a flat in Limehouse, in the former docklands area of East London. Patrick approved. Operation Limehouse was set in motion.

Sam and Rebecca had been told about the new developments while they were driving down to Warsaw. With Sandy and

Pinenut in the car hearing them speak on the phone, Sam and Rebecca had a problem: what to tell their fellow travellers.

Rebecca just said, "We may have to be in Warsaw for a little longer than planned. But you two can go your separate ways whenever you want."

Pinenut beat Sandy to it. "No way, Goldilocks. We'll stick with you guys. You'll need us."

Sandy nodded. Rebecca looked at Sam and shrugged her shoulders.

***

Gerasimov waited for ten minutes outside Park Kultury Metro station, wrapped in a long coat, a grey woollen scarf around his neck. He began his risky waiting game at seven thirty on Wednesday evening. He had no belongings with him. He didn't stand still; he tried to look occupied, while all the time looking out for the taxi with the registration Y799YA. No such taxi arrived. Gerasimov had taken more than an hour to reach the Metro to shake off FSB watchers but to his surprise he hadn't spotted any surveillance, and didn't see any now. He wondered whether the FSB had been warned off by the Kremlin because of the president's personal decision to include him on the special delegation. He doubted it, and was even more unnerved.

He waited another three minutes and then went down into the Metro. He had deployed two strands of the Operation Lion escape plan: the potted plant, which he had duly put back on the kitchen windowsill, and the message in the jar in the tree trunk. Now he had three days to impress on his British controller that he needed evacuating *before* he boarded the aircraft with the rest of the delegation on Saturday morning.

Gerasimov repeated the journey to the Park Kultury Metro the following evening. This time he waited longer, nearly forty-five minutes, during which he became increasingly nervous and found himself shivering with tension and fear. He expected, as each minute went by, to be bundled into the back of an FSB 4x4 and delivered to Lubyanka Square for the special treatment they reserved for suspected traitors to the motherland. There was no sign of the taxi.

What he didn't know was that David Kimche had been issued with new instructions.

The top secret cable he had received from London read:

URGENT. Imperative Redruth boards delegation aircraft. Operation Lion now officially redundant. Repeat, Lion is cancelled.

At 10:20 p.m. on Thursday November 28th, Gerasimov used one of his last-remaining burner cell phones to make a call. It rang and then went into message mode.

He left the agreed message: "Sorry the visit to the zoo had to be abandoned."

Kimche was in the citadel in the embassy basement when he heard Redruth's voice on the phone. And the message.

He took no action, as per London instructions.

One of Kimche's agents in Moscow had eventually spotted the potted chrysanthemum and reported back. Kimche himself had double-checked by going to Neskuchny Garden and had removed the message from the jar. He had returned to the embassy and begun the process of putting Operation Lion into action. Just twenty minutes later he received the new orders from London. Operation Lion was off.

As Redruth's handler and controller, Kimche felt pangs of guilt that he was under instructions not to activate Operation Lion. He knew that Redruth would be in a state of bewilderment, confusion and anxiety, and he had grave doubts about the London decision. In the past, if a secret agent cried for help, MI6 felt obliged to act. It was part of the trust that developed between the agent and his case officer. But Redruth now was a key player in a much bigger strategic game. London's argument was that if there was a secret deal going on between Moscow and Warsaw, it had to be exposed in flagrante, and the only way of discovering whether the new Polish leader was about to betray the rest of the alliance was to present him with the prima facie proof – the arrival of the Lavrov-led delegation at Warsaw airport. Redruth had to play his part. But in Kimche's view, it put Redruth's life in grave jeopardy.

CHAPTER TWENTY-NINE
OPERATION LIMEHOUSE GETS UNDERWAY

Rebecca and her companions arrived in Warsaw on Thursday November 28th, a day later than planned because the driving had been tiring for everyone. They drove straight to the hospital, where Rebecca was examined and given the good news that her stomach injury was healing well. The following morning, Sam and Rebecca were to go to the British embassy in Kawaleril Street in the Ujazdów district of central Warsaw. Sam had rung Geraldine on her cell phone and been told to go there to meet up with George Gardiner.

Sandy could smell a story in the making, but Rebecca shook her head.

"It's a private meeting," she said. "We'll meet up at the hotel later."

George Gardiner, MI6 station chief in Warsaw, and Jack Swift, veteran MI5 officer, newly arrived from London, met Sam and Rebecca on the steps of the embassy early Friday morning.

The MI6 man didn't look like a spy. He was more than six foot tall, with a bald head and thick-lensed heavyweight glasses. Jack Swift was different. He was only average height but he looked tough. His hair was cropped short and he had exceptionally wide shoulders. Rebecca thought he looked like a rugby player.

Swift hesitated when he was introduced to Rebecca, seemingly unsure whether to kiss her on each cheek or shake her hand. Geraldine had told him about Rebecca and her somewhat unusual role in MI5. He had not known what to expect. Her blonde good looks and shapely body had taken him by surprise. He grinned and shook her hand.

Down in the basement of the embassy, George Gardiner briefed them on the operation ahead. Rebecca, surrounded by three male professionals, hoped they didn't all feel she was an unnecessary amateur. She desperately wanted to be accepted as part of the team, but as George Gardiner outlined the risks and challenges of Operation Limehouse she wondered what she would be able or allowed to contribute. She still felt weak from her injuries. While Gardiner was speaking, Rebecca found herself mesmerised by his eyes which, behind the thick lenses, seemed double the normal size.

"We have to split up, obviously," Gardiner said. "Sam and Rebecca have worked closely together leading up to this moment, so I think it's best they stick together. The two teams will be Alpha and Omega. Alpha, Sam and Rebecca, will keep eyes on Redruth wherever he is taken. Rebecca knows Redruth better than anyone in this room, and that will be crucial if the Russians try some sort of decoy operation using a lookalike or whatever."

Sam looked doubtful.

Gardiner smiled. "Don't worry," he said, "you won't be on your own. You'll have a driver, and I've got a backup squad of six guys who will follow you in two vehicles. You will all be radioed up and in contact throughout.

"Team Omega will be me and Jack and one backup car, to eyeball Lavrov and the rest of the delegation when they arrive, and follow them. I should, of course, say *if* they arrive. It's still not one hundred per cent certain they're coming to Warsaw, in which case we are all wasting our time. But the best analysis available is that Warsaw is the destination. Omega has to provide photographic proof of their arrival.

"My instructions are that as soon as Lavrov and party arrive, I have to ring London. What happens next is up to the policy plods in London and Washington, but I assume the secret mission will be blown sky high and Lavrov will have to make a fast exit back to the airport. Omega will follow them and make their presence felt at the airport to underline to the Russians that we know who they are and what they're doing. We don't want any trouble at the airport but we do want the Russians, especially Lavrov, to feel uncomfortable, if not humiliated. I think Jack and I can do that without too much effort."

Jack smiled and looked at Rebecca. She smiled back.

"The other reason Rebecca is needed in Team Alpha," Gardiner said, "is that there is a strong possibility Redruth will be driven off to pay a call at Warsaw's main prison where a certain FSB officer is being held. Again, Rebecca knows this Russian. He is Major Pavel Kozlov. He has been leading the investigation into Redruth and other suspects for the Sevastopol leak. Thanks to Rebecca, he was stopped from returning to Moscow with damning evidence against Redruth and is in Mokotów Prison. I know from my own sources that he is to be released and deported to Moscow, but it looks like the Kremlin may have some bizarre scheme for Kozlov to confront Redruth. If this takes place inside the prison there's nothing we can do. But I'm pretty sure that whatever deal has been hatched between Moscow and Warsaw for Kozlov's release, there's no way the new Polish leadership will sanction an assassination of Redruth inside the prison perimeter. So that means Redruth will be brought out and taken elsewhere for disposal."

Rebecca looked shocked.

Sam had a question. "What if they bring him out, shoot him in the head in the back of the vehicle, drive off somewhere and dump the body? Our duty is to save Redruth but the Russians will have all the cards. He'll be dead before we can do anything."

Gardiner thought for a moment. "This is supposition on my part," he said, "but I don't think the Russians will do that. If it's right that Putin wants this suspected traitor to be eliminated here in Poland, and not returned to Moscow to be charged and put on trial, it will be done more subtly. I don't know how, but this is why we will need maximum eyes on whatever vehicle they use to take Redruth away."

"Sounds a bit iffy," muttered Rebecca, just loud enough for everyone else to hear.

"Rebecca?" Gardiner queried.

"Sorry, but we seem to be leaving a helluva lot to luck," she said.

Sam was about to speak but then thought better of it. He knew that Rebecca, more than anyone else in the room, had a personal investment in Redruth. The Russian had approached her first with the proposal to work for British intelligence and she had handled him with skill and considerable courage. Sam sympathised with her, although he felt no personal loyalty towards Gerasimov. Even though the Russian had probably saved his life, and that of the others, he had shown in the past that he was a ruthless GRU operator who was prepared to kill without hesitation.

"Surely," Rebecca continued, "even if we manage to follow him once he leaves the prison, it's going to be difficult, if not impossible, to stop the Russians from finishing him off. Don't they have poisons and stuff? At what point do we block them and rescue him?"

Gardiner looked put out. He knew it was a perfectly reasonable question, but he hadn't expected it to come from Rebecca Strong, someone he had previously never heard of. Jack Swift had told him she was a favourite of Geraldine Hammer and was not to be underestimated.

"In my view, Rebecca," Gardiner said, "they'll want to leave no trace of Redruth because of the embarrassment it would cause the new Polish government. Moscow thinks it has an ally in the NATO camp, so the Russians in this delegation will want to be very careful what they do while they are on Polish soil."

"But they're still going to get rid of him. Why don't we just intercept the car at the first available opportunity and grab him?

Sam can sort out the other Russians in the car, can't you, Sam?" Rebecca said.

"Rebecca, the plan is to intercept the vehicle as soon as we can," Gardiner said. "But the instructions from London are to pick the moment with care. We don't want to cause a massive scene in Warsaw, with people taking photographs, for example, leading to wild allegations in the newspapers. It has to be done with as little fuss as possible. That will mean choosing our interception point somewhere quiet and out of the public eye. I'm sure Sam could deal with the other Russians in the car, but my six blokes will be there to do the main muscle stuff. Like Sam, they're all ex-special forces."

"All I'm saying is, the longer we leave Redruth in the back of their car, the less likely he is to emerge alive," Rebecca said, feeling herself growing in confidence.

"What about the prison? How many entrances and exits are there?" asked Sam.

"Mokotów Prison is in Rakowiecka Street, south of the city centre, and has only one entrance and exit," Gardiner said. "Security is tight, but as it's a prison used for prisoners on remand or awaiting sentence, it isn't the highest category."

Rebecca had a thought. "You probably know," she said, "I have a boyfriend who works for Sky. He's with us here in Warsaw, along with the guy who drove us from Kyiv. Wouldn't it be a good idea for him to report on the presence of the Russian foreign minister in Warsaw? Local reporters and photographers will soon get wise to it anyway. It would be a good way of exposing the dirty deal, and the whole world will follow it up if it's on Sky."

Gardiner looked interested. "Let me check with London. In the meantime," he said, "everything is to remain secret."

As everyone stood up to leave, Gardiner's phone pinged.

"We have confirmation," he told them. "A flight from Moscow is arriving tomorrow at 9:50 a.m. at Frédéric Chopin airport. The manifest says there are thirteen passengers. The flight is not officially registered but a source at the airport has just confirmed it."

***

Sandy was kept in the dark. For a reporter, there was nothing worse than knowing there was a great story in the making and being unable to even ask about it. Rebecca returned to the hotel with Sam and just said they would both be busy the following day. Sam had already changed the flight booking to London for Sunday for him and Rebecca. Sandy had also changed his flight because he wanted to return with Rebecca.

"You and Pinenut might look around Warsaw for the day."

Sandy was annoyed. "I might go to the airport and fly home after all."

"Sandy, it might be worth your while to stick around," she said. "I can't tell you why, and anyway, I want you to stay. I know we can't … you know … but I'm getting better and it won't be long."

Rebecca had a way of disarming him with her coquettish remarks. He gave up the idea of going to the airport and kissed her.

"So if, as you suggest, I wander around Warsaw tomorrow, I might see something to my advantage?" he asked with a grin.

"I'm sworn to secrecy," she replied. "I'd love to tell you, but—"

"Can I just follow you and then, if something happens, I'll be in the right place?"

"I don't think so, although it's just possible you could play a role. I've already asked for you."

"It's sounding more and more intriguing. Should I get a cameraman?"

"Have one on standby, in case."

Sandy made a call to Sky and asked the foreign desk to fix him a freelance cameraman for the next day. They asked what the story was, to which Sandy replied: "No idea at the moment, but something's up."

An hour later, Sandy received a text from Sky. A local cameraman, Jakub Ilinski, would be in the hotel foyer at 7:30 a.m.

***

Sandy and Rebecca were in bed and falling asleep when her phone rang.

It was George Gardiner. "Rebecca, London says OK."

"OK to Sky?"

"Yes."

"Thank you."

She gave Sandy a long kiss. "It's your lucky day. Looks like you'll be going to the airport after all," she said.

***

Saturday November 30th, 6:45 a.m.

Gerasimov was sitting on his own at the back of the Learjet executive aircraft. In front of him were two GRU majors who were studiously avoiding talking to him. Sergey Lavrov was sitting in the first row of seats and the rest of the delegation was scattered throughout the aircraft. Gerasimov listened out for any conversation that might divulge where they were heading, but there was no hint. The two majors were silent throughout the whole trip.

Gerasimov had said goodbye to his wife and two children, who got up early to see him off. He was realistic; there was a strong possibility he would never see them again. His wife was tearful, even though he assured her he would be away only a short period. He never spoke about his work, so she was used to his secrecy, but Gerasimov was afraid he had given something away which had alarmed her. A look in his eyes, the kiss on her lips rather than the usual hurried peck on one cheek, maybe the way he hugged his kids. He had tried not to show emotion, but after the failure of the British embassy spies to come to his aid, he felt more alone than he had ever experienced in his life. He had always taken his wife for granted and yet he knew he was lucky to have such a devoted woman to care for his children. As he kissed his wife for possibly the last time, he felt an overwhelming sense of doom and despair. Maybe that was the look his wife had seen in his eyes.

***

The Learjet landed at Warsaw Chopin Airport, twenty minutes early. Gerasimov stood up and took one step forward down the aisle, but his way was blocked by the two GRU majors. One of them said they would wait until everyone else had disembarked. Gerasimov's stomach lurched. Throughout his military career, he had always relied on his own abilities to handle every type of hostile scenario, but this time he felt helpless. He was unarmed. Worse still, he had no idea what the GRU majors had in store for him. Would they join the rest of the delegation or would he be taken off somewhere else and dispatched? He feared it would be the latter.

He didn't know yet that they had arrived in Warsaw. He looked out of the window but it was like every other airport. He could have asked the majors but he didn't see the point. Wherever they were, he was in their hands. The fact that he was a full colonel, two ranks higher than them, was not going to help him. He didn't know if they were armed but assumed they were.

Once Lavrov and the rest of his team had left the aircraft, one of the majors turned to Gerasimov and said, "Follow me." The other waited until Gerasimov had passed him and then followed on behind.

The one in front said, "We have another task and will then join the rest of the party."

Gerasimov knew if that were true, the major would have referred to him as "colonel"; even GRU majors were capable of respecting rank. But these two had a mission to complete that would not involve returning to the delegation, Gerasimov was sure of that, and began working out how he could avoid the fate that awaited him. Knocking them over and running across the tarmac was one option that came to mind.

He resolved to make a break for it and found himself holding his breath, as if in preparation for a sprint to freedom.

However, just as he was about to step off the plane, he felt a sharp pain in his neck and he stumbled. The two GRU majors grabbed him and frogmarched him down the stairway. Gerasimov lost control of his limbs.

A Transit van drew up, and Gerasimov's limp body was thrown into the back. The two majors climbed in, one in the front with the driver, the other in the back with Gerasimov's prostrate form.

They drove round the perimeter of the airport and exited farthest away from the terminals through a back gate, which was open for a steady stream of trucks and lorries. The exit route had been pre-arranged as part of the secret deal with the Polish government. The driver fed "Mokotów Prison" into his phone. It was a journey of just three miles. They would be there in less than twenty minutes.

There was no sign of Sam and Rebecca, nor their two-car backup.

***

George Gardiner counted ten Russians as they came out of the terminal and walked straight to a line of Mercedes waiting outside with their engines running.

Sandy hadn't been told who was arriving at the airport, and the cameraman had already filmed numerous people coming out of the terminal. The two were sitting unobtrusively in Pinenut's car. Pinenut was almost as excited as Sandy. He was just a passenger, Sandy was driving, but he felt he was part of the reporting team. He kept on asking Sandy who they were looking out for but he got no answer until the group of ten people emerged together, all wearing hats. Lavrov kept his head down and had a scarf wrapped round his neck, partially hiding his face.

Sandy's contract cameraman, Jakub Ilinski, swore under his breath, but then caught the Russian foreign minister looking up briefly. The scarf slipped enough for him to make identification beyond doubt.

"Bloody hell, that's Lavrov," Sandy said. "Jakub, did you get that?"

Jakub gave him a look and carried on filming as the ten people were driven away.

Gardiner and Jack Swift, sitting in a car not far from Pinenut's, both spoke at once.

"No Redruth."

Gardiner made two calls. He rang Patrick Littlefield with the agreed coded message.

"Limehouse has landed."

Then he rang Rebecca.

"No sign of Redruth. Two others in the party missing. Are you in position?"

"Yes," Rebecca replied.

"Let me know as soon as they arrive."

"OK."

Seven minutes later, a Transit van arrived at the entrance to Mokotów Prison. Sam and Rebecca were sitting in a car down the street. Sam watched the van through binoculars. There was no sign of Redruth. He turned to Rebecca.

"It could be the one, no way of knowing for sure. My instinct is that it is. If so, what state is Redruth in? He'll be in the back, which is not good."

"There's nothing we can do, right?"

"Sit and wait. I'll tell the backup."

The driver had got out and was speaking to the guards. He then returned to the van and the gate opened.

Nothing happened for twenty-five minutes. Then the gate opened again and the Transit van appeared. There was only one thing different: there were now three people in the front, two of them squashed together next to the driver.

Sam quickly passed the binoculars to Rebecca.

It took her time to focus her eyes.

Unable to contain her excitement, she shouted: "It's Kozlov!"

CHAPTER THIRTY
GERASIMOV FACES HIS ACCUSER

Where was Agent Redruth? Was he still in the back of the Transit van or had he been left behind in the prison? Both Sam and Rebecca agreed they had no alternative but to follow the van. Sam rang the backup units and told them to do likewise but to keep their distance.

The van was heading north-east and travelling fast. Sam and Rebecca's driver stayed three vehicles behind. One of the vehicles was a bus. Suddenly, without giving any indication, the van veered to the left and went down a side street. At the same moment, the bus directly in front of the chasing car signalled left and braked at a bus stop. It took Sam and Rebecca's driver three minutes to manoeuvre round the bus and go down the side street. The van had vanished. Sam rang the backup vehicles to warn them.

Rebecca was beside herself.

"We can't lose him," she cried. "Where's everyone else?"

Neither of the backup vehicles reported seeing the Transit van. For the moment, Operation Limehouse, at least the element that covered the rescuing of Agent Redruth, had ground to a halt.

The other part of the operation had gone ahead according to plan. The arrival of the Russian foreign minister and his delegation had been witnessed, photographed and filmed. Sandy Hall had been told by George Gardiner to hold fire until he was given the green light to send a report back to Sky News in London. He was advised it could be several hours before he could tell the world what he had seen. Gardiner promised to ring him when the embargo could be lifted.

Sandy hated embargoes. It would only take some local TV reporter and camera crew to see or hear about the special delegation from Moscow and his scoop would be blown. So far, he had the barest of facts. Lavrov's arrival in Warsaw was bizarre enough, but Sandy needed to know what it was all about. Gardiner had agreed to fill him in but only once the embargo had been lifted by London. The Sky News foreign desk had rung twice, demanding to know whether there was a story or not, but each time, Sandy had stalled them. He didn't dare hint at what it might be and didn't tell them about the embargo.

It was now late morning. He suggested to Pinenut and Jakub, his cameraman, that they go for lunch somewhere. Jakub recommended the TEMBO restaurant in the Elephant House at the city's Zoological Garden. Pinenut put the details into his phone and they set off for the centre of Warsaw, with Sandy driving.

***

A frantic search for the Transit van had drawn a blank. Had it been a normal police car chase there would have been helicopters up in the air by now, searching for the van. But Sam, Rebecca and their backup teams were under orders to keep the operation as low-key as possible. So, for an hour, three cars headed off in all directions in the hope of spotting the vehicle, but all to no avail. Rebecca said what everyone else was thinking: Redruth was probably dead. It wasn't her fault but she felt personally responsible. She wondered where Sandy was and was tempted to ring him. But since there was nothing he could do apart from commiserate, she decided against it. She also had a nagging feeling in her head that perhaps she wasn't cut out to be a spy after all. She was too personally involved.

***

Agent Redruth was still alive.

He had been dosed with benzodiazepine and had been in a sedated state for more than half an hour. He was aware of what was going on around him but was unable to speak or make any effort to change his circumstances. The injection in his neck had disabled him totally.

The van he had been travelling in had veered sharply to the left and then stopped violently. His body had been thrown from one side of the van to the other. He was aware of the GRU major keeping him company in the back. Nothing happened for a few minutes. Then the back door opened and Gerasimov was pulled out unceremoniously. He looked around him and saw they were in what seemed to be a large garage. The lighting was poor.

The two GRU majors dragged him towards a Mercedes estate and pushed him into the boot, the floor of which was covered with an old blanket. They then climbed into the rear bench seat. Major Pavel Kozlov settled into the front passenger seat, and the driver went to open the garage door. Twenty minutes had passed.

After another five minutes, the Mercedes headed for central Warsaw.

His body bruised from the rough handling, Gerasimov had time to think about what had happened at Mokotów Prison. It was there he had realised he was in Poland. Once he had been dragged out of the back of the Transit van, he had been led past the main security desk and into a large room, which had a picture of the new Polish prime minister on a wall. Next to it was a photograph of Warsaw.

There had followed a bizarre ritual. He had lost all sense of time and place. Various thoughts entered his head. For a reason that made no sense he wondered whether he had been taken to a CIA-style secret "black prison". Even though he was barely conscious, he remembered the shudder of terror that had swept through his body. He was never going to see daylight again. He was never going to see his wife and children again, and his brief time as a double agent for Britain's secret intelligence service was over. Rebecca's face had appeared in his mind. He would never see her again.

Through the gloom of semi-consciousness, he saw a man in handcuffs being brought towards him. The man then had the handcuffs removed.

Gerasimov had never met Major Kozlov of the FSB. Kozlov introduced himself.

The two GRU majors held on to Gerasimov as Kozlov walked up close to him.

"Thanks to you and your friend Rebecca Strong, I have been held in this hellhole," he had said, spitting his words out. "I now have the pleasure of being your accuser and executioner.

"Just so you know, it has been decided back in Moscow that you don't need a judge to decide whether you have betrayed your country or not. I have been delegated to do that. So, I formally pronounce that you are a traitor, that you plotted in a conspiracy with the West to assassinate our president, that you sold your soul to hand over our country's secrets to a foreign intelligence service and, finally, that you murdered six members of our illustrious special forces by leading them into a trap in Kyiv in which you, and only you, survived."

Gerasimov heard every word of Kozlov's diatribe, although the list of accusations emerged from his mouth like a muted trumpet. The impact of his words, however, was not lost on Gerasimov. He was going to die, but here in Poland, not in the basement of a Russian prison. He had no idea why this Major Kozlov was in jail, but his reference to Rebecca had brought clarity into his befuddled brain. Kozlov was clearly an FSB investigator and he had uncovered his continuing relationship with Rebecca and worked out what it meant.

Suddenly, Gerasimov had gone cold. Had Kozlov also signed Rebecca's death warrant? He knew what the Kremlin was capable of. If Rebecca was being targeted, it was his fault and his responsibility. Despair overcame him. He was prepared to die. He had, as Kozlov said, betrayed his country. But Rebecca was a wonderful free spirit who had had the misfortune of getting mixed up in his world. He wanted to plead for her life but found he couldn't get the words out. His lips moved but nothing emerged.

After Kozlov's accusations, the two GRU majors had swivelled Gerasimov round and walked towards the door. Kozlov followed. Gerasimov was again bundled into the back of the Transit van, along with one of the GRU majors, while the other major and Kozlov climbed into the front.

Gerasimov had lain on the floor with his knees up to his chin.

After he was transferred to the boot of the Mercedes, he had overheard one surprising word spoken by someone sitting in the back of the car:

"Zoo."

CHAPTER THIRTY-ONE
DRAMA AT THE ZOO

Sandy, Jakub and Pinenut had been at the restaurant in Warsaw's zoo for half an hour. Sandy was getting itchy. He kept looking at his watch. He couldn't stand the suspense, waiting for George Gardiner's call and knowing he had to ring his office before too long to tell them what the story was going to be about. As far as he could see from reading social media on his phone, there had been no reports or rumours about the arrival of the Russian foreign minister at Warsaw airport. He still had a scoop.

Jakub wasn't so concerned. He was being paid whether there was a story to send or not. He had his camera with him as he hadn't felt comfortable leaving it in the car. Besides, you never knew what might happen that would lead to saleable footage, so he took it everywhere. He and Pinenut were enjoying their lunch, while Sandy picked at his food.

Another thirty minutes went by. Still no call. Sandy decided they should leave. He paid for the lunch and prepared to go. At that moment there was an announcement over the tannoy system that the zoo had to close early. Everyone was asked to make their way to the exit and leave as quickly as possible.

"What's going on?" Sandy asked Jakub. "Is this normal?"

Jakub asked around and was told the zoo had to close because of a special visit by VIPs.

Sandy thought, *Could they be Russian VIPs? But why would Sergey Lavrov want to visit the zoo?* He knew it was highly unlikely, but his reporter's instincts told him to stay hidden in the zoo to watch.

The three left the restaurant, and Sandy shared his plan to stay. Jakub said there was a public toilet close to where the lions were kept and suggested they could hide in there. He thought there was a window they could peer through.

"But if the VIPs aren't coming to see the lions," he said, "it will be a waste of time."

"It's a start," said Sandy. "It lets us stay in the zoo."

The zoo wasn't crowded. As Sandy and the others made their way towards the lion enclosure, people were heading to the exit in small numbers.

They waited for forty minutes inside the toilet. Sandy was just tall enough to peer out of the wide window, high up in the wall, and get a glimpse of the locked gate into the lion enclosure. A lion and two lionesses were lying on a raised rocky platform above a grassy area. The zoo was silent except for the occasional high-pitched screech from the monkey cage and sonorous squawk from a peacock.

Sandy was beginning to feel they were wasting their time when he got the shock of his life. Five men were walking towards the lion enclosure. One of them was wearing a green outfit and looked like he was a staff member of the zoo. Three wore dark suits. Sandy didn't know any of them. The fifth, also in a suit but looking dishevelled, and seemingly held up straight by two of the men, was a large, well-built individual with a square-shaped face. Sandy couldn't believe it, but he was pretty sure the fifth man, stumbling as he walked, was Colonel Mikhail Gerasimov.

Keeping his eyes on the five men, Sandy reached for his phone. He texted Rebecca.

"Gerasimov is here, at the zoo. Looks weird. Four others with him. Where you? X"

Sandy whispered: "There's something bad going on here."

He didn't elaborate. If it was Gerasimov, he didn't feel he should tell the others. He needed to hear from Rebecca. She would know what to do. But there was no return text.

"What is it?" said Pinenut. "What's happening?"

"Shh!" said Sandy. He continued watching.

The man in the green uniform retrieved a bunch of keys hanging from his belt. He used two keys to unlock the gate and then turned round to the others as if asking a question. One of the men pointed in the opposite direction. Sandy made the assumption that the man had told the zookeeper he should go. After a moment's hesitation, the zookeeper walked away and disappeared round a corner. The two men holding Gerasimov appeared to take a firmer grip on his arms. The third man then took two paces towards the gate and began to open it slowly.

Sandy whispered to Jakub, "Get this on film."

Jakub raised his camera to his shoulder and peered through the lens. He had to go on tiptoes to see out.

The lion and two lionesses hadn't moved, but as the gate began to open, all three sat up abruptly as if they had woken from a deep sleep. The lion slowly raised itself until it was standing with its four legs straight, ready for whatever action might be necessary.

The man holding the gate looked round nervously. Gerasimov began to wriggle furiously, attempting to break free, but despite his large frame, he couldn't wrench himself away from the grip of his two escorts.

"Shit!" Sandy whispered loudly. "They're going to throw him to the lions!"

"What?" Pinenut whispered back.

"Gerasimov, they're going to chuck him in!" Sandy couldn't hold back from mentioning Gerasimov's name.

Pinenut wasn't tall enough to peer easily through the high window; he went up on tiptoes and gripped the bottom edge of the frame to pull himself up to full stretch.

"What the hell's our Russian friend doing here?" he whispered.

Jakub kept filming. Two of the men in suits were pushing Gerasimov into the lion enclosure. He fell heavily onto the grass. All three men jumped backwards and the gate was slammed shut. The lions didn't move.

At that moment, there was a noise from the public toilet across the way. Pinenut had fallen backwards. Kozlov looked startled and must have said something to the others because they all turned away from the lion enclosure and ran off.

Sandy grabbed Pinenut and they ran out of the toilet. Jakub followed with his camera.

The sight before them was so terrifying that the three of them came to a halt before they had even reached the gate to the enclosure.

The lion and lionesses had now jumped down from their platform and were circling Gerasimov's body. He was lying down, shocked by the hard shove he had received from his captors and also still affected by the drug injected into his neck at the airport. Sandy couldn't see his face because it was turned away, but his head was raised, and he could imagine the look of terror in his eyes.

Pinenut was the first to react.

"We all go in!" he shouted. "Sandy, you and me stand in front of the lions and wave our arms in the air. It will make us look taller and bigger. Jakub, put the camera down and grab the man under his armpits and drag him out, and stay outside the gate. Keep it open for as long as you can."

Sandy and Jakub stared at him in astonishment.

"Go, go, go!" he shouted at them.

As if in a trance, they followed Pinenut into the enclosure. All three lions stopped meandering around Gerasimov's body and focused their attention on the three new intruders.

Pinenut began wildly waving his arms in the air. Sandy followed suit after a few seconds. Jakub put his camera on the ground, grabbed hold of Gerasimov and began heaving him along the grass towards the gate. Before reaching it, he dropped him, exhausted. The lion and lionesses hesitated, as if they were making a decision whether to leap on one of the intruders or run for the open gate. Sandy and Pinenut began backing away, mesmerised by the lions but still waving madly.

Suddenly, there was a shout. Sam and Rebecca were running towards the enclosure. Neither Sandy nor Pinenut dared look round.

Sam shouted to Sandy and Pinenut to get the hell out of the enclosure and to take Gerasimov with them. He then burst into the enclosure, ran to the right, away from the gate, and started jumping up and down and waving his arms in the air. The lion and lionesses appeared confused by the sudden change in circumstances and glared at Sam. But at six foot six inches and with his arms adding another three foot three inches, the sight of such a big obstacle in their environment stopped them in their tracks.

It gave Gerasimov's rescuers just enough time to haul him out. Rebecca held his head, Sandy and Pinenut, his shoulders, and Jakub, his legs. Jakub then grabbed his camera.

Sam shouted at them to close the gate.

Rebecca screamed at Sam to get out.

Sam now had his back to the high fence. The three lions were about eight feet away, all facing him. It looked as if they were about to leap on him, but there was a sudden distraction which caused all of them to whip their heads round.

Rebecca was running up and down inside the enclosure and shouting her head off. While the lions were focusing on her, Sam hurled himself towards Rebecca, picked her up, and ran to the open gate. Pinenut slammed it shut as the three lions, wakened from their confused state, leapt towards them and crashed against the gate, snarling and roaring.

CHAPTER THIRTY-TWO
SANDY GETS HIS SCOOP BUT THERE'S A DELAY

For five minutes, they all stood there, exhausted. Gerasimov had struggled to his feet and was staring at the others. He shook his head as if to clear it. The drug was wearing off but was still affecting him. Sam and Rebecca gave each other a hug. Then Rebecca hugged Sandy and Pinenut, and Jakub, after she had been introduced to the Polish cameraman. All of them had been through a unique and terrifying experience. Finally, Rebecca turned to Gerasimov and gave him a hug, too.

The lions were still roaring and clawing at the gate. The same thought came into everyone's head at the same time: the gate was closed but unlocked.

"Let's get the hell out of here," Sam shouted.

He grabbed Gerasimov's arm and started to walk away, heading for the exit. The rest joined him, except for Pinenut, who said he was desperate to relieve himself and promised to be quick. He disappeared into the toilet from where he, Sandy and Jakub had witnessed the Russians throwing Gerasimov to the lions. Sam, holding Gerasimov's arm, with Rebecca, Sandy and Jakub following close behind, vanished round the corner.

Pinenut was two minutes in the toilet and then ran after them. But suddenly he heard a loud voice shouting in Russian. He stopped at the corner and peered round. Not for the first time that day, he saw something that made his blood run cold.

A man with his back to Pinenut was pointing a gun at the others and waving it in Gerasimov's direction. He heard him shouting: "Move one muscle and I'll shoot the lot of you. Leave the Russian traitor and the rest of you go! Except the bloody woman. I want her to stay as well."

Pinenut didn't speak Russian but he had no difficulty understanding what the gunman was saying. Pinenut reckoned he was about twenty yards from him. None of the others moved. They were about twelve feet from the Russian with the gun. The gunman said he would count to three. Then he would shoot "the bloody woman".

***

After running from the lion enclosure, Major Pavel Kozlov and the two GRU majors had reached the exit gate. No one else was around. The zookeeper, who had been paid a thousand dollars to keep quiet, was not to be seen. The main gate to the zoo was still unlocked. The Mercedes that had brought Gerasimov in the boot was waiting on the other side of the road. As soon as the driver spotted them, he turned on the ignition. The three Russians climbed in, and the driver accelerated away.

Within seconds of their departure, Sam and Rebecca arrived and ran into the zoo. The front gate was still unlocked.

Five minutes later, the Mercedes was back outside the zoo. Kozlov had told the two GRU majors he wanted to make sure the lions had done what was expected of them. He asked for a gun. The driver removed a gun from the glove compartment and handed it to Kozlov.

Kozlov ran across the road, opened the zoo gate and went inside. He walked back towards the lion enclosure and then came to a sudden halt. In the distance he could see a group of people hugging each other. He saw Gerasimov standing up. He saw Rebecca Strong. Kozlov was staggered.

He quickly hid in a doorway and waited. After a few minutes, he could hear them approaching. They walked past him without looking in his direction. He counted five people: four men and the woman. He could have sworn there were six when he first spotted them standing outside the lion enclosure, but he didn't have time to think about it, he had to act. He stepped out of the doorway and shouted in Russian at the five people, ordering them to stop. He raised the gun and pointed it at Gerasimov, who had an expression on his face of shocked resignation. He had been through the worst experience of his life and survived, but the nightmare was still not over.

***

Sam, fluent in Russian, spoke to Kozlov in as calm a voice as he could. "Steady, steady, there's no need for such drama. What exactly is it you want?"

Kozlov shouted back. "Gerasimov and the bloody woman. I want the bloody woman to come towards me with Gerasimov. I will shoot them both if the rest of you don't get the hell out of here. I'll count to three."

"What's he saying? This is Kozlov; you know that, don't you?" Rebecca whispered to Sam.

"He wants us all to go except you and Gerasimov," Sam replied.

"No bloody way," Sandy said.

Kozlov began to count.

He reached "three" when suddenly he fell forward as if he had been struck by lightning, or by a huge blow from behind. He crashed to the ground and was unable to save his face from smashing onto the path. The gun flew from his hand as he tried to protect himself.

Wrapped round his lower legs was a gasping Pinenut, who had hurtled from his hidden position round the corner, completing the final stage of his rescue in midair as he flew towards Kozlov for the only rugby tackle he had ever attempted in his life. And with one broken arm encased in a plaster cast.

Sam retrieved the gun and pointed it at Kozlov, who was writhing in pain. Rebecca ran forward and helped Pinenut up. She kissed him fully on the lips and hugged him until he could hardly breathe.

"You are a crazy bitch!" she said, with a huge grin. He grinned back.

"It was worth it," he said, licking his lips.

Even Sandy laughed.

Sam knelt down and placed the barrel of the gun against Kozlov's bruised and bloodied forehead.

"I'm going to take you to your colleagues, who I assume are waiting for you," he said. "If you play up or do anything that annoys me, I'm going to take you back to the lions and throw you in, just like you did to your compatriot here. The lions must be ravenous by now."

He pulled Kozlov up. The man's face was in a bad way, and he was holding his right arm and wincing in pain. Sam beckoned the others to follow him and marched Kozlov towards the exit. As they left the zoo, they could see three faces looking at them from a Mercedes across the road. Sam told the others to wait. He then pulled Kozlov towards the Mercedes. The driver looked petrified.

With the gun raised, Sam indicated to the driver to put the window down. The two GRU majors were sitting in the back, their faces expressionless.

"You can have your comrade back," he said in Russian, "a little the worse for wear. I'll keep the gun as a souvenir. I suggest you go back to whatever sewer you came from. I shall give your descriptions and the registration of the car to the Polish police, just to encourage you to get out of the country fast. Now, open the door."

The GRU major nearest to where Sam was standing with Kozlov pushed the door open. Sam picked Kozlov up by his belt and threw him into the back, onto the two passengers' laps. Kozlov yelped in pain.

The nearest GRU major stared at Sam for a few seconds but said nothing. Then he turned to the driver and said, "Go."

The Mercedes screeched away from the kerb and accelerated down the road, a blast of smoke belching from the twin exhausts.

The driver who had brought Sam and Rebecca to the zoo was waiting outside. But Sam told him he could leave. He and the others all squeezed into Pinenut's car. They wanted to stick together after the traumatic experience in the zoo. Sam was in the driver's seat.

Sandy's phone pinged. There were four of them in the back, and it was so tight he could hardly get the phone out of his pocket. It was a text from George Gardiner, telling him to ring as soon as possible. After all the excitement and shock of the previous hour, Sandy had pushed into the back of his mind that he had a job to do. It was time for his latest scoop. But the even bigger scoop, the attempt by Russian intelligence officers to assassinate an MI6 double agent by throwing him into a cage full of lions, was a story he assumed he was never going to be allowed to broadcast. He realised he would need to have a conversation with Jakub. Somehow, the local cameraman would have to be persuaded to keep quiet about what he had filmed. Sam and Rebecca, he was sure, would be involved in suppressing the most dramatic story Jakub had ever witnessed.

Sam was told to drive to the British embassy. George Gardiner had been apprised of their imminent arrival. Gerasimov spent the whole journey thanking everyone for saving his life. He was sitting between Rebecca and Sandy, and feeling a lot better. The final numbness from the benzodiazepine had worn off, but the recollection of what he had been through kept filling his mind with terrifying images. The sight and feel of Rebecca next to him helped to dull the tortured thoughts.

They arrived at the embassy. Gardiner was waiting in the foyer and guided them all in without getting them checked by security. He took them down into the basement. He rang the embassy medical staff to come and check on Gerasimov.

Jack Swift, Geraldine's man from London, was still at the airport, ensuring the exit of the Russian delegation. He had reported back that there were two missing from the delegation, apart from Gerasimov, and no sign of Kozlov. It was another half an hour before Swift rang to say that the two missing Russians, accompanied by Kozlov, had arrived at the airport just in time to board the private Learjet bound for Moscow.

Gardiner congratulated everyone for the spectacular rescue of Gerasimov, although he still didn't have the full story. He then asked Sam, Rebecca and Sandy to follow him into his private office, leaving Pinenut and Jakub with Gerasimov. A doctor and nurse were on their way.

The MI6 man briefed Sandy on what had happened following the Russian delegation's arrival in Warsaw and gave him enough detail for his report to Sky News. Sandy said he would need to leave immediately and would take Jakub and Pinenut with him. Sandy gave Rebecca a look of adoration, and grinned at Sam. He then left in a hurry.

Sam and Rebecca told Gardiner about the lions. The MI6 station chief sat there shaking his head in disbelief.

Two hours later, Sandy's report was broadcast live. Incredibly, no local reporter or photographer had spoilt his scoop. The Russian foreign minister and his delegation had somehow managed to arrive in Warsaw and return to the airport without anyone else spotting them. There was also not a word about an incident at Warsaw's Zoological Garden.

Sandy's report went out at 6 p.m., London time.

Moscow has been engaged in a bold and extraordinary attempt to plot a covert deal with the new Polish government to force Kyiv and NATO to accept a peace settlement and end the war in Ukraine,

Sky News can exclusively reveal. Sergey Lavrov, the Russian foreign minister, arrived at Warsaw airport this morning with a special delegation selected by President Putin. The new Polish prime minister, Aleksy Malinowski, who campaigned for a deal with Russia to stop the war, had agreed to meet the delegation in secret without any prior discussions with Washington or other NATO allies.

According to diplomatic sources here in Warsaw, such a deal between Moscow and Warsaw, while not binding on the alliance as a whole nor, indeed, on President Zelensky, could have put huge strains on the US-led coalition, which has shown signs of wavering in their support for Ukraine.

Western intelligence services got wind of the plot and were ready for the Russians when they arrived this morning. The diplomatic sources said the American secretary of state rang the Polish prime minister and requested he inform the Russian foreign minister that he would, after all, not be welcomed as previously planned and that the delegation from Moscow should turn round and go back home. It is understood Sergey Lavrov received the message on his private phone while travelling in a car from the airport. The delegation duly returned to the airport. Security sources said they left for Moscow after a two-hour delay.

The diplomatic sources told Sky it had been a potentially damaging attempt by Moscow to undermine the coalition supporting Ukraine. They said the new Polish government had also got the message loud and clear that secret plots with Moscow were totally in breach of alliance procedures and that any repeat of individual acts like this would put at risk Poland's continued membership of the alliance.

Sandy Hall, reporting from Warsaw.

Jakub Ilinski's film showed the arrival of the Russian foreign minister and his delegation at Warsaw airport, and Sandy reporting from Pilsudski Square in the centre of the city.

Within half an hour, the story was running on all the news agencies around the world. Moscow put out a statement denying that Sergey Lavrov had flown to Warsaw and claimed it was a fake news story, made up by the CIA.

CHAPTER THIRTY-THREE
REBECCA GETS AN AWARD AND A SHOCK

Rebecca and Sam were sitting in Geraldine's office. The mood was triumphant but sad. Operation Greengage had been a huge success, but short-lived. Gerasimov had been brought out of Warsaw in a chartered private jet and was now at a secret address in Surrey. He had been told he would need to go through an extensive debriefing period and would then be given a new name, a safe house guarded by MI6 security officers, and a future role in advising the director general of MI5 on issues including Moscow-inspired espionage overseas and Putin's strategy on assassinations. Gerasimov had asked to stay in London for a few days and told Rebecca he wanted to take her out to the best restaurant in the city, but he was whisked away in a black Range Rover. The issue of his wife and two children was hardly discussed.

However, what was unsaid was clear to everyone. Once Kozlov and the two GRU majors had returned to Moscow with the delegation, the Kremlin would be informed that Gerasimov was still alive. His wife and children would then become pawns in a battle of wills between Moscow and London.

Geraldine had already received a full report on the drama at the zoo and had been in touch with Adam Goldstein in Langley to inform him of the latest developments. Goldstein, in his usual dismissive manner, had suggested that the whole Gerasimov saga had been of limited value. He acknowledged it was fortunate he had survived Moscow's outrageous plot to feed him to the lions at the Warsaw zoo, but he seemed unmoved by the extraordinary courage displayed by those who had rescued him. Geraldine had put the phone down quite abruptly.

"So, my hero and heroine, it sounds like you two should be receiving a medal for what you've done," Geraldine said.

"All in the line of duty," Sam replied.

"Well, hardly," said Geraldine. "When did you get training on how to survive in a lions' cage?"

"We weren't the only ones," Rebecca reminded Geraldine. "Everyone played their part." Rebecca had insisted that the report Sam wrote on the plane back to London should include the roles played by Sandy, Pinenut and Jakub.

Pinenut had driven back to Kyiv after an emotional farewell with Rebecca and Sam. Rebecca and Pinenut had vowed eternal friendship, and he had received one more of her full-mouth kisses. He climbed into his car for the long journey home with the biggest of smiles on his face.

"What happens to Gerasimov now?" Rebecca asked Geraldine.

"He will disappear for the next six to nine months," she replied. "It's the way it is. Even I won't see him. He will be ensconced with a dedicated team. There will be no contact. I'm sure he will be asking for you, Rebecca, but that's out of the question."

"Why do you say that?"

"I think he still likes you, a lot!" Geraldine said.

Rebecca laughed. "I'm taken," she said.

"Taken?" Sam chipped in.

"Sandy proposed on the plane," Rebecca replied.

"And?" Sam asked.

"I told him I'd think about it," said Rebecca.

"Of course you did," said Sam with a grin.

"Well, what about you and Geraldine? Isn't it time you went on one knee?" Rebecca asked.

They all laughed. Geraldine visibly blushed.

***

Eight weeks later, at a secret ceremony in Buckingham Palace, Rebecca and Sam received the George Medal from King Charles. The monarch told them he had been informed of their exceptional bravery in the interests of the country's national security.

***

Rebecca still hadn't given Sandy the answer he wanted, although halfway through dinner in a restaurant near his flat in Isleworth, she came close.

"I'm definitely not saying no," she told him.

He laughed. "I'll go with that for the moment. I never really expected you to just say yes outright. It wouldn't be you."

"Meaning?"

"Well, you're always full of surprises and you do things differently. And now you're a super spy, or whatever you are, maybe getting married to a boring television foreign correspondent with some pretty spectacular scoops to his name is not enough for you."

Rebecca leaned across the table and planted a perfectly shaped lipstick kiss on his right cheek. He instinctively put his hand to the cheek as if to rub off the lipstick.

"Remove it and you're dead," Rebecca said.

Sandy grinned and put his hand down. "You see what I mean?"

"Marrying me might be too crazy for you."

"I think I'll survive."

"I mean it, I can be crazy."

"I know. Like at the zoo. Totally crazy."

"You should have got a medal, too."

"What, get a medal for something I can never talk about, let alone broadcast? I don't think so. But I'm very happy you and Sam got one."

Rebecca reached across and gave him another lipstick kiss on the other cheek. Sandy kept his hands on the table.

Rebecca said, "Come on, lover boy, let's forget pudding and go back to your place."

***

Geraldine offered Rebecca a full-time job but said she would still have to complete the entry course. After that, it would be fast-track all the way.

Rebecca had suspected the offer was coming and had already decided to turn it down. There were aspects of the spying world that she knew she would be good at. She had proven that beyond doubt. But there were elements of the job in MI5 that she didn't fancy at all, such as spending hours on surveillance duties, monitoring suspected terrorists or right-wing extremists plotting anarchy. She had loved working alongside Sam Cook, and everything she had been involved in with Gerasimov and the Agent Redruth saga had been exciting beyond anything she had ever experienced. But she didn't want to be a fully paid-up member of His Majesty's security service. She actually decided she would prefer to work for the "other service", the spies housed in the exotic building across the river from MI5. A job with MI6 sounded more glamorous. But when she met Patrick Littlefield a few weeks after returning from Warsaw, the director of operations never mentioned potential job prospects, although he did admit she would make a good spy.

Above all, she needed some time away from life-threatening situations. She looked forward to a period of calm and tranquillity. No more dramas around each corner.

So, Rebecca decided she would return to her old life as a commercial artist, but promised Geraldine that if she needed her at any time, all she had to do was ring. Geraldine reminded her that she would be covered by the Official Secrets Act for the rest of her life.

Rebecca stayed living in her flat in Notting Hill but spent most weekends at Sandy's place. Every weekend he reminded her that he adored her and wanted her to marry him. She seemed to be coming round to the idea.

***

On a cold, late January morning, Rebecca left her flat early to meet a new potential customer for her large oil paintings. She was wrapped up warmly in a huge fur coat, a red scarf covering her mouth. She walked down the steps from the front door and turned left while searching for her travel card in her oversized bag. She bumped straight into a man who was approaching her from the other direction. They both stumbled and put their hands out.

"I'm so sorry," Rebecca said.

The man in front of her was tall and had a pockmarked face.

Rebecca jumped backwards with a look of unbelieving shock on her face.

It was Kozlov.

The End

AUTHOR PROFILE

After sixteen years as a reporter on the *Daily Express*, Michael Evans moved to *The Times* in 1986, where he became Defence Correspondent and then Defence Editor. He developed a reputation for having some of the best contacts in the defence, military and intelligence world. He covered six wars in the field, including Bosnia, Kosovo, Iraq and Afghanistan. From 2010–2013 he was Pentagon Correspondent for *The Times* in Washington DC.

Back in London, Michael still writes on defence, foreign affairs and intelligence issues for *The Times* and also for the *Spectator*. He is the author of five fiction books, one of them for children, and four non-fiction, including a memoir, *First With the News*. He is married with three sons.

Michael writes a daily blog on world issues – michaelevansbook. blogspot.co.uk – and he tweets every day from @MikeEvansTimes. You'll also find him on Instagram (Michael_evans1945) and LinkedIn (michael.evans@the-times.co.uk). His website is www. michaelevansauthor.co.uk.

PUBLISHER INFORMATION

Rowanvale Books provides publishing services to independent authors, writers and poets all over the globe. We deliver a personal, honest and efficient service that allows authors to see their work published, while remaining in control of the process and retaining their creativity. By making publishing services available to authors in a cost-effective and ethical way, we at Rowanvale Books hope to ensure that the local, national and international community benefits from a steady stream of good quality literature.

For more information about us, our authors or our publications, please get in touch.

www.rowanvalebooks.com
info@rowanvalebooks.com